DOMITIA

LAUREN LOGAN

COPYRIGHT

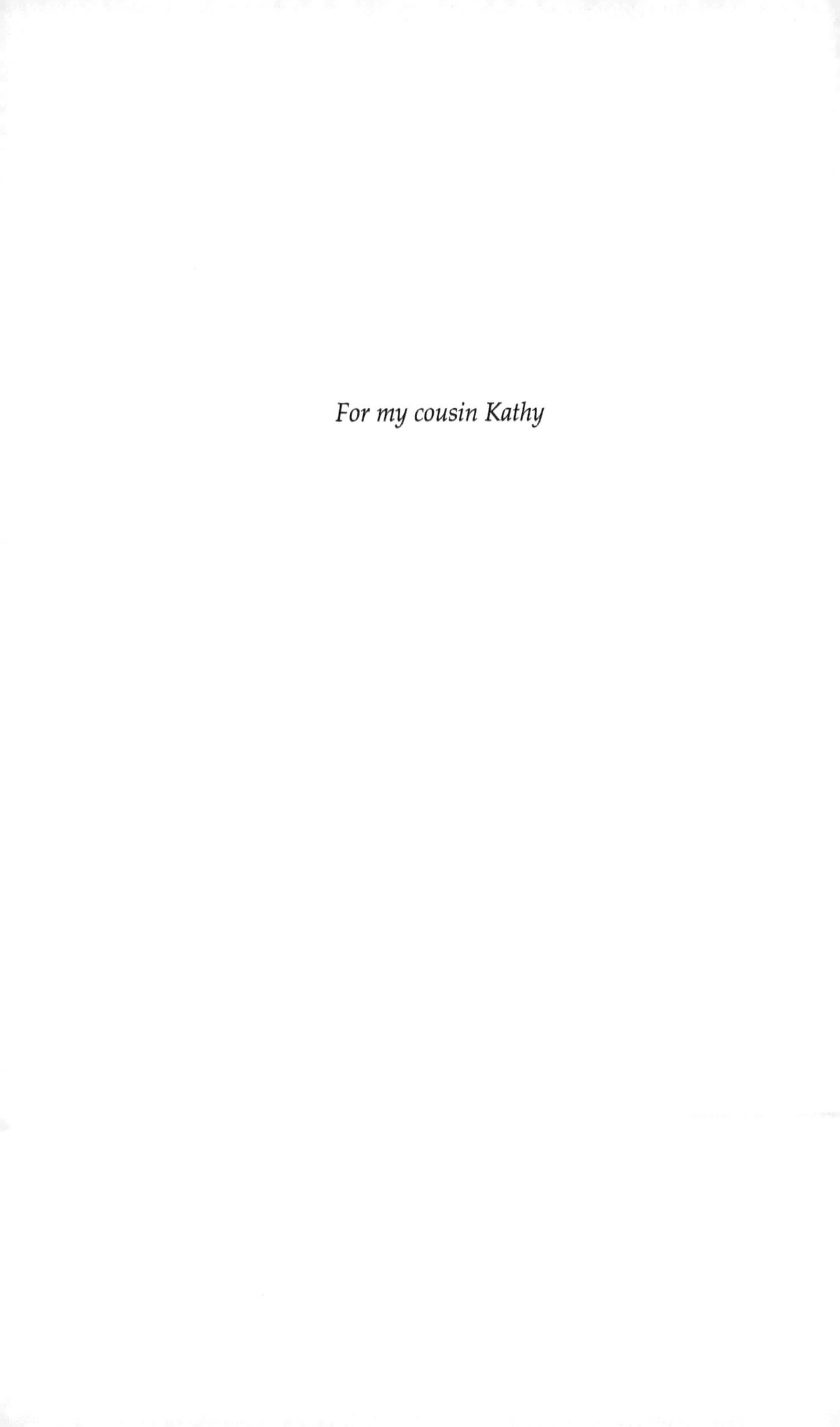

For my cousin Kathy

CONTENT WARNING

Trigger and content warnings for Domitia are listed on
www.authorlaurenlogan.com

Domitia is strictly from mature readers of 18+

Please protect your mental health.

INTRODUCTION

Domitia is a stand alone story in the same universe as the Reticere Series. Domitia follows the events of Reticere book three, Janus, but it is not necessary to read the entire Reticere Series before beginning Domitia.
Please be aware, Domitia contains some spoilers of the Reticere Series.

This work should never be used as representation of any kind. The thoughts and feelings of my disabled character are a small part of what it means to be disabled. The disabled community is not a monolith, and our experiences vary significantly.

Latin
Translations by Amanda Fox
This work includes Latin dialog which is written within quotations and formatted in *italics*. Any Latin dialog will be directly followed by the English translation.

CONTENTS

PROLOGUE
PLANET T-45031

I need to know who broadcast that message! I must know who dare spoke the words! Find all who are involved and drop them on the prison planet! *"Necesse sum scire quis divulgat illum nuntium. Necesse sum quis contemnit loquens verbos. Inveni omnes implicavit et demitte in carcere planeta!"* The disgraced First Human empress cried out into to the bleak room of wanted commanders. A blood vessel on her temple looked like it would burst under her pale skin. Having evacuated as the war began, they had reconvened at the secret base a paranoid emperor constructed many years prior for just such an occasion.

With her strident orders, all scattered to their stations along the walls and sent files to their teams hiding out all over the galactic center. The chilling air in the room formed frost on the corners of any faced outside windows. The rouge planet lacked a viable atmosphere, and was too far from any star, nebula, or black hole for any solar energy.

The desolation of the planet inflated the desperation within the overthrown commanders.

Her boots clanked against the polished cement floor as she stormed into her office and slammed her communicator on the plain metal desk. A bit of grey hair from her bun came loose during the commotion, and she neatly tucked it behind her ear. They wouldn't stop being the First Humans just because they were 'wanted' now. The FH would re-unite as soon as she could find a more suitable secluded world. This one was far too close to the galactic center systems, and still had an occasional cargo ship pass by. She could not risk accidental discovery if they were to continue functioning and regain their power.

A knock sounded at the wooden door behind her and a dark-haired commander stuck his head inside. We have found those to whom the voice belongs. It's a woman in the surrogate program. We had her voice on record. *"Invenimus hos cuius vox pertinet."*

With a joyful smile on her aging, beautiful face, she reclined in her desk chair and asked *"Quis est nomen eius?"* What is her name?

Tressa Powe. She has a sibling named Cinis, and they both live with a grandmother in an exceptionally poor part of Emendo. Cinis was a former UTC base S-3 surveillance team watch commander, and they were reported missing by us before we evacuated, *"Tressa Powe. Ea habet fratrem cum nomine Cinis, et vivent cum avia in paupillimos partes Emendo. Cinis fuit prior UTC dux S-3 inspectionem, et rettulerant omittendus ab nobis ante vacuefecimus."* he replied.

She spun around in her chair to face him *"Interfice aviam. Trade duos fratres ad carcerem planetam. Habe Commandus Dolion capet illos. Scio habebit iocum cum illis ante perficet pensum.*" Kill the grandmother. Deliver the two siblings to the prison planet. Have Commander Dolion take them. I'm sure he will have some fun with them before he completes the drop.

The door shut as he retreated to the hallway, and she leaned back in her seat, resting her feet up on her metal desk. The sound of her boots striking the metal made her cringe.

It must be a sign from the gods. I will make a sacrifice to Jupiter and Mars for their guidance. They surely are behind this good fortune. Maybe I will use the man who broadcast the message. I could have his entrails scooped out and spread over The House of Jupiter's steps. That would surely please Jupiter. "*Erit signum ab deorum. Faciam sacrificum ad Iupiter et Mars nam deo ducente. Certe faciunt hanc bonam fortunam. Fortasse uti virem quem divulgat nuntium. Habui eius viscera excavit et extendit trans scalas domos Iuppiteri. Sibi placet ad Iuppiter.*" She reached up and grabbed her drink off the desk. Tipping the gold liquid back, she wondered if she should kill Rungi that damn underground arms dealer too. Who are her friends? She should have someone find out. Maybe they should die too. She reached for her tablet to send the request.

They all needed to pay after interrupting a million years of the First Human's progress. What their ancestors built was right, ensuring their survival as a people. The humans numbered more than the stars and their existence was more than ensured, but they could always do more. Humans were evolving on many worlds and that future could be in jeopardy now. She wouldn't let a damn thing happen to them.

All of those evolving human worlds deserved to

develop. The First Humans spent generations enacting and protecting this plan. She would do anything to make sure her ancestors plan remained true.

ONE

EMENDO – VENUS DISTRICT 7 – UTC SURROGATE CLINIC 184

In the stark white med room, as she lay back against the chilly stainless-steel table, she wondered if the surgeon would cut through one of her old scars or if they would give her a new one. Whatever they decided, she just hoped they didn't slice all the way down her side like they did last time. She couldn't understand why they did that other than to further mark her skin for the hell of it.

Crossing her arms over her swollen chest, she lifted her gaze just in time to see her own blood spray the glass shield placed just below her mid chest. Rolling her eyes, she wondered if they had hit an artery.

"Dumbasses," she muttered as she tilted her head up, her light brown hair slid from her shoulder with the action. She peered over her large, split open belly just in time to see them pulling her bloody intestines out and set them in the bowl on the table.

"Are you watching?" The human nurse to her left asked, his brow creased.

Sliding her blue eyes over to him, she flatly replied, "This is number nine. I could perform the surgery on myself."

His gaze reflected a mix of disturbed and confused. "You've done this nine times? Who in Pluto's realm would willfully sign up for nine? There is something wrong inside your head."

Tressa gave him a saccharine smile, "First off, it's none of your fucking business. Second, you are not telling me anything I don't know." Irritated, she turned to check the progress of the baby removal. A tiny, deep brown newborn was lifted from the gaping incision she noted ran the entire length of her abdomen.

"What the fuck did they do?!" Tressa cried out.

Fluttering his eyes, the nurse spat, "You chose this."

"No, I did not but thank you for assuming. You better not fuck up the pain meds," she directed.

"Or what?" The nurse asked, his eyes narrowed at her.

Tressa sighed roughly, hoping he didn't call her bluff as she lay back, "I have a UTC advocate, and I will call her."

The nurse scowled at her and reluctantly filled the little reservoir on top of a pain patch with a strong narcotic drug. He slapped the patch on her arm, making a loud smack.

"Take that Iris attitude somewhere else," Tressa breathed as he stalked out and slammed the door. A laser fused her inner muscles while the tech prepped her to be sewn up.

As the pain medication began to work, she ignored the rest of the procedure. Her body shifted a bit, so they must be sewing her up now she thought. She didn't want to look. This incision was by far the worst they had ever performed. Her entrails would likely end up in a knot with how they shoved them back in. She hoped the pain plug in her spine held up long enough to at least make it home, but she knew that was not likely. It usually popped out on its own when she stood up, but just once she wanted no pain for the walk home.

They lifted the glass shield, and she looked down at the mess they made of her already scarred body.

"This removal was by far the worst. Can you not get some decent surgeons in here?" Tressa asked the old surgical tech standing with her hand out for to Tressa to aid in standing.

After taking her hand and leaning up, she felt the block slip out and the pain instantly shot through her body. She swayed a few times and swallowed down a groan before trying to take a step.

"If you can't walk, you can't leave," The woman reminded her, holding her up as the pain took away her breath and balance.

"I know," Tressa replied, trying not to come off rude. The woman was likely to drop her if she was. Releasing a deep breath, Tressa took a step, and the tendon under her foot popped with the weight she added. Another step and the same thing happened. The pain in her feet was always there, but today it was worse. It had been drizzling outside, and she was miserable when the weather changed.

With a few more steps, the tech let go of her arm. "You're free to go. Any sign of infection, let us know and you will get one round of antibiotics for free." The tech began cleaning the room behind her in preparation for the next patient.

Tressa slowly padded over to the exit panel and pulled her meal card from her bag. Worry swirled inside of her as she slid her card into the receptacle. It always killed her to give the card back. It had kept her well-fed for the last ten months. She knew the next two months would be filled with hunger since Cinis was now home and in hiding after helping the Iungo win their freedom.

Their family always relied on Cinis' income from their job with the UTC to feed them. She loved her sibling and what they did for their family, but she always missed them so much. Cinis was her best friend and the only person in the galaxy she could truly trust. They were everything to Tressa. "Do you have food to spare?" As she's struggled down the street a voice came from under a heap of blankets.

Tressa put one foot in front of the other, trying to force herself to make it down the street. "No. I don't even have food for myself."

"You bleeding. Be careful. Some creatures smell blood for miles. You could end up a meal," the wrinkled face peered down at the blood seeping from between Tressa's legs.

After narrowing her eyes in pain and determination she shuffled along and refused to look down again. She knew a trail of blood followed her and it would draw in all the local predators as the sky darkened. After the mile walk down the dark sidewalks in the light rain, she finally reached her building. A vehicle, shiny, new, and clearly not belonging in her neighborhood, was parked on the street, but she was in far too much pain to care. They had diced her up like a piece of meat, and her insides screamed with every step.

It was so much worse than the usual pain she experienced. The last time she felt this way she ended up with scar tissue connecting her insides together. Waddling onto the lift, she finally looked down and her eyes followed the trail of her blood all the way to the front door of her apartment building.

They had given her several bags of blood during the surgery or she would be worried. Lightly placing her hand on her aching belly, she felt the warm blood seeping through her shirt. They had done a terrible job sewing her up. *Do I have any glue left from the tube I found in the apartment dumpster? Maybe I can glue it shut like before.*

She hated being pregnant, but since she had all that trouble, she hadn't been given a choice. In fact, it had been Cinis who negotiated her agreement. She contracted to have six genetically engineered UTC babies in exchange for keeping her hands. She held up her hand, now ruddy and smeared with her blood. The other three surrogate contracts had been necessary, not just for her, but also her grandmother. The food access had kept her from starving on more than one occasion.

The lift door slid open, and Tressa didn't look up as she shuffled out into the hallway. Slipping her key in the door lock, she heard a muffled clatter. *Was that sound coming from inside her apartment?*

"Nan, if you are in the kitchen eating salt out of the jar again, I'm going to have to hide it. You can't eat salt like that," Tressa leaned in as she opened the door. The tiny apartment felt eerily quiet as she shut the door behind her. Wondering if the pain meds were making her loopy, she checked herself in the mirror hanging in the hallway. Her eyes were steady, and she didn't feel like her mind was all that cloudy.

A diffused light filtered in from the tiny window at the other end of the room, but the apartment was otherwise dark. They couldn't afford many light bulbs or their consequent electricity charges.

Something was wrong, the hair on her body all stood on end.

"Nan?" she asked, concern growing with every step down the hall.

A shadowed figure emerged from the dark causing her to turn her head. Behind the hulking figure was a crumpled, round form on the floor.

Her heartbeat pounded in her ears as her eyes adjusted to the low light. Nan was convulsing with blood spilling from her throat. A pool of crimson formed under the elderly woman's body.

"Nan!" Tressa cried out as her world went dark.

TWO

UTC PRISON DROP SHIP S.98 – LOCATION UNKNOWN

Head pounding and belly aching, Tressa exhaled roughly. Chilled air rushed into her lungs as her mind began to clear. A sound caught her attention. No, it was a voice. What was it saying? She couldn't understand it yet. Her headache slowly faded along with the haze but not quickly enough. She strained to hear as the rattle of a transport ship entering an orbit slowly registered in her fuzzy state.

"Sorry about this, soldier. Don't take it personal or anything. I need to collect my trophy. You know how it is."

The crackling of a rail gun discharging echoed through the small space. Tressa froze in fear. Where in Jupiter's house was she? Who was shot, and more importantly, who shot them? A sick feeling enveloped her as she realized she could be the next victim of that same gun.

Cracking an eye open just slightly, she let enough light pass her lashes to see a large man dressed in a First Human commander uniform dragging a limp, lifeless man toward the trash chute down the hall. His body left a smear of blood under his boots. The contrast of the fresh, red blood was striking against the light metallic sheen of the floor.

Furtively looking about while the commander was busy, she evaluated her surroundings, and her heart sank when she recognized a confirming UTC emblem on the wall.

She knew exactly what kind of transport ship they were on, the sudden familiar sound of the ship engines made her stomach turn. The UTC maintained a prison dropship storage yard three blocks away from her apartment, and she had listened to them moving the drop ships around for years. She was fucked, Jupiter spare her soul.

They were taking her to the prison planet.

She must have been discovered. How did they know it was her voice on the broadcast? The hacker had disguised it under layers and layers and layers of harmonic tones. The ship creaked as the hatch releasing trash opened and the victims and contents were dumped into the upper atmosphere.

When she thought the FH commander was far enough down the hall, she reached her hand up to check her body. She had just raised her hand far enough to check her hip before the footsteps headed back toward her. She dropped her hand back down, hoping he couldn't see.

"You won't make ten minutes down there bleeding from your gut and between your legs like you are. Those blood thirsty Resper aren't the only monsters on the planet," his voice boomed directly above her. "Your eye is twitching, Tressa Powe. I know you are awake," he whispered in her ear.

"We have you and we have Cinis. They are prepped and ready in the drop pod next to you. Lucky for you, I love polished toenails." His words chilled her to the bone as he hauled her out of the open pod.

Her eyelids flew open, and still only half aware, she met Cinis' terrified gaze peeking over the seat of the sealed dump pod. Their short dark blond hair was a mess on their head and their wide blue eyes were desperate.

The commander pulled her back to look him in the eye, "Behave or I'll take something from them next." She nodded, she knew exactly what he wanted. All that mattered was Cinis was spared. While she knew she couldn't trust anything he said, she didn't have a choice and had to hope Juno and Mars would project Cinis.

If the FH commander wanted a piece of her, blood flowing and all, then she would just take her mind somewhere else for a while. Being attractive and poor in a planet sized city was a beacon. She had been through everything except the worst violence already. In the back of her head, she knew it was only a matter of time. Rape statistics on Emendo's population was so high at one point the UTC finally stepped in and did something to stop the brutality.

The UTC went straight for barbaric and removed all sex organs from any creature who committed the crime, every organ down to their nipples. It only lasted a year as a law, but it was enough to scare off the worst of them temporarily.

Her focus shifted quickly when he forced her on a metal table and pointed a rail gun at her face as he tossed the end of a strap over her leg and tightened it over her thigh. He tightened it down so hard her knee locked, and she was completely immobile. He grabbed her hands and slipped them into a metal binding behind her back.

Behind her back? Confusion filled her as she tried to

sort out what the hell was happening. What the fuck was he doing?

He didn't want sex. She brought her eyes up to the commander as he pulled a plasma tool from a cabinet above her and slipped it on his hand. The room lit up as it hissed to life.

Realization dawned on her and her stomach fell to her feet. *He was going to cut her fucking foot off?!*

"Mars, help me! What the fuck are you doing?!" she screamed as he approached her ankle with the plasma torch lit and glowing hot. She thrashed against the table, rocking it.

"Hold still, or I will make this much worse," he maniacally smiled at her. He brought the torch down on her ankle, and she released a blood searing scream that echoed through the ship.

The ship tipped to one side, causing the commander to lose his footing. It took him several steps to regain his balance. He stalked forward, and again, the ship tipped to one side, but this time it had tipped much further. Falling backward and catching the corner of the next table, Dolion growled in frustration.

Tressa stared at her ankle. The skin was burned away on the top. She gasped to take in a full breath as she desperately worked through the pain.

Tressa could see Cinis pressed against the glass of their pod, crying, and pounding but no sound was escaping the airtight seals.

Seeming to face a microphone in the ceiling somewhere above him, Commander Dolion yelled, "Captain, what is your name?"

"B'lake Ringers," the intercom replied, not offering anything further.

"Explanation!" The commander demanded.

"Oh, that was just some pockets of turbulence in the upper atmosphere. We should be clear of it soon," Ringers reported casually.

His commander's face was snarled, "Don't let it happen again."

"I have no control over turbulence, sir." Ringer replied in the same flat tone as before.

Tressa loved B'lake. She didn't know why he was helping her, but she *knew* he was. The lights above them blinked a few times before turning completely off and flipping back on a second later.

The commander furiously approached Tressa's bound leg with the plasma torch, his gaze set on her ankle. She had been tearing at the bonds on her wrists to no avail. Her gut ached as she fought to release her hands from the metal digging into her skin. Blood dripped down the table from between her legs as she shook with the adrenaline coursing through her. She nearly had her thumb out of its socket as she continued to yank her hand upward.

The binds on her hands finally slipped down over her thumb before the ship tilted again, this time shifting all the way on its side and sending Commander Dolion rolling. With her hands free, she frantically worked on the buckle over her leg, but it was too tight, and he was returning, now more furious than before. "Hold the ship steady you useless fuck!" Commander Dolion screamed as he leapt the last few feet toward Tressa.

The ship tipped to the right and the commander fell over Tressa, giving her the opportunity to punch him in the temple with her fist before she slammed the end of the metal bindings down onto his forearm. He turned and growled at her as she bashed his arm again with the bindings trying to force him to release the plasma torch.

"Fuck you! You stupid cunt!" Dolion exploded in rage.

With a final smash from the metal bindings, he cried out as he loosened his grip on the torch and the metal table. The ship tilted so far to the side Dolion was now hanging from the tabletop, his feet peddling for traction but finding none.

With the torch slid all the way down to his fingertips, Tressa tried her luck and grabbed it. It was searing hot at the end, and she singed her fingers, but it was worth it. She gripped it, and bright heat erupted as she pressed the trigger. Tressa leaned in and thrust the torch forward, blazing commander in the side of the head. The tendons in his jaw snapped from the heat of the torch and he bit down on the end of his tongue. Blood spurt from his lips as he slid from the table, desperately trying to hold his face together as blood squirted from the steaming, open hole.

"When I damaged the thrusters, it took out shields, and we were hit with a satellite EM Pulse. We are losing altitude quickly. Free yourself and I'll manually send you and your friend down to the planet. Hurry, you only have two minutes until impact. I can eject your drop pod from here," Ringers reported over the com.

"What about you?" she asked as she cut through the thick strap over her leg.

"Don't worry about me; I'll be fine. You don't have time! Just go!" Ringers yelled as he turned on the emergency settings, lighting up her path to her pod.

The plasma torch blinked, it was out of fuel, and she tossed it away. She ran to Cinis first and slammed her hand down on the manual launch lever before she climbed into her own. Before she closed the glass over the top, she cried out, "Thank you, B'lake. I'll never forget what you did for me!"

Slamming the lid down on her pod, she heard its basic thruster engine ignite, and she shot out of the launch tube before she could react. Her head slammed into the rigid plastic seat, and she ached all over again from the impact. She knew she had about seven minutes before the pod landed, so she lifted her shirt under the harness to see what they had done to her.

She had one long bloody incision running right down the middle of her abdomen. Sliding her tunic style shirt back down, she noticed the blood flow had slowed a little since she wasn't moving as much though. Blood soaked right through the thin pants she wore. She still had her pain patch, but it was already half empty, and she only had a day of medicine left in it. Her eyes sought relief from anything in the pod, even though she knew it was empty, but she couldn't help it.

It was more than empty. It had even been cleaned out of the standard emergency drop ship ration packs. This was worse than a death sentence. She had grown up hearing her Nan tell stories about the hellish planet. This was the place the UTC sent you when you were convicted for crimes against the empire where death wasn't enough. The prison planet was where those condemned were meant to suffer at length before death. Suffering was the point. Death became a release.

This planet wasn't just to kill those sent there, it was so they were extensively tortured first. Over a thousand years before, the UTC helped the fruit Resper species escape from the planet of terrors they evolved on. The planet was volatile at best with giant cave systems, canyons from plate tectonics ripping the land in half, mountains reaching above the atmosphere, and prolific vulcanism.

As a child she brought home one of the schoolbooks she had stolen from a bag she found on the street. It was all due to that one planetary science book and her older sibling that she could read at all. Cinis had taught her everything they knew before they left for the academy. Everyone was tested, though. The only people chosen were people intelligent enough for the formal education program when they enlisted in the UTC military, or those who could afford private school.

The smartest, like Cinis, were recruited. Those who didn't test well, like her, weren't enlisted and were left scrounging for food. Cinis supported her and Nan by themselves for a few years before Tressa grew enough to find work as a street cleaner around Venus's temple block in district seven where they lived.

Working age started at ten, so things were hard until she was of age and could work legally. The UTC program began to move hungry smart kids off the street, and for a free education. The income was only survivable if they didn't have to support anyone else. Everything on Emendo, everything humans were in control of, all seemed to have a catch under the surface. Nothing good was ever what it seemed, so even with Cinis's help, starvation was never far away.

Even as a pocket of wind and turbulence rocked the pod, her mind was unable to focus on her current reality. Her past felt more present than her current state. Her hand absently rubbed her neck along her implant scar, thankful beyond reason.

After Cinis met Rungi, she gifted them each a translator implant. Account credits would appear in at random, and boxes of food or medical supplies would be delivered to their apartment. Tressa wasn't sure if she wanted to know why Cinis received the additional gifts, but she wasn't going to question it now they were both headed down to the doomed Resper world. She hoped she would have the chance to thank Cinis should they both survive this fall. She also didn't exactly have room to talk considering she had likely done more, for much less. Her stomach rolled thinking of the repulsive dates she accepted, and what pieces of herself she had to give up to eat. She was jealous of people who enjoyed such colorful, yet invasive, work.

She held her hand over the poorly sutured wound down her body. Thankfully, they bond the interior incisions, so her guts weren't at risk of falling out when she needed to run. That fear seemed far away in her mind, but the squeeze in her heart told another story.

Her drifting thoughts and dizzy waves made her wonder if she had suffered a head injury. She needed rest to heal, but the instant the pod landed, she would face the fight of her life.

She begged Venus to spare her and end her afterbirth bleeding.

The pod slowed down, the tops of the trees raced by, and an entire planet of bloodthirsty creatures would be hunting her as the wind carried the scent of her blood. Pleading to the gods was her only option left.

THREE
UTC PRISON PLANET –
NORTHERN CONTINENT

The landing gear dropped vibrating the pod, and Tressa met the ground without a bump. As the lid slowly opened, the scent of sulfur hit her nose, an unwelcome reminder of what lay ahead. The pod was stripped of all navigation software, so she had no idea where she was or where Cinis landed. She hoped they were alright, but she also knew better than to hold onto much hope in this place. Cinis might already be gone. Her heart broke at the thought, and she ached inside for them.

Pulling herself out of the pod, she cautiously surveyed the area. She was unexpectedly surprised to find a bubbling hot springs with billowing steam on one side of her and a dense evergreen forest on the other. Aside from the putrid scent of the sulfuric hot springs, the environment seemed peaceful. She knew she could not be that lucky.

Further away, she could see a runoff pond. She peered up at the night sky and hoped morning light wasn't far.

The darkness was enveloping here, the shadows in the woods moved and swayed as she took in every angle, she was accustomed to the bright lights of a city, not this raw, natural world. She thought she remembered this planet having a large ice-covered rocky moon. It must not be visible tonight, she guessed. So far, the only light was from a sky full of stars, one that was mesmerizing and so new.

Although there were thousands of stars which should have been visible, one couldn't see even a single star on Emendo at night. There was far too much pollution in their atmosphere. Searching through the trees for a hint of the moon, she found herself entranced by the thick band of stars stretching across the center of the sky like a diffused radiant stripe.

The stars were breathtaking, but she didn't have time to waste. Blood was a beacon on this planet, and if she didn't wash her pants and body clean, she would be dead before she ever had a chance to fight. Sucking in a sharp breath as her ankle throbbed, she refocused on her steps.

Slipping her pants off her hips, she grabbed her lower abdomen as she leaned over to remove them. Her knees and feet were aching and inflamed, she couldn't wait for the relief she sought in the warm water. She had never been able to afford a full bathtub of water before, just an inch or two a week at the most. Sometimes all they had was a single bowl, depending how much the drinkable water cost for the week. Prices changed at the tap daily, and one had to watch the price tickers on the billboards to keep track if you were too poor to buy a ticker for your apartment.

Her mind stopped racing as she held her burned foot up and eased her lower half into the putrid scented, warm water. Bringing her hand up and out of the water, she inspected her skin. Had it been a great idea to just jump into a volcanic spring fed pool? No. Tressa counted her blessings when her skin didn't peel off in strips. Scrubbing her pants against a rock, she held them up and squeezed them out to see if they were clean enough.

Shaking her head at herself as she stood there half nude, she didn't know if this water could help. Blood free flowed down her legs, as the afterbirth blood would flow for weeks. Plopping back down in the soothing natural pool, she searched her mind for what to do while the warmth eased her pain. Nothing, there was nothing she could do. The deep cramping subsided for a few minutes, but she knew it would be back when she left the haven of the pool.

A cold breeze slid through the woods and even in the warm water, the hair on her body stood on end. Knowing she needed to hurry, she did just that. Scrambling to wring out her wet pants, she squeezed them as hard as her aching hands allowed before slipping them back on. It was chilly but she knew it wasn't the cold that would kill her, so she grit her teeth to keep them from chattering.

Another crisp breeze slid against her skin, and she shivered. There was something more behind that shiver though, she thought as her eyes searched the ominous trees.

Something was watching her; her skin prickled and her heart pounded.

Alarm coursed through her as she prodded around for a stick or rock she could use in defense. A tree branch snapped to her left, and her eyes shot in the direction of the sound. Backing up carefully, she checked to be sure she wasn't backing into the hot spring.

When she turned back, terror gripped her by the throat.

A batlike creature crawled out of the shadows between the trees, sniffing the air. This monster was not what they described back home. It was built like a Resper, but seemed more primitive and wilder. Was this one of the blood Respers? Under her breath she muttered, "Jupiter spare me," and the creature turned its head in her direction, its beady black eyes staring right through her. *Oh gods.* It stalked closer. What in Venus name was she going to do? The bat outweighed her by over a hundred pounds at least. As it closed the gap, she could see it wasn't a normal Resper. It had a snout. Its face protruded forward like a wolf, and its bat like wings were enormous, far larger than any Resper she had ever seen back on Emendo. Long sharp claws grew from its hands and its hair covered body was thick with muscle. It stopped and sniffed the air again before resuming its foul intentioned approach.

Her back hit a tree, and the impact made a slight crackling sound where her body met the bark. Tressa knew this was it. The bat rushed for her. She was done for, and she had only been on the planet for a few hours at most. Had it even been three? She had spent too much time in the water. Was this beast going to kill her now or bring her somewhere to drain her like she had always heard in the stories? Was she going to experience the horrific death her Nan had always warned her of if she didn't behave? The monster sniffed the air again, and she noticed it opened its mouth, but she didn't have the capacity to wonder what it was doing. She was too busy trying to figure out how to survive this or if these were her last moments. Its sickly sweet, rotten meat breath hit her, and her stomach turned. Sniffing with every step, it slowly approached. Less than two inches from her face, it opened its mouth and released a high pitch cry into the night. Tressa whimpered in terror and the creature struck, sinking its teeth into her shoulder. A scream erupted from her as the creature bit down, tearing open her flesh. The pain was explosive as the beast slammed her back into the tree, and she groaned with the impact.

A high pitch shout came from deep in the woods behind them, and when Tressa looked back, the bat creature was gone. Relief was temporary as the shouting grew near. She cupped her bleeding shoulder and slid down the rough bark of the tree onto the ground.

"I hear a proto-bat in this direction," someone spoke in a deep voice.

They were moving much closer. An entirely different form of distress set in as she could hear more of their voices. It was men, several men from the sound of it.

"There! Grab them!" one shouted at the same time another high-pitched tone hit Tressa's ears.

She braced herself as a winged Resper man crashed into her, knocking her over from her place at the tree. She let out a grunt of pain as he flipped her, the movement jarring her insides. She was sure something tore as she whimpered painfully and grasped her belly.

"It's a female human. She's injured. No, she's just given birth," the Resper sniffed the air over her.

Remaining silent, she intended to maintain the rouse she didn't know their language. Sliding her hand to her lower belly, she groaned as she felt the area and found it too painful to stand, something was wrong.

Another Resper seemed to be checking her over, "She needs a healer if we're going to salvage this one. The other one recovered was in much better condition. We made more than usual on them at the auction. Maybe this one is valuable, too."

She couldn't see much but when they moved their faces to the sky, she could see ridges on the top of their noses and under their ears. Their ears pointed straight up and were taller than their heads.

The Resper standing over her sniffed at her shoulder, "The other one sold to Domitia the moment we walked them in. This one will go quickly too, with some repairs."

It appeared they were talking about Cinis, and she hoped what they said was true because that meant they were alive. Momentarily mental relief washed over her as they pulled her from the ground, yet pain made it all but impossible to stay aware. These were nowhere near normal Resper she thought. These men had enormous wings, much wider and thicker than the Resper she knew from home. The kind of Resper she knew hadn't flown in thousands of years, and she bet it was because their wings had shrunk too much to carry them.

They began slipping a leather harness over her arms and legs and seemed to be oddly careful as they tightened it under her rear.

One of the larger men turned to the smallest one who was tightening a strap on her leg, "Be careful. We don't want to damage her further. This one smells delicious. I bet she will bring us even more than the last one."

"I think they smell similar. Do you think they're related?" the smaller, young one asked.

Nodding, the tallest one agreed, "Most likely. I bet Nera Domitia will buy her at auction like she did the last one. That was the quickest sale we've ever made."

The tallest of the three leaned over and sniffed between

her legs, "I can smell fresh blood. She is bleeding internally. Forget the auction house. We need to put her in front of the butcher at House Domitia before she dies."

As soon as her brain registered what he said, Tressa lost consciousness.

FOUR

UTC PRISON PLANET - DUNGEON CELL III

If only their legs were shorter. They weren't sure they've ever wished such a thing. Cinis grimaced at the small cot they were stuck in but guessed it was better than the first place they ended up.

It had all happened so fast. They had been stuck in a grimy dungeon cell in what was some kind of ancient prison after being plucked from the ground like a rat in eagles' talons.

They had no idea what grabbed ahold of them, and they promptly screamed, which led to being knocked out. They awoke minutes later and found themselves urine soaked and crumpled in the corner of a stone room with other frightened humans. All the humans were dirty and destitute. They and their sibling were clearly not the only recent prisoner drops. They must have been dropped close to where this facility was located. The moment they stood up, a hulking Resper man in the corner leapt to his feet and dragged them through the cell doors.

After they were removed from the stone cell, the impossibly dark auction room they had been thrust into had been humiliating. After a few offers made in gold, a rich Resper woman decked in leather with an insignia of wings on her shoulders purchased them. The way the regal woman sniffed the air in their direction made their skin crawl.

Were they going to end up a blood cow for a wealthy Resper family? The thought made their stomach roll into a knot from what they knew of rich beings. Wealth meant cruel and ruthless in the galactic center.

Directionally, they still felt out of sorts. The entire journey had been in a box in the back of some kind of mechanical vehicle which made a lot of whistles and clicks. The cell they were now in was cramped and damp. With no way to tell time, they were toiling over how long they had been on the planet. They couldn't have been there long. Their clothes were still damp from the moisture and urine in the first dungeon. How far behind had Tressa been? Had the same hunters plucked her from the ground like the group had done to them?

It was everything they could do not to think about Tressa. All that blood on her, how could she have made it? Their heart was broken.

They tugged at their sweat soaked shirt from behind and wished their hands were untied. Their shirt was becoming uncomfortably twisted and needed to be adjusted.

"What's wrong with you?" The guard asked as he toyed with a small wooden box.

Trying not to huff, Cinis replied, "Nothing. It's none of your business."

"Do you need your hands unbound so you can adjust yourself?" he asked without looking up, sincerity in his offer.

"I need to unbind you to take your blood. If you cooperate, I'll exit after I'm finished, and I won't bind your hands back," he explained.

Cinis thought for a moment and decided if they were going to live, they needed to act right. A piece of hair touched their forehead, and they shook it out of their face before agreeing, "I'll cooperate."

"After your blood is drawn, they will take you upstairs, and you will be interrogated on why you're here. I don't suggest lying," Vin took the metal cuffs off their hands.

Cinis stuck their arm out and admitted, "I'm a shitty liar."

They knew they shouldn't be telling this blood sucking fuck anything, but they were too tired to pretend they were street smart. As Tressa always said, they didn't know shit from shit. They rolled their eyes as the needle went in their vein and hissed at the prick of pain.

"If that hurt, you're not going to fair well here," he passed Cinis a flat stare.

They lowered their head but confidently replied, "I've had to live a life trapped at a solitary desk on a hidden planet so my sister and grandmother could live and eat. They had it hard and she lived a rough life, but Tressa was fed. If I die because I'm weak for it, and she lives because she is tough, it will be worth it."

Cinis recalled only being allowed a short, monitored leave of absence to step away from their post for a few months when Tressa was in trouble. Cinis could still feel a ghost of the ankle monitor they put on to detect certain key words. It would notify the base command if they spilled any secrets.

Flashes of Rungi filled their mind, and their time together, and the deal they had made for Tressa in exchange for whatever Rungi had wanted of them.

"You don't belong here, do you?" he asked quietly, bringing them back to reality.

Shaking their head, "No. I don't think so. We helped these people called the Iungo, but we were somehow caught. I'm worried about my sister. She just had a baby, and one of the commanders may have done something terrible to her before they put us in the dump ships."

"I believe you. I just hope Nera believes you. She will have lot of questions. I'm not sure what to tell you about your sister. She may already be dead if she's bleeding. The diseased proto-bats arrived in this area years ago," he explained.

Clearing his throat as he held the blood vial as it filled, "My name is Vinston Domitia, but you can call me Vin."

"I'm Cinis. Thank you for being so kind. They tell us stories about the Blood Resper and the prison planet so that we will behave as children on Emendo where I'm from," they admitted.

"My planet has a name," Vin replied, seeming to take some offense.

"Isn't that what the planet is called? The prison planet?" Cinis asked.

He laughed at their naivety, "No, it's called Alisot. They changed the planet's name to *the prison planet*?"

"Do you not usually talk to the humans?" Cinis wished they hadn't asked that.

Smiling deviously, Vin leaned in and softly replied, "No. I am far too busy eating your kind. You're lucky Nera likes the way you smell. I probably would have emptied you of blood before I could think twice. So delicious"

Rearing back Cinis's eyes widened, and they asked, "What? You're, uh, you're joking right?"

Flashing his teeth, Vin slid his red forked tongue around his mouth and flicked out at them before it receded behind his lips, "Humans have a fantastic vascular system in their inner thighs. The blood moves so quickly that draining your kind there becomes rather thrilling."

Cinis's heart pounded, and their false sense of security slipped away like the air from their lungs.

"I'm finished. Hold still and hold this here," he pulled the needle out and put a strip of fabric over the crook of their arm.

A drop of their blood pooled at the tip of the needle, and he swiped it off with his finger, immediately popping it in his mouth and making a delighted mmm sound.

"That was disturbing." Cinis couldn't help but say under their breath.

He grinned as he laughed, "We are going to have fun with you. I'll be back in a little while when it's time to bring you to Nera."

He continued to chuckle as he exited the cell and slammed the door.

Cinis was going to throw up. They searched the room for something to puke in, but there was nothing. Cinis swallowed it down and begged their body to calm before they made a mess of the small cell. Bending over, they put their head between their legs and took slow deep breaths.

This was not the time to panic, or maybe the anemia they always seem to have had was rearing its head at the worst possible time. They didn't know and didn't care. All that mattered was they felt like they were dying and didn't know how to make it stop. Lightning seemed to dance in their eyes, and a wave of euphoria pass over them.

The door opened, and they heard a deep huff from Vin, "Lie back."

Cinis didn't rebel in the slightest and slumped over onto the cot. Before they could think, their legs were in the air and blood was rushing back to their head.

"When was the last time you ate something?" Vin asked from between Cinis's lifted legs, his brow furrowed.

"That's a funny question," Cinis laughed. When was the last time they had eaten? It had most likely been days ago with Rungi. They hadn't had even a can of cooked beans in their apartment. Was it yesterday or the day before when they had eaten a handful of mixed nuts they found stashed in Tressa's room? Their mind was foggy, and they were unable to recall.

"That long ago, huh?" Vin asked as he sighed and dropped Cinis's legs on the cot.

Rolling his eyes he didn't wait for them to reply, "Nera is probably going to have my balls for dessert, but we are crashing her private dinner. You're as pale as a nightworm."

"Thanks," Cinis replied flatly as they took Vin's hand so he could lift them up.

Cinis feet were swinging up again as Vin lifted their long, but lean, body into his arms and carried them out of the cell. Their bare feet dragged the wall in the narrow hallway until they reached the top of a set of stone stairs with ivy crawling along the inside of the grout.

Passing through a corridor filled with rich tapestries, marble sculptures, and beautiful works of scenic art; however, it all seemed to reach out to them the way every click of Vin's boots caused the finery in the passageway to sing back to them. Cinis was rubbing their eyes trying to take in everything, but it wasn't too many more steps until Vin turned around and pressed a door open with his rear.

A throat cleared as they entered the room, and a strong feminine voice filled the space. "What the fuck do you think you're doing?"

"They're anemic, and I don't think they have eaten regular meals in years. The blood sample sent them into a fainting episode. They need food now," Vin ordered with a flare of authority in his tone.

Scowling, Nera pointed to a spot at the far end of the table. Vin pulled a chair out with his foot and set Cinis down. They fell back into the V cut in the back of the chair and would have tumbled out backward if Vin hadn't caught the back of their neck.

A man spoke from the darkness across the room, "You're right. Good catch. You're learning well."

Vin set Cinis's head on the table and their arms flopped to their sides.

They had not been this desperate for food and water since they were nine. Stars flickered in their vision and their hands were so cramped they couldn't pry them open. The earthy scent of the grand wooden table was all they could register.

Vin filled a bowl at the serving bar and set some stew on the table. Cinis smelled the stew, and their head popped up.

They lifted the spoon and took a sip, the flavor was bright and savory. After devouring one bowl, Vin refilled the bowl, and they devoured all of it too. Setting the second bowl down, they peered around and found two men and one stunning woman with nearly black hair, a perfectly oval face, and tan skin at the other end of the table. One of the men was Vin, and finally seeing him in the lit room, Cinis could see he was the tallest, with dark brown hair and broad chested. Vin was easily six or seven inches over six foot, he towered over Cinis and they were almost five foot ten. Cinis decided Vin had a magnificent jawline and the most beautiful eyes, a light whiskey brown. The remaining Resper man was tall, but not as tall as Vin. He could have been a model on Emendo, with dark brown hair, a square jaw, deep tan skin, and his green eyes were bright like a jungle snake. The woman must be Nera, Cinis thought. This tall, domineering woman radiated enough power to fill any room she entered. It was the same woman who bought them at the auction. Her black eyes seemed to pierce through their soul. They were all clad in battle ready, cherry red-stained chestnut leather clothing with long knives in sheaths at their sides. The leather she wore was more like armor, with scaled layering added on the arms, legs, and shoulders. A carved filigree around the cuffs and collar added a touch of beauty to the sharp, cold leather.

Nera spoke, breaking the silence, "Why are you here?"

These must be the questions Vin warned them about.

"I was caught after helping the Iungo earn their freedom. There are even warrants for the First Human leaders after what we discovered. I'm here because one of the FH commanders found us and dropped my sister and I here," Cinis explained as their voice shook.

With a scowl on her face, Nera asked, "What is an Iungo?"

Cinis answered, "I think they evolved from a scorpion, or its cousin. I'm not sure. I worked for the UTC and was stationed on their home-world for years. At the time, I wasn't allowed to know where I was, and I still don't know much about them. When they rebelled against the First Humans, I stayed behind and helped them."

Nera leaned forward as she picked up a goblet. "Vin, please return them to their cell. Don't schedule another blood draw until further notice."

FIVE

ALISOT – HOUSE OF DOMITIA – DUNGEON CELL III

Cinis walked in front of Vin as he took them back to their cell, "Is there a bucket of some kind so I can relieve myself?"

Vin turned to them and sneered, "Listen, I don't know what kind of life you humans lived on Emendo. I am not here to judge. We might not have electricity, but we do have indoor plumbing. Just knock on the door. There's a bathroom at the end of the hall."

Trying not to make eye contact with Vin, Cinis asked, "Why is it that you've never developed electricity again after the fall? Didn't all the Resper at one time have space propulsion technology?"

"The fall? Never re-developed electricity? They are still telling those same lies?" Vin's irritation marred his handsome face.

Cinis stopped and turned in frustration, "Lies?"

Vin shook his head at them, "Lies. The UTC have targeted electromagnetic radiation which emits a pulse from satellites above the planet. It's designed to cause any electronic device to blow its circuits, charged or not. If it detects anything, the satellites deploy EM pulse bombs and drop them over the area. The rest of the story is none of your business. If you really want to know, you'll have to ask Nera, and she may never tell you."

A bang sounded at the front door, and Vin rolled his eyes, "You know what? Fuck it. You can come. Don't get in the way."

He turned and headed up the stairs, but when he noticed Cinis wasn't following, he turned back, "Are you coming, or do you like it down here?"

Struck with confusion at why Vin didn't lock them in the cell, Cinis followed Vin to the entryway with massive wooden front doors. The pounding from the other side of the door happened again, and Vin didn't hesitate to swing both doors open.

"We need the butcher," a tall Resper man barked.

Cinis froze. It was the same men who found them and took them to auction. They had whispered such despicable things. Clearing their mind and taking a breath, they decided they wanted to see what was so important and took a step to the side.

Cinis gasped and screeched, "That's my sister!"

Tressa dangled limply in the tall Resper man's arms.

Vin turned his head around to Cinis and back to the men, "Bring her to the table, now. I need to ring Lock." Vin tore down the hall and rang a bell somewhere behind a curtain. Within seconds, Nera and Lock were running down the hallway with their wings tucked in tight.

Lock burst through the entry into the dining room, "What's happened?"

The tall man lay Tressa on the dining table, "This one might be dying, Lock. She needs a butcher. Nera paid a fortune for her sibling. Figured you would want this one alive."

At the word butcher, Cinis felt faint and lost all color. Nera approached and pushed Cinis into a chair before they lost consciousness. Turning to face the men, she commanded, "Lock, take her and do everything you can. I have questions that need answers, and I'm damn glad I went with my intuition."

Turning to the group of collectors, Nera offered, "I'll take her for the same price as the last one."

The tall collector nodded, "That'll do."

Nera turned and headed for the door, "I'll retrieve your payment. Stay where you are."

Nera all but ran down to her rooms and headed straight into her changing nook where her safe was hidden. Pushing her robes to the side, she revealed the seven-foot safe door camouflaged into the wall. Pressing on the wall in the right place revealed a dial. Nera turned the dial on her intricate safe lock as she debated herself, "What are you doing buying these human blood cows? You already have a room full of cows, Nera. Their sweet smell alone is not why you bought them. You want more than a little taste. You had to go and buy their sister too, impulsively. What the fuck is wrong with you?!"

SIX

ALISOT – HOUSE OF DOMITIA

After he slammed the front door behind the group of collectors, Vin turned to Cinis, "You know where your cell is. We are going to try to do something about your sister. You need to rest."

"What are you going to do to my sister? Why is he called a butcher?" they asked, bile rising.

Vin rolled his eyes when he noticed the scar at their throat and rambled to himself, "Of course you wouldn't actually know our language, you're using an implant translator. I should have realized the magnetic pulse wouldn't knock out tech that's run with a nervous system. I am not revealing a speck of this to Nera. She would probably rip it out of your throat."

"Butcher doesn't translate well. We are trying to save her life. We have a medicine we put in her spine to keep her from feeling pain, and we have another one to make her sleep." Vin tried to explain and shifted on his feet in thought.

Cinis clarified, "Surgeon?"

The word was also not translating directly from their throat like it was supposed to, or they assumed that is what was happening with the device. They knew it was wrapped around their vocal cords and they clearly felt part of it crawl up to wrap around their ear canal. It was a disturbing experience.

Vin widened his eyes with his lips protruding, "Serrrgeeeooon?"

Cinis bit their lips together before asking, "Can I stay close?"

"No. If Lock knew you were near, he would be furious with me. Go to your cell and don't worry about your sister." Vin snapped.

Cinis watched behind Vin as Lock carried Tressa down the hall. They solemnly nodded and headed down to their cell. Every step down into the dark and cold dungeon under the house, their breathing became more difficult. They couldn't help but think all the horror stories about the blood Resper might have been true after all. They were just more civilized about it than they had expected, but these Respers were still blood suckers.

Vin watched as Cinis trailed off toward their cell. He turned on his heels, tucking his wings in tight, and rushed to follow Lock in the medical wing.

Lock lay Tressa on the table and began washing up. Vin followed and as they were scrubbing in, Tressa groaned but remained still.

She slid her hand over where her uterus was and gasped as she pressed in.

Lock bumped Vin's shoulder for his attention as they both scrubbed their hands, "I'm glad they have similar parts because I've never cut up a human I wanted to keep alive. This could have been one short procedure."

"Don't get any ideas halfway through. These two are far from the typical humans we buy. Neither are criminals. I don't know how Nera knew, but she did." Vin dried his hands and headed over to prep the tools.

"Vin," was all Lock could say after he cut off Tressa's shirt.

Jagged scars and stretch marks covered her swollen abdomen, and she had loosened skin in the center. Vin leaned against the table as he examined her with Lock. "What the fuck did they do to this woman?" Lock asked as he ran his finger over one of the scars. Tressa didn't move with the contact, and Lock realized she must be as dehydrated and malnourished as Cinis was. What had happened to her? Why was her body mutilated so badly? He prepped her body to cut her sutures as Vin started the sedative medication in her arm. They worked together to turn her to start the line in her back. Blood dripped from the table and trickled down the metal legs onto the floor. "Vin, grab a donor bag and start a line. Her blood pressure is dropping. We need it up before we can begin."

After she stabilized, Lock nodded to Vin.

When Lock began, he followed one of her previous scars. It had been one of the worst, and he made sure to cut along the ridges where she had been cinched together too tightly.

When he opened her up, her insides were a devastated war zone. The scar tissue from her previous procedures had fused her organs together. It took several hours to remove it all, and he had to remove her ruptured uterus. There was no way to repair the rip. By the time he was finished, he had a bowl filled with her scar tissues.

Lock stood over her open body and licked his lips.

"You're joking. I mean, I know..." Vin trailed off as he

stepped back and stared at Lock who was fixated on Tressa's body cavity. Leaning over and opening his mouth, Lock carefully licked every place he had removed scar tissue inside of her. His forked tongue slathered over each area before moving to the next. He lifted the sheet over her legs and licked the burn on her ankle as well. Vin stood by the table waiting impatiently for Lock to finish. After her body cavity, he licked the wound on her shoulder before bandaging it.

After using a fourth of their entire compatible blood supply over many hours, Tressa was carefully sewn up by Lock as Vin cleaned up the implements on the tray table.

Lock snipped the end of the last of the sutures and turned to Vin, "Go inform Cinis their sister is going to recover. She will be awake in a few hours."

Vin nodded and headed straight to Cinis, finding them missing from their cell.

"Cinis?" Vin asked down the dark hallway.

Nothing.

"Fuck."

Where the hell did they run off to? Nera would serve him his own balls for breakfast if he didn't find Cinis before she did. Sprinting down the hallway Vin checked the bathroom and found it empty. "Where the hell did you go?" He whispered to himself as he thought about all the places they might be.

Logic changed his focus, and Vin huffed and headed toward the kitchen mumbling, "Hungry."

He knew exactly where Cinis was. He could hear them in the kitchen all the way from the dungeon. Just as he suspected, he found Cinis standing in the doorway of the pantry.

"Do you need something else to eat?" Vin asked, startling Cinis and sending them leaping in the air.

Cinis grabbed their chest and apologized, "I'm sorry. I couldn't help it. First the stew earlier and now this, I've never seen so much food in one place."

"Your sister is going to be alright," Vin shared.

"I know. I was standing behind the door when Nera left. I heard what you said," Cinis replied, not taking their eyes off the rows of jars filled with meats and vegetables.

"Do you want to explain what happened to her?" Vin softly queried.

Cinis sunk their head. "She was in trouble, I only know it was over a guy and a large theft. Someone died, but she didn't do anything wrong. It was her boyfriend who did it all. She was just there. The only option at the time to keep her from the prison planet was the UTC surrogate program. They issue a meal card for the duration of the pregnancy, so it also gave me a break from having to find a way to feed her and our Nan. She was sixteen when the doctors said she was fully grown and could begin. She was three days from eighteen when she had her first," Cinis explained.

"How many?" Vin asked.

"I think she just had her ninth. She contracted to have six, but she liked being well fed for the time she was pregnant, so she kept signing up. She would have kept having them until she died. It's either that or clean the streets, but I think she has something wrong with her hands and feet. The other options are for stronger people than she and I. People who have the courage to sell their bodies in other ways."

Shaking his head Vin admitted, "We knew Emendo

was bad, but I don't think we paid enough attention to the dying words of all of the humans over the years."

"What do you mean?" Cinis asked.

Vin smiled uncomfortably and looked anywhere but toward Cinis, "We usually buy blood cows at the market and torture them until they die. Mostly for sport though. It's our favorite thing to do when we're hungry and bored."

With their eyes wide and color draining from their face, Cinis whispered, "Oh."

"Are you going to pass out?" Vin's concern was sincere.

Stars blossomed in Cinis vision, "Yes. I think so."

Huffing, Vin reached out and caught Cinis before they lost consciousness, and half carried them to a chair at the table. Leaning their head over, they absently banged their forehead on the table as they put their head down.

Unsure of what to say, Vin tried to make it better, "We have no intention of eating the two of you. Well, no. Let me rephrase. We are not going to kill you and your sister, and you won't experience any pain. Well, um. Maybe a little pain? Shit. I am not very good at this."

Cinis groaned, "Please, stop talking."

Vin mumbled awkwardly, "Sorry."

Lock approached the table and narrowed his eyes at Cinis before asking, "Why are they in the kitchen acting like they need an iron infusion? Why are humans all so sick and mangled before they are dumped off here? We eat most of them right away, so I guess we've never given it any thought before, but now that there's a few we want to make last. It's an odd conundrum. It seems like they've been plucked from actual hell and dropped off here to quickly be put out of their misery. Surely, they aren't sent here to experience *more* misery. I believe the UTC has failed in their ultimate goal of making this a *prison* planet. They severely miscalculated our love for immediately disemboweling humans and drinking the nice pool of warm blood they create."

"Oh, gods. Can you not?!" Cinis pleaded, with their face plastered on the table.

They took a few deep slow breaths.

Vin smiled at Lock knowingly, "Cinis has a rather weak stomach."

Lock laughed, "My apologies, Cinis. I'll try to keep our meal discussions more private."

An ornate clock chimed on the wall, and Lock turned to face it, "Your sister should be waking up soon."

SEVEN

ALISOT –HOUSE OF DOMITIA

Lock returned to the medical recovery room to check on Tressa, but she was no longer there. He began searching the room then up and down the hall. "Where is she?" He called out.

Cinis, still not feeling well and swaying, asked, "You lost my sister?"

"No." Sniffing the air, Lock brushed by them. Sprinting down the hallway with his wings tucked into his body, Lock turned a corner and found Tressa frantically trying to turn the handle of the enormous, wooden front door.

Leaping behind her, he grumbled, "You don't want to do that."

Tressa reared back as she took in Lock. Her back slammed against the giant wood door, shaking the wall around it. Too good looking to be real, this was without any doubt a disguised demon from Pluto who stood before her. Surely he would have crimson skin, long black horns, and a sharp tail under this façade he managed to create.

Was it magic? Horror filled her, and she felt a scream building in her chest.

Cinis came up beside Lock and pleaded, "Tressa please lie back down. You need to rest. You just had surgery." Gritting his teeth, Lock glared at Cinis, then he shifted his attention back to Tressa and took a step toward her. "You had a significant amount of scar tissue we had to remove. Your uterus had a large tear, and it had to be removed as well. I'm not sure how you're walking with the medicine we gave you. When you come back to the bed, I can give you something additional for the pain if you need it. I worked for hours to make sure I put you back together correctly. Have a look at your abdomen and see for yourself. Please don't undo all my work." Tressa searched the room, darting her eyes back and forth, before she turned around. When she finally complied to Lock's request and looked at her abdomen, she gasped. He had fixed the hideous buckling scar running all the way across her lower belly. It looked like normal skin again. She sniffled trying to swallow down the knot in her throat. Maybe it was time to make a plan instead of running. She needed to take him up on those pain meds and rest. She was not ready to escape yet. She and Cinis, could find somewhere to go where there were other humans, at least find beings who didn't want to eat them. Complying, she reached out for Lock, and he took her hand to help her back to bed. His hand was strong but warm and he guided her back to the recovery room carefully. Once she settled, Lock instructed her, "You need to stay in the recovery bed for at least two days. You have a bell if you need to use the restroom. Someone will assist you."

Tressa reared up and scowled, "I am capable of using the restroom myself," before pain forced her back down.

Fury burned behind his bright green eyes as Lock narrowed in on her, "I didn't work for seven hours on a blood cow for you to fuck it all up." Having enough Lock pulled restraints from under the medical bed and strapped Tressa's right arm down before she could say a word.

Pulling at the restraint she yelled, "Fuck you!"

Lock grabbed her left arm and tightened the strap around it too, "If you keep fighting, I'll sedate you."

"Good!" she yelled before she spit in his face.

He radiated murder as he wiped his eyes. Turning to Cinis, Lock leaned in an inch away from their face and seethed, "Your sister is a nightmare. You better end up obedient blood cows, or I'll gut you both myself."

Lock all but leapt to a tray with a syringe and filled it from a vial. He approached the medical bed where he restrained Tressa and slammed the syringe into her thigh. She leaned forward and hissed at him as the meds took effect. In seconds her eyes drooped, and she fell back against the pillow. When she was fully sedated, he turned and abruptly left the room without another word. Cinis took a slow breath of relief as Vin approached from behind and put his hand on their shoulder. "He's just tired and pissed off," Vin explained. Vin tilted his head in thought and continued, "You know, I take it back. I don't think I have ever seen him in a good mood. He's an asshole all the time."

Cinis smiled, "What makes you so nice?"

Vin laughed, "I'm not nice. I'm just happy."

"Oh." The smile faded from Cinis's face.

"I really shouldn't be happy, but I met a guy I like, and it's going really well," Vin smiled bashfully, a bit of flush showing on his tan cheeks.

Cinis's brows raised, "OH! I'm happy for you. I hope it works out."

Vin grinned and shrugged, "Thank you. He's coming by tonight. I plan on telling him I made friends with a blood cow, so maybe I can introduce you. He is not going to believe it. Lock and I both are well known for being exceptionally brutal. This is far out of character for me." Cinis paled. Vin noticed Cinis's abrupt change in composure. "Sorry, I keep forgetting. Just breathe. I'm sure you'll adjust eventually."

Tressa woke briefly and groaned from her drugged state, "Get a room you two flirty fucks."

Vin chuckled boisterously with his fangs shining brightly in the firelight. "You know? I like her too! You are both such interesting people. I think I'm going to love this. Fun, nice humans? What a concept!"

Cinis wasn't sure they could handle any more of the safety-danger yo-yo. "I need to lie down."

Tressa jerked against the restraint mumbling, with her middle finger sticking up. "Lie on this!"

Vin exploded with laughter. "That's it. You two are going to make excellent drinking buddies."

Scooping up Cinis, Vin might as well have skipped down the hall, his wings fluttering haphazardly behind him as their legs bounced in the air with his steps.

Cinis could feel that Vin was beginning to care about them. It was comforting knowing this murderous, beastly-sized male may be on their side, but he wasn't making it easy on their nerves. When he brought them all the way to the dungeon and started to take a step into their room, he stopped and stared at it. "I'm going to talk to Nera about having you moved into the main part of the house. There is a garden courtyard in the center, and all the bedrooms have access from the balconies. Nera keeps the pond in the center stocked and there are big birds which smell like fish. They visit in the summer, and we let them in the back door, they walk right in honking," Vin rambled.

Whispering to themselves as Vin let them down to sit on their cot, "Why does this planet seem so much better than Emendo?"

"Because it is better. Alisot can be deadly, but it's a beautiful planet. We have a lot of earthquakes, but they're mainly small. All our volcanoes are synced to our moon rotation making them predictable. The only real problem is we are trapped here," Vin answered before he closed the cell door. He stood and stared at Cinis for a moment before reopening the door and leaving it cracked. A corner of his mouth tipped up before he headed back upstairs.

ALISOT –HOUSE OF DOMITIA

Feeling rough, strong hands touch the skin on her belly, Tressa's eyes flew open, and she found Lock standing over her checking her sutures.

"Maybe you could warm your freezing hands before you put them on me," Tressa grumbled, watching two versions of Lock separate and fuse back together.

"My hands are not cold. You have a lot of sedatives in your system," Lock explained.

Clearing her throat, Tressa huffed, "I need to pee."

"Can you wait until the nurse returns?" Lock asked as he peered down at one of the sutures.

Tressa shook her head, "Nope. Now."

Rolling his eyes, Lock pulled her gown back down, "Fine. No bullshit. If you act up, I'll spank your ass like a youngling and strap you back to the bed in a diaper."

Tressa smiled deviously, "You promise?"

Lock paused, loosening the straps on her wrists, "I'm not fucking around. Vin might like you, but I don't. I will take pleasure in your punishment. If it wasn't for Nera, I would have eaten you already."

"You're a useless man just like the rest. Fine. I'll behave you curmudgeon," Tressa grimaced, trying to ignore his last statement.

Tressa began wiggling her hips. "Hurry up! I'm going to pee any second."

When he finished removing her restraints, Lock lifted her from the bed and carried her behind a curtain and into a large bathroom. He set her in front of the bathroom and turned around.

"I need help." Tressa was not smiling this time.

"With what?" Lock sharply asked.

"I can't sit down. My legs are too shaky," Tressa admitted.

Roughly exhaling, Lock reluctantly turned back around and held his hands out. She took them with a slap. Putting all her weight onto his hands, she slowly inched back toward the toilet seat. She took as long as possible to sit down and by the time she was seated, Lock was pulling away and trying to escape through the curtain. Chuckling under her breath, she did her business. It was obvious they needed her and Cinis for something and hopefully other than blood. God's help her she was not going to be disemboweled by this monster after he had fixed her. What a dumbass she was being. She really needed to pass these drugs from her system. Nope, she took that back, the drugs were nice, and she wasn't hurting at all. Wait, he said Nera was why he hadn't eaten her. She was in charge, not Lock. *He had been making empty threats!* Oh, this gave Tressa so many ideas.

Staring at the back of his head between the curtains, she sat there thinking a moment. She made a conscious decision to wheedle her way under Locks skin and was going to stay there permanently. If he wasn't allowed to eat and kill her, annoying him would be incredibly pleasurable.

"Lock!" she obnoxiously cried out after she had finished.

First peeking through the curtain with his green eyes turned down, he stalked in and put his hands out for her like his swiftness would reduce the time of his forced contact.

Rising from the seat, Tressa made sure to put all her weight on him. Irritation flaring, Lock scooped her up and carried her back to the bed. He acted like her skin was acidic and her body was somehow too toxic to keep contact with.

Sliding her off his arms, he wrapped the strap around her wrist and cinched it. He efficiently did the same to her other wrist before she could say anything.

"Uh...," was all she could utter as he shut the door behind him.

What the fuck was that all about? she wondered. Did he really hate her that much? This was going to be entertaining. The drugs made her mind shift again as she thought when Nera wasn't looking, he would probably beat her and drain all her blood as punishment. Why did the prospect of dying sound fantastic at the moment? What odd people, those Resper are. They do have good painkillers though. Speaking of Resper people, what was up with Nera? Were they about to become long term snacks for that terrifying woman? Did Vin like Cinis more than just a friend? Something made Tressa wonder if they were going to have to give more than their blood and fear slithered down her spine. What if that was true?

They needed to escape *the fuck out* of this house of horrors before Cinis was caught up in something they couldn't flee.

Or didn't want to.

She trembled thinking of how impressionable Cinis could be, and Tressa had always been scared of Cinis's complicated involvements. Tressa might be a sucker for a cute guy, but Cinis was a sub across the board. Tressa cringed inside at the idea of losing her sibling to a blood sucking abuser. Red flags with spotlights on them flashed everywhere in this place. Just because they hadn't been filling up their blood bags yet didn't mean it was not where this nightmare was headed. The sedatives were wearing off, and she would put on her best performance to escape. She had already built a hate-hate relationship with Lock, so she guessed it was time to be sweet to Vin. Maybe he would fall for it and let her out of this bed. As if she was drawing him to her with her thoughts, Vin appeared in the doorway. "Are you hungry? I made Cinis more stew, and they were asleep when I brought it by. I can't eat regular food like Nera and Lock, just blood. Do you want it?" Being nice to Vin might not be too hard after all, she thought as she smiled at him. Tressa lifted her hand, "I might need some help eating." Vin shook his head as he brought the stew over, "I am not spoon feeding you stew. I can hardly stand the scent of cooked meat, and this steaming bowl is making me nauseated. I can let you out. Lock is a prick. You're not going to run away. It's not like you have anywhere to go." He laughed at his last statement, and Tressa screamed inside. Setting the bowl down next to her, he promptly loosened the straps on both of her hands. He handed her the bowl and a napkin before pulling a spoon from his pocket.

"Don't worry. I wear freshly cleaned clothes every day. I'm not anything like the collectors. They are the lowest of our society and certainly smell like it." Vin explained, his mouth in a superior sneer.

"But humans are all scum and deserve to die?" Tressa couldn't help but say as she took the first sip of stew.

Vin nodded agreeing, "If you met the humans I have, you would have hated them all, too. They were hardly worth the blood and sinew inside of them, tasty but useless beings."

"Why do you like human blood so much?" she asked.

Shrugging, he replied, "Blood is blood for the most part. Unless we hate you or you're scared, then you're extra tasty. We hate humans because they helped trap us here. Chasing down, ripping into, and draining your kind is a highly pleasurable experience. All the great houses purchase them at the collector's auctions. Some torture them for a long time, others kill them on the spot. It can depend on what the human admits or says. Nera kept one hung upside down in the dungeon during the first six years after she became the head of her house. I should mention, she took over house Domitia when she was just eight years old. That stupid fuck told her she was just the right age to suck him off after she had just bought him at a southern auction. I was standing next to her, and I'll never forget the smile on her face. That human suffered more than any being I've ever heard of and the more he admitted, the more she wanted to keep him alive to keep going. She really enjoyed it. So much that she had a room built in her private quarters. I was surprised since she was so young, but nothing stopped her. He finally broke loose one day and jumped over the balcony and threw himself onto the stones below. He didn't have all his skin, so when he landed his insides sort of exploded out of him like a squished bug."

With her mouth open so wide her throat was drying, Tressa coughed then struggled trying to find words. Nera had skinned him, and he had remained alive.

Vin grinned at her as if he had not just told a thoroughly disturbing tale, "We're a lot. I know. You'll grow accustomed to it. Eat up before your food cools."

Tressa stared at her stew, unable to decide if her stomach would allow her to eat after what Vin revealed. These were not just average killer types. These people loved pain and suffering although seeming to be well-adjusted and stable. This place truly was damnation embodied. *She was trapped here,* and she needed to befriend Pluto's demons if she wanted to claw her way out.

Vin opened the door to their cell, letting the firelight of the hallway stream in, Cinis crankily awoke, wondering if they will ever sleep again.

"Do you ever sleep?" Cinis groaned, vision still unfocused.

"Yes. Better upside down though. Generations ago, Nera's house had many fruit bats working in it, but since they lost their ability to fly and hang upside down thousands of years ago, most of the rooms have beds instead of bars. Only Nera's and Lock's rooms have sleeping bars."

"Why did they lose their ability to fly?" Cinis asked, the thought of the loss seemed profound in that moment.

Vin bit his lip before facing Cinis, "Their ancestors thought they were too good for it during the rise of technology and space travel. They eventually lost the ability altogether after just a few generations when wing size began to decrease. If you don't use them, you lose them. The blood bat families saw it happening and we started our flying lessons at three years old. I couldn't imagine having useless wings. The flying is what I think started our divide."

Cinis was struck with confusion. "They all walk the streets and act like humans do on Emendo. I don't understand why they would give up flying or their own home world."

"The blood bats have always been shown to have more grit compared to the fruit bats if you want my opinion. They were always desperate to be better than us, but they have always lacked in the arduous work. I think they condemned us here because they were jealous. Nera thinks all these political things were in play. We know they were offered a gene edit to remove all their blood craving genes to effectively remove us from their population altogether before the final divide. I think they just became too envious to look at us anymore. The dumbest part is many of the fruit bats and blood bats intermarried thousands of years ago when our planet was prosperous and part of the economy of the galactic center. None of us are fully one or the other, or that's how it used to be. The way to tell the difference now is wing size or if they have manipulated genes, but before we were all a nearly identical species of just various skin and hair colors depending on where our ancestors originated on the planet. We were all just born with different dietary preferences depending on our parents. We were one intermixed and successful society until we made deals with the First Humans.

Long ago, we had massive cities and universities covering miles of land. There are still ruins of industrial buildings so wide I could fly from one end to the other without grazing one of my wings on a wall. They studied the vulcanism of our world, biology, physics, space travel, literature, and the arts. Music halls were constructed in caverns to send the choir's voices broadcasting out to a sea of our people waiting to hear the melodies on the surface. My mother used to tell me stories of our old world when I was a boy. How beautiful it was."

"I had no idea," Cinis whispered, sadness for the blood Resper washing over them.

Vin leaned against the wall. "Now we are condemned to our own planet as bottom dwelling blood suckers and parasites used by humans to dispose of their scum. Stories are spread about our world, lies of only horror and hate. We eventually became the monster's humans made us out to be, yet the same humans were surprised when it happened. Anyway, enough of all that negative history talk. Tressa should know we can sense body temperature fluctuations and slight changes in your voices. I know she's planning to run. I've been hunting humans all my life. Please explain to her if she takes off, she's dead. Lock can't control himself, and he will go wild with rage, no matter what Nera orders. He never cares about anything, but for some reason, he put a lot of effort into her repair. It was out of character. I think he's going through something, but he won't talk about it. He's a loose cannon until he sorts his shit out, which honestly, could be never."

"I'll talk to her," Cinis replied as they wiped the sleep from their eyes and rubbed their sore knees from sleeping cramped up in the small cot.

Vin bounced up from the wall. "Oh, right, why I came down here. I talked to Nera, and she said you can move to the room next to mine. She even said when we allow Tressa to walk around, and we trust her, she can move into the room on the other side of you. Just talk to Tressa please. I don't want to have to lock your sister in the dungeon permanently."

Cringing inside at the subtle, not-so-subtle, message conveyed, Cinis nodded and wrapped their arms around their middle.

"Why do you always seem like you're going to lose your lunch?" Vin asked.

Cinis closed their eyes, "You don't want to know."

Vin grimaced, "Ouch. I'm that bad huh?"

Cinis stood and faced Vin, "It's not just you. It's the way this planet works. I was not built for this."

Vin's eyes went wide, "What are you stressed about? We are friends now, right?"

Cinis smiled at his genuine care, "Yes. We are friends."

Vin wrapped his tattooed, muscled arm around them, "Good! Now let's get you set up in your new rooms."

They we so glad he was calling them a friend because they were scared out of their mind. Vin seemed to genuinely like them, but the way he spoke about ending life so casually, profoundly disturbed Cinis to their core. Gripping their own elbows, they tried to keep up.

Following Vin down the hall and up the dungeon stairs to another set of stairs at the end of a hallway they hadn't been down before, then taking a left at the top of the stairs, they headed to the end of the hall lined with periodic doors and took another left. Each hallway had original art with paint applied so coarse and thick it jumped from the flat canvas; they seemed to tempt Cinis to reach out and touch them. Everything in this mansion appeared to have a unique texture. Vin slowed down when he approached six doors in the hall along the left side with windows along the right. Beautiful bright daylight streamed in, making the space much warmer than the dungeon. Cinis dropped their arms and peered outside to the lush forest of evergreen trees and rolling green hills. "Your sister's room will be this door," Vin pointed to the second one in the row. Vin turned toward the third door and pointed to it, "This is your room and that one is mine, Lock is next, and Nera's back door is at the end before the corner. Her rooms take up the entire left wing of the house on the second level so she can fit her personal blood... ahem, see I stopped myself! I am getting better! Anyway, the third floor is the library, observatory, and flight gym. The first floor is the butcher's wing with the attached recovery rooms, the kitchen, dining and entertaining rooms, staff living quarters, and guest rooms. It's a big square with a courtyard, so you can't really get lost."

"What about outside?" Cinis asked, avoiding the little bit about how Nera keeps humans for their blood in her rooms.

Vin turned, warning in his eyes, "Don't go outside without one of us."

Confused Cinis asked, "Why?"

"Do you not have wild animals on your world?" Vin asked.

"No," Cinis answered, honestly. They had seen cats, rats the size of cats, and dogs, but that was all.

Vin paused a bit, "I'm sorry. You're going to have to trust me on this one. The wild animals here will eat you in seconds. We used to conduct hunts, use gas, and even bombs to keep what we call the protos numbers down, but they're smart and hard to kill. They are what animal the blood bats evolved from. The fruit bats had a similar beginning animal, but it went extinct millions of years ago. The protos now have overpopulated since fully automatic, system guided weapons haven't worked in a thousand years. We've resorted to using poisonous gas to clear out all the local caves more recently, well, before most of the

Resper moved south. The protos just move more in, breed like wildfire, and we must do it again. They're slowly taking over the planet, and there is nothing we can do. We are sick of having to fight for our lives with no chance of having a normal existence. It's always all about the fight."

Vin turned the knob, and they both entered the large room, Cinis slowly spun around in awe at the beauty of the space. The deep, rich chocolate walls surrounded regal and decadent furniture.

"Why are the protos so attracted to the places your people live?" Cinis asked.

Vin answered flatly, "We have the same food sources."

Cinis' color drained from their face, "Oh."

"We can feed on anything containing blood, not just humans and other bats. We eat and drink from deer and other forest animals. The stew you ate when you arrived was not human, it was deer. We do often have human stew. It's not common to be like me and only drink blood," Vin explained, like human on the menu was a normal occurrence.

Disgust rolled through Cinis as they put a hand over their mouth. "Would you have fed me human meat and not told me until afterward?"

Vin nervously laughed, "I'm fucked up, but I'm not that fucked up. Well. I may have fed some blood cows one of their friends, but I swear I won't do that to you. That was honestly just because the skinny guy bit my hand, so I fed him to his friends who had been cheering him on. It really served them all right."

"Good to know that's your line." Cinis could feel their insides turn green with disgust.

Walking about the elegant suite, Vin pointed out features.

"You have your own bathroom and small kitchen through that way. The balcony is connected all the way down to Nera's where there is a gate. She doesn't like anyone on her balcony, so don't venture over there. Oh, there's Lock. Lock!" He yelled out after strolling through the large, ornate room.

It was a giant room, and Cinis had never seen so massive a place for one person to stay. They just stood in the center trying to make sense of the horror and disgust mixed with such luxury.

"When can Tressa walk? Cinis wants to know," Vin yelled toward Lock who was passing through the center of the courtyard.

He stopped and stared up at Vin, "If she doesn't cooperate, I'll make sure she never walks again." He all but flew to the back of the courtyard by the exit heading toward the greenhouses. His massive wings fluttered behind him as he went.

Vin turned to Cinis and frowned. "Lock is such an asshole. We should probably check on your sister."

Running down the steps of the spiral staircase to the courtyard, Vin laughed, "I hope he only has her gagged and tied up and we don't find her parts all over the med room."

Cinis wanted to crawl in a hole and die. This place was filled with so much commonplace violence they didn't know how much longer they could keep up the act of being calm, keep acting that they were fine, that all this was *fine*, and nothing was outrageously wrong.

Following Vin, they reached the doorway and saw past his wings that Tressa was, in fact, safe. Strapped to the bed, and pissed off, but fine.

Vin turned and seemed to sense Cinis's rattled nerves, "Are you alright?"

"I'm fine," they answered shortly while they stared at Tressa, and she stared back.

"Liar," Vin countered with a smile.

Scowling, Cinis finally snapped, "You know what? I'm not fine, not in the slightest. I am not a rule-breaker. I can't even bring myself to kill a spider, and I just was dropped off on a planet filled with monsters. You're kind to me, but you're still the Resper I grew up hearing horror stories about. By the way, it turns out the truth of this place is just as frightening. You scare the hell out of me, and so does everyone else here. I constantly feel like I am minutes from death. I am in Pluto's clutches in this house, but then you tell me something worse is outside. I don't think my body can keep up this stress. I think… I just…"

Vin took a step toward them, "Breathe deep, come here. Sit down. Dammit, I knew this would happen. Hey Lock, go get Nera, please."

Lock replied, "I was listening. I'm already on my way."

"Why? What is she going to do?" Cinis asked, their heart pounding to the point of pain. They grabbed their chest as stars exploded in their vision. Vin kept checking the doorway and turning back to Cinis, he worriedly grabbed their hand and held it tight.

"What the fuck is going on?" Tressa asked from her spot on the bed, not appreciating the lack of explanation or her restrained state.

Nera appeared in the doorway without a sound, and Cinis's breath caught in their throat as she neared them. The air pressure in the room seemed to increase with her presence. They were sweating through their clothes and beginning to have serious trouble breathing. The adrenaline was just too much. They were close to losing consciousness as Nera leaned over them with a puzzled look.

"Fuck. You're right. You need to author a book on the proximity of humans in relation to our pheromones. What about her? Is she panicking too?" Nera asked, turning to Tressa.

"No. Why would I be panicking?" Tressa asked, glaring at Nera.

Nera shook her head, "Lock."

Tressa was confused until she felt Lock slip his hands over her face, and his fingers firmly covered her eyes.

"What the fuck!" Tressa cried out as Nera leaned over Cinis who was frozen with fear.

Tressa bowed up from the bed and thrashed at her bonds as if she were a wild cat caught in a snare.

Taking Cinis's shoulders gently in her hands, Nera leaned into Cinis's ear and seemed to purr, "This will only hurt for a second, and you will feel much better afterward. Trust me."

Sweat burst from Cinis's brow as Nera's breath whispered against their skin.

Nera's lips moved closer to Cinis's neck, feeling the heat of their blood pumping just underneath. Desperation to do much more to that perfect neck distracted her for a moment before she gently licked the spot she was aiming to bite. Cinis shook as she sunk her teeth into their skin, piercing their flesh and drawing beads of blood to the surface. Cinis remained tense for a moment before the chemicals in Nera's saliva did their job.

Within seconds, Cinis was a blob of contentment, without a care in the world. Nera drank only what blood trickled out by licking up their neck, and she wiped their skin clean when she pulled away. By this time, Tressa had burns forming on her hands from fighting the bindings. Lock crawled onto the bed and lay over her to keep her from busting through her stitches, his wings hiding Nera's actions.

Tressa shrieked, "If you hurt them, I will kill all of you!"

Nera stood up and licked the blood from her mouth, "We produce a controlled pheromone to induce terror in our prey so their vascular system will freely pump all their blood into our awaiting mouths as we feed. We also produce a hormone in our saliva which we can choose to excrete if we want to spare our prey's life, slowing down their blood flow. Lock and Vin had an educated guess humans might do the same thing as our animal prey in regard to the pheromone reaction, so we all kept our pheromones high. We've never waited this long to feed on humans, so it was a good opportunity to test the hypothesis."

Tressa was filled with fire and fury. "You're just making excuses to bite Cinis, you blood sucking bitch!"

Lock had had enough of Tressa and grabbed a wad of gauze from a table next to them and stuffed it in her mouth. He reached for a loaded syringe and plunged it into her thigh before he crawled off the bed in a mass of wings and limbs and swiftly exited the room.

Vin peered over at Tressa and her boiling red face as she faded into a deep sleep, "See Cinis, I knew Lock wouldn't undo all his hard work."

TEN

ALISOT –HOUSE OF DOMITIA

After about fifteen minutes of euphoric floating, Cinis finally grasped reality. "No one thought it was a good idea to warn me before she bit me?" they slurred.

"Would you have let her?" Vin retorted.

Cinis narrowed their eyes at Vin, "Good point. I do feel a lot better now."

Cinis turned to their sister, her angry eyes regaining focus on Lock who had come back and sat at a desk at the far end of the room, "Tressa, I feel a lot better. You don't have to be mad anymore."

She pulled groggily against the restraints, so Vin loosened them for her.

She peered over at Vin. "Thank you."

"What is going to happen to Cinis when the effects wear off?"

"The drunk effect will fade quickly, and they should feel fine, permanently. I think?" Vin shrugged his shoulders as he seemed to look at anything but Tressa.

Tressa blinked away her irritation, "Should? I think?"

Vin gave her a nervous smile, "The humans we experiment on don't usually live long enough to find out."

Realizing her naturally high anxiety was likely inflated due to the pheromone and because she had not been bitten yet like Cinis, she decided to act right before she was bitten next. Tressa made an effort to use logic and calm herself, so she nodded, "Noted. When will I be allowed to walk?"

Lock answered from the lab stretched along the back wall, "You can now if you didn't pull anything loose with your last tantrum and you take it easy."

With her blue eyes flaring, Tressa slowly turned to Lock and back to Vin.

Vin stared at Cinis a bit, who just smiled without a care in the world, before he approached Tressa, "I'm going to show you to your room. I'll carry Cinis."

Vin seemed to wait to see if Lock objected before he helped her up.

"What? I can walk!" Cinis claimed right before they stood and promptly fell back in the chair, they had been sitting in, giggling all the while. Cinis' eyes went wide, "Oh."

Vin grinned as he helped Tressa down and she swayed momentarily. When she felt balanced, she froze in place for long enough that Vin thought he better wait for her.

Slowly taking her hand and running it down the full length of her abdomen, she had an increasingly puzzled look on her face. Twisting to one side and then the other, her insides felt strangely loose. She didn't feel the pulling and uncomfortable stretching of her organs like she usually did when she stood. Leaning back, would have been far too painful before. It had only been a few days, and she felt, healed. How? Not daring to shift her gaze back at Lock, Tressa peered up at Vin whispering, "You fixed all of me on the inside, too?"

Vin nodded with his lips slightly parted. "We did say it took several hours. You were filled with large lumpy scars which had healed all wrong. Your gut was a mess. We had to pull your intestines all out and put them back together the right way. It's amazing you didn't end up with a knot in your small intestines the way they had them wrapped in a ball. There was a lot more, but I'm not sure you want to know." "Can we go to the room you mentioned?" Tressa asked in a soft tone she hadn't used since she had been a small child, a tone she had once used when she had still been innocent and kind, untainted by her harsh world and upbringing. She didn't dare check behind her to see if Lock had heard any of their discussion. She still hated him, even if he did repair her internally. He picked up Cinis like they were nothing but a pillow and headed up some stairs and toward the hallway with their bedrooms. Taking a right, and passing Nero's doors, there was a line of six doors and Vin pointed, "Yours is the door right before the end. Cinis is in this room." Opening Cinis's door, he walked in and set them down on the plush couch in front of the fireplace. After handing them a blanket, he went over to the windows to the courtyard and opened them up to let the light in. He loved to feel the warmth.

Tressa didn't like the idea of having her own room. "I can stay in here with Cinis."

Cinis nodded and Vin agreed, "I don't think Nera will mind. The room next door is open for you when you want it. You should both rest. We are having guests in from Waxe city tonight and you will be expected."

Furrowing her brow, Tressa asked, "I thought I was supposed to be resting?"

"Listen, I don't fully understand it, but you two have a scent that is irresistible. They *will* be able to smell you and when they do, they will demand to know who we are hiding. It will not go well. If we present you as Nera's and Lock's new pets, you will be much safer." Vin explained before he headed to the door.

"Wait, what does *new pet* mean?" Tressa asked, her eyes narrowing.

"You both are Nera's and Lock's new pets. That's what happens here if you want to keep a human alive, one that you enjoy feeding on exclusively. It's sort of like a promotion to being a house's locked up blood cow," Vin elaborated, like that was a simple thing to understand.

Cinis scrunched their nose, "But they don't feed on us."

Vin put his hand on the doorknob and laughed, "Yet. Be ready at six. You have two hours. The housekeepers should have left you plenty of clothes. We had them alter some for your wingless shoulders."

As Vin shut the door, Cinis slowly turned to Tressa, "Wait. He just said yet. Does that mean what I think it means?"

"Are you ever going to develop common sense? How the hell do you think we are going to repay them for saving us from being eaten alive by giant, wild, blood-sucking bats." Tressa lectured.

"What?" Cinis asked, wondering where the hell their typical anxiety response had fled.

"Oh, when I first landed, before the collectors found me, this huge feral bat sniffed at me and then bit my shoulder. I thought I was dinner," Tressa explained with her eyes wide, remembering the scary moment and rubbing her shoulder where the scabs were still healing.

Cinis, with their demeanor uncharacteristically calm

interrupted, "I feel like I should be quite upset right now, but I'm just not finding it."

Glaring at them with her brow furrowed and ignoring what they had just revealed, Tressa continued, "I think they washed my hair when I was out, but I want to take a bath anyway. You can go next."

After a long pause, Tressa blurted, "I wanted to make a plan to escape but now I'm thinking that is a really bad idea."

Cinis looked at Tressa with a straight face and argued with every ounce of sincerity, "Stupid idea. Tressa! That would be a *stupid idea,* and I would not go with you. Gods! Vin is so awful to listen to sometimes, but I will not leave him. Like all the prison advice stories, we just became bitches to the scariest inmates. We are in a particularly advantageous position right now."

"Pluto's two headed dogs, Cinis! You're such a fucking sub. Are you still high?" Tressa cursed with a frown.

"Probably. I feel fantastic. Better than ever," they admitted, remembering when Nera bit them. She was a terrifying goddess, and Cinis shivered thinking about her breath on their neck.

Grumbling under her breath, Tressa headed for the bathroom and shut the door behind her. She was done with listening to Cinis justify their circumstances. This was *not* about Vin, and Tressa knew that! Nera was going to die if she harmed Cinis.

Lock, on the other hand, was a clear threat. Tressa squeezed her eyes shut while she turned the water on. She was positive he would attempt to drain her in the night. Sticking her hand under the stream, it became warm in seconds, and she wondered how they had such excellent indoor plumbing without having power for over a thousand years. Maybe the answer was in all those books around the fireplace. She wondered if her language translator implants would be able to decipher the words on the page or if she would have to read them aloud. Probably read them aloud she decided, which would be pointless since she didn't know how to pronounce their symbols.

Slipping off the backless recovery gown she wore after her surgery, she turned to face herself in the full-length mirror. Freezing in shock, she tipped her head to be sure she was seeing the same body and not some holographic image.

Her stomach lay flat again. Before it had bulges in different areas from scar tissue holding her organs in various places. It had been that way for many of the people who had been forced into the program because there was nothing any of them could do about the subpar medical care. Botched surrogate deliveries were much more common than Tressa was first led to believe when she had been recommended for the program. Other stories, or what she hoped were stories, made horror movies sound tame. One person died because their intestines had wrapped around their kidney. They had become constipated and bled to death internally when their kidney had been pulled until it ripped. True adoption was illegal, so the rich needed other ways to have children without having to physically birth them. That would be far too much to ask of the rich women on Melior. After all, they had their figures and social lives to consider and couldn't be inconvenienced by the physical strain of carrying their own children.

She slid her foot in the filled tub and sank into the luxuriousness. She reveled in the warmth, reminding her of the hot spring she landed near. That sulfur scented pool had been wonderful, despite the horrid scent, and this was even better. Every aching muscle relaxed as the heat seeped into her body, relaxing her tension, easing her recovery. Saving the moment, she rolled her eyes at her flesh under the water. She wasn't supposed to submerge her incision even if it did look almost healed.

Reluctantly sliding her toe to the drain, she flipped it up and turned the shower on. Unprepared for the drips of a heavy rain from above, Tressa moaned with excitement.

"Cinis!" she yelled.

Cinis opened the door and came straight over to the shower, "Yes?"

"Look at this shower! It's like rain! You can come in with me if you want," Tressa offered.

"Sure. It's big enough for four people." Cinis dropped their clothes in a pile on the floor.

Tressa started to tire of the water spraying on her back, so she sat down as Cinis came in, and sat down next to her, the comfortable quiet extended for some time before Cinis cleared their throat, which usually meant they were about to reveal something Tressa didn't want to hear. "Nera is hot as fuck," Cinis admitted under their breath. *There it was.*

Tressa gasped dramatically, "Oh, for Venus's sake, already?"

Widening their blue eyes, Cinis asked, "What? She's powerful and has the nicest body I have ever seen, I am absolutely screwed if she bites me again. I might cum."

Tressa banged her head on the tiled shower wall, "Do you have any dignity left? Who took it all? Why is that meter always on empty with you?"

Cinis knew what was coming out of Tressa's mouth

next as they said it along with her, "You don't know shit from shit!"

Cinis smiled gleefully at Tressa's scowling face over them matching her words, "I love strong women. I can't help it."

"That's not what I meant at all, and you know it." Tressa did not attempt to hide her irritation.

Cinis laughed, "You're not going to make me say it. I know what you want me to say, but I'm not going to."

Tressa whacked the back of her head against the wall again. "I hate you so much sometimes."

"I hate you, too. I wish you would calm the fuck down, but we can't all have what we want," Cinis admitted sweetly as they leaned over and washed the two inches of hair on their head.

Trying her best not to bang her head again, Tressa followed suit and washed her hair. It was fairly clean, so it didn't take long, but Cinis was out of the shower and finding something to wear before she had even finished rinsing the conditioner out. "Oh, I like this." Tressa could hear Cinis from inside the dressing room. After she turned off the shower, Tressa padded in with her towel wrapped around her and sat down on a bench to survey the clothes in the room.

Cinis pointed to a rack of dresses, "I think those are for you." Tressa dropped her towel and faced the mirror, still shocked at how healed her incision was as she ran her hand over it. She was more than a little surprised it seemed like they could remove her stitches in the next few days. "How did this heal so fast?" she wondered under her breath. Cinis was too busy looking at themselves in the pantsuit they had tried on to hear what she had said.

She turned back to the rack and began flipping through

the dresses. They were all gorgeous flowing gowns and seemed *Melior* expensive. She felt like a high-end prostitute and desperately wished that was all they wanted.

She feared what Lock wanted. *How much blood she would have to give him, would he accidentally take too much?*

A chill spread down her arms, and she shivered despite the warmth of the balmy room.

She selected a light mint green dress and slipped it on. It was a simple floor length summer dress, made of silk from the looks of it. Slipping it on, she decided she loved it. Finding some sandals, she questioned the uselessness of them before slipping them on. Searching the closet, she couldn't find any better shoes for her or Cinis. Nothing seemed sturdy or a good option to run in. These people were too smart she thought. She would have to be smarter.

They both finished dressing, and Tressa was pleased to find makeup in a drawer in the bathroom. It was probably ancient, but it didn't look used. Who knows how long it had been in this cabinet? It left a dust ring when she picked up the powder. She hadn't ever been able to afford makeup and only knew how to wear it because Rungi had let her play in her makeup collection a few times. She cringed thinking about Rungi. Tressa knew Rungi had used Cinis's body in exchange for setting up her surrogacy contract, but she also knew they were more than willing. It still made her uncomfortable because it had been Tressa's fault. That stupid boy, and her stupid young heart.

Her preparations and memories were interrupted when from the other side of the door, Vin asked, "Are you two ready?"

ELEVEN

ALISOT –HOUSE OF DOMITIA

Cinis opened the door. "Do we need to know anything about the people coming to dinner?"

"Just eat as soon as the food comes out, and don't listen to anything they say." Vin coached as he shifted on his feet.

Confused, Cinis snarled, "If it's a private meeting, why are we coming?"

Tressa laughed entering the room, "Wise up. They're probably going to be talking about gutting humans half the time we're eating, maybe all of it. Eat quickly and ignore the conversation. He gave you some golden advice."

Shrugging, Cinis followed Vin, and Tressa trailed behind, the door clicking shut behind them. As they entered the dining room, Tressa focused her eyes to find steaming hot bowls of blood with a freshly killed buck suspended from the ceiling. The creature was upside down and cut in two places on its neck, the blood running down the many points of its antlers and into serving bowls.

Vin tried to block Cinis's view, but failed miserably. Cinis slapped a hand to their mouth, and Tressa grabbed their other hand to guide them to the end of the table, as far away from the bowls of blood as possible.

After they sat down, Vin leaned over Cinis, "Please just try not to pass out. They will be here any minute."

Cinis grabbed his arm as he passed by Tressa, "Please. Who is coming?"

Understanding, Vin did his best to explain, "They are people who think they are further up in hierarchy than Nera. She, Lock, me and my family, and a few elder cousins down south make up one of the top ruling houses. Her house used to be the most powerful before the fall, and these others they always come knocking when they have a problem they can't solve. I personally think Nera should tell them to fuck off until they make her Queen like her tenth great-grandmother was."

"Wait. Why is there not a royal line anymore?" Tressa asked, genuinely interested.

Vin slid his eyes around the room, "Don't ask any more questions about that. All I'm going to tell you, is this was the guest home to the original home that was burned to the ground by the great Resper houses. The great houses all still blame the Domitia's, no matter what it is that goes wrong. Nera assumed the role of head of house as a young child because her parents didn't survive an uprising over the protos."

Understanding fell over Tressa, and she nodded. Cinis needed to shut the fuck up and act right no matter how disgusted they were. This was one game Tressa knew how to play. There were no painkillers in her system, and her mind was sharp. This was life or death, and she was going to do anything to survive. No more games.

Pushing her chair back, Tressa strolled over to Nera, who had just entered the room, "I think you need to bite Cinis again."

Scowling, Nera asked, "Why?"

"I know your guests are important, and Cinis is not doing well over your new bloody chandelier. If your guests even mention disemboweling anything, Cinis might fall out of their chair and mess themselves on the floor. Not everyone can handle blood," Tressa explained as she tapped her foot.

Nera peered over her shoulder, "They're lucky we didn't suspend a human up there. I won't bite them before they arrive. They'll know what I did. I know how to fix this."

Fear spread in Tressa's chest as she watched Nera approach Cinis and pulled them out of the chair like they weighed nothing. Grabbing a ladle, Nera poured a large amount of steaming blood into a cup before leading them down a dark hallway off to the side of the dining room. Taking a messy gulp with blood running down the sides of her chin, Nera slammed Cinis against the wall, bringing her face close to theirs. Cinis felt her hand wrap around their neck. Nera was taller than them, she was at least six feet. Her breath was hot against their skin, and their heart was beating out of their chest. "You're going to behave tonight. Do you understand me?" She leaned in close, so close that Cinis could smell the metal and smoke on Nera's breath.

Cinis shook in Nera's grasp, "I, I'm trying."

Nera tipped her head to the side, and her forked tongue slithered out of her mouth and slid by Cinis full lips, only fluttering against them, "You're going to behave, or I am going to thoroughly punish you if you don't. I'll do it in front of our guests and again later."

Cinis shivered with fear and delight, "Yes. I'll be good."

Without taking her eyes away from Cinis, Nera ran a single finger up Cinis inner thigh, stopping just over their screaming center before abruptly turning back down the hall. She had left Cinis breathless and desperately wanting to rub their thighs together.

"Fuck me," Cinis whispered to themselves, right before someone shoulder checked them.

"Watch it. Why don't you go sit down? Why are you in the serving hall?" A feminine voice asked as she sniffed Cinis.

"Oh sorry, I'll move out of the way." Cinis quickly made their way to their seat and didn't once look up at the dripping buck.

A pounding noise at the door startled them, and they wondered if this night was going to end with them dead. Cinis did everything they could to not grind into the chair. God's, they could not sit still. Were they sweating? Venus help them.

Lock rose and unlocked the door, swinging it open with his eyes wide with irritation, and his voice filled with forced hospitality. "Welcome. Come in."

Two of the evilest creatures Tressa and Cinis had ever imagined stalked in the room. The first man to enter was hunched over and was clearly elderly. The other man was younger, but in contrast still seemed much older than Nera, Vin, or Lock. They both wore military style dress suits and regal sashes with raised symbols in the Resper language.

Vin stood by the table and spoke in a booming voice, "Welcome to House Domitia. Please have a seat."

Nera stood next to the head of the table and watched with poison in her eyes as the old man sat in her usual place of honor at the head of the table. The elder man with his dust scented, aged regal suit which reflected his community standing, his once grand lands had become unkept and neglected. A once powerful man, too stuck in his ways to hear the frustrated pleas of his children.

Once the two were comfortable, Nera followed, finding a seat. Lock and Vin found seats flanking Nera, and everyone ate and slurped without conversation. Cinis sat frozen until receiving a scathing look from Nera. They abruptly began with the seared venison steak first. Tressa had already finished her vegetables before Cinis had even begun, and within a few bites, Tressa was halfway finished with her steak. Cinis never understood how she could eat so fast. Was she even chewing? Cinis did their best to finish their meal quickly and sat back, trying to prepare themselves for whatever happened next. Aside from the buck dripping blood from the center of the table, the discussion was so boring Cinis was bobbing in their seat. Between the urge to grind on the edge yet scream with disgust and fear, this was becoming a sensory nightmare for them. Wiggling their foot under the table, Cinis fought the urge to flee from the room.

Tressa stomped on their toe and Cinis shot up, drawing Nera's attention. She scowled at them, and they bit their lips together, honestly hoping they were in trouble. They wanted Nera's trouble *so bad.*

"Stop it," Tressa hissed.

"What?" Cinis asked, genuinely confused.

"You always shake your fucking foot when you're thinking dirty things. Stop it Cinis, I bet they can all smell it. Don't be stupid," Tressa quietly seethed.

They *hated* being called out.

Cinis, with their searing face, whispered back, "I can't stand you. You can sleep in your own room tonight."

Tressa turned and found Lock glaring at her from across the table as well as the younger of the two new men, someone Nera called Maeler.

"Found some pets, have we? How much for a taste of the long haired one? Does she do anything else?" Maeler asked with a flick of his tongue.

"No, she's mine. I take all she can provide," Lock snapped, cutting off Nera and causing her to raise an eyebrow.

"I asked Nera, not you. You're a bastard, and I don't care about your opinion," Maeler spat at Lock.

Tressa could see Lock boiling from across the table. Why did his words of possession sway her so? Was she just as bad as Cinis? Surely not. Wait, Lock is Nera's brother?

Nera turned to Maeler, "She was a gift to Lock for his loyalty to our house. He is my legally adopted brother, whether you choose to acknowledge him as such means nothing to me. His name was on my father's inheritance letters before I was ever born, and that's the only document that matters. He is a fully recognized Domitia, and you would be wise not to question him and his relationship to me again in my house. Now back to your little sheep problem. Did you say you lost over a hundred last week?"

Begrudgingly relenting, Maeler sat back in in seat, "They were our large breed too, the giant ones that we sheer and drain at the same time. They feed and clothe a whole village. Now we have over fifty starving families."

"They can hunt the west woods, but no further," Nera offered.

Maeler sunk his head, "Thank you. That does not, however, solve our situation with the protos. They are big enough they are stealing the sheep whole and spreading their entrails and parts over miles. It's bringing in bears and wolves. The diseased waves of the bats have reached our borders, and we can't ignore it any longer."

Nera leaned toward Maeler, gripping her chair so hard it groaned. "Do you recall my father talking about this very thing? The day he lost his head. Your people killed him for this *exact* warning. You said he was starting trouble and causing fear to spread. Lock and my mother collected the pieces of my father in the city gardens at the end of the stone where he was beheaded. The warnings of my house have fallen on deaf ears. Many times over we have been proven right, and just like those times, you should have listened. It's too late now. If they are taking your sheep, you need to round everyone up and head south, beyond the house-controlled lands of the north. You need to take your people to the southern continent and beg the great houses residing in Vintner city for refuge. All the other great houses already relocated their people there years ago and they are living on a seaside coast."

"But only your line lives in luxury because *your* house still holds the location of the royal riches! When all the great houses turned on the Domitia King after the fall, your ancestors should have been forced to distribute the wealth," Maeler's older companion grumbled.

Ripping the old man's throat out greatly appealed to Nera and it was only intensive self-control she didn't. Most of her family had been brutally murdered protecting the location of the Domitia Royal Library and their family's ancient wealth. It was a miracle she even existed at all. To make it sound as if her family hoarded what had cost them so much infuriated her.

Maeler leaned over toward the elderly man as he coughed, "Father, it's all right. They are just trying to help."

Lock guzzled a glass of local liquor and slammed the glass down on the table, "I don't know why you don't move your people out. They will end up victims to the protos along with your prized flocks."

Nera agreed, "Travel home tonight by our car, and you can use it to transport your old and young. I have more of them in the back garages if you need another." Maeler countered, "Why should we have to go so far away? We are all related, so we should be able to come here. Are you not willing to help our people? Only a ride, how generous." "I told you she wouldn't listen. She's no better than her selfish father. Trash begets trash," growled the old man. Lock shot from his seat and reached for the old man, but Nera stopped him with a raised hand. He froze with a hiss. Standing slowly with serene poise, Nera delicately wiped the corners of her mouth, folded her napkin, and set it on the table. "My graciousness will extend to the offer of transportation and to hold my people at bay despite their desire to dismember you. Maeler, you were warned years ago yet chose to ignore that warning – whether it was stupidity or laziness, I can't say. I can say your people are now paying for their poor choices in leadership. My people gave their lives to save our lands, we protect it from protos and other invaders, and we will definitely defend it from your inadequate preparation." Maeler opened his mouth to object, but Lock silenced him with a lethal look. Nera sighed, "Now you may either accept my offer and save what you can, or once again reject the advice and let your people become proto food."

Mealer cocked his jaw to the side and seemed to pick at his tooth with his tongue instead of answering. Maeler's father began to object but Maeler put his hand on his arm to quiet him. Maeler rose to his feet, nodding in acceptance. "We will be on our way then."

A Resper woman with light brown hair appeared at Nera's side, "Would you like for me to pull the car around?"

Nera curtly nodded to her, and she took off down the dark hallway at the end of the room. The two men were already outside with Vin and Lock right behind them. Cinis almost worked up the nerve to look up from their plate when they saw Nera's hand next to it. Leaning down over Cinis, Nera whispered in their ear, "You were good, but not good enough."

Fuck. Cinis was dying inside. Tressa was already halfway down the hallway headed to her room. This was too good to be true. Their nosy sister left them there. "Get up," Nera commanded, and Cinis jumped to their feet. Cinis swore they saw a hint of a smile as Nera imperceptibly sniffed the air, "Go to my room. Now." At a brisk pace, Cinis took off for her door. They were desperate to find out what was going to happen. After that first bite, they had been dying for another, and they didn't care if her saliva was addictive. They just needed to be bit again, to feel those lips on their skin. Cinis stopped at the door and didn't dare touch the door handle; they had played this game before. "Good. Now open the door and stand in front of my mirror," Nera commanded.

Cinis did as they were told and stood in front of the mirror. They felt exhilarated yet terrified. The door slammed behind Nera as she made her way over to Cinis, dropping her leather jacket on a small couch as she approached. She wore a loose cropped shirt that left little to the imagination. Nera had a small waist and perfect hips, her nipples were pierced, and her perky breasts were nearly visible through her thin shirt. Her arms had raised tattoo symbols running down them. Her belly button was pierced, and she had the same raised tattoos disappearing into her waist band of her leather pants that clung to her luscious curves. Cinis was dying to see more of where those designs led. Cinis was about to come undone with this gorgeous woman. Her wings draped loose behind her as she drew closer.

"I need to know if this is going to be fun for you or not," Nera asked as she leaned in to inhale Cinis's scent.

"Yes, it is." Cinis could hardly say the words but knew in that moment, Nera would not have touched them if they had said no or nothing at all.

Something shifted inside of them and Cinis was so hot with need sweat formed on every inch of their skin.

Nera bit her lip with a fang as she grabbed the top of Cinis shirt. She took her nail and sliced it down the middle, leaving Cinis' flat chest bare from the waist up.

They didn't dare move to cover themselves. The tip of Nera's finger slid down the center of their lower belly and she slipped it into their pants. She pulled their trousers off their hips and onto the floor. They had nothing on underneath, and Nera leaned over and sniffed them between their thighs. She peered up at Cinis and slapped their ass three times. Cinis did their best not to move, no matter how much it stung.

Coming back up to face them, Nera demanded, "Spread your legs."

Complying, Cinis did as they were told, spreading them wide.

Leaning down, Nera studied them, "You will do perfectly."

Her hand reached up to touch Cinis. When her hand made contact with Cinis' skin between their thighs, they couldn't hold back the gasp that escaped. Their body trembled with the feel of Nera's fingers, while their heart raged in their chest.

Nera swirled her finger over their sensitive bundle of nerves, and they shivered, unable to take in a single breath.

"You are ready for me?" Nera asked as she angled her face up at them.

Cinis feverishly nodded as Nera smiled and whispered, "Good. Now go back to your room. If you touch yourself, I'll tie you to a tree and whip you until you bleed. I will know; I can smell you from anywhere in my house."

Fucked. Cinis was *fucked*.

TWELVE
ALISOT –HOUSE OF DOMITIA

When Tressa arrived alone in the hall earlier, and realized no one was watching her, her first instinct was to run, but she wouldn't leave Cinis behind. Plus running away anytime soon wasn't going to happen now that she knew about the proto-bats, and she had met the neighbors. She cringed thinking about the dinner guests. Uncertain of her next move she went into her room. Tressa heard Cinis's door open and shut so she knew they were back, but she didn't want to go over there, because she had also heard them go to Nera's room for a little bit longer than she was comfortable with, and she was not sure if she wanted to know what happened. After Vin returned, he went back to his room, and she could hear his door shut too.

Not being tired in the slightest, she spent a few hours picking through the entire room and had not found anything particularly interesting. She was a little surprised at how many ancient looking, but brand-new products there were. Lotions, skin toners, mud masks, and nail grooming tools were a few of the items she investigated. They were all high quality and still worked well, but they were clearly bought off world. Having finished the exploration, she was bored. Was this going to be her new life? Stuck in this house? It was better than being eaten alive by a feral bat, so she did her best to shrug off the feeling of being trapped. At least they were all trapped here together. She better make the best of it before she made herself upset.

Raising her dress, she checked her incisions, and the stitches looked more than ready to be removed. That didn't seem possible. They had only been on the planet a few days. What had those Resper done to her to speed healing like this and why would they want her healed?

Her stomach growled, and she checked the clock. The unpolished gears were all visible behind it, and it read midnight. Midnight? How had so much time passed so quickly? Surveying the mess she made inspecting the room, she realized she may have let the time move away from her.

There was no food in her small kitchen just like there hadn't been any in Cinis's rooms. Thinking of Cinis, she didn't want to wake them, and she decided it was time to test a few boundaries anyway. Rebellion was in her blood.

Slipping out of her room, she turned around and made sure to ease her door shut quietly. The windows lining the hall flashed her reflection back at her until her eyes adjusted. She paused to appreciate the sliver of moon lighting the area. Moving on, not daring to pass by the row of doors, she turned right and headed down the long hallway toward the front of the house and took another right to access the stairs. She knew the kitchen was on the far front corner. Why did they have to put the kitchen so far from her rooms?

The walk shouldn't have been tiring, but her feet had been especially sore lately, so she stopped at a bench in the entry way to rub them and rest before continuing to the kitchen. As she leaned on the stone wall, she investigated the dining room and found it spotless, not a trace of blood remained. Nothing came for free in the center, how could their blood be enough to pay for all of this? Why were she and Cinis lounging around like royalty in nice rooms when there was work that needed to be done? She felt like a doll being kept in a box. She hated it, the guilt of feeling useless, it felt like a sour stomach.

She wished she understood more of what was happening and why Nera had moved so many people to the south. What did that help exactly? Would everyone leave? What happens when there's nowhere else to move? Questions filled her mind, and she hoped Nera wouldn't make them stay when the worst of the feral bats made it to this part of Alisot. Tressa had a nervous feeling staying was exactly Nera's plan. They would be the decoys to give everyone else a chance. She had heard this hero's story before, and she didn't like the end.

Nausea over being eaten by one of those awful protos filled her as she stood back up and headed toward the kitchen. Her hunger over-rode her fear. The fires still burned in the lamps, so she could easily see she approached the island countertop where food was laid out. She grabbed a fresh batch of bread and a jar of jam before finding a seat at the table.

A whoosh of air was all she felt before Lock plopped

down in the seat next to her and dropped a small block of cheese on the table. He didn't say a word as he reached across her and ripped some bread off before breaking the cheese. A few bites later, he leaned back in the chair and stared at Tressa. She could feel his eyes burning into the side of her head.

Why was he here?

"Did I wake you up?" Tressa asked, avoiding looking at anything but her bread.

Lock released a long breath, "No, I wasn't asleep."

Taking a bite herself, Tressa didn't say anything else. She kept her eyes forward and chewed in silence until her small meal was gone.

"Try the cheese," Lock offered as he broke off a piece and handed it to Tressa.

Taking it from him felt strange. She knew what was coming. The incredibly intimate act she would have to perform for him. If it was just her body in a sexual way, she could easily do it. Lock was more than handsome enough, and gods know, she had been with plenty of far worse looking men. If she had to guess, she bet his body was a ten out of ten on a bad day.

She really needed to stop thinking about his body. The room had grown silent, and Tressa was feeling even more awkward than usual.

Needing to gain any sense of control in the moment, Tressa turned to him and asked, "Why are my incisions healing so fast?"

He didn't meet her eyes as he answered, "You don't want to know."

Tressa raised her eyebrows, "Oh, gods! There is a reason! I shouldn't have asked, but now I need to know."

"I'll tell you, but you're going to regret it." Lock met her gaze with a smirk.

Tressa briefly closed her eyes, "Whatever it is, I know you enjoyed it, and that makes it all so much worse."

Lock scoffed with a smirk, "You're right, I did enjoy it. Our saliva does some interesting things."

Tressa's eyes went wide, "No, please tell me you didn't." She motioned to her insides as Lock gave her a devilish grinned and flicked his tongue at her. Gagging, Tressa set her head on the table, "Gross. Gross. Oh gross. You fucking licked my insides." She slid her arms around her middle and groaned.

Lock gave her a dazzling smile as he broke off another piece of bread. "Your stitches come out tomorrow."

Tressa gagged again. "I don't know how I'm going to look you in the eye after this."

Lock thew his head back and laughed, "You're welcome."

Tressa lifted her head from the table and tried to change the subject. Her insides felt like they were crawling around. "A proto bit me, but it took off when the collectors found me. I thought it was going to eat me."

"It would have. They don't like their meals interrupted or to share. Was there anything in the area to tell us where you were? A landmark?" Lock asked.

"Yes, it was near a hot spring. Which smelled like shit," Tressa explained.

"Sulphur? I know of the place, but there are several hot springs. We need to investigate it tomorrow. It's close to here. Go try for some sleep. We will have a lot of work to do if we find more of them that close," Lock instructed, his lips slightly parted. Something had shifted in him, or maybe he was responding to the shift in her.

Tressa nodded, "alright."

Lock stood up and left the kitchen, not waiting on her. Well, she wouldn't be bored after all, just in grave danger. Maybe she should have shut her damn mouth. She stared at the small piece of cheese left over. She imagined a mouse trap, but she was tied down where the cheese would go. She was the bait. Great.

THIRTEEN

ALISOT –HOUSE OF DOMITIA

A bell rang near the door, and Tressa confused, stumbled out of bed to turn the handle in half-asleep haze. Checking both ways down the hall, she saw no one. The system star was just coming up over the horizon and the sky was a shade of periwinkle. She shut the door and turned around to find the time. Six in the morning. That must be her wakeup call she thought as she rubbed her eyes, remembering what she and Lock had discussed the night before. She headed straight for the bathroom and showered before heading into the dressing area to throw on some appropriate clothing for the day, a long sleeve tunic over thick leggings. The only thing she seemed to be missing were sturdy boots.

Checking the clock, she read it was now six twenty-nine. Vin banged on her door at precisely six thirty. She opened the door, and he stood there with a pair of boots that seemed like they would fit her.

She glared at Vin, "So you were aware you gave us nothing but inadequate footwear."

"I am aware we know runners when they see them," Vin explained as he smirked at her.

Tressa couldn't help her next question, "Have there ever been others like us?"

Vin matter of factly replied, "Not usually, humans are just sustenance here."

Narrowing her eyes at him, Tressa grabbed the boots and sat down on a bench next to the door to put them on. When she laced them up, she stood and followed Vin to the hall junction, finding Cinis, Nera, and Lock waiting. Lock as always, seemed like he was in the mood to skin and eat someone. Nera seemed inpatient and ready to continue her day. Tressa guessed Nera had already been working for hours before the rest of them awoke. Cinis, dressed much like Tressa, stood to the side, clearly uncertain about why they were there.

Following Nera, they headed to the third story up some stairs at the end of the hallway. The area at top of the stairs opened to massive aviary. There were several tall trees, multiple perches, and balconies randomly placed throughout the room with netting for a ceiling. The netting seemed to be anchored to two large mechanical arms with multiple gears, attached to a lever on the side wall. What Tressa didn't see were birds.

"Cinis, you are with me. Tressa, you are with Lock," Nera commanded.

Without any further warning, Lock walked up behind Tressa and grabbed her waist startling her. With his arms wrapped firmly around her, he strode toward an open balcony at the back of the room and picked up speed. It dawned on Tressa what was about to happen, and it took everything she had to hold in the scream gathering in her throat as they approached the edge.

Before she had time to think, or scream, they were in the air, and she fought to keep her body straight. If she had any question about her internal healing, it was answered in that moment with Lock's powerful arms firmly around her. He had been careful to grip her body in such a way that he didn't touch her stitches, but her abdomen underneath his iron grip seemed to be fully healed. She hated to admit it, but she was thankful he had accelerated her healing. She still wished she didn't know how he did it though. She was sure she was going to add that knowledge to her growing nightmares about this planet.

Looking over to see Cinis a frozen board in Nera's grasp, Tressa tried to hold in a laugh. They were white as a ghost with their eyes squeezed shut and hands clenched in tight fists. Lock must have felt Tressa tensing. Tressa felt him look over to Cinis too, and it didn't take long for his deep belly laugh to fill her ear. When he started, Tressa couldn't hold hers in and laughed along with him. With the wind whipping around, no one else could hear them. Nera must have sensed something and increased her speed, beating her grand wings against the wind. These beings may be murderous, but they were easily some of the most magnificent and graceful people in the galactic center.

It took around twenty minutes to reach the general area of the hot springs, and Tressa noticed Lock worked up a bit of a sweat while flying.

Pointing to a clearing below Nera circled to allow Vin to land first. Nera sat herself down gently next and Cinis stumbled from her arms. When Lock and Tressa landed, Tressa didn't seem to have any issue at all moving about after the flight. Cinis recovered in a few steps but still looked pale.

Lock approached Tressa as she scanned the woods. "Does anything seem familiar around here?"

Turning and surveying the clearing, Tressa decided she didn't recognize anything, "Nothing here looks familiar. It was a double pool with one that seemed far too hot. It was bubbling. The other one was cool enough for me to climb into."

"I think I know where she's talking about." Vin abruptly took off to the north.

Lock scooped Tressa up and Nera grasped Cinis around their middle. As the group followed close behind Vin, Tressa did not recognize any of the surroundings. The pine trees and flat ground all seemed identical.

"I think part of why I don't recognize anything is it's daytime now, and it was nighttime when I was here," Tressa explained to Lock.

"I'm sure we'll find it." Cinis yelled in encouragement. Nera told them to be quiet.

After several minutes of flight, Nera called out from somewhere behind Tressa. "I found Tressa's drop pod."

Nera pointed to the pod below and the group landed again. Tressa enjoyed the second flight, but Cinis still looked nauseous.

"You climbed in that water? What if your skin had fallen off from acid?" Cinis asked, their brow furrowed, as they approached the pod and the pools behind it.

"I knew you were going to ask that. It was either that or be eaten immediately. I was covered in blood when I landed. I'd like to think it bought me some time," Tressa explained.

Lock turned and gave her a brief look of respect. "Good call. That was smart."

Cinis shrugged as they approached Tressa's pod and

noticed a small blinking light. Cinis leaned in and pointed as Vin approached, "The pod still has a light on it. It'll explode during the next electromagnetic wave." he explained.

Lock stretched out his wings, "I'm going to take to the air and see if I can spot any activity. Vin, I want you to take the north."

"I'll keep searching around in this area and see what I can come up with," Nera stated.

After many hours of searching, they couldn't find any trace of the bat den, or any trace of the proto Tressa was bit by. "Do you think they've found a new cave we don't know about?" Vin asked Nera as she appeared from between the trees.

Nera shook her head, "No. I think they've become smarter, and faster."

Lock leaned on a tree and huffed, "Nera, you know where we have to go to find the trail right?"

"Don't say it. I know." Nera snarled.

Vin leaned over to Cinis. "We're going to the local tavern. Nera hates it in there. We are some of the cleanest Resper in the area. I mean cleanest like we take baths regularly, and we value oral hygiene. Many of the locals in small towns don't know what a toothbrush is and only drink blood, even if they have other options."

Cinis cringed, "Do we have to go with you?"

Vin bashfully smiled at them, "That's why I'm going to apologize in advance."

"What? No!" Cinis objected, their fear and confusion visible.

"They are using us as bait to attract their bounty hunters." Tressa blurted as she stared at Lock, who stared back at her solemnly. He didn't seem as eager to turn her into dangling dinner. Something had changed after the evening before, and the hair on Tressa's arm stood on end with the way Lock looked at her, his lips slightly parted. "Well, if we have to be bait, let's get it over with," Tressa stated turning to Lock, ready for the flight back to the house.

FOURTEEN

ALISOT –HOUSE OF DOMITIA

Tressa dressed for the evening with a set of leathers she altered to make much more revealing, and the boots Vin so graciously let her keep. When she walked out, she expected Lock to react, but he too kept his cool. Maybe he didn't actually *like* her after all. That thought stung and she realized he hadn't so much as pretended to care other than to keep her from being bat food.

The confidence she had five minutes before in her room melted. She knew it was time to show off since she was supposed to be bait, so she did her best to fulfill that role. No matter how degrading she felt it was, the idea of Lock wanting her had made the overt outfit feel worthwhile, but now reality set in, and she knew how childish she had been. She wanted to return to her room and put on the longer leather jacket.

Huffing, she peered down at the low-cut leather top she wore. Being the damsel in distress was not on her bucket list, but she also didn't really have a choice. She wanted to keep her nice rooms, and she knew she had to earn them here, or become someone's snack.

Nera seemed to be enamored with Cinis although she wasn't sure Cinis had any real idea yet. They were always oblivious to any kind of honest advances. She was fairly sure the only reason she was alive was because Nera wanted Cinis. Her sibling was brilliant beyond reason, but they would become lost going on a walk around the block.

The only reason Tressa ever felt like it was alright to tease Cinis was because she was constantly creating her own trouble with her impulsive mouth. She only hoped she could keep it under control in a few hours when she was used for bait.

Critically evaluating Tressa from her head to her feet, Nera nodded, "I guess we're ready. We are taking a car. It's too far to fly in the cold."

"Cold?" Tressa asked, rubbing her hands up her bare arms.

Vin nodded at the window with dark clouds in the distance. "The weather has turned; A cold wind is blowing in, and we expect rain later."

Tressa turned to run upstairs to grab the jacket, but Nera commanded, "Let's go," as she began heading toward the front of the house.

As they stepped outside, Cinis couldn't believe their eyes. A steam engine car was parked out front. Unable to help it, they went straight up and knocked on the hood, turning to Nera with pleading eyes. She signaled to the driver, and he pulled the lever for the large, curved hood. It popped open to the side, revealing a mass of polished gears causing Cinis to gasp. Nera leaned over Cinis and whispered, "You like steam engineering?"

"Obsessed," was all Cinis could say as Nera carefully shut the hood.

"We have a garage almost the size of the house in the woods behind the greenhouses. My grandfather Nero, who I'm named after, loved to build steam engine cars, and there are hundreds of plans he drew up but never had the chance to build. Our gardener Pole is our mechanic now, and she spends a lot of time back there. She doesn't talk so don't expect a conversation; however, she will let you look through things. It's time to go." Nera guided Cinis to the open door, lifted high above the car.

Cinis climbed in next to Tressa, and Vin passed them both long leather coats he had grabbed on the way out. The wind was blowing, and they were both shivering. Lock pulled the handle and shut the door after he climbed in.

With a small jolt, the car took off, and the driver tilted his head to the side toward the open window between the passenger compartment and driver's area. "Scouts say our journey to town will be clear, but the way back we might have a storm. Pole slipped the rubber tires on and bolted up the lightning rod just in case. If it rains hard enough, we will be stuck until it passes."

After Nera nodded, the driver rolled up his window and focused on the drive. Cinis kept their eyes on the scenery and their mind as far away as possible. The last thing they wanted was to think about anything about to happen in a dirty bar.

Just then, Cinis felt Nera's hand slip around their thighs to separate them and lightly ran her pinky finger over their most sensitive place, up and down, then pressing in at their bud before easing her hand away. Why had she just done that? Was she doing it on purpose to make Cinis go absolutely mad? They were already turned on within an inch of their life. They had their answer when Nera sniffed the air and seemed satisfied. Noticing Cinis change in disposition, Nera leaned over and whispered in their ear, "You smell delicious. Be good, and you might be rewarded."

Before pulling away, Nera flicked her tongue under Cinis ear against their neck causing a spark to shoot down Cinis's nerves. Crossing their legs, they knew they were going to be a mess. Nera was a dark manipulative goddess who set off every warning bell there was and yet, they had never met a more perfect woman. They wanted Nera to do her worst to them and they were not sure they felt ashamed of that. Who the hell was there left to judge them? Their sister? Tressa could honestly fuck off.

The rocks under the tires drove Cinis mad. When the road smoothed, they sighed with relief, but they sensed it was only temporary reprieve.

After a silent drive down dark roads twisting through the dense forest, they slowed to a stop. Tressa wondered what was going on ahead. The foggy glass between them and the driver made it impossible to see anything. The windows to the sides of the car were foggy, too, and covered in drizzling rain, so she reached up and wiped the condensation with her arm. The system star, under the edge of the rain clouds, was setting and the sky was a fiery orange, giving an eerie glow to the city. Tall buildings, appearing deserted and decaying, stretched high into the lower clouds rolling in. Tressa couldn't bite her tongue and blurted, "You have functioning cities?" Not daring to slide her gaze around the car, she wished she could have held that one back.

Lock leaned toward her and gave a curt one-word answer "Had."

After an uncomfortable pause, Lock continued, "There are not many of our people left in Waxe City because the great houses already evacuated their people."

"Why are you staying if it's so dangerous that your people are evacuating to this extent?" Tressa asked, afraid she already knew what the answer would be.

Nera turned to Tressa with pain in her eyes, "Someone must stay and fight for our ancient homelands. My family reigned over these lands for thousands of years, and I'm not just walking away. I have an heir appointed, and I have plenty of old cousins who will become the next guides for the house seat after I'm gone. Lock was my parents' ward before I was born, making him next in line by my father's decree, but he chose to stay with me instead of taking the house seat. We must stay to save our home."

Tressa turned her gaze toward Lock, but he didn't meet her eyes. His solemn expression said everything his words could not. He loved Nera dearly, and he would stay with her no matter what. Tressa peered over at Cinis, and a stone formed in her gut, she knew that feeling of love.

Sliding her focus to Vin, she asked abruptly, "Why are you here?"

Tipping his head to the side, he shrugged and smiled, "I'm the only young Domitia cousin, and I am an exceptionally talented violent person."

Nodding understanding Tressa accepted their explanation. She hoped she had enough aggression in her too, because she had a feeling, she would be fighting along with them soon. She had known these wretched monsters had smelled of honor.

The car came to a stop and steam billowed out in a low whistle.

"We're here. Lock?" Nera gave him a knowing look.

He exhaled roughly as he reached for the door handle and opened the large metal door, swinging it up. He blocked Tressa, allowing everyone else to exit and head toward the door. Lock then turned to face Tressa, "I don't play Nera's fucking sex games. You need to lure us a hunter so we can get out of here. Think dirty thoughts or whatever you do to make yourself hot on the way in. I'm not touching you."

Abruptly exiting the car, he held his arm up and waited for her to slide out before slamming it shut then directing her toward the front door.

Thunder cracked in the distance, and she hopped her way to the door as quickly as she could. Hearing Lock's footsteps behind her was all it took, and her mind filled with thoughts of him on her, his body against hers. The heat forming in her lower belly felt wrong. She knew at the end of an experience with him would be teeth, not soft lips. He couldn't stand her, but her body overruled her mind. She craved Lock's touch, and she wanted to resist her attraction to him even if she was beginning to hate herself for it.

Her bare arms shook in the frigid wind as she climbed the three stairs at the entrance. Before she could reach for the door handle, Lock slipped the coat she forgot over her shoulders. She didn't even see him grab it.

The wind picked up, and she felt drops of rain along the part of her hair as she opened the door into the dark entryway. When he stepped inside and the door shut behind them, Lock sniffed the air and twisted toward her with his eyes wide.

Smiling at him deviously, she asked, "Where did they go? It's too dark in here for me to see anything." She wasn't lying. The room was so dimly lit she could hardly see anything. *They must have good night vision*, she thought as Lock took her firmly by the arm and pulled her through the filled room.

The stench of the room seared her nostrils. Tressa wasn't sure how her state of arousal was even identifiable in the mucky haze. Finding the reserved area Nera, Cinis, and Vin were already occupying, they sat down on the circular black leather couch.

It only took seconds before a server appeared at the table asking, "What can I get you to drink?"

"I want a double Devil's Gold on ice," Lock replied as he turned to Nera and she nodded, as well as Vin. "Make that three." Lock amended.

"Do your pets need anything?" the server asked.

"Water. They need to be clean. They are both being given to the hunter who can find the most recent infested den for us to cull. Please make an announcement to the tavern," Nera requested as she handed over a rolled piece of paper with a raised design of symbols on it.

The server went directly to the nearest bar and passed on the order to the bartender. The voice of the bartender filled the room. "House Domitia has two prized human pet siblings as a reward to the hunter who can lead them to the recent infestation. They are both petite, pretty, and smell delightful. Inquiries are to be made to Nera directly. They are located in booth twenty-six for the next hour."

No matter what they had told them beforehand, Cinis was scared out of their mind, especially when a line of blood Resper formed by their table. Nera grasped them on the thigh under the table in a bruising hold, a silent command to calm down.

"I know where the den is. I been there. I can show you," the first man claimed as he stared at Tressa, unblinking.

"Her scent is exceptional, isn't it?" Nera asked as she kept her eyes on the man.

Nodding he agreed, "She smells better than any human I've ever come across."

"Since we have a crowd gathering, let's see which one of you can produce an actual location you can describe with words?" Nera directed.

Several of the people shuffled away, and the rest seemed hesitant to approach.

Five remained, three women and two men still stood around when Nera finally announced, "I'm tired of waiting. It's been thirty minutes, and we've finished our drinks. How about you five just show us since you think you know. Those who are right can share the two siblings."

At that, the group of bounty hunters began chattering amongst themselves. They all passed a drink around, mumbling to work out their plan, and then nodded to one another.

"Good. We have a car with a trailer. You will ride behind in the trailer. It will be dry. You will stay in the guest house. This will take less than seven days. Do you accept?" Nera asked.

They all nodded in unison, and Tressa's heart sunk. She knew someone was being played, she just didn't know if it was the bounty hunters, or if it was her and Cinis.

FIFTEEN

ALISOT – HOUSE OF DOMITIA

Staring at the ceiling in her room, dread and need filled Tressa. After returning from the disgusting bar, Lock told her to meet him in the medical room. Lock's rough hands against her skin when he took out her stitches caused her heart to beat out of control. Lying under him as he gently touched her healing belly made heat explode low inside of her, she had been internally begging for more.

This situation was unbearable. There was no way he hadn't noticed, but he said nothing. She slammed her head back against the pillow. It was bad enough to desire a man who could literally eat her, but she also didn't know if Nera really *was* giving them to those hunters.

Those awful people terrified her. Tears filled her blue eyes as the reality of her situation sank in. She needed to do something, but didn't know what the best plan was. Cinis was safe, at least temporarily, but she was not by a long shot. Drastic, she needed something drastic. She needed to be sure Lock wouldn't give her up. *I just want him to touch me again, even if it's rough.*

She knew what door was his through the balcony. What if he hadn't locked it? The thought alone had her burning inside with need. She leapt from the bed and shivered in the cold as she reached to open her balcony doors. Opening them quietly, she checked both ways, relieved to find the courtyard empty. The glass ceiling above the courtyard still had rain pattering onto it and the sound was soothing, but not enough to curb her fears.

Tip-toeing over to Lock's doors, she found them not only unlocked, but open. It took a few seconds, but when her eyes adjusted, she had to hold back a gasp.

Lock was hanging upside down from a bar anchored from the ceiling in the center of the room where a bed would have been. His wings were wrapped around him tightly and she couldn't even see him breathing. All that stuck out were his ankles and his feet wrapped around the bar.

This was not going to be easy, but she knew exactly what she was going to have to do to secure this bat's attention. Her original plan to crawl into his bed was quickly altered as she lay down under him and raised her sleep shirt up to her neck. Sliding her hands down her chest, she stopped at her nipples and moved her fingertips over them. They pebbled, and she arched her back, spreading her legs. Sliding one hand down her body, she ended between her legs and slipped a finger inside before twirling it around her bud.

Lock moved his wings above her, and she exhaled slowly as she kept twirling her fingers. She could hear a rough breath as the top of his wings parted, and she could just make out the tips of his hair. Feeling herself becoming slick, she ran her fingers through her heat and back up to her bud. She moaned softly, and Lock opened his wings enough she could see his face.

He whispered, "Fuck."

Tressa closed her eyes, and she groaned as she moved her fingers, bringing her close to climax. Tipping herself over the edge, her eyes flew open, and she found Lock's wings were flared out, and he was staring at her as she imploded into a thousand exquisite pieces underneath him.

Her mouth opened in a gasp as he fell from his perch, covering her, but didn't make so much as an inch of physical contact with her body. He hovered over her, leaning into breathe in deeply at her neck.

"Tress, what the fuck are you doing?" His breathy question heated her skin, his lips gently touching her ear.

Tressa's voice shook as she whispered, "Please don't give us to them."

With a smirk growing on his face, Lock positioned his lips over hers and softly hissed, "Go to bed, Tressa."

Terror exploded inside of her and her heart pounded in her chest as if it would burst. Lock leaned even closer and lowered his ear directly over her heart. "That's better. So scared. So deliciously filled with fear. You should be, Tres. Now go back to bed before I become upset with you and think of ways to make you behave."

With her heart threatening to tear a hole in her, she began to sit up. Before she could think, he was already upside down on his perch with his arms crossed over his chest and watching her intently as she scrambled up. He was stark nude, and Tressa's eyes all but bulged out when she caught sight of his erect length. "Now be a smart girl and go to bed." Lock closed his eyes and relaxed his wings to wrap around himself.

Tressa wasn't sure if she helped her situation or hurt it, but one thing was absolutely certain. She wanted Lock so much it took her breath away. Tressa wondered if maybe she was experiencing the phenomenon where kidnapping victims fall in love with their captors. Rolling her eyes at herself, she decided if it saved her, it was worth it.

As she passed by Cinis's room, she heard, "Pst!"

Twirling around she saw Vin and Cinis watching her from the darkness of Cinis's doorway.

Shaking her head in disbelief, she tip toed over and whispered, "What are you doing?"

Sniffing the air, Vin grinned deviously and quietly teased, "I know what you've been doing!"

With their mouth gaping, Cinis opened the door and pulled Tressa inside before shutting it. "What are you two doing in here? Are you spying on me?" Tressa asked again as Cinis turned up the lamp.

Smiling, Vin showed Tressa the card game they had going on the table and explained, "It's a child's game we play. We each lay one card face down in the middle. The idea is to call out the other person for lying. It's supposed to hone our skills for hunting, but it's fun. I used this set with numerals to learn them when I was a kid. It was nice having a reason to bring them out."

Vin and Cinis sat down around the table, and Tressa joined. Vin shuffled and dealt the cards.

Sensing Tressa's unease, Vin grinned at her, "Lock is not an easy nut to crack."

Tressa blew out a breath, "Nera isn't really going to give us to the hunters, is she?"

Cinis scowled, "I highly doubt it."

Trying not to laugh, Vin admitted, "I don't know what it is about you two, but you smell way too good for her and Lock to let you go."

"What does that even mean?" Tressa asked, her eyes narrowed at Vin.

Vin explained while he dealt the cards, "The scent you give off tells us your blood tastes like heaven. There's nothing a Resper loves more than a terrified human they can fuck *while* eating. You two are a dream come true for them. You have no idea how much Nera paid for you, a small fortune at least."

Cinis and Tressa faced one another with wide, fearful eyes, and Tressa timidly asked, "But why does fear smell so good to you? I don't understand."

Vin shrugged. "We've tried to figure it out. It's something with your stress hormones. The UTC sends mostly typical criminal type humans, and they're hard and fearless. We almost never have them soft and sweet like you. Humans are usually cheap and disposable because they dump shipments regularly, but lately it's been slow. Then you two are dumped out of nowhere."

Cinis huffed, "It's been *slow* because the Iungo stirred up the UTC council. They had to scratch their entire agenda for the year and re-write the slave and genetic ownership laws. The prison dumps must be on hold because of that. I know the senate must clear them since being sent here is considered a fate worse than death."

Vin scowled at their words. "I'm sorry you were sent here. It *is* a fate worse than death. Nera's father tried to warn everyone, but they killed him for causing unrest. This planet was better when I was little, but after the first wave of protos passed through and killed Nera's mother, everything changed. Her parents were pillars in the city, and their chosen role was to unify the houses even though they hadn't tried to reclaim the throne in generations. A second wave of bat's passed through and thousands of our kind died. Waxe has been a ghost city ever since. Nera was so young, and Lock was just old enough for her elder cousins to take most of the remaining people of the house and the people of the Domitia lands to head south. The infestation of fast breeding bats will eventually reach them, but it will be generations from now. I'm still certain Lock can come up with a way to stop their overpopulation and put them back to normal. It's just going to take time and better equipment."

"Does better equipment exist? I know you can't run electronics," Cinis asked.

"We've heard rumors of an underground base with a lab that was left intact by the UTC and the fruit bats, but we have no idea where it could be. It's supposed to be so far underground the sweeping electric charges don't reach. We've looked into it and had no luck. They were meticulous in grounding us here. What they didn't take or hide, they destroyed to dust."

Tressa picked up her thick playing cards, and she absently noticing the raised roman numerals on one side. The raised edge around each card extended farther than the numerals. "Do you think maybe an old fruit bat city would have had information on an underground facility like that?"

Looking over toward Tressa, Vin stared for a while with his mouth open before he admitted, "You are right. That would make sense. I bet we can find a location in the old-world maps. Most of the land is still the same as it was before except for the bombed areas. Those are over grown and have been for a thousand years. If anyone ever finds that place, it's probably going to be an excavation."

Shaking their head, Cinis pointed at the cards and asked, "Who goes first?"

Vin slapped a card face down, "I go first. It's a thirty. Now it's your turn."

SIXTEEN

ALISOT – HOUSE OF DOMITIA

The bright morning star warmed the dining room as Cinis approached the window. Cinis paused to watch Nera speaking with the group of hunters. They were to have meals with their potential future pets, and Cinis wondered if they would become the meal.

Peering down at the revealing clothing they had awoken to find spread out on their bed, it seemed a real possibility. The outfit was sheer loose pants with a matching top of just two pieces of fabric crossing over their front and tied in the back. It didn't hide much, and Cinis kept their arm over their exposed mid drift. Tressa entered wearing a similar sheer outfit, but hers showed her legs instead of her middle.

Tressa walked up with a limp, "I don't know why you hide yourself. You have a perfect body, and I know you are not modest."

Dropping their hands to their sides, Cinis huffed, "Is your foot hurting again?"

"Shut up. Shut up, and don't talk about that again," she

snapped at Cinis. Tressa's eyes burned holes in Cinis as she continued, "We should be seated before they come in. I don't want them near me."

"That's wise," Lock agreed as he entered the dining room, and his sharp gaze met Tressa's. Patting the side of the chair he stood in front of, "You're sitting here next to me and Cinis is next to Nera. You two better be ready to perform. If they think we are setting them up, it will be a blood bath, and Nera doesn't like messes."

Cinis crossed their arms and sat quickly. What the fuck did perform mean? They eyed Tressa and she was just as confused but seemed relieved to be sitting next to Lock.

Vin passed them and plopped down on the other side of Lock. "What our friend of not enough words means, they are going to pretend to feed on you. So, when they bite down, you better act excited about it. The hunters are only going to want well-trained pets," he explained as he leaned back in his chair.

"Oh," was all Cinis could exhale as the front door flew open.

Nera stared at them through the pillars in the entryway as she stalked forward, not breaking eye contact. The five hunters entered in behind her, each one wearing leather and adorned with weapons. "Sit here," Nera directed as she gestured to the other side of the table from everyone already seated.

Continuing to her seat, Nera rang a small bell on a wall switch, and a door at the end of the room opened. Several servers came out with bowls of blood and set them at the table in front of the hunters and Vin. The next wave of servers came out with meals for Lock and Nera as well as food for Cinis and Tressa.

Bottles of golden liquor were also poured, each hunter

holding up a cup with ice in it. They each grunted and growled, guzzling their drinks, and demanding more, all while slurping their bowls of blood.

Cinis shook at the mere presence of these gruff people. Nera must have sensed it because her hand slid between their arm and their body, gently rubbing her finger down their side. Within moments Cinis began to calm and Nera began rubbing the back of her fingers along the top of their pants, then lower.

While Cinis and Nera were close enough to the table so no one could see, from the sniffing across the table, the hunters knew something was going on. Nera stroked her hand lower, and they nearly moaned with need. Cinis dripped as Nera slowly neared the apex of their thighs, causing their legs to shake and part under the table. Flipping her hand around Nera slipped a finger in their loose pants and gently grazed Cinis's bud. A rush of pleasure rolled through them, and if they didn't finish this time, they might scream.

Cinis was wildly aware of everyone in the room, and especially the fabric that was rubbing their nipples so gently they might explode from that alone. Was this part of the breakfast performance? The chair leaned back as Nera's whole hand plunged inside Cinis's pants. When her hand slid down to their bud, Cinis couldn't contain a soft groan. Nera pressed her finger down on Cinis's center and when her hot breath met their throat, they realized exactly what this show was about. Cinis let themselves loose and leaned back, trusting Nera to balance them. With that, Nera made delicate circles over Cinis's swollen heat.

After a gentle lick, Nera's fangs plunged into Cinis's neck where it met their shoulder, and, in that moment, they fell into oblivion. Cinis fought for a breath as Nera stroked them so gently the waves of pleasure crashed one after another. Gently pulling her hand from Cinis's pants, Nera leaned the chair up as she lapped up the trickling blood from the small bite.

They had never been an exhibitionist, but after today, that was staying on the list of most enjoyable. That was as close to a spiritual experience as they had ever had. If this goddess asked them to fall on their face in worship, they would obey.

Once she was satisfied with the small bit of Cinis's blood she took, Nera leaned back. She glared at the hunters before sticking the fingers in her mouth that she had inside of Cinis just seconds before. Her forked tongue wrapped around her fingers, and she licked them clean.

The hunters all elbowed each other whispering their thoughts only loud enough for their side of the table to hear, but from their expressions they were hungry for more.

Tressa faced Lock, and his narrowed eyes and pursed lips told her it was her turn. *He isn't going to stick his hand in my pants, is he?* She wasn't sure she could handle so much of a public show.

With a whoosh, Tressa was leaned back in the chair, and Lock's fangs sank in at the base of her neck. His hand rested on her collar bone, and he rubbed the small valley of her throat gently while he licked her neck. His lips against her neck were sending her into a tailspin. The small pinch of the bite, and the way his hand held her neck was enough to do her in. *What was with these horny bats?* Lock shifted his hand to grasp her shoulder, but in doing so grazed her nipple. She shivered with the touch and could feel herself becoming wet with anticipation.

As Lock's lips lingered at her neck, his hand moved

lower on her chest, and she silently begged him for more. She understood her body was mangled, but she hoped she at least smelled good enough to him that he would eventually put more than his fangs on her. Tressa lifted the shoulder his hand had been grasping, and he reached down and cupped her breast over her shirt before setting the chair back down. Her heart leapt and the evidence of her pleasure now dripped down her inner thigh. Lock met her eyes, his bloody mouth parted, and his nostrils flared. His heated breath against her skin created a wild need, but the look in his green eyes frightened and enthralled her. She may let this monster bleed her dry after all.

The hunters across the table, now satisfied with the authenticity of their prize, chugging their bowls of blood and chatted amongst themselves. Tressa was sure as fuck convinced as she shifted uneasily in her seat.

SEVENTEEN

ALISOT – HOUSE OF DOMITIA

The hunters left to rest, as they all had a long day ahead of them. Vin went into the courtyard to review maps while Tressa and Lock retreated to their rooms to rest.

Nera grabbed Cinis's arm as they tried to stand up, ordering, "You are coming with me." Cinis heart pounded in their chest as Nera led them to the center of her room. "Stand here."

Nera went around her room and opened all the blinds and curtains before standing in front of them. "You want this? All of this?" Nera asked as she came so close that Nera's boot rested in between Cinis bare feet.

"Yes," Cinis breathed, their peaks so rock hard they might crack.

"You will not touch me. Do you understand?" Nera's hand slid up around Cinis's throat and she gently squeezed.

Cinis shivered with excitement. "I understand."

"Good," Nera acknowledged as she fluttered her wings behind her.

Breathing heavily, Cinis almost came undone when Nera pulled the sheer fabric off their shoulders. Nera hooked her fingers in their pants, pulling them down.

When Cinis's clothes dropped on the floor at their feet, Nera took a step back and eyed her chosen captive as she decided, "You are just the right height."

Nera began ripping her leathers off and tossing them in a pile. This was the first time Cinis had seen Nera's whole nude form, and they were shocked to find the rest of her body covered in raised tattoo symbols. They lined her arms and legs. More of them ran along her torso from her collar bones down her chest. Her body was curvy but strong like Cinis had only seen in fitness advertisements. Nera's tan skin was perfect, and the shape of her legs was making them shake with anticipation.

"Stand here," Nera demanded as she grabbed something out of a drawer. Cinis did as they were told and felt Nera move them back closer toward the pole, "Here." Nera took their hands, and tied them to the pole.

They stood still as Nera leaped upside down onto her perch. Before Cinis knew what was happening, Nera's face was between Cinis's thighs, and her hands were pressing them back into the pole as she took one of Cinis's legs and lifted it to gain more access.

Nera flicked them with her tongue and found them dripping wet. She would move slow and steady, but when Cinis's moans became nothing more than sharp breaths, her tongue moved quicker and deeper.

They weren't certain, but at one point they thought Nera had her tongue all the way inside of them. As soon as their delicious waves began, they shook and leaned their head back, smacking it on the pole. "It's always so good upside down," Nera stated as she licked her lips.

Cinis rubbed the back of their head on the pole. It was aching from hitting it. A spot of blood dripped from their head, and Nera swung from her perch at the scent. Spinning around and grabbing their head, she tilted it down and Cinis didn't understand because she wasn't even angling their head toward any light. There were certain things about these people that were still unexplainable.

"It's just a tiny bump. May I?" Nera asked, giving them a look of desperation for that little drop of blood.

Cinis asked, "You want that drop in my hair? Why don't you just bite me?"

Nera scoffed, "I would love to bite you and drink from you, but you're not healed, and your red blood counts were very low when Lock checked. We know human anatomy, and no number of vitamins or iron will replenish your blood quicker, it takes time. I'm asking to lick your wound so it heals faster."

As realization hit them Cinis gasped, "Oh wow. That's why Tressa healed so rapidly. I was wondering about that." After untying Cinis, Nera finished with the wound on their head. Cinis sat up, "Can I ask you a question?" Nodding Nera stopped and waited. "What do your tattoos mean?" they asked.

Nera peered down at her body and smiled, "They are symbols written in our old language with various meanings. They're usually the story of our lives, our house affiliation, or sometimes commemoration for loved ones we've lost. It also depends on the area. Some places they're limited to arms, necks, and faces. Other places they're like mine and full body. We begin shortly after our first major flight."

Listening and watching the way Nera spoke was mesmerizing. Her voice seemed surreal.

"My last markings are from a loss. My uncle died protecting Lock and I from a group of proto-bats with an infection that caused them to go mad. It's something that has evolved on many worlds, and it attacks the brain lining. We are susceptible too, but we've all been vaccinated as infants. Our people are given boosters through many of our bought food or drinks in cities. It's standard and required. Too many blood borne illnesses pass through our people to not be hyper vigilant about disease."

This was the most Nera had spoken since they had met her, and they were going to do whatever they could to keep her talking. It was nice to hear her say more than just commands.

"Can I ask you something?" Nera asked.

Cinis nodded.

"Do you like this? This game we play."

Cinis couldn't help but crack a smile.

"Good," Nera breathed as she guided Cinis onto the floor and crawled up their body.

Sitting on their pelvis and pinning their arms above their head, Nera leaned forward and twirled her fingers feather light around each one of their taut peaks. "We have three more hours. I want to know every place on your body that makes your heart race, so I'm going to tease you for the first two and lick you for the third."

Cinis arched their back and moaned as they mumbled, "What do you mean tease?"

Nera smiled as they tried to pull their hands away and

realization dawned on them. She leaned up and tied their hands to the pole as they squirmed.

"Oh gods." Cinis's breathing quickened as Nera sat back down on their pelvis to twirl her fingers around their nipples, but only just enough to drive them wild.

EIGHTEEN
ALISOT – HOUSE OF DOMITIA

Tressa was ready and decked in the leathers she had worn when they had flown to the hot springs. They had several places for knives, but she had not been given anything sharp. One thing she was thankful for, from her terrible experience when she was younger, was her boyfriend at the time had taught her to hold a knife.

She remembered her crash course, although short, and hoped he had taught her correctly. Cringing, she recalled in that moment that his sentence was to be condemned to this planet. She wondered how long he made it after being dropped here. If he hadn't killed the two attendants at the front desk of the heist she accompanied him on, he would have only had to do time at a work camp and she would have never ended up a surrogate.

A knock at the door brought her out of her tumbling thoughts, and Vin stuck his head in. "Are you ready Tressa?"

Smiling she said, "Everything but knives."

Vin grinned, "Lock told us this morning you were safe for a knife. I don't know what changed with him, and this is one time I do not want details."

The door shut after that comment, and Tressa laughed as she raised her hand to open it. Lock may have told her to leave his room, but her little show had done *something*.

Her nipple still ached from where he touched it. How is it that she is dropped off in the middle of a prison planet yet she manages to find a gorgeous man-bat, except he would not fuck her. Maybe this was Pluto's playhouse after all?

Turning the handle, she knew she had to meet them in the hall, or someone would start knocking again. The natural light pouring in from the windows lit up the hall and she was able to see some of the art a little better. Different textures emphasized the shapes and colors. Each piece was deeply etched, creating patterns within patterns in the depth. The attention to detail was astonishing, and she couldn't stop staring at the twisting shadows the natural light created.

She refocused and moved to the back landing deck as she heard Nera talking to Lock about the crack developing in the left high bar. She found Cinis, rather calm and content, and she knew exactly what that meant. They had been in Nera's room for a while.

She had to admit she wasn't even slightly apprehensive about saying whatever Nera was doing to her sibling was a good thing. She had never seen them look calm. She might be in Pluto's paradise currently, but Cinis sure wasn't.

The group moved out ahead of her, but Tressa caught up as everyone headed toward the front door, and she wondered if they were taking the car. She really needed to wake up and stop daydreaming.

Lock slowed as they all walked ahead and allowed her to catch up to him. When she did, he handed her a bound-up leather knife case filled with knives.

"If one of them touches you, Kill them. You strike here, here, or here." Lock pointed to his neck, right below his ribs in the center of his abdomen, and right below his groin in his leg. "Those are all our major arteries, and they are fairly instant kill points. Don't hesitate, or you will die."

"What is going to happen when they find the bat den?" Tressa asked quietly.

Lock glared at her and slid a single finger over his lips, gesturing for Tressa to shut up. Taking the hint, she sealed her lips and made a mental note not to ask again, no matter how scared. Cinis was safe, but Tressa still had no idea if she was or not, not really. Tressa was still just the sister, no matter what Vin claimed.

They filed out of the front door, and she saw a long car that reminded her of the long-wheeled vehicle Rungi had sent to Tressa and Cinis's apartment when they helped the Iungos. Vin climbed in, and Nera had to nearly pull Cinis inside the door as they were so intent on studying the vehicle.

Cinis was obsessed with vehicles run on steam engines, not the electric kind like on Emendo. Cinis, eagerly asked for a look under the hood every chance they had to study the water engines but still had no clue how it worked. They loved all the gears and metal parts, and the sounds it made when they were traveling were still new and interesting.

Tressa ducked into the car and decided this mode of

travel was far better than flying in the cold as she settled comfortably in her spot.

Lock slid in next to Tressa, and they all watched the door at the other end open and the hunters file in. Noticing only four now, Tressa turned to Lock, and he tipped his head, no, very slightly, just enough for her to notice and take the hint. Don't ask about the missing huntress.

The car took off with a whistle and a small jolt. Like before, the road was rough for a while, but became smooth as they left the property and turned on the main road. They traveled for about an hour in uncomfortable silence before the driver pulled off the main highway and onto a rough dirt road. Another thirty minutes, they finally came to a stop.

Vin opened the door, and they climbed out, but Tressa and Cinis remained next to the car. All the Resper had their wings stretched out, and Tressa loved watching. Vin's wings seemed to stretch further down his back than the rest of them. He also seemed to have larger fangs and a wider wingspan. Lock and Nera both had more compact and swifter moving wings. They all had defined, muscular backs, and she bet it took a ton of muscle to flap those wings.

Cinis approached Nera comfortably, but Tressa just felt lost. Tressa could feel Lock behind her, and she turned to face him. "You must be used as bait again to lure the bats out of their den to find the exact location. We need a way to draw them out and fortunately for us, your blood smells like heaven."

The plan solidified in Tressa's mind, and she sighed as she leaned her head to the side, "Make it quick."

He leaned in by her ear and whispered, "Do you want me to dose you?"

Shaking her head, no, he raised his eyebrows. "Suit yourself." He bit down at the base of her neck. It stung for a split second, and she felt a hot trickle of blood run down her skin. Lock only took a small drip, and she noticed his eyes widen just a bit. He pressed a rag to her neck and licked his lips. Swallowing roughly, he whispered, "If you change your mind, let me know."

He tied the bloody rag to his ankle, and Tressa saw out of the corner of her eye, Nera doing the same with some of Cinis's blood. He pulled her body to him, and he began flapping his massive wings. Thankful for the recent rain, the wind they all produced in the clearing was intense. If it had been dry, they would all have needed masks for the dust.

Rising above the tall trees, they spread out over the area. Lock and Tressa going in one direction and Nera and Cinis going in another. The wind was cold, and Tressa's long hair was coming out of her braid, thrashing her in the face. She ignored it but decided on double braids next time like Nera always wore.

As they flew, she noticed the Resper hunters flying higher up and Vin flew the highest, above everyone. Cold seeped down into her bones with every minute the wind beat against her. Her body began shivering when she heard Lock breathe, "Shit."

Leaning over so his mouth was by her ear he explained, "Hold onto me. We will be on the ground soon." The warmth of his face was overwhelming, and she couldn't help leaning into him. For a moment, he didn't pull away, and her heart pounded. Maybe he didn't want to pull away or maybe he just wanted to warm her up, but either way it was kind, and she appreciated it. She desperately hoped he wanted to do more than just drain her of blood.

She hated this stupid standoff he was doing if that's what it was. Who knew at this point. The man was completely unpredictable, and that was the only thing she knew for sure about him.

A high-pitched sound came from somewhere above and Tressa pressed her ear to his chest as Lock made a similar sound in one direction and again in another. The sound continued from the other Respers, and in an instant, they all flew quickly in one direction, it was so fast she couldn't open her eyes and wondered how the hell they could see where they were going. She couldn't even pry her eyes open with her fingers if she wanted to. Her lips were open, and cheeks flared out, and she just knew her face looked horridly embarrassing. She nearly chuckled at herself when the most terrifying sound she had ever heard caught them. She felt Lock tense his arms around her as she realized what they were flying away from.

They had found the den, and the protos had poured out and met them in the sky. This had not been their plan, had it?

NINETEEN

ALISOT – HOUSE OF DOMITIA

No matter how much of Nera's magic spit was in their blood, nothing could have prepared Cinis for the hoard of hungry proto-bats following the group. It would have taken a sedative strong enough to knock them dead.

The screeching from the protos differed behind them as Nera beat her wings so rapidly, they couldn't even detect the individual flaps anymore. The wind was cold, and their heart pounded keeping them just warm enough to not chatter their teeth. They were gasping for air under her hold, but they weren't about to start complaining. Thankful Nera had an iron grip and strength beyond reason, being where they were, in her arms, gave them a sense of security although they knew they were in imminent danger.

A powerful screech came from Nera, and they turned their head to the side, so it wasn't unbearable. Feeling her tense above them, Nera dove down and Cinis knew the ground was coming up quickly, when they met the ground, it was abrupt.

Nera snapped, "Tuck!" and Cinis rolled somewhere dark and dusty with their eyes closed tightly. They came to a halt and rubbed dirt from their face before trying to figure out what was happening. The hissing, growling, and high pitch screeching seemed to be coming from every-where. How many of those protos were chasing them? The frantic yet calculated way everyone was moving told them to rise the hell up and assist, or they might not make it.

Vin, Lock, Nera, and two remaining hunters scrambled to roll large rocks into the small opening of the cavern. As Cinis checked around them, their heart sank. The sides of the cave were filled with large bones, some seemed human, while some were too difficult to place. Trying not to focus on the bones, they watched as a hulking bat with a long, sharp face landed outside and ran for the opening. They had never seen something so horrible. Deep slow breaths, they needed to take *deep* slow breaths, or they were going to pass out. *Help or die*, is all Cinis could chant in their head.

Lock pulled a knife out and released a high-pitched sound as he jammed it through the bat's head from under its chin. Blood dumped from the bat's snout and gaping mouth. When he pulled his knife out, he shoved the bat out of the ever-shrinking hole as five more bats hit the ground outside of the cave. Ear piercing screeches filled the air as they charged at the hole and clawed at the rocks.

"Fuck!" Nera cried as she pulled her knife from her waist and stabbed a bat under the ribs as it tried to crawl inside.

Kicking it out of the hole, Lock tried to push a boulder to block the way. Nera fell to the ground as one of the bat's reached inside the gap in the rocks and grabbed her foot. Kicking wildly, she clawed at the rock, and Cinis ran toward her. *Those fucking bats are not taking Nera!* The growling proto-bat yanked Nera further out of the hole as another bit down on her calf. Nera released a ferocious growl as she kicked her feet and clutched at the stone.

Cinis grabbed the nearest rock and threw it as hard as they could, hitting the bat in the forehead and the impact caused the creature to snarl and snap. Lock continued struggling with one of the hunters to force the last bolder to move while Nera used the distraction of Cinis's throw to continue her fight. Cinis checked behind them to find Tressa knocked out and sprawled out in the dirt.

Vin dove for Nera, and he climbed over her back to grab her somewhere under her folded and tucked wings. With his iron grip, they knew he wasn't letting go, and Vin pulled with all his might while Lock and now both hunters pushed the boulder. The giant stone boulder started to move, and Cinis panicked Nera would be crushed.

Grabbing another rock, Cinis leapt onto the rocks above Vin and spotted the head of the bat who had Nera. They heaved upward and came down with all their weight, slamming the rock onto its face. The bat screeched in pain as Vin and Nera went tumbling into the cave. Cinis leaped out of the way with them as the boulder rolled into place, sealing them inside and away from the horde of bats that had followed them to the cavern.

They rolled to one side as Nera and Vin landed on the other in a heap of wings and limbs. Once they untangled, she grabbed her legs and hissed, "That bat den is diseased. My legs are shredded, and we don't have time to do anything but wrap and run. Lock, did you bring the bandages?"

In the pitch black of the cave, Cinis made their way toward Nera by her voice. When they were in arms' reach, Nera reached out and grabbed them. Pulling them close and leaning over their head to wrap her wings around them.

Lock worked quickly wrapping Nera's leg with a strip of fabric. "I think Tressa was knocked out during the dive into the cave. I need to go check on her after I wrap your legs."

"Vin, he's almost finished, help me up." Nera held a hand up for Vin and he took it, pulling her up.

Cinis stood and helped taking her other hand, surprised at how light Nera was to lift. They expected her to weigh much more than she did. Grabbing their face, Nera panted in exhaustion as she pulled them so close their noses were touching. She wrapped her arm around Cinis, rubbing her thumb against their jaw as she whispered in their ear, "I will never forget seeing you leaping over me with that rock." They absently searched the darkness with their eyes and felt Nera's hand pull them in, what they assumed, was away from the cave entrance and toward their way out.

One of the hunters, a woman, spoke from somewhere in the darkness. "This cave has a crevasse that will slow them about a mile from here. If we can make it across the wide crevasse, we will squeeze down a narrow passage and exit out of one of my hunting cabins."

"Lead the way." Nera didn't trust the hunters, so they would be walking ahead of her and Cinis.

Lock held Tressa close as she woke up and whispered, "Why is it so dark?" She wiggled her legs to be let down, and he put his arm around her, "We are in a cave, you were knocked out from the force of us flying down toward the entrance. I had to roll you to the back when we landed."

Her heart raced in her chest, and Lock moved his thumb against her shoulder, slowly calming her with his caress, she hoped they didn't have to walk for long but knew better than to think this would be easy. Her feet were already sore, and she dreaded how badly they would ache later.

After the first hour passed without any sign of an end to their trek, and only minimal communication Tressa couldn't help her mind racing. She wondered how long they would be in the cave and if she and Cinis would have to keep everyone fed. The idea sickened her, and her heart rate soared again.

When she stumbled, Lock spoke up. "We need to take a rest. We are far enough from the entrance of the cave, and we've passed by several open passages leading to other directions. Vin, can you hide our footsteps please?" Lock asked as he guided them to what she wondered was the cave wall.

Tressa could hear Lock untie the bloody rag on his ankle and hand it to Vin. Vin headed back down the way they had come. He traveled a short distance before Vin spread his wings and beat them as if he were flying at top speeds to create a tunnel of wind. With those powerful wings, their scent would be dispersed by a whirlwind.

Helping Tressa sit down first, Lock sat down on the ground and pulled her onto his lap. It was not at all what she was expecting, but she was not upset about it. He leaned forward and grabbed her legs swinging them over his and yanking her toward him to sit sideways on his lap. With one arm around her middle and the other on the top of her chest, he pressed her into him. Lock leaned his head forward to put his lips on her ear, "You must stop being so frightened. Do you understand me?"

When he pressed his hand gently against her chest again, she finally understood what he was doing. She was scared out of her mind, and the hunters were growing ferociously hungry. They were drawn to her stress hormones and her fear intensified the scent. If the hunters were vying over her scent and blood, then Lock must also be ravished with her close proximity.

Listening to the other end of their small group, Lock could hear the hunters breathing and heartrate had increased. Fighting his own impulse to sink his desperate fangs in her flesh, he couldn't imagine the blood thirst of the hunters. They would rip her in half. The thought made him boil with anger, and he tugged her closer, wrapping his wings around her firmly.

Taking a long slow breath, Tressa nodded slightly steading her breathing. His grip was strong, and she knew he would defend her, but she also knew they didn't need that kind of trouble. When he shifted under her, she felt him grow hard and press into her behind. His breath shuddered at her ear when she moved against his lap. He gripped her firmly and softly bit her ear with his blunt front teeth, a warning to stop before he lost his control.

"The bats should give up for now and go back to their den. We need to sleep here for a few hours before moving on. Once night falls, we need to be well on our way, before they bring their friends back." Nera pulled Cinis next to her and began wrapping them up in her wings.

"I'll keep first watch. I'm not tired," Vin offered.

"If we're sleeping, I am going further down in the cave." Lock stood up and set Tressa upright at the same time. He grabbed her around her waist to steady her, and they headed past the group and down until the cave turned. It was far enough Tressa could hardly hear the others talking. She had no idea why they were going so far down but she agreed. It seemed much safer to be farther away from those hunters.

Surprised to find her back pressed to the cold rock wall, Lock was up against her, she didn't know how he had moved so quickly. He leaned over and pressed his full lips to her ear, "I'm going to touch you now. Do you understand?"

Tressa had never said "Yes," so fast.

Lock grabbed her face with one hand and kissed her as the other went to her lower back where her pants buckled. He expertly undid them and slid his finger between her butt cheeks as he peeled her leather pants down. Easing her down onto his outstretched wing, he wrapped the other wing around them and tucked it in behind her. Hovering over her, he didn't pull his lips away from hers, his forked tongue explored her mouth feverishly.

Tressa was doing her best not to be stunned. He was *kissing* her. No one had *ever* kissed her like this. It was rich and thorough, he acted as if he desired to reach deep inside and taste her soul. It was all consuming and she was gasping for breath.

He started on the buttons at her collar and undid them just enough to pull her breasts up so that just her tips were set free. Pressing her breasts together he slid his thumbs over her nipples and rubbed them gently, making her shiver with need. She couldn't help rubbing her thighs together. She felt his wings tug her closer to him as he continued to twirl his thumbs against her sensitive nipples. He pulled her hips to him and kicked her pants off her feet to slide his hand between her legs. She moaned as he felt how soaked she was.

His forked tongue in her mouth had set her on fire, his attention to her breasts was thrilling, but what he was doing between her legs with his fingers was heaven. She had never come undone from a man's hand before, a woman's once, but never a man. His movement was soft as he gently rubbed around her bud, running his fingers through her slick center before sliding back and forth over her most sensitive place. Her thighs trembled for more as he continued to slowly bring her to the edge.

Leaning over her chest, he slid his twirling tongue along both of her nipples while he hit just the right rhythm with his fingers. When her head leaned back and she tipped over, he anticipated her moan and slid his hand over her mouth to muffle it.

Lock brought his trembling lips back to her ear, "Tress, I'm starving."

She gladly showed him her neck and he grinned against it, "Not there. I need to gag you first. You can't make a noise." He lay his hand over the middle of her thighs, and she gasped before nodding slowly with under-standing. Reaching into a pocket on his vest, he pulled out a wad of fabric and slowly pushed into her mouth and followed with another one to wrap around it.

He slid his hand to her hips and pulled her up where he could roll them both over. He inched her up until his face was positioned over her thighs, but he made sure she would still be lying on his wing. When she felt his hot breath on her bud, she expected a quick, sharp bite. What she received was something else entirely.

He lifted her hips up and gently crossed her arms under her body, behind the small of her back before kissing her down her lower belly and into the crease of her hip. His soft lips were making her arch towards him, and when he started with his tongue, she understood why she was gagged.

She screamed inside as he licked his way to her most sensitive place and twirled his tongue around. When he finally bit down right above her swollen bundle of nerves, she thought it was too soon for her to fall over the edge again, but Lock drew her to the precipice while he drank the blood that trickled down the center. He feasted on her, and she shuddered, her legs forced apart by his hands holding her center to his mouth.

Lock caught her trying to pull her arm out, so he shoved it back in and ran his fingers down her side making her squirm. She wasn't sure how much more she could take and didn't understand where the hell her orgasm was. Lock had her right there, at the edge, so close it was all she could think about. It was bending her perception of reality, it felt like an eternity of pleasure had passed by in moments.

With his wing stretched out wide above them, he began dipping down. When the membrane grazed Tressa's breasts, she shattered. Her body arched with the convulsing waves. Lock held her down and teased her with his tongue until she slowed. Her body was slick with sweat, and he couldn't help but slide his long forked tongue over her and lick up every drop of dripping salty sweat from the valley of her hip. She stretched out with his touch; she had never had a man so thoroughly satisfy her like that. He hooked a finger in her mouth to pull out the gag and stroked the back of his hand along her jaw.

Lock gently pulled her pants up and buckled them back before carefully pulling her back down his wing to face him. He leaned in, his lips grazing her ear, whispering, "Do you understand now?"

The heat of his breath against her ear twirled through her body like a blazing cyclone. She understood more in that moment than she had since she arrived on the planet.

Lock did not rush.

TWENTY

ALISOT – NORTHERN CONTINENT CAVERN

Waking up with a slam and Lock grunting in pain, Tressa rolled over and shoved her breasts back in her top before taking a knife from her side. Lock retracted his wings around to his back as she rolled off onto the dirt, her body hitting a set of legs. The scent of the man was vile and sickly sweet. She felt hands reach for her and not hesitating, she slammed a knife up into his gut and yanked down.

A gurgling grunt came from the hunter above her before he began to fall forward. His blood and entrails spilled out onto Tressa as he fell over her. She sat up just as behind her Lock yelled, "Duck!"

Not having anywhere else to go, she fell backward and covered her face as Lock dove over her and tackled the other hunter. Pushing back up, she wiped something hot and sticky off her leg, quickly realizing it was the innards of the hunter she killed. She kicked the rest of it off her legs as it sounded like Lock fought with the woman.

"Share your pet, you greedy Domitia!" The huntress grunted in pain.

Tressa heard a loud snap and something large dropped onto the ground with a thud as several sets of footsteps approached.

"Did they attack you in your sleep? The hunters were supposed to be relieving themselves. Lying pieces of shit." Vin jogged the last few steps over to Lock.

Lock was out of breath and sound like he was in significant pain, "Bore kicked me in the side before I fully woke and could roll us out of the way. I know I have a broken rib. Tressa gutted Bore, and I just broke Poley's neck." Lock limped over to Tressa and lifted her from the ground to slam a kiss on her bloody lips. He licked the blood off her face as he grumbled, "You vicious woman." Kissing her roughly a second time he pushed them both into the wall behind her and his hands roamed her body.

"Lock, listen to me. I know you're ready to feed and fuck after a few fresh deaths, but we need out of here. I could hear the bats working on the door already. They're out before the system star's last light. You know what that means," Nera ordered.

Turning back to Tressa he huffed but relented, "We need to run. That means you're going to have to trust me to lead you."

She couldn't so much as see his face and the idea of running in the dark wasn't exactly pleasant. She guessed he must be able to see in the dark much better than she did and agreed, "I trust you."

Without further discussion, they all took off and Lock practically drug Tressa behind him for the first several yards. She finally found her footing and allowed Lock to guide her steps. It felt like she was moving far faster than she knew she could run, but it may have been a trick in the dark. Her feet were aching, but she pushed through. She had to.

They ran for what seemed like half an hour when Nera demanded, "Stop." They all skidded to a halt and Tressa held her breath for Nera to listen. "They're through. This is a deep crevasse. We need to fly over, but it's going to be difficult because there is a low ceiling on the other side. We have one chance and carrying someone else, it's going to be rough. Cinis and Tressa need to face forward so our arms can be free to help launch us over the ledge. Once we are on the other side, we fly for almost a quarter mile with a sharp down wind. Follow me the rest of the way. I think I know the way the huntress was talking about. Now move, the bat's will be here soon," Nera quietly gave the orders as she grabbed Cinis by the arm for them to crawl onto her.

Tressa climbed onto Lock and held on for her life as he lined up after Nera. Vin was at the back. She held her breath as she heard Nera take off running from her crouched spot and then leap over the ledge and unfurl her wings. When she heard them land with a grunt on the other side, her heart finally unclenched. Cinis was safe.

Her stomach dropped to her feet once again when Lock leapt from the ledge, and she felt them free fall the few feet before his beating wings caught up. The wind pressing down on his wings was pure terror, and she bit her tongue to keep from screaming. When she felt his powerful arms shove them up and over the ledge, her heart was threatening to beat out of her chest. They almost didn't make it.

"Breathe, Tressa. Your heart is racing, and it's driving me mad with blood lust. Your terror is making you smell so fucking delicious. Unless you want me to bite and dose you, you're going to need to learn how to control it better," Lock demanded as he ran with her still holding on tight.

In seconds they were lifting off again and his wings were beating so rapidly she couldn't hear the individual beats. It began to sound like a hum. The flight was only a few short seconds before he was landing, and she scrambled off. Vin landed in a whoosh, and everyone held their breath so Nera could hear.

"Fuck! They're pouring into the cave, and I can't tell how close they are. We have to find a way out of here or die." Tressa felt useless as they all seemed to just be standing there. Not understanding what was going on, she just held her breath in case they were trying to hear the bats down the cave.

With urgency Nera grabbed Cinis's arm and ran to the left, "This way!" Lock followed, pulling Tressa with Vin at the back. The spot between the rocks was narrow, but they moved as quickly as they could. They ran through the narrow cavern in the pitch black until Nera whispered, "Yes!" under her breath.

Dropping Cinis's arm, they could hear her move toward something in front of them. They heard the creaking sound of an old door and dim, evening light poured into the small, cavernous area. As her eyes adjusted, Tressa passed by several old barrels and some mining equipment.

"Go!" Nera yelled and they all ran through the old door.

From the small entryway, Nera began rolling barrels into the cave, "Grab that lantern and the matches." Lock lit the lantern from a box of matches on an old wooden table, seeming to know precisely what she was planning. He handed it to her as she handed him the axe she had unhooked from the wall. Just then the loud screeches of bats met Tressa's and Cinis's ears, making them both twirl around to face one another. Remembering what Lock said, Tressa did her best to breathe.

Lock slammed the axe into the side of one of the barrels and kicked it into the darkness as Nera tossed in the lit lantern. The way they were both running, Tressa braced herself for Lock to grab her as he ran by. When he did just that, she knew this next part would be rough.

Within seconds, they were airborne, and Lock's wings beat so powerfully his body was rocking. She opened her eyes just in time to see the barrels explode and a column of fire to shoot out of the small building below. The ground shook violently and rumbles of falling rock in the cave came echoing out of the small clearing and up into the sky. The ground continued to shake below as billows of ash and acrid smoke rose high into the air behind them.

Lock leaned in and pressed his lips against Tressa's ear, "You're safe. We're going home."

TWENTY-ONE

ALISOT – HOUSE OF DOMITIA

After waking up in their own bed, Cinis was confused to say the least. They had been stripped nude and tucked in. They didn't even remember falling asleep. If anything, they thought they would be waking in Nera's room, and it was admittedly a disappointment to find themselves alone. Had they fallen asleep on the way home? They dressed and walked downstairs to look for the others.

Entering the dining room, Cinis found everyone else already at the table, no one had any food in front of them yet. They had all grown quiet when they walked in.

Nera pushed her chair back and approached Cinis, "What would you like to eat? We have a full kitchen again, and I hired a chef who says he makes human food." She pushed a chair out for them and when they sat down, she rounded them and pushed it in. They were a little surprised at her attentiveness, but they enjoyed it.

Vin restarted the conversation they had been having before Cinis came in, "We don't have the option to buy explosives without heading down south to pick them up from the houses who have already fled."

Lock countered, "We could just steal it."

Squeezing his eyes shut, Vin slowly lay his head down on the table and groaned loudly.

Scoffing, Lock asked him, "Is there anyone even guarding the warehouses anymore? Didn't House Bellereaux leave last year? Take now; explain later. We can send a messenger with our plan and how the other houses are going to all split the cost. It's our necks. That's the least they can do."

"Why is it *your* necks anyway?" Cinis asked, and they all froze.

After a tense moment of silence Nera spoke, "Lock and I don't have our own children under the law. We are the only nobles out of all the houses without official offspring of some kind under our direct care. We don't have immediate families, so we are considered expendable and the first line of defense." Lock cleared his throat, and Nera turned to him. "I said official offspring. Pyra is legally your ward not your heir. She's almost old enough to have her officially sworn in. When she is, I'll keep my word and allow her to legally be your heir and the House Domitia's official third in line. Legal or not, our elder cousins know she is the next in line."

Lock glared at Nera, "That's great. You think we're going to make it back for any of that to actually happen. Let's think realistically, though, because the chance of us dying is certain. You're going to have to make a House decree and send it with instructions to open when we don't make it out of this."

Nera closed her eyes briefly, "Fine. Vin, please have the scribe make the document and I'll sign it. Pyra is to inherit the Domitia name along with the head of house position. Don't forget that addition. She has written me six letters since she and her mother moved to our southern home, every one of them signed Pyra Domitia."

Chuckling, Lock tried to seal his lips but failed, and Nera glared at him. "You know how I feel about her grandfather's house. We are not discussing this again with her mother either. Pyra wants it this way, and no one is going to convince her otherwise." Lock raised his eyebrows at her as he lifted his bowl and chugged the rest of the warm blood, with it dripping down both sides of his mouth.

Pyra had been hopelessly obsessed with Nera since she was a toddler.

Nera turned to Cinis to change the subject, "What do you want for breakfast?"

"Can they make flat cakes? I've only had them once," they asked.

Tressa beamed hopefully waiting for the answer, and Nera replied, "I think he mentioned something like that. Do they contain cinnamon?"

A man with a scarred and permanently broken wing approached and Nera ordered, "Two plates of flat cakes. Bring fruit and coffee out as well. The rest of us will have our usual bowls."

With their eyes wide Cinis asked, "You have coffee?!"

Nera smirked, "I should have said something sooner. I didn't know you liked coffee. I'll order more from the south."

Conversation returned to the plan until a server came in with bowls of warm blood for Nera, Lock and Vin. The scents coming from the kitchen were making Cinis so excited they nearly missed Nera's hand on their leg. When they did notice, their body temperature flared. Her hand might has well have been sparking against their skin. It was all just a reminder of a passion they hoped would not come to an abrupt end.

Nera started to explain, "We need to steal a truckload of explosives later today," but stopped and softly asked, "Are you alright?"

All Cinis could do was blankly stare at Nera and the conversation about plans ended. They knew what was coming after this little heist and no amount of cheery attitude could make them forget. Nera pulled her hand away and quickly gulped down her second bowl of blood as she rose from the table, "Eat your breakfast and come to my rooms afterward. Lock and Vin, please retrieve the city map and make us a decent plan. Vin also, find a scout and send them to see if anyone is at the warehouse." Vin and Lock finished their bowls and nodded as they rose from the table.

Lock leaned down to Tressa, "Meet me in the courtyard after you're finished eating."

"Sure," she agreed before he walked off with Vin and Nera down the hall.

Trying to swallow down their dread, Cinis asked, "Are we really about to eat flat cakes? I'm going to have to work out a lot more if we keep eating like this."

Tressa laughed, "You're telling me you don't burn enough calories in there with Nera?!"

The man with the broken wing set down the plates of food and burst into laughter, "Oh, now I see what they like about you two." He chuckled as he went back into the kitchen.

Cinis's face burned as they turned to Tressa, "Fuck you, so much."

She laughed again, but stopped when she noticed a small decanter, "Is that *syrup*?"

Slowly peering over at the auburn decanter, Cinis swallowed roughly, "Tressa, I think that's real syrup."

"Oh, gods! It's soft butter. I've never tasted butter before." Tressa cut into the pancake and poured syrup all over it.

After taking entirely too big of a bite, Cinis turned to Tressa talked around it, "I'm honestly not nearly as worried about dying now. Sugar is a hell of a drug."

"I mean you're not wrong. Do we fit in here more than we have admitted to ourselves?"

"I think so. Good talk. No more talk though. There is sugar to be eaten." Cinis shoved a folded-up bite of pancake in their mouth. They nearly cried it was so delicious. How could sugar be so powerful? They shoved in another bite. The scent of coffee made Cinis squeal as they lifted the cup, "These scents and tastes are incredible. How in Pluto's hell do they have all these things? Do they grow them and make them?"

Tressa took a sip of her coffee, "I think so. Nera was talking about truck shipments and mail before you came in."

Chewing another bite, Cinis lost themself in the meal, and Tressa did as well. Before they both knew it, they waddled from the table so stuffed they were uncomfortable.

Tressa went toward the doors to the courtyard, "I'll see you in a few hours," and winked as she walked away.

Rolling their eyes, Cinis headed to Nera's room to find two Resper men setting up a bed next to her sleeping perch. Nera stepped behind Cinis and leaned in close to their ear, "For you."

Cinis smiled, "I wondered why I didn't wake up in your room. I didn't even think about how you didn't have a bed."

The two men filed out after the bed was made and Nera commanded, "Take your clothes off and lie on the bed." Cinis heart soared, and they did what she said. With her lips slightly parted, Nera moved to the side of the bed. "Now that I know all the places on your body that make you squirm, it's time to find out what makes your mind spin."

Already wet without knowing what the hell Nera meant, Cinis obediently nodded, "What does that mean?"

"It means I'm going to fuck you while I eat you." Nera grabbed Cinis's hands and held them down at their sides. She leaned over and slithered her tongue around Cinis's already pebbled peak and the other before climbing on top of them. They were shaking as Nera pulled her shirt off and tossed it to the floor.

Moving up their body, Nera brought her lips up to kiss them. They kissed her back and cut their tongue on Nera's fang. She didn't end the bloody kiss and stroked her hands down Cinis's flat chest to their pebbled nipples, concentrating her thumbs on them again. They softly moaned into her mouth with the perfect circles but Nera didn't linger this time. She followed a line down Cinis's body, nibbling and kissing them all over before descending between their thighs. Whipping her tongue back and forth against Cinis's bud, they arched back and their hips rocked.

With her wings splayed wide, Nera grabbed their hips in her hands and devoured their center, lifting them off the bed. Nera's tongue was a flurry orbiting Cinis to another planet. Their feet dangled over Nera's back where her wings joined while their hips shook with the approaching release, and when they shattered, it was all encompassing. They saw stars as she bit down on their inner thigh, drinking and continuing to rub the tip of her thumb around their bud. Her thumb kept the rhythm until after she finished feeding on Cinis's blood, and she replaced her thumb with her mouth. The first release had not ceased, and Cinis wasn't aware it was possible what Nera was trying. What was she trying exactly? Did they know what was going on? No. Did they care? Absolutely not.

"Breathe deep and resist the urge of your second orgasm. I promise when it finally happens, it will be the most pleasurable experience of your life."

Cinis arched up to watch Nera as she brought her mouth back down on their center to twirl and suck, and they didn't know how long they could dam the second wave. As Nera continued to take them higher, they felt something cresting, was it a second orgasm about to hit?

As they questioned the possibilities, the most intense orgasm slammed into them, and their mouth dropped open in a silent scream. It was so much. A brilliant light show blasted through their head and all Cinis could comprehend was pleasure, intense, pulsating pleasure. Nera's bruising hold contained Cinis's hips and her tongue flicked over them until Cinis couldn't take it anymore and screamed, their legs began flailing around wildly.

Pulling away, Nera dropped them, and their body flopped onto the bed. "What was that?" Cinis could hardly speak.

Nera lay next to them with their blood running down her face, "That's what happens when you have an orgasm on top of another orgasm. The next time we do that, I'll remember to tie and gag you first. You almost kicked my wing."

Heart slamming in their chest, Cinis almost tipped over again with her words.

Nera cocked her head, "Oh, you like that idea?"

With wide eyes, Cinis asked, "No one can get anything by you, can they?"

Rubbing her finger around one of their nipples, Nera whispered, "Never."

TWENTY-TWO
ALISOT – WAXE CITY

In the back of the box truck, Tressa and Lock were ready with their knives on their belts and thicker leather armor Nera had ready for everyone.

"Do you really think we'll all die when we set up the explosives and try to take out the den?" Tressa asked.

Sliding over to sit next to her, Lock paused a moment, "I think it's a strong possibility. That tavern we went to finally closed and the rest of the lingering people from other houses are evacuating. No one is staying to help. I just want my daughter to have a chance to live her entire life in peace. Not just until she grows up and has to face this problem again."

"I didn't know you had a daughter."

He stared at the floor. "She is not from me, but she is very much mine. I courted her mother Kellin for all my young adult life. We eventually called it off, and she traveled, probably to be away from me. When she returned, she was pregnant. Kellin had some complications, she stayed on the Domitia grounds for the end of her pregnancy. Since I have been the only butcher in the area since I was a teen, I delivered the baby. I loved Pyra the moment I held her. The sadness in his eyes was enough to bring her to tears, "You loved her? Kellin?"

"Not really." He stared at the floor again.

"Turns out I didn't really know Kellin all that well. It was just a superficial attraction. I could have grown to know her, I guess, but as adults we didn't have a lot to say to one another. I helped raise Pyra until she was six when they had to move south with the rest of House Domitia. She's living with her mother and doing very well. Her aunt lives nearby and knows what it means to be my daughter and what that brings to a tied in family. Nera was Pyra's role model, so you can image how she acts." Lock half-bragged.

He gave her a much different smile than she had seen before. She was surprised Lock had a side like this at all, and it was thrilling to see.

He narrowed his eyes at her and leaned over to her ear in the noisy truck, "Why does this make your heart race like fear does?"

His searing words against her ear made her shiver, "I'm not sure if I'm ready to say."

"No?" he asked with a smile.

She melted and finally built up the courage, "Am I always going to be just your pet?"

He stared at her and didn't smile as he leaned in and kissed her before whispering against her lips, "What's wrong with being my pet?" He kissed her again, and she was destroyed inside. Did this man want her or not? Unable to control herself, her heart felt like it was tearing in half. Was he just trying to make her afraid? She could already tell her heart would be shattered.

She was nothing but a pretty meal to him.

The truck stopped and Lock turned to Tressa, "We will finish this later. There are only a couple of guards to kill if we have to. This will be quick."

"Only a couple, huh?" Tressa asked flatly.

She rose up to climb out, and he slapped her ass. "Quickly. We need to move."

Nera opened the back, "Hurry, the guards are on break. Cinis and Vin will lock them in the dining area."

Lock nodded. "Meet you around the side."

He and Tressa leapt out of the truck and dashed to the side door of the warehouse and waited for either Nera or Cinis to open it.

Moments later Cinis opened the door. "Vin trapped them in the kitchen, but he said they would be through the door in less than ten minutes. We need to run!"

Taking off into the warehouse, they joined Vin as Nera backed the truck up. Cinis ran up and opened the back door. Vin approached with a tall stack of boxes and placed them inside the back. Nera jumped out and ran to grab a load.

Once they had the truck packed up, Nera slammed the door shut and yelled, "See you at the house!" Cinis and Tressa jumped in beside her while Vin joined Lock in the sky above. The engine burst to life and the truck rumbled out. Nera looked back toward the warehouse, "Dammit! They've almost broken down the door." With that, she floored it, and the truck went flying. The roads were brightly lit with highly reflective material, and it was hard for Tressa to concentrate. It seemed ridiculous to be blinded like that while driving. It must be a Resper thing, she thought. She looked out the window and at all the abandoned buildings instead. It was row after row of empty streets.

"Lock and Vin have clashed with the guards in the sky. It sounds like we will need to treat them for injuries when we arrive home." Nera scanned the sky through the open window. A crash on top of the truck had Cinis whipping around to look at Nera who casually replied, "It's Lock. He'll live."

Lock from on top of the truck groaned, "Don't be so sure!"

Nera laughed and a second lighter crash on top of the truck must have been Vin though she just continued like she hadn't heard it. When she arrived at a turn off, she pulled onto the side road. Speeding as far away from the warehouse quickly as possible.

Shortly, she came to a stop, and a man landed in front of the truck. Tressa recognized him as their usual driver. "Thank you, Wintel."

He approached the door as Nera opened it and leaned into Cinis for them to make room. Cinis was slender, but Tressa had hips. "I can only squish so much over here."

Nera narrowed her eyes at them, "We will fit. It's only for a few minutes."

When they arrived at the house, Nera stepped out and climbed up on the side of the box truck to Lock and Vin, "Do you need help getting down?"

"I think I can manage," Lock grunted before promptly falling off the side of the truck and landing face down on the gravel with his wings fluttering behind him.

Leaning her head back in annoyance, Nera scoffed, "I hate when you're more hurt than you let on. Can't you just ask for help?"

Vin leaned against the truck laughing hard enough to shake the driver's door until it shut. Tressa was terrified and crouched next to him while Cinis was wide eyed with fear.

"He will be fine. We will carry him to your room. I need you to let him feed. He has an open wound on his stomach, but it should be closed by tomorrow," Nera explained as she turned him over. Nera leaned down and licked his gut wound as Cinis and Tressa stared at one another in disgusted disbelief.

When Nera rose, Tressa gasped at the torn open flesh on the left side of Lock's abdomen. Nera hooked under his arms, and Vin grabbed his feet. He was covered in dust from the gravel; Tressa ran ahead of them to throw a blanket down on the bed. Her and Cinis had the door propped open and the bed prepared when Nera and Vin carried him in and lay him on the bed. Vin tipped him to one side and tucked his wing in underneath him and repeated it on the other side. Nera and Vin didn't seem concerned, but Lock seemed like he needed emergency help.

Tressa in a panic asked, "Are you sure he's, alright? He doesn't look alright."

"We heal fast. Just go to sleep, and he will wake you up at some point. He will be hungry. No one will bother you, and we will have your meals brought to your door," Nera assured her.

Tressa smiled the best she could, but she couldn't muster much of an effort. She was terrified Lock was worse than what they thought.

Nera came up behind her after she turned to him, "He is not dying today." Something about her words set Tressa at ease as Nera herded everyone out of the room.

Tressa sat on the bed and started to take his clothes off, but wondered if he would mind. Looking down at his boots, she decided she didn't care if he was mad. He looked uncomfortable. When she pulled on his boots, she was astonished at how flexible the sole was. She guessed it would have to be since he used his feet to perch upside down. After slipping his boots off, she pulled his socks off and marveled at his feet. They were fascinating to her, and she ran a finger on the top along the curve. His foot twitched, and she yanked her hand away, the last thing she wanted was him waking up to her touching his foot.

She undid the buckles at his sides, and it took a grand effort to peel the tight leather pants off the big deadweight man. When she finally managed to remove them, she looked up to find him without any kind of underwear. Wondering if he would want her staring at him when he had not chosen to show her, she decided to toss a blanket over him before she started on his vest and shirt underneath. After taking off his arm armor, she undid the buckles on his vest and eased it away from the wound. She began lifting his shirt and was halfway before she gave up and grabbed scissors to cut it down the middle and down the arms.

With a pot of pre-boiled water Nera had delivered, she took a soft cloth and cleaned his wound. As she rubbed away the blood, she couldn't seem to find any open wound. There was one laceration from below his ribs to his side, but it seemed like it was already beginning to close. She swore she had just seen an open gash.

He groaned as he moved and the wound opened again, bleeding. This time the deeper laceration was evident. She pressed the rag on it until it stopped and cleaned up the blood. Had he really healed that fast? She could only hope it was true.

The relief at his rapid healing combined with the adrenaline crash from the physically and emotionally exhausting day did her in. Drained, she slipped on a nightshirt and crawled in next to him. *Please let tomorrow be a better day,* she prayed to the gods.

TWENTY-THREE

ALISOT – HOUSE OF DOMITIA

Walking through the verdant greenhouse, Nera reached over and linked her arm into Cinis's. After growing up in the concrete desolation of Emendo, the lush gardens were a sensual delight. The warmth of the room drew out the honey scents of the rainbow of flowers surrounding the stone pathway. Every few steps a new intoxicating floral scent enveloped them. It was the most fragrant garden imaginable. "I wish we would have met sooner," Nera admitted softly.

Cinis's heart lodged in their throat, "What do you mean?"

Nera smiled, "There is no way out of this for us. For you, and some of the house staff, yes. You're heading south soon. A letter has already been drafted. As for Lock, Vin, and I? We have a task that requires our lives."

"Is there really no other way?" Cinis asked.

Nera shook her head. "The den is too populated. When it blows, there will be plenty left to chase us down. The end goal is to destroy the den they return to every time we think we killed them off. The cavern we just destroyed was too small. It was just where we hid to draw many of the diseased in who were willing to follow during the daytime. The main den still exists, and we didn't come close to killing enough of them. Before, when we had the resources of the other houses we had a chance, but now they're all gone, and it's just us."

"How did you kill them before?" Cinis asked.

"We used gas bombs. The chemical we used was a remnant from the days when the UTC was here. They had left several hundred canisters of a deadly gas. They tested the impact, and it was environmentally neutral after a few days, so we used it until it was gone."

"You're saying the only plan possible is one where you drive the truck with the explosives next to the den, detonate the bombs, and die trying to fly away from the mass of giant bats pouring out?" Cinis asked, more emotion than they knew how to deal with rushed around in their heart and pain seeped into their voice.

Nera stared back at Cinis solemnly, "Since the attacks of our people increased substantially about ten years ago, we have been focused on total relocation. Our people found out about the wave of bats that seem to breed faster, about fifty years ago. A team went to the far north of the continent where they found the largest den ever recorded by a long shot. Out of fifty-two, only three made it back. One refused to ever speak again. The other two were never the same.

We planned constant scouting trips to track them, and we knew they would eventually end up here. We just didn't always know they were moving the whole den in large numbers. Dens usually begin with a few mated pairs and grow to thirty. This one was a madhouse of a thousand. There is something wrong with these proto-bats, and we can't figure it out."

A deep pit formed in Cinis's gut. This all sounded too familiar. "The First Humans probably did something to their genetics. They were behind a galactic eugenic program the Iungo uncovered. The FH were sending meteors and rockets to planets with life and altering the course so that the planets developed humans halting natural species development there. They committed the crime on over one hundred worlds. Now all the worlds are developing humans and not their natural species. I wonder if the changes in the bats are something they developed.

The Iungo made it to the UTC science station with the proof they found on Janus. The only reason I even know any of this is because they left me with an electronic tablet to keep me updated. The final message about them reaching the UTC came in an hour before I was taken, but I received their evidence file a day before. I had just finished reviewing what they found on Janus when I heard a knock at my apartment door. I don't remember anything after that. I never even read the last message. I'm sure our involvement is how we ended up here. The way we were dropped, wasn't protocol. I know that FH commander somehow found out we had helped the Iungo and sent us here. The sadistic bastard tried to cut Tressa's foot off before he put her in the drop pod."

"The First Humans involvement to that degree never crossed my mind. The protos breed fast and have multiple births, which should be rare. The only kind of twins we have is identical. These bats are producing males and females in one pregnancy. I wish I knew where that old UTC base was. I had scouts search the city for a map, but they haven't had any luck. I know there is tech

Lock could use to find out for certain. If we did find it, we may be able to create more of the chemical we used to use to kill them before. We could save the planet for the next generation, and they may even be able to move back to their ancestral homes. The issue is everyone we need to speak to about it is hundreds of miles away. We only have a week or two before the den's food scouts start reaching my lands. We know they are close because almost all the wildlife is gone. They strip all life from an area, then move on. They have likely eaten everything. We will rely on reserves from here on out. To be safe, you and Tressa will leave in a few days with the rest of my house's staff."

The verdant beauty was a harsh contrast to Cinis's growing heartache. As the two continued in the disheartened silence, they peered up and noticed the workshop behind the greenhouse they were strolling in.

An idea hit Cinis, and they could have sung as they offered, "I'm not going anywhere yet! I'm going to build us an armored getaway truck! There are plans for one. I know I saw some when I was poking around in there."

Not waiting for Nera's response, they ran from the greenhouse and down the path. Blasting through the workshop doors, they sprinted to the drafting table in the office dug through the stacks of blueprints until they found the plans. The sheet of schematics was peeking out from under a water run generator plan, and it had caught Cinis's eye as they toured the workshop earlier. It seemed perfect for this situation, and they knew they could build it. With the right protective armored vehicle, they could all come back alive. *Nera could come back alive.*

Cinis heard Nera's footsteps behind them. "I am going to need a lot of coffee."

"You are leaving in three days. If I have to drug you, I will," Nera replied flatly.

Cinis looked back at her, "Not if I finish this in two days. I need a team, I need you to trust me, and I need that coffee."

Trust was something Nera had truly little of, but something told her she could depend on this beautiful human's plan. There was something about this lithe human that sang to her. They were like the spring winds twirling over the distant grasslands, giving Nera a hope she thought she could never experience.

"Fine. Take a team from the house staff. I'll round them up and send a few of them out here. I'll make sure you have a wait staff as well, but you have exactly two days, nothing more. When you wake on the third, we will spend our last day together. On the fourth, you will leave even if the vehicle is not finished in time," she ordered.

"You mean you will risk it if I can finish in time?" Cinis beamed with hope.

Relenting, Nera nodded, "If there is a chance we can all make it out and survive, I will allow you to stay. You will not leave the safety of the truck, no matter what. If I don't make it, you are to head south with those of us who do and live your life. Do you understand me?"

Cinis's voice shook with possibility, "I'll agree to that."

"Good. You don't have a choice." Nera turned to return to the house.

They knew they never had a choice about anything regarding Nera, they didn't care in the slightest. The only thing they did care about was saving her life. They wanted a chance with her, dammit! Even as a lowly pet, Cinis would gladly remain at Nera's feet.

With the whirlwind of the last week, Cinis finally cried.

Tears flooded out, realizing their fear and emotional exhaustion all while they blurred the schematics as they desperately formed their plan of action. Vin opened the door and walked in as they futilely attempted to hide their tears.

He threw his big arms around them. "Nera told me your deal. I'll do everything I can to help."

The tears flowed again, and Cinis admitted, "I've never been happy before. I've just now found a few moments of it, and I can't bear the thought of losing the chance for more so soon."

"I've never had it. I just want a chance to find it," Vin agreed, his face void of any feeling.

They both focused on the plans and went to work. Vin and Cinis had far too much to lose to fail at this.

ALISOT – HOUSE OF DOMITIA

With the curtains pulled shut, the room was pitch black save a few streams of light under the door. Tressa woke but didn't dare move. Lock's hand rested on her hip, and it had not been there for long. It was the most he had moved since he had been hurt.

A soft groan came from him and Tressa rolled on her back so she could check on him. He kept his hand in place, and it slid between her thighs. Leaning in closely to see if she could see his face in the darkness, she found his eyes open, and a thrill burst through her. She whispered, "Are you hungry?"

He nodded, and she moved up to hand him her arm. He didn't remove his left hand from between her thighs but rubbed it along her leg. He gripped her thigh when she moved closer to him. He held her forearm to his mouth, and she could feel the heat of his breath. He rubbed his teeth on the area before he bit down, and she noticed they were sticky. When he sunk his teeth into her, she didn't feel a thing. While he fed, she tried to clear her vision so she could see him better. What she could see of his thick muscled body was enough to make her hot on its own.

He licked the wound thoroughly and pulled her arm over him. When her face was even with his, he licked the blood off around his lips and kissed her. As she kissed him back, he pulled her over him so she was straddling him.

He moved and Tressa gasped, worried she had harmed him, "Oh shit, did I hurt you?"

Grunting softly, he whispered, "Shhh. I don't care. This is worth it." Grabbing her hips, he pushed her against his hard length, and she ground down on it. Groaning, he leaned his head back in the pillow. Tressa put her hands on his shoulders and felt the raised tattoos adorning him. She ran her hands down his arms and chest before leaning down and licking his nipple. Rubbing her hands down his stomach, she could feel his rippling muscles, and it was enough to make her wet. He was perfect for her, bulky, but not super cut. Moving down his body, she licked him along the crease above his thigh, and he tilted his head up to watch her.

He was already nude, so Tressa took his length in her hand and stroked it once. Lock breathed heavily as she licked her lips before putting her mouth on him. His eyes widened in pleasure, "That's good. Oh. Fuck." Tressa used her hands with her mouth to caress him, and rubbed her finger up and down over his back entrance.

"Damn, already?" he whispered, more to himself as his ecstasy built quickly. Moments later he squirmed, and his hips clenched right before his release exploded into her mouth. Swallowing it down, she leaned up, and he grabbed her hands.

There was a flurry of limbs and Tressa had no idea

what he was trying to do. Pulling her up his body, he swung her leg over his shoulder. With her hips in his grasp, he guided her entrance onto his awaiting mouth. Tressa cried out as he sucked her swollen heat into his mouth and twirled his tongue around wildly. It was so much stimulation she couldn't help but fight his iron grip on her hips to pull away. He was devouring her, and she was thrashing around above him and bucking uncontrollably, the only thing to hang onto was the headboard.

It was too much. Her nerves screamed with the assault and sweat dripped down her body. He continued twirling and whipping his tongue so fast that she couldn't catch her breath. When her climax approached, she almost didn't want it to happen. It was all consuming and she hopelessly wiggled in his bruising grip. Her vision blurred as her orgasm crested, and she leaned her head back in a silent cry as she was flung over the edge. Frozen in time, she just curled over as pleasure pulsed through her.

Stars filled her vision and her breath quickened, as the waves flooded her. He licked her up and down, lingering on her center and sending heat through her as the ripples slowed. By the time he loosened his grip, she was so exhausted she fell over onto the bed face down. Sweat dripped from her body.

He leaned over and slid his forked tongue up her sweaty spine causing her to arch and shiver, "Oh gods! Why?"

His lips found the edge of her ear and whispered, "I love when your body trembles. I can taste the thrill in your sweat."

Gushing with emotion again, Tressa's voice broke when she asked, "How much longer do we have together?"

Silence fell over them, and he finally whispered, "Three days."

He pulled her into him, and he kissed her down her neck, "I'll make sure it's three days that will carry you through the rest of your days."

"You don't understand, I want more than that. I want you forever! I need more than that. I don't think I can leave you," Tressa repeated, her heart constricting so hard her face began burning.

"Tress, you don't have a choice. Nera and I already have the sedatives prepared in case you don't comply," Lock admitted.

Tressa's desolation finally spilled over, "Being sent to this planet has truly turned into the worst nightmare I could have ever imagined. Being eaten alive when I landed would have been a mercy."

Grabbing her face, Lock kissed her, "Don't grieve yet. Wait until after it's over."

She took a deep, slow breath, "I'll try."

Lock whispered against her skin, "I'll just have to keep you distracted."

Kissing down her throat, he pulled her shirt up and over her head. He took her breast in his hand and kissed all over it before moving to the other one. He moved on to her hips, kissing her gently. Her heart raced as he spoke, "I want you to tell me about your life. I'll go slow this time, but I'll stop if you don't keep talking. I'm going to bind you. Do you understand?"

She nodded, not knowing if she could even play along with her cyclone of feelings. "Yes. I understand."

Taking her hands, he lifted them and grabbed a chain with a small belt at the end from behind the bed. After he adjusted the length, he put her hands in the belt together and tightened it.

Tressa was already shaking and trying to rack her brain on what she was going to tell him. She needed to think now before he descended on her.

He gently pulled her down to stretch her body out and crouched over her, "You can't see anything can you?"

She replied, "Not really, I can a little but not much."

He made his way over to the window facing the court-yard and opened it a crack to allow light in before coming back over. He crawled on top of her and wedged a pillow under her head.

"Don't take your eyes away for any reason," he demanded as he lifted her breast to his mouth. Twirling his tongue over her peak, he peered up at her expectantly.

Tressa groaned, "Oh fuck. I wanted to be a dancer. I have never told anyone that."

He moved on to the next breast, again, twirling his tongue and driving her mad with need. She was so sensitive, and his tongue was a contradiction of rough and smooth, and she shook as it rolled over the tip of her nipple. He brought his hand up and played with one as he licked the other.

"I took care of our Nan and cleaned the streets around the Venus temple as a teenager." Tressa's body writhed under Lock.

He moved down, kissing and licking along her right side. Her sore muscles ached, and he seemed to notice as he rubbed her ass and thigh. Kissing lightly along her inner thigh had her speech sounding like she was speaking into a fan.

"I liked. To run. But it. Was way too. Dangerous. Where. We. Lived," she managed to squeak.

He twirled his tongue down between her thighs and rubbed her most sensitive place as she continued to speak in segments, "My feet and hands. Began hurting. When I was twenty. But I didn't. Have money to find help for it."

His rhythm steadied and she felt the waves cresting rapidly. When it hit, it was different. It was relaxing and gentle. He softly licked her through the rushing waves, drawing out her pleasure.

Lock licked his lips and crawled up her body so he could face her, "You have a joint disease that's undiagnosed? Why didn't you say something. You know what a butcher is right? We practice medicine. I am a doctor who specialized in butchering."

Tressa cringed, "The word my translator is using is not accurate, and in our language it's a word that means you cut up animals for their meat."

Lock leaned back and howled with laughter, "No wonder you looked at me so strange when I said that. I am not a meat processor. I was trained as a child in medicine, by Nera's former house butcher. She taught me everything I needed to know to become a butcher myself by the time I was a young teenager. I fixed my first set of broken wings when I was sixteen. When she left, I kept teaching myself."

"I am thirty this calendar cycle. How old are you?" Tressa asked.

"I turned forty this year. I am five years older than Nera. You're too young for natural joint pain," he answered with concern in his voice.

Tressa bit her lip, "Do you really think you can help me with my pain?"

"I don't know until I can look it all up. Humans are different than us, but our immune system likely functions somewhat similarly. Is it your immune system or wear and tear?" he asked as she reached up and massaged her wrist.

"I have never been hard on my hands and feet. I always have a low fever, and I don't really feel all that great most of the time." Tressa admitted.

His concern deepened. "Fuck. So many times, I have wished I wasn't part of this damn suicide mission. It conflicts with my desire to give care. I know there are other doctors down south. Many actually, but I know I am one of the best. I could probably find a way to develop a treatment. Fuck fate. I'm going to go find Nera. Stay here and stay naked."

He released her wrist then stormed out stark nude and didn't seem to care in the slightest.

Within fifteen minutes, he rushed back in, "I take it back. Dress now. Cinis came up with a plan that could work, and they need help. They're in the workshop with Vin and some of the house staff."

Tressa met his eyes and saw the hope in them. "Listen. Fuck worrying about my condition for now, and fuck wasting time. If they found a way, we need to dedicate every moment to it."

"I'll do anything it takes if it buys us more time," Lock admitted as he slipped on his pants as quick as he could.

Tressa pulled on a pair of soft pants and stood watching Lock slip a shirt on. Was Lock aware of what he just said? Tressa couldn't help it as her heart soared.

TWENTY-FIVE

ALISOT – HOUSE OF DOMITIA

Bolting a sheet of precision cut alloy onto a new truck, Cinis looked up as Tressa and Lock appeared in the doorway of the garage where they were working.

"How do we help?" Lock asked as he approached the project.

Cinis tightened a bolt as they answered, "Go review the plans and start assembling. We need to put two layers of welded armor on this truck. We might not be able to finish in time even working around the clock since I haven't cut the rest of the alloy sheets yet. All that's finished is the reinforced suspension, and I beefed up the engine with a hotter burning fuel system and reinforced the boiler to withstand the extra pressure and temperature, but there's still so much to do."

Reviewing the plans, Lock acknowledged, "Got it. We need to cut down the bolts that stick up and round them off, make the exterior as smooth as possible."

"Great idea." Cinis agreed, not looking up. Everyone

worked with intense focus for the next few hours. The sense of urgency pushed them all to concentrate more than any of them had before.

As the day passed and the light faded, a woman from the kitchen staff came in with a tray of food and set it on the table. Vin and Lock headed over set down their tools to eat. Vin had a bowl of blood and Lock made a plate of raw meat and some kind of cooked root vegetable.

Realizing she too was hungry and in need of a break, Tressa joined them. When she reached for some of the vegetable, Lock grabbed her hand. "You do not want to eat that."

"Why?" she asked.

"Back when my world had technology, we developed multiple high vitamin root vegetables that taste a lot like blood, and that meat is human."

Grimacing she made a mental note to only order human food. The idea of eating something tasting like blood made her stomach curl, but human! Oh, absolutely not! She tried not to be sick. Moments later another tray was brought out. This one clearly had human food on it.

Finally taking a break, Cinis made a plate, "I have a weird question."

Vin asked, "Why am I not surprised it's a weird one?"

They laughed, and Cinis blurted, "What happens when you just have *blood cows* and not one you also have sex with?" Tressa tried not to groan. Cinis always asked the most inappropriate random questions. Questioning their captors about masturbation was something clearly not a topic for the moment.

Lock stopped chewing and looked at Vin before swallowing and asked, "You mean if we don't have a partner or mate? We use our hand like everyone else when they need to cum." Shrugging, Cinis accepted the answer.

Tressa, intrigued now, had more questions since it had been brought up, and found herself blurting. "Do you usually give yourself a hand job right side up or upside-down?"

Lock reached over and kicked Vin in the shin as to silence him. Grinning Lock answered as Vin tried not to spit out his food. "Both, and yes, before you ask, I've squirted cum on my face more than a few times. Once it fell in my nose, and I am not ashamed to say I almost cried. It was ten years ago, and sometimes I swear I can still smell it. We have an exceptional sense of smell, and the full scent was in my nose for a month." Vin held his hands over his mouth to muffle a belly laugh as he eyed Tressa and Cinis who were both busting at the seams.

Sliding his eyes over to Vin, Lock laughed as he admitted, "That wasn't the worst part, when it went up my nose, I fell off my perch and busted my head on the ground."

Vin howled first, and everyone in the room followed with raucous laughter. "Any Resper with a dick has done it. We've all had a nose full of cum a time or two. I didn't fall off my fucking perch though!" Vin managed to tease through a tight bloody grin and his boisterous laughter.

Cinis's stomach ached as they wheezed, "I think that's the funniest thing I've ever heard."

Lock re-filled his plate as Tressa was just finishing hers. Vin scarfed his blood down and went back to work. Cinis quickly ate the last of their plate and returned to cutting more panels.

They worked late into the night. In the early hours of the morning, Cinis knew it was far too late, and they still weren't even close to finished. Watching Nera enter the workshop to collect them they slid down the side of the unfinished truck. Lock and Tressa had worked until they both began to doze off while standing and making dangerous mistakes. Cinis had insisted they try to have a few hours of necessary sleep and they went off to bed. Vin was sprawled out on the floor and snoring at his workstation. Cinis had kept going when everyone else had fallen out with exhaustion.

"You are a noble human, and I admire your endearing drive. I am truly sorry you couldn't complete your armored truck in time." Nera held out her hand. Cinis couldn't bear to reach up and take her hand. They leaned their head back against the metal panel as tears poured down their cheeks. Kneeling down in front of them, Nera put her hands over theirs. "Your time to cry is not now. Save it for later. This is my time, and I want every minute of it."

Cinis peered up at her through their tears and wiped their face. She was right, and they could cry later. Taking a moment to collect themself, Cinis conceded with a nod before they allowed Nera to help lift them from the floor. She lifted Cinis into her arms and carried them all the way to her room.

Lying them on the bed, she leaned over and kissed them. Something was different, and Cinis was melting inside. This kiss was sweet and revealing, soft, and tender. In this moment, there was nothing domineering about Nera. She kissed down their neck and held them close for a long while before continuing down their body. She stopped at their nipples and took her time, admiring their fit body.

Spinning and twirling her tongue along their body it seemed her hands were everywhere at once. Every touch, every kiss lit a desire they had not expected in this moment of goodbye. Nera savored every taste of Cinis's heated skin. She wanted to remember their scent and sweetness. Cinis shivered with desire, and Nera grabbed their hips in a bruising hold before showering them with fervent kissing and licking. She closed her eyes as she closed her mouth over Cinis bud and ran her tongue along the nerves slowly, building to a perfect rhythm. A strange vibrating began and Cinis strained to hear. Nera was humming, but at a high frequency. The gentle vibrations created an unreal intensity, and they began shaking. They knew exactly what she was about to do.

A sorrowful thrill burst through Cinis as the vibrations changed and went back and forth. Waxing and waning. They were already cresting and writhing through the first orgasm, knowing Nera didn't plan to stop. She was going to take Cinis into a second climax without allowing the first to ever end. Their legs were shaking so wildly they knew their muscles would be sore later but did not care. Nera increased the vibrations of her tongue as well as her rhythm, and they were at a point of breathlessness.

Nera reached up and pressed on Cinis's chest, forcing the air from their lungs so they would inhale. As the air filled their lungs, they felt the waves beginning to crest, slowly, just like before. As they tipped over, it felt like time stopped as they leaned back and released a cry of deep pleasure.

The moment the second set of waves slammed into them, Nera hooked two fingers inside them and tapped them forward. They were lost somewhere in the stars and between exhaustion and pleasure. It was all too much. Blackness creeped in their vision as their waves slowed.

Before the darkness took them, Nera whispered, "I'll wake you in a few hours, my little human."

TWENTY-SIX
ALISOT – HOUSE OF DOMITIA

The darkness was still heavy in the room when Tressa sat straight up in bed, "Fuck! Lock! Wake up. We have to finish the armored truck before the morning."

Groaning as he lay on his stomach, "Nera said Cinis had two days. This is day three. You both leave in the morning." Realization hit him, and he sharply sat up as he turned to her, "Oh. Yes, I see. Let's go now."

Scrambling off the bed and dressing in the clothes from the day before, they were out the door in less than a minute.

"What time is it?" Tressa asked, aching feet popping and clicking as she walked.

Lock reached over and took her arm to alleviate the pressure on her feet as he answered, "It's four. We have all day and night."

When they reached the workshop, Lock went over to Vin, who was still asleep on the floor and kicked his leg. "Get up!" he barked.

Vin opened one eye, "Fuck off, cum sniffer."

"We have to finish the armored truck, so we don't die." Lock was hovering over Vin.

Growling, Vin staggered up, scratching and stretching with sleep encrusted eyes, "Oh! Getting up. Wait, isn't it day three? Aren't we too late?" Vin asked.

Lock stared at him, "Not for us, just for Cinis."

Realization dawning on him, Vin excitedly leaped to his feet, "Getting to work!"

They worked all day and into the night, bolting the plates on to the entire outside of the truck. Heavy tires were installed to cut down on the possibility of flats and a retractable guard was attached to protect the glass. A periscopes was installed with 360-degree vision to ensure the driver could navigate all times.

As darkness fell, Vin took a gulp of his cup of blood as he turned to Lock, "We are almost finished." Lock agreed, and they started the final welding. The two worked through the night as Tressa slept on a travel cot brought out by the house staff when she couldn't stand anymore.

When the first light began peeking over the horizon, Lock leaned over the side of the truck to check on Vin who was back asleep on the ground and Tressa who was just rousing. He was sitting on top of the finished truck when Tressa peered up through her sleepy eyes and whispered, "You did it." She shot up and jumped to her feet. "You fucking did it!"

Lock slid off and stumbled as he approached her mumbling, "I'm exhausted and can't walk, but yes, we are finished. I just called for Nera. She will be here any minute."

Just like that, Nera walked in with hope blazing in her eyes, followed by a swollen eyed Cinis. Slowly approaching the armored truck, Nera gasped, "I didn't think it would be finished in time. I was wrong. I'll go ahead and give the staff their seventy-two-hour evacuation warning. We leave for the den at the same time. We need to prepare our bodies and minds for what we must do if this is going to have a chance of success."

She turned to a relieved Cinis and gently smiled. The two passed by Vin sleeping on a cot as they headed back into the house, likely so Cinis could finally sleep.

With that, Lock went over to Vin and kicked his leg.

Vin leaned up, "Fuck you!"

Laughing, Lock hovered over him and replied, "No, fuck you!" Vin shot up and tackled Lock to the ground as Lock yelled, "We finished the truck!" Lock laughed uncontrollably on the ground as Vin stood up and rubbed the sleep out of his eyes.

When he finally looked down at Lock on the floor, Vin kicked him in the ass, "You're a prick!"

"I'm the prick who finished the truck!" Lock yelled as Vin scowled from waking.

His expression melted and Vin turned around to Lock, "You did it. We might not die now?" He sighed with relief, "I'm going to kick Manx ass when I see him. That fucker didn't say a word and went south."

Tressa dropped her jaw, "Wait the guy you just started dating?!"

Vin nodded, "Asshole didn't even leave a note. Just ghosted."

"I hope he breaks a fang." Tressa crossed her arms.

Vin smirked, "Thank you."

"I'm starving." Lock walked over to Tressa and took her hand. "Let's go to the kitchen since the staff are all off packing." Vin suggested.

Agreeing, Tressa nodded, and they all headed to the kitchen. Walking in, they found Nera making Cinis something to eat. Tressa went over and asked, "What is that?"

"My father had a human he cared about alongside my mother. He was a chef on Emendo who had been in trouble for giving away leftover food to the poor. The UTC framed him for a murder and sent him here. He used to make this meal for me when I was a child," Nera explained as she opened the cabinet to get out a bowl.

"This has no name, but it's a broth with bird meat and noodles. He used to add carrots and celery to it as well, but we don't have any fresh, so I had to use jarred from the pantry. You are welcome to eat as much as you want," Nera offered as she filled the bowl.

"What happened to him?" Tressa asked.

Nera peered over at Tressa before heading back to her room with Cinis's soup. "The old staff were all gutted together in the front yard after my father was beheaded."

Lock went over to sit by a now gloomy Tressa. "I miss them a lot. Tuhn was a kind human man, and her father was a great man. I miss them all."

"Didn't they raise you?" Tressa asked.

Lock smiled with the memories. "I was their ward and their only child before they had Nera. They didn't know they could have children and had an elder cousin appointed heir until I was of age. When Nera was born, her father wrote a new heirship decree making her heir. Her father made sure I remained in the line of succession when they officially changed my surname to Domitia and made me their legal child."

"What about your parents?"

Lock cleared his throat, "My birth parents were blood, um, human hunters and addicts to a strong, synthetic pain medication. Both overdosed. I never knew them. The Domitia's took me in as a small baby."

"If we live, will we see your daughter?"

Lock nodded, "We can absolutely do that."

Vin asked, "If we make it, won't we still be in the same situation?"

"True, but we will have a lot more time. There isn't another single cave big enough for their population to move close to here, but I'm sure they will eventually find other ways to infiltrate the lands and settle in. They will find a way to come back eventually. They may just go around this area and keep heading south until they figure it out." Lock speculated.

Nera appeared back in the kitchen doorway and went to the drawer in search of a spoon. "If we live, we are going to find that ancient underground base of the UTC's. I've gone over my father's map notes for the last few days, and I found a place he marked with a UTC symbol. It was near one of the ancient space port cities of Alisot called Banyona. It's a long way from here. We would have to drive and then we might have to walk for a long while. It will be several weeks of travel, maybe months."

They all agreed and as Tressa blew the steam from her soup. She was doing her best to ignore the weeks or months of walking of that plan. That part simply terrified her, and she didn't have the energy to be frightened at the moment. Nera grabbed a napkin along with a spoon and headed back to her rooms.

Vin leaned back in his chair and tapped his finger on the table, "We will need some recruits for that kind of a journey."

Lock turned to face him, "I agree, but we don't have

many who will likely volunteer. We just have us for certain."

"Lock, how about that treatment and maybe I could be more than just someone you drag around," Tressa requested as she gulped down some of the delicious soup.

Locks brows shot up, "That is a great idea. Let's go to my lab right now."

"I'm going back to sleep." Vin yawned and pushed in his chair.

Lifting her bowl to refill and bring it with her, Lock took it from her and washed it out before setting it down. He pulled a tall mug out of the cabinet and filled it with the soup from the pot. Lock handed it to Tressa, "Nera hates messes." She laughed and took a sip before she followed him out of the kitchen. As she passed the drawer she knew held the kitchen towels, she opened it and grabbed one.

His lab, which was just a room on the other side of what Tressa now knew was the clinic, was always well lit and clean. Tressa took in the seemingly modern medical equipment. "Sit down in the chair with padded arms. I need to take a little blood. Our equipment is basic and adapted for Resper. I can't tell much, but I want to at least do some white blood cell counts."

In awe, Tressa swallowed roughly, "You can do that? I have to be honest. I was terrified about you operating on me. I genuinely thought you were going to put me under to cut me up and eat me. We had been told so many horror stories about your kind. To find out your people have been having an arguably civilized life down here is a bit of a shock. No wonder the First Humans messed with the bat DNA. They must have been upset your civilization didn't fully collapse."

"It did for a few hundred years, but we recovered and rebuilt a new one. Nera's ancestors were the Resper who re-united our people and established a new civilization after we were left in ruin. I don't understand why the other houses are so critical of the Domitia's. All we've ever done was try to make things better. Lean back. This won't hurt much. Take a breath and slowly exhale."

She did as he asked and after her blood was drawn, he lifted her arm and licked away a drip of blood. "I still cannot believe you licked my insides! Ick! Could you not have just spit in there or something? Ugh, I don't know if that's any better." She shifted uncomfortably in her seat.

He looked at her like she was a sweet treat before leaning in close, "And pass up a chance to taste you that intimately? I don't think so. Don't forget, at the time of the procedure, all humans were still nothing but food to me. I have to admit, you are lucky I didn't eat you. You have no idea the restraint I had to use."

Her eyes flared wide and her pulse shot up, causing Lock to hum as he turned to put up the tubes of blood. When he returned, Tressa's heart was still racing as her mind went wild. The disturbing thoughts running through her mind made her sweat and she couldn't deny, she was horrified to her core. This man was a predator, and she was truly his prey. His *pet*.

"Damn, you smell so good when you're scared." He leaned over and sniffed the skin of her neck. He licked her and she shivered, causing him to smile against her flesh, "Not yet. I have some work to do." He leaned up and kissed her and over her lips whispered, "Go rest. I'll see you in a few hours."

TWENTY-SEVEN

ALISOT – HOUSE OF DOMITIA

The house was quiet. Dread filled their gut as Cinis entered the kitchen. Each one of them kept finding reasons to extend the evening, knowing this will be the last meal they may have together.

Slowly walking to the table, Cinis saw Nera had cooked again. She had prepared a sliced ham and some kind of mashed root vegetable along with a spread of cheeses and jams and a variety of wines and liquors. Pulling their chair out, they asked, "Are we drinking tonight?"

Nera put her hands on the table and leaned forward. "Tressa can drink alcohol to her hearts content. You can have some but you're driving tomorrow, so only a few. Vin, Lock, and I need to be ready for the morning which includes draining the last blood cows. You two are not leaving the truck, no matter what."

Knowing they would leap out to fight for Nera anyway, they just avoided an argument and nodded a false agree-ment. They reached for the wine and poured a large glass before handing it off to Tressa who did the same. She looked like she needed it. Tressa was as white as a ghost. She must be just as worried, Cinis thought as they began cutting into their enormous plate of food.

Everyone ate in silence. It would be a long night. Nera, Lock, and Vin would need to try to sleep some after their large meal. When daylight broke, everyone needed to be ready to move. The den was hours away, and in the few hours after the light spread over the land was the best time to set up the explosives. When everyone had seemingly finished eating, Nera stood and looked around the room, and at these people she felt responsible for.

Nera addressed the room when she knew she had everyone's attention. "After a day of digging in the library, I found the old cave surveys for the area. I have a map of where all the explosives need to go. There will be scouts asleep outside of the den, so we will need to watch for them, and be prepared to take them out before they can raise any alarms."

Taking a slow breath, she continued, "Vin, you are staying with Tressa and Cinis. Lock and I decided that if things go bad, we are placing you in charge of their well-being. If anything goes wrong, you are to haul them away. You have our blessing and the seal of House Domitia to use any means necessary to keep them safe."

Pausing, Nera waited for any disagreement, and when there was none, she continued, "We are going to need as much time as possible to set up the sets of explosives. They are on timers, but they are only two hours at maximum. When we finish with the set-up, Lock, and I, will fly to the farthest point and start the timers. With the sizable area we need to cover, it will take exactly two hours to set them. Each one will be set fifteen minutes apart. That means only having fifteen minutes between stops. We will be racing against the clock, and it will take thirteen minutes at max speed to fly from one stop to the next." Nera turned to Lock, "If we fumble, we die."

"Understood." Lock slid his hand onto Tressa's knee. She was trembling. Her heart was racing, and she couldn't stop it. Gulping down her wine, Lock rubbed her leg in reassurance. The chance of either of them not making it plus the bit about the blood cows weren't exactly calming thoughts.

Nera's warning and planning was thorough, but Tressa was still scared out of her mind. She was sure her heart would break before the first hints of morning light. She knew she needed to stop this cascade of terror running through her mind, but she didn't know how. Besides Cinis and her Nan, Tressa had never cared about anyone so much as this unlikely group.

This was a suicide mission, even with the armored truck. It was clear Nera and Lock weren't expecting to walk away. This entire plan was still a dark chance in hell. She looked over at Cinis, and they were wide eyed and agitatedly tapping their foot on the ground.

Nera turned back to Cinis and Tressa. "If we had more people, we wouldn't have such a tight window. Three guards are traveling up from the south, but they won't be here in time. They are instructed to meet and escort you three south. We don't have the luxury of help. I'm sorry you two were dragged into the proto war. In another life, we could have all been incredibly happy, but we need to face the reality that one or both of us will likely not be making it back to the truck tomorrow. I need both of you to give me your word you will leave without argument." They looked at each other, seeing each other's true intentions, but Cinis spoke first and whispered, "Fine."

Tressa choked out, "I fucking hate this. Fine."

The room grew silent, and the air became thick with sorrow. Vin was sitting in his usual place, down from Nera and Lock. His heart and frustration were the heaviest, and Cinis knew it. The man he liked abandons him and now he can't defend his best friends. He was cursed to let his two best friends die because he had to care for their helpless human pets.

Cinis shook with fear and rage. They had been sent to this planet to die and they felt like this was a fate worse than death. The last thing they would do was show it though. They would never let Nera see how devastated they were. They would never try to convince her to abandon this doomed plan and run south. They knew why it was important to destroy this den specifically. They understood her honor to her people. They could see how it had to go, but why Nera? Why Lock? Why now?

Sensing their heightened emotions, Nera lead Cinis to the gardens, pointed to a padded bench, "Sit here." She approached a small stand and opened the door to retrieve a long box. Setting it on the table, she pulled a few items out and began tapping on various jars to empty them onto what sounded like paper. "Have you ever smoked leaf?" she asked.

Cinis vaguely remembered the one time they did smoke it. "Yes. I couldn't afford it, but I did when I was with Rungi."

Nera raised her eyebrows and asked, "You and Rungi were more than friends?"

Cinis stared at their hands. "I have a thing for strong women. What can I say?"

Laughing Nera licked the edge of what they now saw was a rolled leaf cigarette. It had been a long time since they had anything other than alcohol or coffee. Nera lit the leaf cigarette and hit it a few times before sitting down and passing it over to Cinis. "I'm surprised Vin isn't already heading this direction. He loves to smoke." Nera laughed as she leaned back on the bench. Grinning at Cinis, she leaned to the side and tilted her long pointed ear, "And there he is."

Vin's footsteps could be heard approaching as Cinis handed the rolled leaf cigarette back to Nera. When he came around the bin of vegetables and leaf growing all around the bench, he already had his hand out. Taking two large drags, Vin coughed, "This was a good idea."

Nera threw her head back and laughed in a way Cinis had not heard before. It was deep and genuinely happy, carefree. It was who she really was inside, and they had been dying to meet that person.

They all passed around the leaf and smoked until they were red eyed and smiling at nothing. Vin sat on the ground and ended up lying on his back with his wings spread out under him. "I know I'm getting my wings dirty, but I just cannot care right now," Vin admitted as he stared through the glass ceiling of the greenhouse.

Nera tucked a bit of hair in her face behind her pointed ears. "I'll brush them off before we go inside. Your wings are always a little dusty, anyway."

Reaching out and trying to grab her with his foot, Nera pulled her legs up as she yelped, falling halfway off the bench. Laughter exploded between them before Vin glared at her, "They are not always a little dusty, you *asshole*."

Leaning over with lazily blinking, semi-closed eyes, Nera whispered to Cinis, "Sometimes our wings become dry and look dusty. He does not properly moisturize and…"

Vin cut her off as he sat up, "One time, when we were in our early twenties, we drank too much, and we had a big meeting with one of heads of a major house the next day. We woke up that morning covered in mud in the middle of the forest. Nera had a bad stomachache, and Lock could hardly climb into the sky. To make it home on time, we went as high as we could so we could catch the faster air streams."

Cinis peered over at Nera who had zero expression on her face and did not seem amused at all with this story.

Vin continued, either oblivious to her interest or ignoring her, "When we came close to the house, Nera couldn't hold it back and threw up midair. She spewed everywhere. It was so disgusting Lock almost fell out of the sky. When we made it to the house, we went around the corner and one of the staff told us there had been an incident."

Nera groaned next to Cinis as Vin began laughing so hard he could barely speak. "We went around the side of the house and found the man we were meeting was covered in vomit."

Cinis gasped, "Oh no! It wasn't?"

"When we faced him, and he smelled us, he knew it was us. He cursed us up and down and stormed out. He had little kids, and they were laughing so hard they peed in their pants." Vin rolled in the grass, giggling almost uncontrollably as Nera glared at him. "I've never heard of someone getting puked on like that before. Only you would do something that awful!"

Finally speaking up, Nera shook her head, "House Seri is still feuding with us over it."

TWENTY-EIGHT
ALISOT – HOUSE OF DOMITIA

After the others had disappeared into the gardens, Lock leaned over to Tressa. "Let's go look what the lab tech reported on your blood work before the staff left."

Feeling him press against her, she admitted, "I think I need a distraction."

"I have plenty." Lock rubbed her leg gently.

Rising up, they went to the lab, and she sat down in one of the chairs as he grabbed her results off his desk. Behind him sat a curiously large microscope. She wondered to herself why the viewing mirror was so wide. He sat next to her and read the report as his hand slid down the paper. "You have a very high white count for being cancer and infection free." he muttered softly, more to himself.

"How do you know I am infection and cancer free?" she asked as she turned to him.

Lock didn't look up from the paper. "I can smell many diseases and all cancers. We all can."

"You can *smell* infection and cancer? That's some intense sense of smell. I've heard of dogs on Melior doing that, but I didn't know the Resper could," she admitted.

"I doubt the Resper you met on Emendo were anything like us. What did they say when you had checkups?" he asked.

"I've never been to an actual doctor for a checkup before. Healthcare is a luxury where I lived. Cinis and I are extremely lucky to have good teeth. We had a neighbor who wanted to be a dentist," Tressa cringed with the memories of him digging in her mouth.

"That's sounds terrible. The almost dentist I mean, and you never once saw a doctor until you had a baby?" Lock asked as he peered at her with a shocking amount of unexpected sympathy.

"I still never talked to a doctor, though I carried nine pregnancies for the surrogate program. The only doctor I saw was through the glass when I was delivering." Tressa had her hands wrapped around her middle.

Lock just stared at her in disbelief. "I grew up on a prison world and it was still better than your upbringing. No wonder you both have a panic disorder. You must have developed some kind of immune system disease which attacks healthy tissue. Your joints are the only thing that hurt?"

Tressa thought before she answered. "No. The tendons around them hurt too. They have lumps on them."

He took her hand and felt all around. "I'm not sure how to make your immune system stop attacking the healthy tissue yet. We don't have many of these kinds of diseases here. We hardly have working UTC microscopes much less any of the Resper's medical diagnostic equipment we had saved in the former Domitia home. The FH made sure to level all our medical facilities when they trapped us here."

"You need to live so we can all go to the UTC base, and you can run more tests there. I bet they have particle replicators. You could make a medication for me. What if the treatment you have been looking for is down in that base?" Tressa hoped he understood the loud meaning.

He paused, choosing his words carefully. "I want more time with you, Tressa. I don't need more convincing. I was already going to do everything I could to survive. I never *wanted* any of this. For years I have had pills filled with a fast-acting poison to kill us instantly before we were torn apart by the bats. We keep them in our leathers. I accepted my fate years ago and so did Vin and Nera, but I have another reason to live now. I won't fail. I can't."

He took her hand and sniffed the air before standing up. Tressa was unable to respond. What could she say? "Nera has Cinis in the greenhouse, and they're smoking leaf. Do you want to join them?" Lock asked as he rubbed her knuckles with his thumb.

"No. They used to do that with Rungi too. It's not something I want right now." She decided she wanted to remember every moment, unclouded.

Lock helped her up from her chair, "Let's go to your room for some rest."

"Don't you need to sleep upside down?" she asked.

"Not always."

"Don't you have the best sleep that way?"

Lock nodded.

Tressa couldn't help it as she smiled, "I'll meet you in your room then."

"Alright." They arrived at his door, and he watched her prance off to her room, wondering what she was doing.

In her room, Tressa grabbed a pillow and a few large soft blankets before backing out of the door. Lock bit his lips when he saw her heading toward him with a pile of bedcovers so tall she couldn't see over the top. He held the door open as she went in and dumped her pile of covers on the floor with her pillow. She made herself a small pallet under his perch while he stood watching every second of it. Slowly approaching as she curled up, he leaned over her and kissed her. "It surprises me I can find so much delight in a human. I used to feel nothing but anger. You've done something to me." He kissed her again before flipping upside down to hang from his perch. He curled his wings around himself, and all she could see was his hair poking out of the top in the dim light.

Curling up in a ball underneath him, Tressa stared at the wall and desperately tried to think of nothing to keep her heart calm, so Lock could sleep. When she knew from his breathing that he was asleep, she lie back and stretched out. Worry filled her, but she did her best to soak up this moment. This room. Everything about this man and how he shouldn't have to risk his life all because everyone else had to evacuate. It wasn't fair.

But oh, life isn't fair, old Nan would say. Guilt filled her when she remembered her grandmother on the floor in a pool of blood with her throat slit. She had loved her Nan, no matter how crotchety she was. Memories of her old life trickled through her head as she focused her eyes on the man she was quickly falling for. It was so much more than her just trying to seduce him to survive. She genuinely cared about him and wanted a future with him, one she begged Venus and Mars to give them. She was even willing to pray to Jupiter if it meant they would all live.

Her thoughts reeled until she finally gave in to exhaustion and slept.

TWENTY-NINE

ALISOT – HOUSE OF DOMITIA

Tressa and Lock stood tensely in the hallway adjacent the dining room with Nera and Cinis waiting for Vin. They were dressed in their leather flight armor and strapped down with weapons. Nera had decided Cinis would drive, and they were busy mentally preparing. Lock and Nera looked well rested, but when Vin walked out, it was clear he hadn't slept. He seemed as if he had spent the night in a pit of despair. Cinis knew he hated that he had to live either way, and the guilt was eating him alive.

Vin slumped against the wall in the hallway, "Nera, are we draining the last two blood cows or what?"

Shrugging Nera nodded in agreement, and the two moved toward her rooms. Cinis thrummed with anxiety. Could they handle watching the Resper kill two humans?

Nera and Vin emerged with two bound angry men with gags and brushed past Tressa and Cinis, heading to the courtyard.

Before Lock followed them, he turned to Tressa, "You two are going to want to stay inside for this."

Tressa looked to Cinis, and they closed their eyes briefly before sitting at the dining table. Tressa waited for a few minutes after Lock shut the door before she snuck up to the window to watch. If she was going to fall for a monster, she needed to know exactly what type of monster he was.

Nera and Vin shoved the two men to their knees, and Lock took one of the men by the neck. The man tried to head butt Lock, which prompted Lock to pull his knife from his side and begin slicing the man's arm off at the shoulder. The human man released a blood curdling scream as Lock hacked into him, separating his shoulder. Once his arm had been severed, Lock peeled back the skin and bit into the muscle underneath to rip it away with his fangs. Blood poured from the man, and he whimpered as Lock devoured his arm in front of him. Vin took a knee and leaned in to feed on the man's neck as Lock tossed away the rest of his arm.

A flock of dark carrion birds circled overhead and one dove for the arm. Tressa swallowed down her disgust that such birds would frequent the area for such an occasion.

Nera bent the next man backward and began feeding from his neck, blood spirting from the artery she pierced. Vin finished off the man with the severed arm as Nera passed Lock the sluggish man she had been feeding on. He bit a chunk out of the man's neck before drinking him dry.

Once both men had been drained of all their blood, the three Resper approached the steps and cleaned their faces in a small fountain before Vin dragged the bodies off leaving wide streaks of blood on the ground.

Nera and Lock headed toward the door, and Tressa

sprinted away from the window to stand by Cinis in the dining room. When Lock rounded the corner, he stared at Tressa as he ran his tongue over his wet lips. She forced a deep breath and a smile at him, but he knew she had seen everything. This is who he was, and he wanted her fully aware her presence wouldn't change his lifetime of brutal conditioning. Not to mention anyone sent here was sent for the very reason of suffering until their end.

Lucky her.

After collecting Cinis, Nera headed toward the truck and grabbed backpacks off an entryway table before passing them around. "These were packed for each of us before the staff left. They have food and supplies for your journey south if it's necessary," Nera explained as she handed them out.

Cinis heart pounded as they moved toward the armored truck next to Nera who was carrying an extra box of explosives. It wasn't even time to leave yet, and their chest was already tight.

Prepping their spot in the front seat, Cinis did their best to smile at Vin as he plopped in the passenger seat. Tressa threw her bag in the back and leaned against the truck with her head back and eyes closed. She was exhausted from a mostly sleepless night and more so after what she just witnessed. Tressa was questioning her sanity in considering a relationship with Lock or this suicide mission.

Nera and Lock stowed their gear and said their last goodbyes before the long drive. When they arrived, there wouldn't be much talking.

Nera leaned into Cinis, "I'll see you soon."

Holding back everything, they whispered, "Liar," as

they moved in and kissed her. They could still taste the blood on Nera's lips.

On the other side of the truck, Lock didn't say a word as he pulled Tressa to him and kissed her head. Leaning her head back, he kissed her lips and stroked his thumb along her neck before he helped her back into the armored truck. Lock walked back and climbed in the passenger seat of the truck.

Breathing was difficult, and her head screamed for her to run, run far away and escape before it was too late. Logic repeated, *you're in danger. You saw what he did to those men. He's a monster and won't change. One day he will eat you too.* Her heart though? Tressa's heart was broken. Not because of what they had now, but what they could have, the chance to explore this passionate man and the possibility of a true relationship. Her emotions were stretched out too far and she felt as though they could snap her in two at any moment. Tressa did not know when it would happen, but she did know if this went awry, it would forever change her.

Tressa had shed a few tears here and there in her life before, but she had not had a chance to grieve for her Nan. There just wasn't time after being dropped in the middle of a planet filled with monsters of all kinds right before being rescued by a whole different kind of monster, the kind that dives under your skin and steals your breath with just a look, the kind that makes you do outrageous things, things you would never do. Then to be caught up in this maddening plot to save the same monsters who wanted to eat her and Cinis – would she even have time to sort out her feelings?

Those emotions would just have to wait a little longer. For now, Tressa made a few choices about her word she had given Nera about heading south as she sat in the armored truck. Leaning her head forward, she began tightly braiding her hair. Cinis saw what Tressa was doing and smiled at her. They already knew the plan. If there was anything Tressa loved about having a close sibling was their ability to have an entire conversation with no verbal communication. Cinis handed Tressa two strips of leather to tie her ends before starting the armored truck with a rumble. They couldn't help the little thrill over how good the engine sounded after all the modifications.

The truck with the explosives pulled off onto the gravel road, and Cinis shifted into gear and pulled in behind it. As they reached the main road, Cinis leaned toward Vin in the middle, "You know you're going to have to kill us or sedate us to keep us in the truck, right?"

Sliding his eyes over, Vin stared at Cinis before closing his eyes and dropping his head back on the headrest with a huff. "I can't believe they left me in charge of you two. They should have known this was not going to work."

After a long pause, Vin opened his eyes and turned to Cinis, "For the record, I cannot stand either one of you right now." Cinis and Tressa both grinned nervously making him laugh. "But really though, please calm down if you can because I can hear both of your hearts pounding, and it's making my head spin."

All three spent the next few hours doing all they could do to stay calm.

When they arrived, Nera pulled off and signaled to Cinis to park in a specific place in the clearing. They turned the truck around to face the road and took a slow, steady breath. Watching as Nera and Lock drove off to set up the bombs, Cinis wondered what the plan was for when Nera and Lock arrive to the clearing, likely with a mass of bats behind the both of them.

Vin leaned over Tressa and rolled down the window to listen before rolling it back up, "They're far enough ahead that they won't smell you get out."

"What if we had needed to go to the bathroom?" Tressa asked, leaning away from Vin's wing in her face.

Vin dug in his bag between his legs and held up a large-mouthed jug with a lid, "Nera handed me this for when you or Cinis asked that exact question."

Tressa's mouth dropped open, and Vin laughed as he waved his hand for Tressa to get out of the truck.

After he squeezed his wings into the v in the seat, he shut the door. "Cinis, you have to stay in the truck to drive, but Tressa and I could stand by the open doors and just wait for them."

Distressed to the point they were twisting their fingers, Cinis garbled out "What kind of plan is that? What happens when you are all outnumbered?"

Vin shrugged, "We will be outnumbered no matter what happens. Our best plan would be to just make sure they both make it back into the armored truck and someone is available to drive away in that instant. We can't waste any time. It will take over an hour to lose them during the day, maybe longer if they're diseased. We might have to drive away from the house for a few hours to stop and kill the followers before we can go home. Any survivors will return to their den mates, and they will bring back the entire colony."

Tressa eyed Vin incredulously, "You and I are waiting with what weapons? I only know how to use a knife, but just a few basics, kind of!"

"I brought this and you can use these as backup." Vin

pulled out a large sword from under the seat along with a large leather bundle filled with long knives. They split the roll of knives, sliding them into the holders all over their leathers.

"Is there anything I need to know about how they fight?" Tressa asked.

"Since you don't have wings, they love to duck down and ram their victims when they're on the ground. It's their thing. Once they ram and knock their target over, they will tear through them with their claws. I would say aim for where the shoulder meets the neck and imbed your knife as far as it will go. They will go down and stay down. They can't fly without that muscle intact, and they cannot run far."

"Got it, sure, no problem. Stab in the shoulder, hard." Tressa leaned to one side of the v in her seat and ran her finger down the edge of one of her knives. *This was a terrible plan*, and she knew it.

THIRTY
ALISOT – NORTHEN CONTINENT CAVERN MISSION

Lock and Nera placed the sixth bomb, and she was almost finished wiring the timer when they heard a crunch somewhere in the distance. Sniffing the air confirmed a bat had woken up. They hadn't heard a warning cry, so they knew they were still safe, for now.

Lock went off to investigate and found a tottering bat in the woods. By the smell, it was diseased and in the last stages. When it finally smelled Lock and charged him, it reached out for Lock's wings. Lock was ready and had his hand on the hilt of his sword behind his back. Drawing it out at just the right time, the monster impaled itself as Lock swung his other hand up with a knife and sliced its throat. The beast fell to Lock's feet and its blood spilled over the ground. His gut twisted at the idea of how many were still sick in this colony.

Returning to Nera, he found her finished and ready to drive to the next stop. They made their way through the woods and all the way to the truck. Thankfully, it was a magnetic engine, and it was nearly silent. It was one of her grandfather's famous designs that made their family a fortune on top of the one they already had. Today, it was priceless.

Nera turned to Lock back inside the truck, "Only two more to set up."

"I know we've stayed behind to see if we could find a solution, and if not, to die trying but it's different now. I can't pry Tressa out of my head." His fists clenched with his frustration.

"That's why it was only supposed to be single people, like we were before. We never dreamed we would find those two humans in the midst of this. They were supposed to just be like all the rest. Disposable. A distraction." Nera spoke in a soft tone as the truck slowly took off.

Lock turned to face the woods, not wanting her to see the emotion in her face. "It feels unfair, but I guess nothing ever is. I'm glad I had a taste while I still had the chance."

"Me too," Nera whispered.

They rode in silence to the next stop and set up without incident. When they pulled up to the final place to plant the explosives, Nera took a few moments before climbing out of the truck. "Thank you for everything, but especially for raising me when our parents died." Nera held onto the door handle.

Lock turned to her and replied, "I still remember the first time I held you when I was five. Mother was so worried I would squeeze you or fly off and I tried to do both."

Nera smiled her gratitude at him as she opened the door.

For a long moment they both just stared out into the woods together, not thinking of their vibrant childhood or their wild times as teens growing up alone as heads of a great house. They thought of the two humans they just met and how desperately they wanted out of this grand sacrifice. Nera was filled with despair and finding it hard to concentrate. It took a few minutes, but the work was done, and they headed to the truck for their second set of swords. Once every weapon was secured at their backs, they faced one another one last time before they both nodded solemnly and took to the sky.

Lock headed for the farthest point as he watched Nera aim for her first stop. Dread filled him where once he held honor. This was no longer a sacrifice he wanted to make, but it was far too late. The other great houses would never have accepted a Resper-human union anyway. He desperately tried to push Tressa out of his mind, but nothing he could do would remove her grip on him. He had never felt this way before.

When the hands on his watch hit one o'clock on the dot, it was time to move. He knelt down and set the timer. After he had turned all the right gears and knobs, he leapt into the air, flying as fast as his wings would take him. The muscles in his back already ached with the effort. His wings were strong, but this would push him to his limits each time.

He landed at the next stop and checked his watch, perfect timing. Heading over to the timer, he set it more quickly than the last. It took a few minutes like the last one, but his fingers remembered the action, and it was smoother. When he was finished, he didn't stand as he shot into the sky. The cross wind hit his wings, and he fought it with all his strength. He hoped it was the last blast of wind, but he couldn't rely on that.

Flapping his wings as fast as they would move, his

back screamed at him the last few moments before he landed at the third stop. This was like a sprint and a marathon at the same time. His body was in agony as he made his way to the bomb and the timer attached. Spinning the knobs, he hardly had time to catch his breath before it was time to leave for the last timer. He closed his eyes as he shot into the air, already dreading this next stop.

The first bombs would be going off as he was setting the timer on the last stop. His stomach lodged in his throat. He knew the bats would begin pouring out as he flew the last stretch toward the truck. His heart pounded in his chest as he put every ounce of his energy into his flight.

He knew he was slower this time and dread filled him as he approached the final stop. He landed in a full run to the timer, and slid to a stop in front of it. He grabbed the dial as sweat dripped into his eyes. Wiping it clear, he saw his time was already up. The ground shook as he spun the knobs. The blast reached his ears as he flew for the waiting truck.

Grabbed from behind, he hit the ground with a thud. Above him, a diseased bat gripped his wing. Her snout was foaming, and she growled at his attempt to pull his wing free. His world came crashing in when he heard the crunch of the delicate top bone in his wing. Pain laced through him, and he cried out.

There was no way he could reach the truck now. He took out his sword and cut her head off as he pulled his broken wing away from her hands and hissed with pain as he tried to fold it up. He screamed in anger as he took off running, knowing he could hardly run half as fast as he could fly. With his movements, pain shot through his wing and down his spine. It was agonizing. He told himself to turn his anger to fuel, but it was too much. With every step he pounded into the ground, he wanted to use his powerful vocal cords and release a scream. He could already hear the bats' wings flapping behind him. There were so many.

He held his arm up and read his watch. It had only been ten minutes. Lifting his head to listen, he could tell Nera was almost to the truck. A sense of peace fell over him knowing Nera would make it, and he begged himself to keep running. His legs were screaming, and his broken wing was now sending electric jolts of pain through his body. Pulling his watch up to his face, it read fifteen minutes. They all deserved to know he wasn't going to make it. He used his high-pitched voice to signal to Nera, no. He repeated it three times over the next few minutes of running.

Listening behind him, he knew they were closing in. When he heard them approach from above, he pulled his swords out and skid to a stop. As he turned to face them, he saw the hoard of bats above him blacked out the sky.

THIRTY-ONE
ALISOT – NORTHEN CONTINENT CAVERN MISSION

Nera slammed into the ground next to the truck, tucked in her wings, and stopped to listen. Vin came around the back of the truck and watched Nera standing there trying to breathe silently so she could hear. Her mouth dropped open, and she raised a hand to it as she turned her head toward where Lock was supposed to come from.

Nera twirled around to Vin. "Get in! Lock is down!" She shoved Vin toward the back, and he pulled Tressa in with him. They both found a seat as Nera slammed the back shut. Nera ran around the armored truck as Cinis moved over and she leapt into the front seat. The truck's tires spun as Nera slammed on the pedal and popped it into gear.

The truck flew, even with all the extra weight, and Nera drove over dips in the road with such speed they were catching air. No one dared speak as she flew through the woods.

Turning the wheel sharply and sliding to a halt, Nera

dashed out of the front door and ran into the woods. Vin and Tressa popped open the back and followed Nera.

Tressa's feet screamed at her to stop as she pounded through the woods. She wasn't far behind Vin as she saw Lock and Nera both slashing away at the mass of bats closing in on them and surrounding an embattled Lock.

Tressa could see part of Lock's wing hung at an odd angle and knew it was broken. She knew she had to do something. There were so many protos. How could they all survive? They wouldn't unless she did something drastic.

Making a split-second decision, she raised her bare hand up, pulled out a knife and slashed her hand across her palm and turned towards the blood hungry monsters. Remembering the one science book she read as a child, she knew exactly how to draw the bats away from her friends. They could smell blood from a great distance, and she wasn't far.

Sheathing her knife, she clapped her hands, causing her blood to spray in the air. She turned toward the direction of the main road and let out a blood curdling scream before she took off running.

Tressa sprinted desperately and cringed as she heard Lock roar from behind. The bats must have already diverted toward her scent. Not wasting any time, she calculated her path and stayed true knowing the bats had to run through the thickest trees, instead of swooping from above to catch her. She begged the gods her friends understood what she was doing.

Hearing the steam engine of the truck pop as it kicked into gear, Tressa beamed with hope but didn't dare check behind her. She could hear the bats approaching, and she kicked up her pace, but the stench of the protos reached her and she knew they were almost on top of her. Pumping her legs harder, she could hear a soft hum of the truck coming closer. She could see the steam and hear the engine more clearly rumbling to her left. A whistle met her ears as she braced herself as Vin reached out from the passenger door and grabbed her by the waist. Just as she felt a proto touch her hair, the air around her whooshed as Vin hauled her into the truck. She was tossed over the seat, landing roughly on the floorboard. She raised her eyes to find herself at the feet of a raging, furious Lock.

A proto slammed into the top of the truck and Cinis pulled several levers, shutting all the metal guards on the outside and locking them into place. The truck grew dark, and Cinis used the periscope view to navigate as they flew through the woods. Sounds from outside of the truck reverberated around them, and Cinis tensed with the noise. The bats slammed into the truck, one after another. Some landing and pounding, others screeching as they slid off. Their claws scratched at the metal causing Vin, Nera, and Lock to snarl and cover their ears.

Vin crawled over the seat to the back of the truck, forcing Tressa to sit closer to Lock. He moved away from her so they were hardly touching. Tressa's heart felt like it was being squeezed in a vice as another bat slammed into the truck. This one was much harder than the others. A creaking and tearing sound came from above, and they all prepared themselves in case one of them broke through.

Cinis kept their eyes on the mirror as they thought aloud, "It sounds like they have broken through the first level of armor, and it has slowed us down a little from the drag. I think we're still alright though."

After a solid hour of pounding on the truck, the furor finally stopped.

"I don't trust the quiet," Nera admitted.

Vin leaned toward the front, "I agree. I think we should go to the backup stop to make sure we weren't followed."

Nera agreed, "Cinis, take us right at the fork and not left. I think we have some stragglers hiding on our roof."

Cinis nodded, "We have about three more minutes until we turn."

After they made the turn and slowed to a stop, Vin pulled his sword out and Cinis flipped the inside latch to open the back of the truck.

The moment Vin climbed out, he shot into the sky as Nera opened her door, following him into the sky. It was just one proto-bat, and the body hit the ground a few feet from behind the truck with a thud before Nera and Vin landed on either side of it. It had been disemboweled and its insides were splattered out over several feet.

Tressa tried to look at Lock, but he wouldn't meet her eyes. She knew her little stunt would piss him off, but she didn't regret it. They all would have died if she hadn't distracted the mass of bats that had descended on them. She created a way for all of them to live. Lock would just have to deal with it.

After kicking the dead bat once, Nera leaned her head back and took a long slow breath before she turned to Vin, "Let's go home."

Vin settled in the truck and Cinis released the windshield guard as Nera sat down. Vin shut the back from inside and sat next to Lock.

"I'll help you set your wing," Vin offered. Lock didn't respond. Tressa knew he was too angry to speak, and she was fine with that. He was alive, and that was all she cared about. Everyone was alive.

Everyone was alive.

THIRTY-TWO
ALISOT – HOUSE OF DOMITIA

When they pulled up to the house, Nera went wordlessly inside. Vin opened the truck door and explained, "She's going to send a pigeon to the southern settlement. Lock, let's move you inside so we can splint your wing. Eh?"

Vin helped Lock out. He limped past Vin and slowly made his way toward the front doors. Tressa stepped out and gave Vin a sorrowful look. She followed Cinis and the group inside and to the house clinic.

Lock crawled onto the table as Vin prepared the necessary supplies. He headed back over with a tray in hand which had multiple different tools and a syringe. Vin took the syringe and motioned with his finger for Lock to lean over. He sighed as he tipped to one side, and Vin yanked down his leather pants before stabbing him in the rear.

"Fuck that was cold!" Lock narrowed his eyes at Vin.

Vin just shrugged, "Don't be a baby! You'll feel better in a minute."

Vin checked the clock on the wall and tapped his foot

waiting. Lock crossed his arms and leaned on his side. Fury was still chiseled in his face.

Tressa knew exactly when the mild pain drugs began to work when Lock growled, "Everyone but Tressa, *out.*" Cinis cringed and stepped closer to the door, only stopping when Tressa gave them a beseeching look.

Vin dropped his head and groaned before turning back to Lock and protesting, "Not until I'm finished." Shaking his head, Vin grumbled something about "Regal assholes," as he turned to collect what he needed to make the splint.

Lock glared back at him as he turned to Tressa.

"You should have stayed in the fucking truck like you said you would," Lock seethed.

"You Vin, and Nera would all be dead if I had," Tressa shot back.

Lock, filled with fury, shouted, "I don't give a fuck! *You could have died*! It was supposed to be me that fucking died, not *you!*"

Vin stopped and reacted to Lock like he was meeting someone he had never met before. Vin slid his attention to Tressa and her expression changed slightly. Did he just say what she thought he said?

Vin heard it too because he held nothing but kindness and love in his eyes. With much more compassion, Vin went back to work and prepared to set the wing, "Lock…"

Cutting him off, Lock interrupted, "I know. Just do it." Vin sighed as he took in the broken section of Lock's wing, the thick tendons pulling it far past the bone where it was supposed to line up. Whispering, "Fuck," under his breath, Vin turned to Lock with a grimace. "This is going to fucking hurt. It's been out of place for a while." Vin admitted.

Lock turned to Vin with his eyes narrowed, "You're not helping."

When Nera came in, she rounded the exam bed as Lock crossed his arms. She leaned down and wrapped her arms around his shoulders before anchoring her knees under the edge of the bed. Vin prepared his hands on either side of Lock's two broken bones, cringing at the resistance. Lock took a few deep breaths and grabbed his own elbows. With all his strength Vin yanked the two bones apart, stretching the tendons out so he could put them back in place.

Pulling away from Nera's iron hold, Lock shot his head back and released a high pitch scream as Vin connected the two bone ends back together. The bed creaked and popped with Lock pulling against Nera.

Cinis and Tressa held their hands over their ears as the piercing sound echoed through the room. Tressa's heart was pounding as the sound of his scream slowed, and it became a sorrowful moan.

Nera grunted and Lock shuddered as Vin placed the splint and put the clamps around it to keep it in place. When it was over, Lock collapsed face down on the bed.

When Vin passed by her, Tressa grabbed his hand and whispered, "Why didn't you put him out for that?"

"We had already used the last of the anesthesia on another patient." She knew it was her he meant, and guilt filled her. "He needs to rest. I'll let you know when he wakes up. The worst is over." Vin gave them both a tired smile.

Cinis and Tressa headed out into the hall, and Cinis threw their arms around Tressa. Nera caught back up with them halfway down the hall, "Tressa, I know Lock is furious, and I would be, too, if it had been Cinis. I have to admit to you the truth. What you did was stupid, but you saved the three of us, and I can't thank you enough for that. House Domitia owes you three life debts. You once owed us a life debt, but now we are the ones who owe you. It is interesting how life likes to fuck with us, isn't it? Just when we think all is lost, we are thrown a chance we never expected."

Tressa attempted a smile, but she could tell it wasn't convincing, "I think I want to go lie down now."

Heading down the hall as the light faded for the day, Tressa watched at her door as the days light slipped under the horizon and diffused the world into darkness. Turning the door handle, she went inside and found all her covers missing.

They were still in the middle of Lock's floor.

Oh, well, she thought as she went over to the bed. She took off her leather jacket and tossed it down before the scent of her body wafted up. She decided she needed a shower before she went anywhere near a clean mattress.

Heading into her bathroom, she stripped the rest of her leathers off and stared into the mirror. The events of the day seemed like a far dream compared to the sorrow in her over Lock having his wing set. After what he said? Would he die for her?

She turned on the shower and watched the water as it began to billow steam. She stuck her hand in to test the temperature, finding it perfect. When she stepped in, the heat made her exhaustion worse, and she had to sit down. As she sat on the floor and let the water rain over her, she finally let the flood gates open. Tears poured from her eyes in rivers as she released the emotion she had been holding back.

THIRTY-THREE

ALISOT – HOUSE OF DOMITIA

"I want you to fly high over the cave location the colony was using as a den and evaluate if they've moved on or not. If the cave is not a giant hole in the ground, I want to know," Nera instructed Vin as she walked in the gym.

Behind them Lock was hanging from two suspension lines and trying to complete a rehabilitation routine for his broken wing. He hated to be interrupted, while he was working, and glared at Nera. Vin, who had been spotting for Lock, stepped towards her. Nera ignored Lock's scowl and turned back to Vin, "Be careful, but go now."

Vin flapped his massive wings and leaped off the balcony.

She passed by Lock quickly before going straight to the yard on the side of the house where she, Tressa, and Cinis had been training. When she turned the corner, she met Tressa's gaze and shook her head. Tressa hadn't spoken to Lock in weeks. No one really had. He wouldn't look at her.

Nera approached Tressa and asked, "Are your compression socks on?"

Nodding, Nera took off in a jog, and they followed behind her. Tressa was already up to a mile without a break and that was a record for her. She had speed, just no stamina. She knew she needed to build her strength, but it wasn't the only reason she was forcing herself to run. It was the only thing keeping the nightmares away.

Every time her eyes closed the bats grabbed her and Lock watched as she was torn apart. He screamed and was torn apart next. In those moments, the pool of sweat around her when she awoke screaming was the only thing to remind her she was still alive.

As her feet hit the ground, the deep ache and popping tendons were enough to make her sick, but she pushed through anyway. Breathing deep, she pushed everything aside and did her best to enjoy the beautiful land. Until a few weeks ago, she had no idea there were miles of up kept lands belonging to Nera and Lock. The beautiful, long grassy areas were separated by trees lining stone pathways, creating long stretches of greenery. Hidden fountains with small furnished patios to hide away and read or listen to the birds were dotted among the thicker wooded areas. Now that the house staff had temporarily returned, they had guards outside, and they were able to use the grounds. Diseased bats were known to fly down and snatch their prey right off the ground in broad daylight, so Nera had been training them to listen and react better.

Sweat dripped down Tressa's brow as she did her best to breathe through each few steps. After they ran, they gathered in the dining room for a meal and planning. Nera had work to do, mostly dealing with the other houses and making them pay for the explosives they had stolen. After that was completed, she still needed to detail her plan to locate the exact position of the ancient UTC base. The plan would be copied and sent to the other houses before they left. She was leaving her house staff to decide if they needed to head back south this time and wanted to make sure the mail courier was still making trips to the property.

Nera had been avoiding the task she detailed the previous week, and they all knew it. None of them wanted to take on this next journey, but after Vin returned from his scouting mission.

They knew they couldn't delay. The bats had one of the biggest colonies on record in a massive cave system a short fly north from the recently leveled cave. He maintained a high altitude so the bats wouldn't spot him. He had to turn back before he came close enough to survey because his wings began to freeze in the frigid air. He had seen enough to report, there was still too many for the five of them to destroy.

After their meeting, Tressa headed to her room to clean up. She passed by Lock's room and stood outside of the door. It was the third time this week she heard his alarm and knew he was about to emerge. She wanted to knock on his door with everything in her being. She missed him. Everyone did.

She stood at his door preparing to knock as the door swung open. Lock wore clothes Tressa hadn't seen. They looked thin and cool, for warmer weather. Something about his fresh appearance made her uneasy. He had grown a short beard, and it was meticulously groomed. His hair was slicked back, and he had a leather pack at his side.

Lock froze in place as their eyes met. His mouth parted and he scowled before he pushed by her.

"Lock," Tressa tried to reach for his arm, but he pulled away.

He stopped in his tracks a few steps away and turned sharply to her, rushing forward. She retreated up until her back hit the wall.

Lock, so close to Tressa's face, she could feel his hot breath on her skin, "I don't want to talk. Not to you. Not to anyone here."

As he stalked off, Tressa just leaned against the wall. Had they all lost him? Was he ever going to forgive any of them? Was he ever going to forgive her?

Bringing her eyes up to the clock in front of her, she noticed for the first time that it didn't have glass over the face. The hands all had some kind of texture on them as well. She knew her mind was searching for a distraction, and she gladly took it as she studied the clock. The longer she was here, the more curious the décor and aesthetic of the home became. She liked it. It was just always a bit different than she would have expected.

Accepting there was nothing she could do in the moment, she went into her room. After a cool shower, she headed out to the greenhouse to help the staff pick vegetables. She loved it no matter how badly it hurt her hands. Feeling useful was far more important than a little pain.

Heading down the stairs at the corner of the hallway, she could still smell the body wash Lock used swirling through the air. Her heart was hanging on by a thread and she didn't know what else to do. She hated this. She knew how he felt! Why in Pluto's hell was he acting like this? Tears wet her eyes as she arrived at the greenhouse, where the staff stopped and peered at her strangely.

Catching her breath, and wiping her face, she angled

her face to the sky and saw Lock leaping off the balcony with outstretched wings.

She knew he was just now able to fly again, but the clothes? The pack? Was he leaving for the south?

Her breath left in a whoosh, and she sat down on the garden bench. After a few moments she rose up and headed toward one of the vegetable beds. Finding her newest favorite, bright red tomatoes, she grabbed a basket and picked several before finding where the onions were buried. She had just plunged her fingers in the cold dirt when she could feel Nera standing behind her.

Tressa turned around to face Nera, "I know. He's gone."

Nera's face was a picture of sadness, "This is the longest he has ever gone without speaking to me. He said he was going to visit his daughter. He will be back before we depart in a week."

One more week without him. One more week, and then she would be stuck riding in an armored truck and hiking with him for weeks, possibly months. She didn't know which one was worse.

THIRTY-FOUR

ALISOT – HOUSE OF DOMITIA

Nera kissed a trail down Cinis's back. "I don't ever want to leave this bed."

Cinis smiled into the pillow, "Why can't we stay another week? I could put in some more work on the new truck."

Nera slapped their bare, round ass, "No. We can't put off the inevitable, but I can fantasize." Nera leaned down and stuck the end of her forked tongue between their butt cheeks. Just as Cinis began to buck, she pushed them onto the bed with her hand on the small of their back. Lifting one of Cinis's legs, Nera leaned down and put her face between their thighs.

Cinis squealed with the anticipation and their legs trembled as Nera held them in her grasp. Nera wasted no time and flicked their center mercilessly as they moaned into their pillow.

When they shattered, Nera watched Cinis raise their hands up from where they were gripping the pillow and flail them. Nera lay back and laughed as Cinis flipped over with a look of absolute shock on their face. "Where the hell did that come from?" Cinis asked, catching their breath.

Licking her lips with great satisfaction, Nera had no intention of answering.

"Why won't you let me eat your pussy?" Cinis asked mustering in the courage.

"I don't like it. Feels like a slug. I would much rather have your hand. One day I'll introduce you to some of my wearable toys, but until then, I would prefer your hand."

Cinis leaned over and kissed Nera's shoulder as she lay on the bed next to them. She had hardly allowed Cinis to touch her, so this shift was significant. Reaching over, they took her round breasts into their hands and Cinis asked, "Can I put my mouth here?"

Nera breathed with anticipation, "Yes. You can do that."

Smiling, Cinis took a nipple into their mouth and stroked it lightly. Something told them Nera had a softer side when it came to her own pleasure as she leaned into Cinis. The way she was breathing, Cinis sensed this approach was working. Slowly moving from one nipple to the other, Nera was already panting. Easing their hand across Nera's belly and down between her thighs, they found her soaking wet.

Grazing their fingers through Nera's heat, they felt Nera rock her hips in need. When they twirled her bud, her hips shook with the rhythm. Cinis slid a finger inside, and Nera leaned her head back, making a sultry, breathy sound that Cinis needed to hear again. Moving softly but deliberately, Cinis caressed her further.

The metal of Nera's piercings glinted in the soft light. With their tongue, Cinis flicked the ring in Nera's belly button before kissing and licking her nipples. Massaging her with building pressure and speed they felt Nera's heat build until she orgasmed. Nera was pleasured to the point of trembling and Cinis grinned.

Cinis leaned over and kissed her between her breasts, "Are you sure we have to get out of bed?"

Nera brought her head up and angled it, a sign she was listening for something, "Yes. Lock just landed on the balcony. It does not sound like he is in any better of a mood."

"How can you tell?" Cinis asked, their brow furrowed.

Nera tapped her tall ear, "He slammed down onto the balcony. He is usually graceful. He almost sounded as clunky as Vin just then."

Loud footsteps pounded down the hall, followed by a door slamming shut.

"The trip in a few days is going to be fun with him in the car, isn't it?" Cinis asked.

Nera bit her lip in thought. "Let's go find your sister."

As they arrived at the greenhouse, Tressa stood watering the cucumber plants, and her face fell when she saw their expressions.

"Great. What now?" Tressa asked as the water hose dropped to her side and began spilling on the ground. Cinis walked across to the faucet and turned it off.

"He's home. I need you to do something for us."

Tressa rejected Nera's request, "I do not think so. I already tried that once and I am not doing it again."

"You don't even know what I'm going to ask." Nera rebutted.

"I know it will involve Lock, and I know it won't go well." Nera calmly stood silently watching Tressa with a hawk's focus until she caved. "Fine! What do you want me to do?"

"I need you to use your magic *whatever* on Lock and force him out of his bad mood. I have a feeling it's a lot more than just a bad mood this time. He was hard to deal with before, I can't imagine being stuck in a truck with him this way."

With her face void of all emotion Tressa repeated, "*Magic whatever*?" and continued, "You mean pussy power? No. That's what I said no to first. I tried that already, and it was an epic failure. He is un-seducible."

Nera continued her viper's gaze, determined to melt Tressa's resolve. Cinis watched the standoff, knowing Tressa would cave, and she did.

"Fine. One night I fingered myself under him while he slept and when he woke up, he told me to get out. Thanks for making me tell that embarrassing as fuck story. Now if you will excuse me, I have some important things to do like water these future pickles." Tressa whipped around and stalked to the faucet.

Nera smothered a smile, "I knew you would be obsessed with pickles."

"What?" Tressa spun back to them, hose held up like a gun.

Nera couldn't contain her laughter, "Please just try. We have to be in the truck with him and then we are hiking for weeks, maybe months."

"No! I am not doing it."

Nera sighed in seemingly resignation, "Fine. I will just hire him a willing woman from the staff for the night."

"What?! Gods, I cannot stand you. Hire someone else!? Dammit. I'll try. Venus knows I could use some dick anyway. Now both of you leave me alone. Future pickles remember?" Tressa spat as she turned the water back on and returned to her watering.

As Cinis and Nera opened the door to the house, they grabbed Nera's arm and asked, "Did you just overtly manipulate my sister?"

"Yes. What's the problem?" Nera asked sincerely.

"What's the problem? You did it so casually, like you do this all the time." Their eyes were narrowed on Nera.

Nera beamed, "Oh. Thank you. Royal upbringing does have some use."

THIRTY-FIVE

ALISOT – HOUSE OF DOMITIA

As the daylight passed and Alisot's bright star lowered over the land, Tressa lay on the floor of her room thinking about what Nera had asked her to do. She knew Lock cared about her, so, why did it feel like she was taking her life into her hands?

Sliding out of bed, she went into the dressing room and poked around. Opening a drawer, she quickly shut it and turned around to lean against it. Putting her hands over her mouth, she felt like this little discovery was a sign. Turning back, she reopened the drawer and pulled out several sets of gorgeous lingerie. Corsets with folded knee highs and bra sets with matching panties for everything. She dug in and tried the bra sets on first. She hated how her stomach looked, so those went right back into the drawer. Pulling the corsets out, she put each on and those felt much better than just a bra.

Finding a particularly beautiful black corset set made of a spidery lace, she slipped it on, tightened the laces, and turned to see how she looked. After a touch of makeup, she felt hot enough she might actually manipulate Lock into talking to her. He may be angry and mean, but at least he would be speaking again.

She slid on some heels but kicked them off when they made her feet ache. Huffing, she slid them back on anyway feeling her feet pop as she stood. She knew they looked good and completed the look.

Making her way into the hallway, she checked out of the windows and saw a stunning, full moon. It was bright and large, lighting up the land in a silver glow. She faced Lock's door and turned the knob. It was open, and she peeked inside. He wasn't there.

"What the fuck?" she complained. Staring down at her outfit, she whispered to herself, "Fucking hell. Now I have to walk around and find his ass with all this shit on? Dammit!"

Stopping to think, she went over to the windows and admired the giant moon. Hearing a sound coming from the left stairwell, she made her way in that direction. She just hoped it was Lock and not one of the staff.

Her feet were already screaming, so she took off her heels to walk up the stairs. At the top, she slid them back on and cringed as she did. She slid her gaze around the room and saw a shadow move in the wing gym. Closing her eyes, she knew this was not going to be easy. Approaching the glass doors, she pushed them open and found Lock standing in the middle of the room.

He was shirtless and soaked in sweat from his workout. He paused to stare at her. She tried to stay steady as she walked toward him, but her feet kept popping and it was becoming difficult. She gritted her teeth and finally made it over to him without falling or twisting an ankle.

Looking anywhere but at her, he didn't move as he quietly asked, "What are you doing?"

Tressa closed her eyes feeling incredibly self-conscious. "I just want to talk."

"It looks like you're trying to do a lot more than that," His flat tone was almost as painful as his silence.

She swallowed roughly and whispered, "What do I have to do to get you to…?"

"To what?" He answered loud enough his voice echoed around the room.

"To fuck you or talk to you, Tressa?" Lock's brow lowered over his eyes he barreled toward her, and her flight instinct kicked in. On her first step backward, her ankle twisted. The back of her heel fell off and when it did, she had to kick them off as Lock charged her like a bull.

Still stumbling backwards, she pressed against the wing tree as he leaned in, "First off, why the fuck are you wearing heels? I could hear the damn tendons in your feet popping all the way down the hall. Then this?" He grabbed the front of her corset and ripped it in half before throwing it on the ground. The slight breeze and fear chilled her, causing her nipples to pebble.

Lock's voice broke, "You wear this bullshit. This shit that covers everything."

Tressa reached up and put her trembling hand on the side of his face. Smelling her fear, he froze. His eyes closed, and Tressa pulled him into her. He leaned his sweat slicked body onto hers, pinning her to the tree. He leaned over into her ear and whispered, "I can't get it out of my head. I can't stop the image of you running as they rushed you. I can't stop reliving the moment you die. Over and over."

She reached up and kissed him on his full lips,

breathing against them, "But I didn't, and you didn't, and we're both very much alive. I want you to fuck me."

He brought his face up to her with a wild look in his eyes and didn't say a word as he pulled her panties down, and she stepped out of them. With his strong hands, he grabbed her by the waist and lifted her to wrap her legs around him as she held onto his neck.

Without any warning, he ran for the balcony, and it took all of Tressa's will to not scream as he shot into the sky. Her heart pounded as his hands wrapped around her nude body, pulling her in even tighter.

Flying high into the sky, he slid his hand down under her bare ass and pulled his athletic pants down, springing himself free. Tressa gasped when he leaned forward and kissed her as he sheathed his length inside her. She kissed him back feeling his tongue explore her mouth. Tressa moaned over his lips as he thrust into her. He filled her over and over, his thrusts matching the rhythm of his beating wings.

Grabbing her hips as he spread his wings and soared through the air, she gripped his shoulders harder as she leaned her head back. He tipped his wings and began nosediving as her pleasure crested. The thrill of dropping through the sky made her heart skip and a scream bubbled up inside of her. The moment the cry left her lips, Lock bit down on her shoulder and slammed into her with his release.

Sucking at her shoulder and pounding into her, he finally began flapping his wings again as they neared the ground. When his wings caught the air, Tressa shook with the thrill, pain, and pleasure. Her hot blood dripped down between her breasts as he landed onto the ground softly and leaned her back to lick up the blood that had flowed down her body.

He faced her, yet still not fully looking her in the eyes, and licked his lips.

She cocked her head to the side as she peered up at him asked, "Can I ask you an odd question?"

Smirking, he wrapped his hands around her waist to haul her back against him, "Yes?"

"Why does it never seem like you're looking into my eyes? You look at me, sure, but it's not quite directly."

His expression fell, and he scoffed, "Do you not know?"

"Know what?" she asked, confusion written all over her.

He smiled and leaned in close, "Tressa, I use echolocation. Very few Resper see with our eyes. Those who do have sight have severely limited vision."

"What? What do you mean? How have you done? Everything? You can see with sound? You use echolocation? How?" she stumbled on her own questions.

"I am honestly surprised you didn't know. Are the Resper on your home world not the same?"

"No! You did surgery on me!" she screeched as she put her hands on her belly in a panic.

Lock threw his head back and laughed, "I can see just as well as you can with my echolocation. Maybe better."

Tressa felt bewildered as all the clues hit her at once and she asked, "Is that why the clock has no glass on its face, the paintings are all filled with dimension and texture? Oh! Your tattoos are all raised! How did you use the microscope?!"

Lock grinned at her, "I was not the one who used the old UTC microscope. My lab tech and our driver can both see black and white, but they are uncommon. Even less common than that is color vision. You never noticed our mouths opening so we can use ultra-sonic waves to build the world in our minds?"

Tressa's eyes went wide again, "That's how you always seem to know so much. I really need to talk to Cinis about this. Do they know? Oh, I bet they don't!"

"Humans are so curious, yet you never seem to understand much beyond your own skin." Lock tenderly stroked her cheek as he spoke.

Tressa felt silly but still felt the need to rush to Cinis. Maybe Lock was right. Humans never could understand they were not the center of the universe. Human supremacy was a disease, and she was beginning to see it in her own suppositions. She had a lot of work to do, and she was just beginning to realize it.

Lock lifted them into the sky, and he quickly calculated they were over thirty minutes from the Domitia house. Tressa shivered from the cold, and he wrapped his arms around her naked body as he aimed for their home.

THIRTY-SIX

ALISOT – HOUSE OF DOMITIA

Leaning over the maps and plans, Nera racked her brain on how they would cross the large expanse of forest. A knock sounded at the door, and she already knew it was Vin, so she ignored it. He would open the door on his own.

As usual he opened the door a crack, "Nera?" He approached the table she was stewing over. "I have some news."

"From your tone, I'm guessing it's not good." She didn't look up.

Vin went on, "A report came from the south on the major movements of the bat colonies. They have taken over the entire top hemisphere of our world. There is a substantial area before we reach the base where we cross the path of a colony of thousands. We will be passing directly into their territory for over a day. It gets worse though. The remaining protos from the colony we just bombed moved from here and have re-populated an area to the west. There is no single den. They seemed to have settled in the abandoned properties."

Nera's head shot up, "The *west*? Fuck. Are you sure?"

He nodded, and she sat down in her chair, putting her hands over her face and screaming into them. The base was far to the west and the bats they bombed knew how they smelled. This was awful news. It was bad enough they would have to fly over one colony, but two?

"Does Lock know?" she asked, lines forming in her brow.

"Not yet. I'm going to tell him next."

Nera nodded, "I haven't spoken to him, but according to Cinis, he said hi to them at breakfast."

She paused a moment, "You can go ahead and take a break, I can hear him coming."

"Oh good. I was worried he would never speak to anyone again." Sarcasm in every word, Vin headed back toward the door and aimed for the kitchen.

Leaning back in her chair, she knew Lock was always listening. He would be storming in her room at any moment. He managed to surprise her this time by entering in her courtyard door, "You're fucking joking?"

"Not a joke. We might have to go all the way around." Nera stood up and leaned forward over the raised topographical map. She had already plotted out a course, but now she was going to have to make it much longer. Nera whistled when she finished adding up the additional time, "This sets us back another month unless we can find a way through."

"We could fly over and fly as long as we can each day." he suggested reluctantly.

Nera shook her head. "We are not built like Vin. We

will not fare well on that journey. You might not make it at all with your higher body weight."

"It is the only way. We are going to have to cross the mountain area by flight." Lock sighed, knowing it was technically impossible for him to accomplish.

Nera shook her head again. "We need to have a few long-range guards. I had three come back up from the south who will go with us. We will need help hauling supplies, too."

Dreading the flight over the mountains, and now this second long flight, Lock offered, "I'll pack the bands so we can shape up on the way."

Sinking her head over the table, Nera groaned, "Please tell Vin to talk to Bensley and Trajen. See if Halso will go too. We are going to need all the wide range Resper we can recruit to make it over two colonies in one trip with all our baggage."

Lock agreed, "I'm packed. I think Vin is too. We just need to load the truck."

Nera tapped her finger against the wood of the table, "I'm glad you're alright."

He stopped and turned to her, "Pyra? She doesn't even know me anymore. She acted like I was a stranger."

Pain snaked through Nera at his words, "You had to know that was coming. She was so young when she had to evacuate with the rest of our people. Was she happy?"

"She was passionate and vibrant, but she wouldn't come near me. I was there for a week, and she never spoke a word to me," he trailed off, pain in every word.

Nera cleared her throat and chose her words carefully, "Lock, it will just take time once you are reunited. It was part of the sacrifice we signed up for, and you knew that."

"But seeing it? Living it? I had no idea how deep it would cut to find that my daughter had forgotten me." He left out of her courtyard door and shut it behind him.

Putting her hands over her face, Nera leaned over her map and rubbed her eyes. She sighed as she heard Cinis footsteps approaching, and if she had to guess, they were upset about something.

The door swung open, and Cinis came barreling in, "You don't use your eyes? Lock did *surgery* on my sister! How the fuck can you drive?! I am freaking out. Please tell me what's going on."

Nera was filled with disbelief at Cinis's obliviousness, "You just now found out we don't use our eyes? Don't you have Resper's on your home-world? You do realize humans are not the galaxy standard right?"

Cinis, feeling immensely close minded, kept their mouth shut, and Nera sighed with exhaustion before she continued, "I can see some black and white with my eyes, but its blurry. Vin and Lock have no visual sight, and that's why they can't drive on roadways. Why do you think the roads are lined with so much reflective paint? Our vehicles emit a sound similar to ours for echolocation so we can visualize the roadway. We just see differently than you do. We never really needed vision, so we adapted without it. Before our fall, we had entire universities dedicated to echo-technology development, which was all for echolocation centered electronic equipment."

Cinis was stunned. "This is the most fascinating thing I've ever heard. That's why you keep the window down."

"I can see just as well as you, or better, with my ears. Our entire written language is raised for us to either feel or use our echolocation. How could you possibly not notice?"

"I need a fucking drink. I feel exceptionally stupid,"

Cinis blurted out, and Nera laughed as she went over to her bar to pour them that drink.

She handed them a cocktail. "You're not stupid. You're just dense from human conditioning."

Cinis scoffed but accepted the truth and took a sip of the stout drink.

Tressa held the lightweight sword in her hand, "I can swing this without my hand hurting. Is there a way we can change the handle so if I lose my grip it doesn't fall?"

"I can make the guard wrap around the handle. No problem." Vin took it back from her and handed her the practice wooden sword she had been using.

Returning to the lesson, Tressa lifted her sword, and Lock pointed down, "Feet."

"Shit." She widened her stance and adjusted her overall focus.

Lock tipped up the corner of his mouth, "Lean into it. You are not getting anywhere only using the weight of the sword like that. You need to use your body weight with the thrusts. Your targets are going to be Vin's size, moving rapidly, diseased, and thoroughly pissed off. We need to work on your speed, too."

"You know I'm not going to grow any faster. That's

hilarious," Yet she leaned forward trying to follow his instructions.

Coming toward her with his wooden sword, he tucked his wings in and spun to hit her sword, sending it flying.

Tressa put her hands on her hips, "Oh, fuck off with all of that."

Laughing, he went over and picked up her sword before he handed it back to her. "Try again."

She didn't know how many more try-again's she had in her. Her hand and knuckles were swollen. Distracting herself from the throbbing pain, she shifted her gaze to the horizon and found a storm brewing in the distance. She watched as thunder struck the ground and Lock turned to watch the storm with her.

"It looks like we need to end our workout for the day. Storm season arrived a week early." Lock moved to reach for her sword.

"Were we going to leave before this storm season? Was that part of the timing?" she asked.

Lock leaned his head to the side and concentrated on listening before he turned to her, "We have difficulty with our echolocation in the rain and fog. It seems like we did miss our window and this sounds like a strong storm. We should all lie in the courtyard, the sounds of the storm there are ethereal. You have to experience it to understand."

"Won't that be dangerous under the glass?"

He smiled, "No. The glass was made with a mix of alloys in it. It's as strong as steel and it doesn't block the sound; it focuses it. The shape causes the music of the storm to become concentrated so we can hear what's happening outside at all times. That's why our homes are designed this way. Plus, for those of us who can see some light, it's nice to have it everywhere possible."

Putting away the practice weapons they turned and walked toward the courtyard as Tressa asked, "How many of your people on average can see at all?"

"Around a quarter, if that. Some of us can see for most of our lives and lose it in old age. Others, like myself, never had it. Nera's mother, and the butcher I learned from, were unable to use their eyes since birth, but Nera's father could see light and shadows until his death," he explained as he opened the door for her.

Humans were never taught any of this on Emendo, even from the random underground teachers she met over the years. As far as Tressa had known, the Resper on Emendo could all see with their eyes. She vividly remembered the few Resper she had encountered, recalling how they made piercing eye contact during communication, a stark difference to the way the blood Resper communicated with little eye contact.

As they entered in the courtyard, Vin spread out a large plush blanket onto the floor and plopped down. Tressa sat on the blanket as Lock stretched out. Nera and Cinis came down the stairs to the courtyard patio and joined them.

Cinis knelt on the blanket, "What are we doing?"

Nera knelt and patted the spot next to her, "Both of you lie down. You will understand in just a few minutes."

The storm rumbled, and Tressa couldn't wait to experience the storm as Lock did, or as close as possible.

As the first large droplets hit the glass above, Tressa could already begin to hear the resonated echo each drop created in the room. Lock leaned over to Tressa and whispered, "Close your eyes." When the rush of rain finally broke? The room sounded like an orchestra of raindrops. It was one of the most beautiful things she had ever heard.

When she did, a whole new world exploded in her mind. There was an incredible mix of bass and treble and the high notes of the smaller rain drops echoing on the metal edges of the greenhouse. The sounds of the rain were dancing behind her eyes like little fairies. She held back a gasp when the sound morphed the dance in her mind as the rain patterns changed. Little fairies of water evolved into fields of water people, dancing and singing, twirling and swinging one another to the beat of the droplets above.

This world had so much beauty to it. What had begun as a prison sentence had turned into something priceless. Her heart pounded with excitement as the rain intensified and the sounds changed again. This time the imagery was a battle dance, synced and intentional, but fierce and strong. Swords of ice slammed into one another as they clashed. Hail pounded the glass like drums, and she smiled as the imagery became the beat of war drums. In her mind a line of people formed of water and pounded on cylinders of ice, defeating their enemies.

The storm raged for half an hour before it began to fade. The gentle rain became two bodies of water, making love as the darkness fell.

THIRTY-EIGHT

ALISOT – HOUSE OF DOMITIA

When they all gradually awoke from their slumber, sprawled on the floor of the court-yard, they found the morning sky glowing from above and knew it was time to leave. They had all been lulled into a deep sleep by the rain and had woken up well rested but sore from the ground. They filed into the dining room after dressing, each sitting in the same seats they had grown to find comfort in.

The morning seemed surreal. One of the house staff brought in their meals as Bensley, Trajen, and Halso entered the dining room all massive men with larger wingspans than Vin. They wore the house Domitia insignia of wings on the shoulders of their leathers and had guard patches with symbols on them. After they sat down, a few minutes later the wait staff brought out bowls of blood.

After the unusually quiet breakfast, Nera stood from her place at the table. "We leave now. Go grab your personal bags and meet at the armored truck outside."

Within ten minutes everyone found their seats in the new truck as Bensley sat in the driver's seat. Trajen climbed in a passenger's seat after Halso sat in the middle. Nera, Cinis, and Vin all filled the back seat, while Tressa and Lock sat in the middle seat.

The truck clutch popped, and they took off with a jolt. The new truck had all the armor folded up, so it seemed less like a tank and more like a regular transportation vehicle. The truck was larger and fit everyone comfortably. Thanks to Cinis, this truck they had built could transform into a tank within seconds. All the armor slid into place by the pull of a lever.

A few hours passed, and Tressa had just begun to doze off with her head resting on Lock's legs when Bensley leaned his ear toward the open window, "Aw, shit."

"What?" Nera asked from the back.

"We have unwanted company." He pointed in front of them as Nera crawled over the seat, pushing Tressa down onto Lock's lap. She didn't hate having her face in Lock's crotch, but did Nera need to smash her head down onto his lap as she climbed over her? Probably not. Trajen rolled the window down on the passenger side and Nera leaned over the front seat to hear.

"Is that a group of them eating something on the side of the road?" Nera asked under her breath, confused at what was happening. Tressa sat up and when she did, one of the protos turned to the truck. "We've been spotted," Nera announced.

Bensley pulled the lever, and the armor slid down to lock into place. As he pulled the periscope down from above his head, he ordered, "Halso, start cranking." Next to him, Halso began cranking a lever. He pulled it down over and over. Tressa counted ten times as something sounded like it was winding up under the hood of the truck.

As the armor closed, several bats slammed into the top of the truck from the sky, clawing at the metal armor as Bensley slowed to a stop.

As soon the small aerial group of bats all made contact with the outside of the truck, Bensley yelled, "Arms in!" and slammed a lever down next to the gear shifter. Everyone pulled their arms away from the doors of the truck as an electric current arced through the exterior armor. Everyone in the truck slammed their hands over their ears as the bats outside screeched while they were electrocuted. From the sound of it, several bodies slid off the angled exterior and plopped on the ground outside to be run over by the still moving vehicle. Only a few moments passed before the electricity faded, and Bensley could listen out of the periscope.

"I think they're all dead." Bensley pulled back the truck armor, causing one more to dislodge and slide down the window, its face smearing across the glass.

Tressa reared back, "Oh gods!" as the steaming proto-bat body slid off and onto the ground.

From the back seat, Cinis surveyed the ground wide eyed and leaned their head back, "Ha! It worked!" Their excitement clearly overriding any disgust.

Nera was motionless with her mouth open, "Can someone explain what the fuck just happened?"

From the front seat, Bensley beamed, "We've been building it with Cinis, but we weren't sure it would really work."

Cinis explained as Nera climbed back over Tressa, again smashing her face into Lock's lap. "I know we can't have electronics, but there's nothing keeping us from using electric currents. We tested it to be sure it was safe. Even if someone touched a door, the most you would get on the inside is a static shock. There is a rubber lining and all non-conductive alloys inside the truck. The outside, however, we made an alloy out of several highly conductive metals to line the center of the exterior armor. Nodules poke through the armor so that the plate will arc the electric current in waves so that all the bats in contact go into cardiac arrest. We decided to set the power level to stop their hearts so it would be somewhat humane."

Bensley was proud beyond reason, "Halso helped too." The generally stoic Halso turned and gave a half grin, which was when Tressa noticed the solid white cataracts in his eyes. Turning to Cinis, Tressa couldn't help but swell with pride at her sibling.

Nera stared at Cinis with her mouth hanging open. Nera was not a person easily surprised, yet this human kept managing to pull it off. "You designed all of this?" she asked in disbelief.

Cinis nodded, their cheeks flush with excitement. "I've learned a lot in your grandfather's office. He was incredible. The details in his notes are mind blowing."

Nera took Cinis face in her hands and kissed them, "Thank you."

Bensley popped the clutch, and the truck accelerated. He excitedly floored the pedal and the truck speed forward, the engine humming as a trickle of steam flowed from the exhaust pipe in front of the window.

Cinis leaned over to Nera. "I built one of your grandfather's prototype engines. It uses alternating magnets to run the triangular rotary pistons. The magnets begin moving when the clutch moves into gear. It just needs to heat small amounts of water to start. Once it's going, we don't need any more water. I mixed your grandfathers' older crank magnetic engine design with his last rotatory design and a steam starter. It was a genius set of designs, and I couldn't help combining them. It's much more efficient and has a lot of power without any use of electric current."

Nera was overcome with pride.

THIRTY-NINE

EMENDO – JUPITER DISTRICT
1 – MERCURY SECTOR

"The hacker was dead when we arrived, an earlier team had already broken into his apartment. His friend was there so we took him. The hacker has no family. Only this friend," the UTC soldier reported through the comms to his commander.

The commander replied, "Get him on the next prison drop ship. We already have a drop pod reserved; no sense in wasting it. We altered his file to show the murder conviction."

Taberi pleaded, "Prison drop?! You have to be kidding! I didn't do anything! I'm innocent! Can they hear me?! I didn't kill him!" Struggling against the soldiers hold, he knew it was useless, but he was going to do anything to keep from going to the blood-suckers home world. He was not a fighter and knew he would never fair well on that sort of planet. Taberi begged them, "Listen, I'll do anything. You can't do this. I just stopped by to see if he was alright! I didn't kill anyone!"

Leaning over him, the UTC guard slammed him in the

side of the head with the butt of his rail gun. "Shut the fuck up."

With stars flying through his vision, he landed on the ground and focused just enough to see a blinking light. He checked to see if the guard was paying attention. He reached over and pressed the button next to the light. The pad read his fingerprint and the door opened. He had not known the hacker's name, and he had set his fingerprints to his lock box? Taberi remembered the hacker offering him a warm drink a few weeks ago on a chilly day. He had wrapped his hands around the cup. That must be when he copied them. Had he really considered Taberi a close friend? A small box was inside the safe as it slowly opened. He grabbed the box with his sticky long tongue, sliding it under the chair next to him. Being a dumped UTC lab experiment had its perks.

Sending one of his eyes toward the guard, he kept the other one focused as he opened the box. When he realized what it was, he almost yelped in excitement. It was a universal translator implant. He snatched it with his tongue and held it in his mouth as the guard yanked him off the floor. It was small and seemed to be crawling around inside of his mouth. Horror overcame him when he felt it was crawling into place, but from the inside. He knew they were painful to install, and he was afraid he had just made a horrible mistake.

He leaned his head back and screamed as the device crawled through his throat in two places. One heading to his ear, the other moving to his vocal cords.

The deep, wriggling pain in his throat and ear overtook him and his vision went dark.

What felt like seconds passed but must have been longer. He was strapped down to a seat and did not recall being moved. His tail was crushed under him, and he pulled it out from under his rear with a groan. He could hear some kind of engine sounds. Where the hell was he?

As his sluggish eyes began to open, he lifted his hands and rubbed the sleep away. Stretching his long, limber hands, he brought them down to evaluate his body. Everything seemed alright.

Moving his eyes around to see where he was, fear spiked inside of him as he could see nothing but sky. What the fuck?

He looked over the side through the window of the drop ship and saw what seemed to be a giant moving black cloud. As he approached the black cloud, it became individual forms, forms he recognized as terror gripped every inch of him.

He was inside of a dropship flying into a mass of giant bats. He released an ear-piercing scream as he frantically searched the pod for controls to maneuver the ship.

FORTY

ALISOT – UTC BASE
DISCOVERY MISSION

Happier than she had been in as long as she could remember, Nera pulled Cinis close to her. "This trip might not be so bad after all."

Around an hour passed by before Bensley huffed from the front seat, "Nera, next time shut the fuck up."

Nera scowled, "Why?"

Tressa leaned forward and peered out of the front window. Her heart raced as what she saw sank in. The sky ahead of them darkened with hundreds of bats pouring into the air. It was daytime, which meant many of the bats were likely diseased, or they were hunting something.

Lock grabbed Tressa and held her to him. Her heart was racing out of control, and Tressa couldn't help but keep her eyes on the sky. "What is that?"

Trajen rolled his window down and angled his head to listen before he whipped his big body around. "That's a single drop pod."

Cinis and Tressa shot up to face one another before they both turned to Nera expectantly. Nera blankly stared at the two of them, "Don't even think about it. We have no idea who could be in that pod. First, we would be risking our own lives, and that's a no. Second, let's say we do catch the drop ship. Do you really want us devouring a human criminal in this truck?"

Cinis reached up and grabbed Nera's arm, pleading, "But what if it's someone like us?"

Nera closed her eyes and licked her lips before turning around in her seat. "Lock what do you say?"

Lock scowled before answering Nera, "Absolutely not. We cannot risk it."

Vin chimed in as he scratched his chin. "If my vote matters, I think we should at least try." The three hulking men in the front all grumbled in agreement with Vin.

Nera crossed her arms. "This is a terrible idea."

Lock blurted out, "If he's a criminal, I'm eating him on the spot. I hope you're ready for that up close." Tressa cringed.

Ignoring Lock and Nera, Cinis leaned over Nera and checked the sky for the drop ship. "It seems like its angled where we could match its speed and catch it on the roof. Those ships are light, and there is a flat area on the top of the truck it could land."

Bensley asked, "What are my orders, Nera?"

Cinis turned to Nera and took her hand. "Please."

Nera gave Cinis a scathing stare. "You will pay for this if you're wrong, little pet." With gravel in her voice, Nera ordered, "Catch the drop ship, Bensley. Vin, move in position to grab the human, and Trajen, can give you cover. I want Cinis and Tressa in the back on the floorboard. Lock, you're in the middle with me as back up."

Everyone shifted into position as the truck left the road to match the angle of the ship. Tressa and Cinis huddled together, trying to keep themselves steady in the wildly shaking truck. Bentley floored the accelerator just as the drop ship could be heard overhead.

Trajen and Vin opened their windows in preparation. Trajen pulled his body halfway out of the window and sat on the edge, pulling his sword from behind his back as the first bat dove toward the truck.

Bensley grasped the steering wheel and kept his ear to the window, "AHA! I gotcha!"

A bat landed on the hood of the truck, and Trajen grunted as he sliced into it, spraying blood all over the windshield. Vin hung out of the back window and crawled up just as the pod landed on the truck with a bang. Hooking his legs against the door, Vin stood up and popped the top on the pod. A man with short brown hair and big green eyes popped his head up and screamed as Vin reached in and grabbed him by the shoulders. Vin yanked the man into the truck through the window as Trajen skewered another bat.

When everyone settled back inside, Halso began pumping the lever to prime it as Bensley pulled the lever to lower the armor. They took a sharp turn, and the drop ship rolled off the top of the truck.

The man from the drop ship curled himself into a tight ball at Vin's feet when the first wave of protos landed on the truck. Vin grabbed his tail away from the door as the electric current arced over the armor outside.

The captured man shot his head up, and Vin warned, "Keep your tail tucked or you might have a shock."

The man looked up at Vin with terror in his eyes and

cried out, "Please don't eat me. I don't belong here. I didn't kill anybody I swear! He was my friend!"

Cinis and Tressa climbed back up on the seat in the back to see the newcomer.

Vin patted the man on the shoulder. "Just stay down."

The man cringed and curled himself into an impossibly tight ball.

Nera leaned forward and put her hand on Bensley's arm. "Report."

Bensley listened as they flew down the road, and two more bats hit the armor with a screech before they fell away. He turned away from the periscope. "I am going fast enough now to outrun them. We will be clear of them in thirty minutes." Everyone in the truck seemed to simultaneously take a breath of relief.

Nera, having decided the newcomer seemed harmless, climbed into the back and signaled for Tressa to help Vin convince the man he was not about to become a Resper snack. Tressa moved around the seat and placed a gentle hand on the back of the man, "What's your name?"

He brought his eyes up and sat up as soon as he realized she was a human. "My name is Taberi."

Vin moved over so Tressa could help Taberi into the seat. He sat on the edge of the seat, as far away from Vin as he could. Tressa grasped his arm reassuringly, "You're safe now. Vin is who pulled you into the truck. He is a kind Resper." Taberi brought both of his eyes up to Vin who was trying his best, and failing, to give him a kind smile without showing his teeth. A kind blood Resper? Was that even possible? He didn't genuinely believe that for one second, no matter how convincing this woman was.

Everyone in the truck could tell without a doubt, just from his scent, Taberi was not a criminal, the man sweated profusely and reacted fearfully to every sound and movement.

Tressa could tell what she said hadn't helped much. "Look, my sibling and I have been here for over a month, and we are still alive and doing well. My name is Tressa, and this is Cinis." He looked back at Cinis and tried to smile but settled on a head nod.

Vin, trying to help, chimed in, "I promise I won't bite you, today."

Taberi brought his horrified eyes to Vin just as Cinis popped Vin on the shoulder, "That is NOT helping!"

Tressa bit her lips and put her hand over her mouth at the interaction as a bat hit the top of the truck and was electrified before it fell away.

Lock leaned up and asked Bensley, "How are we doing?"

"Almost clear. Just a few more stragglers in the sky. Halso, re-charge the current." Bensley leaned forward to listen in the periscope.

Tressa gave Taberi a reassuring look and eased back into the seat. She announced, "You are safe. Just sit back and relax. There's nothing to fear at the moment." Cinis nodded encouragement and Taberi, not believing, set back, but he did not stop looking for an escape. There was no way this was safe.

They continued on for another hour before Bensley lifted the armor, "We're in the clear. I'll find a place to pull off the road."

Moments later the truck pulled to a stop, and everyone left the compartment to rest. As Cinis, Tressa, and Nera headed off to relieve themselves in the woods, the rest of the group stretched their legs. With everyone distracted in one way or another, Taberi inched his way to the line of evergreen trees. He thought himself to be far enough and bolted through the woods.

Changing his skin color to match the surroundings, he yanked his clothes off so he could fully blend it. He couldn't hear anyone coming as he peeled out of his pants and leapt onto a tree to scurry up and hide. Once he found a thick branch and decided he was high enough, he crouched down and blended into the branch. He could hear shouting in the direction from which he had come. Cringing, he tried to slow his heart rate, slow breaths in and out. If he stayed steady, maybe they wouldn't find him, and he could escape. Where the hell was he going to go? He could not just live in the trees. Pluto spare him. This was a nightmare.

Footsteps crunched in the leaves all around, but he couldn't see anyone. A whoosh came from above when he was grabbed around the waist by a set of strong arms, causing a scream to erupt from his throat.

The powerful Resper man he was held against landed on the ground as he heard a familiar voice. "You wouldn't survive a day in these woods."

Taberi turned to a solid tan skin tone before he brought his eyes up to Vin who grasped him in an iron hold. "How did you find me?"

Vin, noticing Taberi's nudity cleared his throat and leaned down to his ear, "Everyone has a scent." He couldn't help it. Vin leaned in and sniffed Taberi's neck. Frozen in fear, he closed his eyes and prepared to die. "Calm down. I'm not going to eat you," Vin whispered, hearing Taberi's heart race in his chest. That didn't help in the slightest, so Vin offered, "Let's find your clothes."

Taberi nodded as Vin set him down on the ground but kept a hold on his arm. After a few yards, Vin bent down and retrieved Taberi's pants off the ground and handed them to him.

After they emerged from the woods with Taberi dressed and thoroughly embarrassed, he sunk his head for his walk of shame back to the truck.

FORTY-ONE

ALISOT – UTC BASE
DISCOVERY MISSION

Hours passed as they followed the wide road, winding around hills and crossing bridges over streams. Tressa had been lulled to sleep in Lock's lap with Cinis in the middle and Nera on the other side of them. Cinis leaned into Nera, and she pulled them close. They felt her hand rub up and down on their arm and Cinis was nearly purring with the affection. Vin and Taberi sat in the middle row with Bensley driving. Halso slept on Trajen's shoulder, and he had been softly snoring.

Taberi watched the scenery pass by as his tail curled and uncurled by his side. Vin was hopelessly obsessed with Taberi's tail, but he was doing his best not to make it obvious. He wanted to touch it so badly his hand itched.

Several more hours passed before the bright daylight star began its decent into nightfall. Bensley pulled off the road and drove down a dirt pathway. After a few minutes, he slowed to a stop, and they all filed out. A small cabin sat a few yards away. The building disappeared into the side of a hill.

Nera pulled her pack from the back of the truck and handed Cinis theirs. "This cabin belongs to one of my cousins. We will stay here for the night. It will be the last time we have a roof over our head for a while, so get some rest."

Bensley grabbed his pack, slinging it in the front seat and waiting for everyone to grab their things and head inside. Once the truck was cleared out, he pulled it around the side of the cabin and into a small single garage.

Nera was the first inside and went to the fireplace, turning on the gas and lighting it to provide some light and warmth in the dark room. The simple cabin was small and had one four pane window in the front next to the door, a fireplace, a couch, and a tiny kitchen with a table for two. Opening a door at the back of the room, Nera lit another gas lantern, and the hallway illuminated. Cinis held back a gasp at how large the room was. There were three sets of bunks with a fireplace at either end of the room. Nera sighed and mumbled to herself, "Shit. I forgot my cousin's family doesn't hang to sleep."

Approaching the bunk to the right, Nera tossed her pack on the bed as the rest of the group came in and found a bed. Bensley, Trajen, and Halso each begrudgingly claimed one for themselves, all of them were large enough they took up an entire bed.

Taberi sat down by the door and made himself comfortable. He had already done the math. There were not enough beds, and he was absolutely not climbing into bed with a blood Resper.

Across the room, Vin sat down under Halso in the middle bunk bed and pulled his thermos of blood from his pack. Vin guzzled down a few gulps of blood before he noticed Taberi curling in a ball by the door. He knew the poor guy's heart had been beating out of control for hours. Every time Vin so much as leaned toward him, his heart would soar in his chest. He couldn't believe he was admitting this but, he felt terrible for Taberi. He smelled just like Cinis and Tressa, which he knew meant Taberi was scared out of his mind. Lock and Nera may have some attraction around it, but that was not Vin's desire at all.

Vin turned to Nera in the bunk next to him, "Did you pack any extra dried food for Cinis and Tressa?"

Knowing what he meant, Nera lightly tapped on Cinis shoulder and pointed to their pack to hand it over. She dug in it for a moment before retrieving a small bag and handed it over to Vin.

Vin took a reassuring deep breath and made his way over to Taberi with the sack of dried fruit. He crouched down and reached his hand out to draw Taberi's attention. Startled, Taberi jolted up and slammed his back against the wall trying to shove away from Vin. "I'm sorry. I didn't mean to scare you. Are you hungry?" Vin asked softly.

Taberi gulped and whispered, "Y-Yes. I'm always hungry."

He had been homeless most of his life and that question, *are you hungry* bounced around in his mind like a dagger. Why did this terrifying man care if he was hungry? No one on Emendo had ever cared.

Vin handed him the bag, and Taberi reluctantly took it with shaking fingers. Vin remained crouched in front of Taberi, his wings angled up so they weren't smashed on the floor. They hung over Vin and Taberi's heads like an umbrella. Taberi's mouth watered when he saw the dried pieces of fruit. He couldn't eat them quickly enough. With his mouth so full he could hardly chew, he finally built up the courage to look up at Vin's face. When he did, he couldn't tear is eyes away.

Vin was strikingly handsome, and Taberi was so taken back he nearly choked on the fruit as he tried to swallow. His tail curled up tightly, and he became all too aware of his own skin. He resisted the urge to hide, and his skin color rippled from the color of the wood behind him and back to tan. Vin seemed completely unaware as he remained knelt. Once Taberi had finally swallowed his enormous bite, he relaxed a bit and whispered, "Thank you."

Vin smiled, forgetting about his fangs, and Taberi stiffened. He did his best to stay calm, but those fangs were way too close for comfort.

Biting his lips together, Vin gave a half smile and whispered, "I told you I wasn't going to hurt you. I have some human friends whom I've grown to love. I know you're not lying when you say you don't belong here. It's pretty obvious."

Taberi had a strange sense of relief he never expected to fall over him as he held his gaze on Vin, "You believe me?"

"If I rapidly lifted my hands and yelled, BOO! you would probably lose consciousness."

Taberi frowned, "Oh, yeah."

"It's going to be cold by the door. If you're set on sleeping on the floor, at least sleep closer to the fire. You can share my bunk if you decide to," Vin stood up and waited for Taberi who finally nodded. He went back to his bunk and could hear Taberi behind him, following. He passed by Vin and when his eyes fell on Trajen and Bensley in the bunk beds to the left, he abruptly turned and sat by Vin's bed.

Vin moved his big, muscled body around in the covers, and once comfortable, he watched Taberi curl in a ball next to his bed. There was a brown blanket folded at his feet, so Vin grabbed it and lay it over Taberi, who snatched the soft blanket and quickly tucked himself into an impossibly tiny ball. Vin listened as his breathing finally slowed and his heart rate calmed. Finally, Vin could relax. Taberi's racing heart had been eating at him for hours. Vin tried not to think of the moment earlier in the day when he had Taberi, nude and in his arms in the woods.

FORTY-TWO

ALISOT – UTC BASE
DISCOVERY MISSION

Vin awoke to a whimper below him. He leaned over the side of the bunk to check on Taberi, who seemed upset. On closer inspection, Taberi was asleep and must have been having a bad dream. He made a sorrowful sound again, and Vin's heart hurt. A few moments went by before Taberi shook and pulled the covers away from his face. His heart rate skyrocketed, and Vin had enough. He leaned down to Taberi and whispered, "You're alright."

Taberi nearly came unglued and tried to leap away but tripped over the covers he was wrapped in. Vin reached his long arms over and grabbed Taberi by the waist and hauled him into the bed. He froze as Vin pulled him close and held him in his arms. At first, it made things worse and Taberi shivered as his heart continued to climb.

Vin sighed and brought his hand up to lay in the center of Taberi's chest. "You have to calm down. Just breathe. Come on. You can do it. Take a slow breath." Taberi fought compliance and Vin couldn't help but rub his thumb against his chest. His breath kept catching, and Vin held him tight, whispering, "Just breathe. I've got you."

Taberi finally took a slow breath and lay his head back against Vin's chest in defeat, "I don't want to die."

Vin began rubbing the top of Taberi's chest, "Just stay with me, and you'll be safe." Taberi nearly sobbed with Vin's affection. How could such a terrifying creature be so comforting? He did his best to relax, but being belly up and stretched out over a blood Resper was not the way to accomplish that.

Taberi felt Vin loosen his grip, and Vin moved to lie next to him. Vin put his arm around him and pulled him close. He chose to curl in and close his eyes. What was happening? How had Taberi ended up in the big scary man's bed? Was Vin rubbing his back now? *Do I like this? Oh gods.*

Thoughts poured through Taberi's head as Vin continued to try to comfort him. Was this how a blood Resper always acted? He had met some Resper on Emendo, and they were nothing like this man. He pulled his legs up and tried to turn and curl in a ball, but Vin pushed his legs back down and wrapped his hand around his waist.

Taberi had a million emotions crash into him at once as he felt Vin slowly drift into sleep. How was he in bed with a man he met just hours before? This was a record for him. He usually couldn't get a date to save his life. No one wanted a poor guy with no confidence.

Shadows danced on the walls for hours before Taberi could fall sleep. When he did slip off into dreamland, he begged the gods to let him rest. He was tired of reliving the awful memories from his time living on the streets as a child.

Hours later, Taberi woke with a start in Vin's bed. There were no covers over them, but Vin's hand had made its way up his shirt, and it was currently resting on his stomach. Vin wasn't moving his hand, but it didn't matter, the contact was all Taberi could comprehend.

Did he just become this big Resper guy's target? Vin's hand moved to wrap around his waist, and he came undone with heated confusion and want. His skin was on fire as Vin nestled his face into Taberi's neck, his hot breath curling his toes. He needed the hell out of this bed and tried to move, but Vin hauled him back against his body and moved his hand up his shirt to his chest. Taberi was absolutely losing his mind when he felt Vin's length harden in his pants.

Vin gently moved his hips forward and ground against Taberi as he slid his hand down his body to his lower belly and whispered sleepily, "Mmm, come here."

Taberi took a sharp breath, and Vin's head popped up with his eyes wide open. He stared at Taberi as he gently pulled his hand from under his shirt, "I am so sorry."

Taberi looked up at him whispering, "Um, it's alright. You were asleep and didn't know."

Vin felt like the biggest creep in the world until he noticed the sweat on Taberi and the evident erection he also had. He bit his lip as Taberi rolled over and gently pulled his shirt back down. Taberi made no move to climb off the bed and Vin put his arms behind his head and leaned back against the pillow. The system star hadn't come up yet, and they were the only two awake.

After a few minutes of awkward silence, Vin couldn't help but ask, "Are you alright?

Taberi had no idea how to answer that, so he closed his eyes and moved closer to Vin. When Vin felt him move against his side and settle, he felt minutely better and tried to stay still.

The two lie together until Cinis sat up and woke Nera for a trip to the bathroom. As Cinis headed to the door, Taberi sat up, "Can I join you?"

Turning and seeing Taberi in Vin's bed, Cinis did their best not to smile as they answered, "Of course."

The three of them headed down a stone path into the woods for the bath house. Around the side of the hill, they found a stone entryway with a large wooden door. The door creaked as Nera opened it, and they all filed inside as she found a gas lamp on the wall and ignited it. The bath house had a steaming natural spring to one side and a hallway with what appeared to be restrooms behind it. Cinis headed to the restroom as Nera and Taberi followed. When they emerged from the back, Taberi leaned down and dragged his hand through the water.

Nera paused as she narrowed her eyes at him, "I think my cousin's wife is around your size. You can wear some of her clothes that were left in the cabin. If you need a bath, please help yourself. We won't leave until we've caught some breakfast." She did her best to leave out anything particularly telling, but Taberi more than read between the lines, and his heart began racing with fear.

Nera turned to Cinis, "Can you stay here with Taberi while I go find him some fresh clothes?"

They replied, "Of course."

The door shut firmly behind Nera, and Taberi turned to Cinis, "I'm scared out of my mind. Can you please explain what's going on?"

Cinis paused then responded, "It's a long story. Basically, we are trying to find an old UTC base so that the doctor can find a way to stop the overpopulation of protos, which are those scary bats you flew into. I can't lie to you. The blood Resper here are every bit as dangerous and murderous as we were taught on Emendo. The only difference is, they are capable of caring. They have feelings and emotions like we do. They've just been conditioned to hate humans for the last thousand years, like we've been conditioned to fear them. You really are safe with Vin, I promise. He seems scary, but he's actually the kindest of all of them."

Taberi stood and stared at them before asking, "Um, can you turn around?"

"Oh, shit. I'm sorry." Cinis spun around, and they heard him sink in the water after undressing.

Taberi made an oddly joyful sound, "I've never been in so much water before."

Cinis understood as they hadn't either until they had taken a bath in Nera's house. "You would be shocked at how much better this prison planet is than where we came from. How did you end up here?"

"I was checking on my friend who hadn't answered his phone in a few days. I found him dead. I guess the First Human soldier accused me of his murder." Taberi watched as Cinis stiffened.

They froze at the mention of the FH, asking, "Who was your friend?"

Taberi slowly answered, "The Hacker."

Guilt flooding them, Cinis turned and met Taberi's eyes, "Tressa and I are why the First Human soldier showed up at The Hacker's apartment. The Hacker made a broadcast for the Iungos and broke into the UTC system to send it everywhere. It was Tressa's voice on the recording. I'm so sorry you were dragged into this."

Taberi stared back at Cinis in disbelief, "I had just been

promoted at the north side UTC data entry office. The Hacker helped me find the job. He had been my friend for the last ten years after he let me stay on his couch for a few months. I was homeless my whole life and had been sleeping in his hallway for a year."

Cinis felt awful. "I'm so sorry."

Taberi ran his hand over the stone along the tub. "I would say it's not your fault, but it definitely was all your fault."

Cinis gave him a smile without joy behind it, but one of sadness and understanding, the way only two children of a sorrowful world could relate to one another.

FORTY-THREE

ALISOT – UTC BASE
DISCOVERY MISSION

Nera knocked before she opened the door to the bath house. In her arms were battle leathers in Taberi's size. "Halso caught a deer, you two may want to stay in the bath house for a little while." She warned, Cinis nodded at Nera and noticed the thick fog rolling in.

When they turned back, Taberi looked like he had seen a ghost, "How can you deal with all of this so easily? Knowing what they do?"

Noticing he had moved by the towels, Cinis turned away and answered, "Oh it still scares the hell out of me, but I've learned to care about Nera, and I acknowledge her physical needs."

Taberi rubbed his shoulders then reached for a towel to wrap around him. "So, you and Nera are together, together?"

Cinis laughed, "Honestly I don't have a clue what we are, but we care for one another, and I think that speaks for something."

Taberi shook his head in disbelief as he pulled the leather pants up. "Do you let her bite you?"

Rubbing their neck where their most recent puncture wound was healing, Cinis answered, "Yes. It's not as bad as it sounds. If they like you, they only take a little bit and they make it fun."

"Fun?!" Taberi was horrified as he approached Cinis and sat next to them.

Cinis just replied, "Honestly, Nera makes it a lot of fun. It's not the bite itself but what comes with it."

Twirling around to face Cinis, Taberi dropped his mouth open, "WAIT."

Cinis slid a hand up to their mouth to help hold in a laugh as they stood to bathe. It would likely be the last time before they arrived at the base, so it was necessary.

Taberi dropped his head in his hands and groaned, "Is Vin going to try and bite me?" Cinis didn't answer but patted Taberi on the back in half-assed reassurance. He just turned and glared at them.

Tressa burst through the door. "Ick, I just passed by Lock elbow deep inside of that deer. I think I'm going to be sick."

She hauled herself to the bathrooms in the back as Taberi huffed and furrowed his brow, "I feel like I'm going to lose my mind. How have you been living like this?"

Cinis shook their head, "You're going to have to toughen up really quickly because you haven't seen anything yet."

Slipping his jacket on, Taberi turned around on the bench so Cinis could bathe with some privacy. When Cinis was dressed, Nera popped her head in the door with blood smeared lips. "You three might want to head back to the cabin and go inside. Cinis, please guide Taberi away from the left side of the cabin. Lock was hungry and made a hell of a mess by the garage."

Taberi slapped a hand over his mouth as Cinis gave him another pat on his back. "Let's go, you can do it."

Tressa groaned and retched again from the back of the bathhouse as the door shut behind Cinis and Taberi. Nera was standing with her face and arms away from Taberi, but Cinis could tell she was covered in blood. *Was it absolutely necessary for them to devour prey like that? Why was Lock such a feral animal about it?* Cinis grabbed Taberi by the hand and led him away from the path to the garage. They peeked through the trees and gagged at the intestines hanging from a tree branch. They pulled Taberi along, taking large strides back to the cabin. When they arrived inside, it was quiet and empty right before Tressa burst in behind them.

"I didn't make it out of the bathroom in time, and I just had to pass by all six of them naked and washing blood off their arms and faces. It's too early for this shit." Tressa shivered as she made her way to her bunk and buried her face in the covers.

A few moments later Lock, his face still wet from washing, found Tressa face down in the bunk. "I can't change what I am."

She scowled at him, "I'm not asking you to change, just maybe don't rip the creatures guts out and haphazardly toss them into the tree?"

Laughing, Lock rubbed his hands down his face, "I admit I get a little too excited when it's time to eat."

Tressa groaned and rubbed her still sleepy eyes, "Has the system star even been up for an hour?!"

Lock combed his hands through his wet hair as Nera and Cinis passed by and began packing up their gear. The rest of the group came in one by one to pack up and within a few minutes everyone was heading outside as Bensley pulled the truck around. Cinis cringed as they noticed the blood on the tires of the truck as it came to a halt in front of them.

The group piled in the truck and Tressa plopped down next to Lock in the back with Cinis climbing in next to her. Taberi sat between Nera and Vin as the three guards climbed in the front, taking the seats they had before. The truck popped into gear, and they took off down the gravel road with a jolt.

Tressa peered back as the cabin disappeared from view, knowing that was the last soft bed any of them would be sleeping in for a while. They had a couple of thick bedrolls already packed, and Nera had taken an additional one before they left the cabin.

The morning was chilled, and a thick fog blanketed the land. The Respers in the truck seemed uneasy. The truck traveled at a slower speed.

Cinis leaned forward and touched Nera's shoulder for her attention, "Is there a reason we are driving so slow?"

Nera turned around to Cinis, "Echolocation doesn't work as well in the fog. Our range is severely reduced just like vision would be."

"Wait, echolocation?" Taberi interrupted and grabbed his chest, "He is not using his eyes to drive? How? I am so confused right now."

Understanding how he felt, Cinis blurted, "They don't use vision like us, they use echolocation."

"The Resper on Emendo and Melior can see, why can't any of you?" Taberi asked, his independently moving eyes roaming the truck for answers.

A realization hit Lock like hail from the sky. "Nera, do

you think the Fruit Resper betrayed us and our planet for eyesight?"

The silence in the truck was thick and heavy. Nera closed her eyes and hung her head as disgust filled her. For the last thousand years her family and her people had been cut off from the galactic center, something they had been a part of for many thousands of years prior. It took less than one hundred years of partnering with the UTC and First Humans for the Fruit Resper to turn on their own people. They had lost their ability to fly and thought eyesight was the answer. Her heart was broken. How could they have not figured out the truth until now?

Nera realized they had been devouring humans for generations, never truly finding out anything other than their personal crimes. Or maybe some of her people had figured it out, but the secret had died with time? Her head spun.

As the day warmed, the fog began to lift, and Bensley was able to speed up. "Nera, we are approaching the drop point."

Pursing her lips, Nera took a deep breath, "When we park, we will begin traveling on foot. We have at least a two week hike before we need to make our long flight over the second colony of protos. They are settled somewhere down in the valley, in front of the mountains. The base we are looking for is on the other side of the mountain range, heading west. It could be as far west as the coast, and I'm betting we will find the base in the city ruins closer to the sea."

Everyone in the truck mentally prepared themselves as Tressa rubbed her already sore feet. This was going to be hell for her, and she knew it.

Bensley pulled the truck to a stop. "I can smell a home

built off this road to the left. They have oil canisters. I'm going to take the truck and see if they have somewhere I can hide it."

Nera raised her eyebrows as she took her pack out of the back. "We will all wait here until you arrive back."

He pulled away after everyone gathered their things. The Respers all separated the snaps on their packs, dividing their bags into three long bags with buckle straps at both ends. They helped one another attach a bag to their backs between their wings. The other two bags they buckled around their hips and secured the bottom at their knees.

Cinis had wondered how they were planning on wearing a backpack with those wings and marveled at the simple design solution. Tressa's and their packs were just one solid bag, and they wondered when theirs had been custom made. They did have wingless backs as the Resper all seemed to say.

The group paused a moment as four drop ships fell from the sky, heading west, across the mountain range they were aiming for. Human criminal drops from Emendo occurred monthly or more. Drop ships would be landing all over the planet over the next few hours. Respers wanting human blood would be following them closely.

Taberi adjusted his bed roll over one shoulder as he wiggled his toes in his boots. He couldn't believe he had the same size clothing and feet as Nera's cousin and was grateful for the coincidence. His old shoes wouldn't have lasted more than a week in the wilderness.

Once Vin was strapped down with his bags, he approached Taberi, "Can I talk to you for a minute?" Taberi, unable to find his words just nodded and followed Vin off into the woods.

When they had moved away from everyone, Vin stopped, turned to Taberi and apologized, "I should not have had my hand in your shirt this morning. I can't remove it from my mind. I'm sorry. If you don't want to sleep near me again, I understand."

Taberi was still speechless and stood there as if he were thoughtless as well. He didn't know what to say. How could he say he kind of liked something but this whole thing also scared the hell out of him? "I, um. I." Taberi started, trying to find the words.

Nera called out from behind them, "Let's go. Bensley is back."

Before he could form a full word, he was saved. Taberi turned on his heels and made a straight path back to the group.

Yet, Taberi couldn't help but watch as Vin came through the trees. He had been thinking about Vin's hand in his shirt nonstop too. He could feel his color shift to match the surroundings as he tried to hide his turbulent feelings.

FORTY-FOUR

ALISOT – UTC BASE
DISCOVERY MISSION

Hours passed as they hiked through the wilderness, the evergreen trees becoming thicker as they traveled uphill. Birds chirped from all around and the sap from the trees perfumed the air. If they weren't on such a difficult mission, their time in the woods would have been refreshing and joyous.

Tressa tried to control her breathing as the pain in her feet settled in. She did her best to ignore it, but as Lock insisted on following behind her, it became difficult to hide. As they passed a smaller tree, he found a tree branch to make a staff for her and stripped it down until it was smooth. It had made a difference, but at their next stop, Lock still took her bag and wore it on his chest.

They continued on until midafternoon when Nera stopped everyone and turned to the guards, "It's time to make camp. We need to catch something for us to eat, but it needs to be something the humans can also eat. Search for either a deer or hog. We can drain it for our dinner and cook part of the meat for them." Nera then turned to face

Lock, "You are not going near it until we've divided things."

Next to Lock, Tressa bit her lips together as she massaged her sore hands.

Lock noticed her reaction. "I told you I can't help it. I get very hungry."

"Don't you think it's a bit much if *Nera* says you might want to dial it back?"

"The taste of meat which was alive moments before is indescribable."

Tressa scowled at him and crossed her arms.

Taberi heard what Lock said, backed himself into a tree, and hit his head. He began sweating in the cool of the air and swallowed roughly. His color shifting to the umber hue of the trunk.

Vin appeared at his side, "What happened?"

How did he know? Taberi blinked a few times before he all but whimpered, "I'm surviving."

Vin sighed trying to shift his mind to something else. "Why don't you tell me about your family?"

That question was a knife to the heart, and Taberi always struggled to answer it. "I was made in a lab. I'm half human and half Vultus. The project lost funding, and the researchers didn't want to kill us as they were instructed, so they released us onto the streets of Emendo with nothing but the lab clothes we had on."

Vin was frozen. He could not fathom this man would have answered the way he did. His parents were down south with the rest of their people. He had been unconditionally loved, they were still upset with him for staying with Nera and Lock. He knew it was hard for his parents, but he wasn't leaving the people he had grown up with and had to fight with to make their planet safe again. But to have been created and abandoned was beyond his comprehension.

What could Vin say? He needed to change the subject. After a painfully long pause to think, Vin shifted his feet, "Do you have anything interesting about you being half Vultus?"

"I know what you're doing, and thank you for trying to make this easier. Yes, I can change my skin color from browns to greens and all shades in between." Taberi explained, knowing damn well he wasn't ready to talk about the other things that made him different.

Vin smiled but tried not to show too much of his fangs. "I wish I could see your colors. I don't think I've ever had the desire for sight before. Being able to change color sounds incredible."

Taberi had not thought about Vin not being able to see his colors. They could use their echolocation to see form and distance, but not color. He had never imagined such a thing.

Doing his best to not seem obvious, Vin was using his echolocation to look at Taberi's face. His doe eyes were kind, and he couldn't tear his focus away from his full lips. They all used hypersonic sound so prey couldn't hear them, but right now he was using it to take a peek at the handsome man standing before him. Taberi was a little under six feet tall, which made him several inches shorter than Vin.

Not knowing what to say Vin awkwardly asked, "So, what is it like having a tail? Do you use it to grab things? I have always wanted to ask someone with a tail so many questions. My parents caught... Oh, I'm going to skip that story."

Taberi's skin shifted colors as he stared at Vin, his heart picking up speed again.

"Shit. I'm sorry. I am awful at this aren't I?" Vin was at a loss at how to make Taberi feel comfortable. He kept saying the wrong things. How had Nera and Lock, wait. No, he was not going that route. Absolutely not.

Taberi's tail curled and uncurled behind him. "It's the thought that counts right?"

"Not when I can hear your heart pounding," Vin admitted as he moved the end of his boot around in the dirt.

Cinis appeared from behind the tree, "They just brought back a hog. I'm going to stand here with you while Vin goes and does his thing."

Grateful for the chance to end his embarrassing ineptitude at conversation, Vin awkwardly gave Taberi a low wave at his waist before hopping away.

When Vin found Bensley, he already had the hog's intestines, lungs, and liver lying in a pile next to it. He had his arms elbow deep inside the pig pulling the remaining innards out as Nera shifted leaves around to form a pile to cover the gore.

Halso tapped Bensley on the shoulder announcing, "It's my turn, hand it over."

Bensley huffed as he ripped the pig's heart out and begrudgingly handed it over.

Lock cleared his throat from behind them declaring, "I better have a leg to myself."

Trajen handed Vin a thermos filled with steaming pig's blood, and the two gulped it down as Nera approached to grab one for herself. She took two and handed one off to Lock. When Halso finished eating the pig's heart, he licked his mouth and headed off to gather more firewood. Nera had already started a small fire and buried wooden stakes in the ground to cook the meat on as the rest of the Respers cleaned up.

When the fire was big enough, Bensley impaled the hog leg onto the wooden sticks, and Nera called the humans to come sit around the fire. Their daylight star had set, and darkness filled the woods save the large moon that would be hovering in the sky soon. The three guards were on duty and had made a perimeter around the camp. They were hanging upside down with metal boot anchors in the trees while monitoring every angle.

Other than the crackle of the fire and soft wind in the trees the camp was mostly silent until Tressa furrowed her brow and asked, "You haven't mentioned one thing about the gods, if you don't pray to the gods of our world, what gods do you pray to?"

The campsite remained silent for a moment before Lock spoke, "We don't believe in gods. Our ancient ritualistic religious practices died thousands of years ago when we left our planet and joined the galactic community. We had all sorts of prophesy about a reckoning of our wickedness and how our world would end in destruction. Most of the religious institutions were nothing more than a business and when we spread out to the stars, no one bought what they were selling any more. We turned to innovation, progress, and aimed to develop into a higher level of society. Our ancestors wanted to create a utopia, and we found religion was too divisive for an ideal world."

The deafening silence after Lock's explanation was only broken by the sound of an owl catching a screaming mouse in the woods. Deep in thought about his answer to her question, Tressa slipped her hand over Lock's, and he leaned into her.

Sitting with her legs crossed next to Cinis, Nera tapped her hands on her knees. "If we can find a way to move Cinis, Tressa, and Taberi off this planet and back home, I think we should try. They are defenseless here."

Cinis protested, "Not a chance in hell. You would have to drug me and shoot me off in a rocket! I am not leaving."

"This planet is doomed if we can't find a solution. I don't know what kind of life we can offer you here. If we find a way to communicate with the Iungo people you helped when we find the old base, you should find a way to go home. Alisot is too harsh for humans, and it's just getting worse," Nera explained.

Cinis crossed their arms, "I'm not leaving."

"There are things I cannot protect you from here. Do you understand that?"

"I am aware of the situation. Do you have any idea what our lives were like before we came here? Do you have any idea how much more we have been fed here than we ever were at home? It's not just the food. It's the fresh air, it's the bright yellow star in the sky, and the people. You're not sending me away. You tried that before, and it didn't work!" Cinis speaking their mind so boldly wasn't something they did often, but damn it felt good this time. "You'll have to make me leave." Cinis looked over to Tressa for her support.

Tressa nodded with Cinis, whispering to Lock, "I don't want to go home."

He wrapped his arms around her, "Nera, I understand your fears, but I think I agree with Cinis and Tressa. Both of their physical conditions are far better than they were when they arrived."

Tressa wrapped her hands around her middle and closed her eyes. She was not leaving. This was her home now, and she would just have to accept all the blood and gore. She didn't care if she had to live as his *pet*. Cinis had caved quickly, but her acceptance had taken a while.

Vin sunk his head next to Taberi. He had heard the way his heart had pounded at hearing there may be a way home. Vin knew he didn't have a chance in hell. Alone as always, Vin's heart twisted, and he stood up to find a branch to anchor his boots to so he could get some sleep. A few feet from the fire, he found a good place and leaped to the branch to secure his boot anchors. He finished and dropped himself down, with his head about three feet from the ground. Vin closed his eyes and tried to block out the world around him by wrapping his wings tightly around himself. A twig broke, and he opened his eyes but didn't part his wings to see who it was.

A blanket was spread out right below his perch, and he sniffed the air. His heart nearly leaped into his throat as Taberi settled down on the mat under him and curled into a ball to sleep.

FORTY-FIVE

ALISOT – UTC BASE
DISCOVERY MISSION

The sky above them filled with a dark cloud, casting a shadow on the woods as they began hiking for the day. Nera halted the group and climbed a tree for a clearer look. Nera dropped down from the trees and landed on her feet in the center of the group directing, "We need to make a quick camp without fire. We only use the supplies we have. No straying from camp. Tomorrow morning, we fly over the colony. There is a cliff-side we can leap from a quarter of a mile from here. Make sure your wings are stretched and ready. Do not forget to put on your ice barrier cream before bed tonight. It needs a few hours to dry, and we don't have time in the morning."

Part of the group busied themselves with setting up camp as the guards made a perimeter.

After setting up her bed roll, Tressa lay down and yanked off her boots. Her feet were screaming, and she rubbed them through her thick socks, but it was not helping much. Lock knelt at the end of her bedroll and gently took her foot into his hand, "Does this area here hurt or the heel?"

He gently pressed into the ball of her foot, and she almost squealed aloud, "Yes, that area. The tendon pops when I walk."

Lock admitted, "I can hear it happening with your every step."

She realized that was how he knew she needed a walking stick. Tressa bit her lip as he massaged her foot, "Don't you have to fly us over the protos tomorrow? How long will that take?"

"It will take several hours."

Tressa was confused. That sounded outrageous. "I thought you could only fly for four or five hours at a time? How long are you going to have to fly tomorrow?"

"It will take eight."

Tressa froze, "You have to carry me too?"

Lock struggled to find his words, "Why do you think we've been working out our wings for the last week and a half?"

Tressa just thought they were wrapping long, stretchy bands around their wings and fighting the tension as a routine. Now that she thought about it, she had never seen them do the exercise at the house's wing gym. Tressa frowned, "What happens if you have to stop?"

Lock couldn't find the words to answer her. They couldn't stop. He would simply fall out of the sky and the two of them would die. He would not let that happen. They had to make it over the colony and his skill was needed to find a way to reduce the numbers of the protos. He also knew, out of everyone, he was the most likely to struggle. He weighed almost twice what Nera did and needed much more energy to move his larger body. Vin had distance wings, and his size didn't make a significant difference. He could sense Nera staring at him from behind, waiting for him to answer Tressa's question.

"We're going to make it across," he answered flatly as he resumed rubbing her foot.

Cinis lay their hand on Nera's shoulder, "I need a bathroom break." Nera turned and nodded, following Cinis into the woods. The woods were singing with birds and chattering squirrels, Cinis was mesmerized by it all. They had fallen in love with nature and wanted to run free between the trees. Breathing in the fresh air, they brought their face to the sky expecting to see the evening daylight, but all they saw far above the trees was a whirling cloud of proto-bats.

Nera could hear the mass of bats in the sky, spreading over the mountain to pick it clean. The mix of the screams of bats above her, and the beat of Cinis's heart in front of her was enough to make her snap. She came up behind Cinis, "I'm glad you want to stay, but please understand. We will have to cross all this land again. I don't know how we are going to accomplish this journey once, much less twice. That's if we are able to find a way to reduce the numbers of the bats and we can find the UTC base. We might not even make it inside."

Cinis turned to Nera and countered, "What if we get to the base and everything goes right? We don't know what we might find there. What if we find a spaceship?"

Nera shook her head, "The EM pulses, remember."

Cinis sunk their head and squeezed their eyes shut, "So maybe we can turn the power on in the base, and if we do, maybe it won't get zapped."

Shifting on her feet, Nera answered, "I know this plan is a stretch and we're going on a lot of hope."

Cinis raised their hands and slid them up Nera's arms. "Remember around the campfire when Tressa asked about your religion? I believe in the balance. When we were talking about who we pray to, I might pray to Jupiter, Juno, or even Venus, but what I honestly believe in is the great balance of life. I was able to see a whole species fight back and emerge as the people who ultimately took down the First Humans' power which has remained in the galactic center for thousands of years." Cinis paused to lean up and kiss Nera, "I know you're worried about tomorrow, but I know we will make it. I know we're going to all get to the other side."

Nera nodded solemnly. "We just need as much rest as possible tonight." Cinis agreed, and they each found a place to relieve themselves before heading back to rejoin the group. As they made their way back, Nera noticed something moving to the left of Cinis but couldn't move fast enough.

Cinis hopped and yelped, "Ouch!"

Nera had her knife out and deftly sliced the head off a snake at Cinis' ankle. Frantically grabbing the head of the snake, Nera ran her fingers over its face, "Fucking snake. Did it pierce your skin?" Nera had no idea how bad this would be for them. She had never known a human to get bitten. The viper was not common in these lands. They were found to the north.

Cinis untied and peeled down their boot to find two puncture marks. Nera's mouth dropped open when she could smell the droplets of blood on Cinis ankle. With the way Cinis heart was beating, Nera only had moments to explain what typically happens with a bite. "You are going to become terribly ill, very quickly. There is no antidote for this kind of viper, and even if there was, we are too far away to make it before your symptoms begin. It likely won't kill you, but you're going to wish you were dead. Cinis, you're going to need to stay very strong. This will likely be the hardest two days of your life. I will strap you to my body tomorrow for the journey, but you probably won't remember anything. Just know I am with you, and I will not leave you. You will survive this. Please be so strong."

Nera cupped Cinis face just as the first cramp began in their gut. They grabbed their stomach and groaned, "I'm sorry Nera, I'm so sorry."

Nera kissed Cinis and pulled them close as another stomach cramp hit. Within moments, Cinis' breath shortened, and they curled their legs into their body. Lifting them off the ground, Nera held Cinis close as she made her way back to camp as carefully as she could. She knew every bump and jostle would be agonizing. Cinis whimpered as the sweat formed on their brow, and Nera's heart broke with the sound. She resisted the urge to hold Cinis close to her and add pressure to their already agonized state.

When Nera arrived back at their campsite, Lock leaped to his feet and approached Nera and Cinis. "What happened?"

Nera could hardly speak, her emotions were eating her alive, "A northern viper bit them through their boot."

Lock froze with his hand on Cinis's head. "Nera," he started.

Nera interrupted, "I know. I had time to explain it to them."

Lock roughly exhaled as he checked Cinis over. "This is bad."

Tressa was hovering over Lock and whispered with gut

wrenching fear in every word, "Is my sibling going to die?"

Lock stood up and took Tressa aside, "Not likely, as long as they understood what was going to happen to them first. The problem arises from not knowing what's coming and how bad it gets. It can be hell on a person's cardiovascular system because of what the venom does. It's not designed to kill its target prey right away. It wants the larger prey to call on all the smaller prey with its cries. The viper eats the smaller scavengers as they arrive. The larger prey is usually eaten alive by small predators while it cries in pain from the venom, but the venom isn't causing too much harm. As long as Nera explained to Cinis how painful the next two days will be, they will likely survive. They just need to remain calm and let their body process the venom."

Tressa nearly fell to her knees and Lock sensed her distress, and pulled her to him. He wrapped his arms around her and held her tight as Cinis let out a pained whimper. Lock turned to Nera, "You are going to need some rest tonight."

Nera nodded as she hovered over Cinis, "Tressa?"

Tressa all but ran over to Nera, "Anything."

"Cinis needs someone close to comfort them when it gets worse. If Lock and I don't sleep tonight, tomorrow won't happen. We can't stay here any longer than one night." Nera didn't know what to do with her hands since she couldn't touch Cinis.

Tressa moved to lie next to Cinis, "I will take care of them. You two sleep. You need to rest."

FORTY-SIX

ALISOT – UTC BASE
DISCOVERY MISSION

They lined up at the cliffside after first light, nowhere near ready to begin their flight but preparing for it, nonetheless. Cinis began rocking sometime during the night and hadn't stopped for hours. Strapping Cinis to Nera was gut wrenching. They whimpered and could hardly manage a full breath as their legs were pried away from their body. If Tressa hadn't seen it with her own eyes, she wouldn't have believed it, but she saw tears form in Nera's big black eyes when they had to pull Cinis legs away.

Cinis was wrapped around Nera, and they had two thick straps holding Cinis under their arms and another over their low back which wrapped around her waist. Their legs were wrapped around her, and Trajen used a stretchy band for their workouts to tie Cinis's feet.

Taberi was tied to Vin, and he was positively terrified. His tail was curling and uncurling over and over, and his color was a mottled beige. He tried to find the best place for his face with Vin's face mere inches away.

Tressa was last and she was strapped to Lock in a similar way. From her angle, she could see the shining layer of barrier cream Nera had spoken about. She hoped it helped. The air was chilly where they were, and she couldn't imagine how much colder it would become.

Bensley approached with thick, short, brimmed leather caps designed with the Domitia house insignia of wings, and everyone slid one on, except for Cinis who was being wrapped carefully in cloth. Tressa was relieved to have something covering her head. Lock instructed, "Lower the brim to keep the icy wind from freezing your eyes."

They each tied their caps under their chins, and Nera approached the edge of the cliff. Lock slid his gloves on and handed Tressa hers as he followed Nera. The Respers all lined up at the cliff and spread their wings to stretch one last time before Nera began beating her wings.

She leapt off the cliff, and Lock followed, then Vin. The three guards launched behind them and found their places behind and to their sides. As they gained altitude, one thing was clear, it was much colder than any of them had anticipated.

Lock cursed as he registered the cold against his wings, "It's colder than we thought. If you're sure your gods will listen, you should pray to them. We need it."

Tressa was at a loss, so she did what Lock asked and prayed. She prayed to every god's temple she could recall visiting: Jupiter, Venus, Mars, Juno, Vulcan, and Apollo.

They had just reached the altitude they needed to remain off the proto's radar when Vin felt something curl up between his legs. Vin focused on Taberi who was wide-eyed and still shaking from taking off.

He felt it again, as something curled around his upper thigh. Speaking up to be heard over the wind and wings, he asked, "Is there something happening between my legs?"

Taberi slowly turned his face toward Vin's. "I am very cold. I may have wrapped my tail around your leg." Vin didn't know what to say. He was so thrilled he could hardly contain himself. Taberi looked up at Vin again, smirking, "I guess we're even now."

Vin couldn't help it as he blurted out, "You can wrap your tail around whatever you want." Pausing to think about his words, he bit his lips together and decided he would stop talking before he embarrassed himself again. Taberi was stunned, but Vin could feel him wrap his tail around his leg much tighter. If he could just stop saying the wrong thing! Vin could have buried himself in the dirt over what just came out of his mouth. He had never been particularly good with his words, but he was on a down-hill roll.

Vin stopped his racing thoughts as Taberi lay his face against his chest, and he nearly melted inside as Taberi began to calm down, his heart leveling out and beating normally. He barely noticed the frost already forming on his wings.

Leaning down, Nera listened for Cinis. All she heard was faint whimpers, and she ran her hand over their head. She knew how painful this was for them, and the timing couldn't have been worse. She didn't understand how this little human had crawled into her heart, but she was overwhelmed by them. She had never had anyone who made her feel the way Cinis did. None of the Resper she had been with before compared in any sense to them. Cinis had done something to her, changed her in some definable way. Nera had spent years filling her life with meaningless hookups and draining blood cow after cow. She always had at least one tied up in her room, half dead. They had mended a wound in Nera she didn't even know she had.

Nera knew she had no room to complain about Lock and his eating habits, she had gleefully participated in many gruesome killings. When her prey was a particularly filthy human, depraved and ruthless, she loved to break them. Lock had taught her where she could cut holes into them, and they would bleed without dying. She and Lock played with their food often, but she felt they deserved it. The human in her arms was not that way. They were gentle and kind. Nera felt a strong urge to protect them and ensure they survived, but she was helpless in this situation. How could she have let this happen? She had hopelessly fallen for a defenseless fawn.

She leaned her ear back and over her wing to listen for Lock, and she could hear a crunch from the ice already forming on the edges of her wings.

A bit of ice fell away from Lock's wings, and he scowled as his wings ached from the cold. His wing was throbbing at the place where the bone was healing from his break. They were barely halfway into their journey, and Lock already struggled to keep moving. He was in bad shape now, meaning the last hour of this journey over the proto-bat territory would be impossible. Every flap of his wings brought more throbbing pain down his spine. He was not built for this; his wings were made for speed. The workouts they had done made a difference, but his agony grew with every down pull. *Why had we even considered this? Was Nera in as much pain?* He tried to shake his wings to dislodge the forming ice, but the action sent agony through his spine and legs.

Tressa heard Lock make a grunting noise as he shook his wings. She knew he was not doing well. His face was a picture of distress. Racking her brain, she tried to come up with something to say. She wanted to be motivating but wondered how she was trying her best to stay calm?

Another three hours of this went on before Lock began to miss a beat with his wings, sending him and Tressa dropping down. Lock fought to climb back up to altitude every time and she knew it was just costing him more energy. He had been flying with his eyes squeezed shut for the last thirty minutes, and Tressa began to fear they truly would not make it. After he dropped down a terrifying length and had to fight to find his place again, Tressa knew she had to do something. But what?

Her heart began to race in her chest, and Lock finally opened his eyes towards her. She did not have a way to help. They were pleading and desperate. That's when it struck her; he was *hungry*. Tressa reached up with her hand and lay it on the side of Lock's face. "Lock, I want you to bite me. I don't think you're going to make it unless you have something to help."

Lock's mouth dropped open as his voice rasped, "Please."

She pulled her leather jacket apart and yanked it down, exposing her neck to the bitter cold. She jolted with the shock of wind and hissed when he bit down on the place between her neck and shoulder. Lock sucked deeply and drew gulps of blood into his mouth, and the draining sensation was dizzying. Tressa did her best to slow her breathing as he finished and licked up the side of her neck. He had taken much more than ever before, and she understood now why he had always been so careful. He could have sucked her dry of blood in a matter of moments.

He trembled as he swallowed down the last drops of blood and licked his lips. Running his hands up to Tressa's face he cupped her head and brought his forehead down to hers as he panted. Tressa brought her lips to his and kissed him, tasting herself.

He pressed his face against hers. "Your blood tastes as if I'm drinking down air and life. Your skin always feels like fire against mine, and your heart is a drum drawing my soul into its rhythm. My existence before you was another life I can't seem to remember, one lost to time."

Nothing could have prepared Tressa for his words. She squeezed her eyes tight as she felt his trembling body calm and settle. He held her head to his chest as he breathed deeply, regaining a bit of strength. The agony in his wings was present, but it was no longer overwhelming him as Tressa's blood satiated his profound hunger. He vigorously shook his wings and much of the ice fell away, giving him a bit of relief.

From her place up front, Nera leaned her head back and released a hypersonic call to the other Respers that she had calculated their destination approaching. Her call was a desperately welcomed sound for the group. The long-range guards were struggling with all the gear they were hauling almost as much as those carrying Cinis, Tressa, and Taberi. Within a few moments, Nera began her descent. Each of the Respers followed her lead, angling their wings as they headed downward on the last part of the journey.

Vin leaned down so Taberi could hear him. "It's almost over. Nera signaled that we are descending." Vin felt as Taberi's tail curled up tighter, still wedged between them. Taberi's tail wrapped all the way around the bulge in Vin's pants, and Vin was not sure Taberi had any idea what he was doing. In fact, he knew Taberi was clueless, and Vin was NOT going to tell him. His penis and balls were quite cozy and warm at the moment. They were pretty much the only warm thing on his body. As they approached the ground, Vin wrapped his arms around Taberi as he angled to land in a clearing behind Nera and Lock. Nera and Lock landed first with the three guards right behind them. Each shook their wings, ice flying off them in every direction before slumping over and unloading their gear. Once all his bags were on the ground, Bensley approached Nera to help her with Cinis as Lock began removing the straps over Tressa.

When Vin landed, Taberi slumped in his arms after remaining tense for the last eight hours. Vin shook the remaining ice from his wings and unbuckled the top of the travel strap behind his neck and pulled it off him and Taberi before reaching down and loosening the lower strap. Vin sat Taberi's feet on the ground, and he grabbed his shoulders when he began swaying.

Vin rubbed his hands up and down Taberi's arms, "Are you alright?"

Taberi was so exhausted he could hardly stand without Vin's assistance. He had not unclenched his body the entire trip and was hardly able to speak, "I'm just tired."

Taberi tried to take a few steps and Vin caught him under his arms, "Nope, sit here and I'll get your bed ready."

Halso handed Vin Taberi's bed roll, and he found a tree branch to set up under. Taberi had been sleeping under him every night.

Vin turned to find Tressa pealing ice off Lock's wings as he knelt facing a tree. His hands were braced on the bark and his head hung down.

The rest of the group continued setting up camp as Nera tended to Cinis and Tressa helped Lock. There wasn't an option to have a fire being as close as they were to the protos territory though they would have all loved to feel the warmth.

Once Tressa had removed all the ice from Lock's wings, she pulled his healing balm out and applied it to the entire top of his wings. He guzzled a thermos of blood but hadn't moved otherwise. After Lock was able to turn and sit, she went to Nera. Nera had finished lying Cinis down and wrapping them in a bed roll when she took a few steps away and shook the last of the ice off her own wings. Tressa approached Nera with Lock's balm, "Do you need some help?"

Nera nodded, "Thank you. Cinis is halfway through the worst of it. They should begin recovering by tomorrow night. We will have to carry them tomorrow so that we can make it far enough away for a fire. They will need a large meal when they finally process all the venom."

After applying some balm to Nera's wings, Tressa made her way back over to Lock who still sat by the tree. "Do you need help getting in the tree?"

He shook his head, and since Tressa didn't know what else to do, she lay down on her bed roll next to him. Lock slowly turned to her and crawled next to her. She moved over as he crawled onto her bedding and slumped against the ground with his arm over her. His wings drooped over them, and as she turned her head to ask him if he was alright, and found he was already asleep.

FORTY-SEVEN

ALISOT – UTC BASE
DISCOVERY MISSION

All of the Resper were sore and had aching backs from the journey, but Cinis still needed to be carried. When Halso watched Nera struggle to lift herself off the ground, he helped her up and offered to carry Cinis.

There was no way Nera would have been able to carry them for another day now that the group was walking again. Nera helped hold Cinis for Halso as the two worked together to repurpose some of their flying straps to help hold them up. Halso was uncharacteristically gentle, and Nera was grateful they all understood how much Cinis meant to her. that all her guards had not questioned why she was treating this human like they were her everything.

Across the camp, Lock was bent over and trying to slip his pack between his sore wings when Tressa snatched it and tucked it under her arm. "You're not carrying that." Lock scowled at her.

Tressa gave him a particularly sassy look. "I'm not entirely useless. It weighs almost nothing anyway." She stuck her hand out to help him up, and he glared at her hand before taking it. He allowed her to help him up and she narrowed her eyes at him, "Why do you feel deceptively lightweight?"

Lock seemed intrigued to share Resper medical anatomy. "My bones are light and flexible. I don't weigh anywhere close to what a human would weigh of the same size."

"Are you telling me you weigh the same as me, but you're nearly twice my size?"

Lock thought a moment before answering, "I probably still outweigh you but not by a lot. We couldn't fly if we had solid, hard bones like humans. When we learn to fly as children, we fall out of the sky many times, and when we hit the ground we bounce. Usually, we are unharmed, but sometimes we will have some bruising."

It made a lot more sense why he and Nera had each struggled so much flying with a human strapped to them. They were by far the most exhausted that morning. Both of their wings drug the ground behind them as they walked around. Tressa patted Lock's bag under her arm, "I'm going to hang onto this one."

He quietly protested but complied as he attached his other bags to his hips. The group began their journey sluggish and never picked up much speed. It was all downhill as they descended the mountain, but that didn't seem to make much of a difference. The air warmed up as they hiked and for the first time in the mission, Tressa wasn't experiencing any pain in her feet. She knew it was too good to be true, and it would start up soon, but the break was needed and appreciated. The forest surrounding them was dense with a mix of foliage in the shade of jeweled greens and the floor was sprinkled with a rainbow of wild-flowers.

Every once in a while, Cinis would groan and Halso would rub their shoulder. By the time their bright daylight star had made its way past mid-day, Cinis had sat their head up and had begun moving without moans of pain. Cinis did their best to breathe through their tremendous pain but wasn't sure how much longer they could do it. It was beginning to affect their mind; imagery of their own death was their only comfort. With each imagined death, they were able to cling onto the edges of reality. As their skin warmed from the air, the venom began to recede, and awareness slowly returned. They cleared their throat, "Water?"

Halso turned to Nera next to him as she pulled a thermos of water out for Cinis. Nera held the thermos up for Cinis to drink. "Not too fast, your digestive system is going to need some time. I know you're starving, but it will cause you to vomit if you take in too much. You should begin feeling better in the next hour." She turned to the other and announce, "We can make camp here." Everyone began finding their places to sleep as Nera and Halso attended to Cinis.

Tressa and Lock both collapsed together on her bedroll as Nera started off into the woods for some firewood.

Bensley and Trajen searched the woods to find something to eat as Vin started a fire with some kindling. Nera appeared from the woods with her arms full of large branches and dumped them next to Vin. Vin could plainly see exhaustion was written all over her, "Why don't you rest until dinner?" Nera nodded briefly and made her way over to Cinis's bedroll before falling on her face next to

Cinis. Halso headed off to hang from a tree and guard the campsite as Vin finished up building the fire for cooking.

Taberi was sitting on his bedroll when Vin approached him. "Do you want to go with me to find a stream so we can boil some water? I can smell water not far from here."

Taberi took Vin's outstretched hand as he answered, "Sure." Vin helped him up and they headed in the direction of the stream, taking their time as they strolled through the woods.

Making conversation with Taberi was difficult, Vin decided as he searched for something to say. He hated surface conversation but was desperate to know more of his thoughts. Vin just had no idea where their middle ground would be. Taberi had lived such a different life than he had.

Unable to help it, Taberi saw a beetle and the urge to eat it was overwhelming. His long, sticky tongue shot out of his mouth and snatched it from the tree on the other side of Vin. Taberi slid his hand over his mouth as he chewed up the beetle and swallowed. He could not believe he had done that in front of Vin. That had been one of his dirty little secrets about being half Vultus, and he was mortified.

Vin halted and slowly turned to Taberi, "Was that your *tongue*?"

Taberi crunched again and swallowed hard as Vin continued, "Did you just eat a bug?"

Taberi, choked out his response, "I can't help it. It's the Vultus in me. When I see one, it's overwhelming."

Smirking, Vin couldn't contain himself and asked, "What else do you do with that tongue?" Taberi gasped as Vin slid his thick arm around his shoulders. Taberi looked up at Vin who was still smirking, but he could tell it was friendly gestures.

They continued on through the woods until Taberi heard the water running and nearly squealed thinking about stripping off his clothes and jumping in. Not thinking before he spoke, Taberi blurted, "We should rinse off in the stream."

When he realized what he said, Vin was already biting his lip. Taberi's heart raced as it sunk in. He had just invited the big sexy bat to get naked with him.

Oh gods! Was he ready for this? Fuck no he wasn't! He had never even had another person touch him. How was he going to go through with this? What had he done?!

Vin pulled him close whispering, "If you're not ready, that's alright, too."

It wasn't that. Taberi was dying for affection, especially Vin's. He grabbed his middle; he was so scared he might be sick.

Vin noticed his change in demeanor and stopped walking. Vin pulled away to face Taberi, "If you don't want this at all? I will understand. If you're just scared of me, and you think you need to be with me to be safe, that's not the case at all. I will leave you al-."

"No, that's not it," Taberi interrupted, unable to say what he wanted.

Vin nervously stepped away from Taberi and the absence left him reaching for Vin's hands. The moment their fingers touched Vin took a sharp breath, "I thought maybe you were just afraid?"

Taberi was so tired of being ashamed as he whispered, "My body is built different than a human, and well, I'm new at this."

Vin felt more nervous than ever, "I like different." Vin's

face fell as he registered the last part of what Taberi admitted, "Wait. Did you just say you are new at this?"

Closing his eyes, Taberi nodded, "I kissed someone once, but that's it."

With that, Vin thought he may come unglued, "Do you want this? Do you want me?"

Taberi couldn't nod fast enough, "Yes," and he swore he saw the tips of Vin's wings flutter and he wasn't sure Vin was breathing.

"Taberi, take your clothes off. Now," Vin commanded. He was out of breath and the end was a wheeze. Vin began stripping his jacket off as Taberi peeled out of his leathers faster than he's ever taken his clothes off.

With Taberi down to his briefs, Vin licked his lips, and he pointed to the ground in front of him. Taberi took the few steps to close the gap, and Vin ran his hands gently down Taberi's sides before he hooked his fingers in his briefs to pull them down. Taberi felt like he was running out of air. He could not recall a time when he had ever been this hard as his briefs fell at his feet. Pulling him close, Vin leaned down to kiss his shoulder. He gently kissed up Taberi's neck and when their lips met, Vin's heart stuttered. He kissed him back as Vin ran his hands down Taberi's chest again and his thumb grazed the fine line of hair running down the center of his abs. Vin wanted to explore every inch of this man with his mouth.

He tilted Taberi's head back to kiss a line down the center of his neck. When Vin reached his chest, he wrapped his arms around Taberi's waist leaned him back as he gently kissed his nipple. Taberi whimpered as Vin licked and kissed his nipple, then moving to the next and doing the same. He twirled his tongue over them, and Taberi was mad with need. He needed Vin to touch him so badly, he ached for it, almost to the point of true pain. Now that it was happening, each touch felt like a thousand at once.

Holding Taberi up, Vin leaned him further back as he kissed him down the center of his abs. Gently kissing below his navel, Vin continued down his body to right above Taberi's length. Vin licked him along his lower belly from hip to hip causing him to writhe in his arms before lying him down on the soft leaves below. Taking handfuls of cold water from the stream, he washed Taberi, causing him to squirm and shiver. Vin stroked his finger under Taberi's length, noticing a valley where he was used to feeling a seam.

Taberi took a breath, "Vin, I need to tell you something."

Vin paused and kissed up his side before answering, "Anything."

Taberi sat up on his elbows and looked down at his erect length, "It's a lot different than what you're used to."

Vin smiled at Taberi as he wrapped his fingers around his length. "I don't care. You're perfect the way you are." But Vin didn't know what would happen when he stroked Taberi's length a few times. Taberi started to explain but Vin leaned down and took his nipple into his mouth and swirled his tongue as he palmed his length. Vin hovered over him as Taberi trembled, trying to keep himself together and wanting to explain before it was too late.

Vin kissed his way across his chest, and Taberi was going to come undone. He couldn't take it anymore. Vin felt something happening to Taberi's length and he paused with his tongue still out and flicking Taberi's skin as he noticed what was happening. Taberi's penis split into two pulsating sides with soft spikes running down the center of the inside.

Vin reared back and yelped, "Well, that's new!"

Beaming, Vin brought his face up to Taberi's, "You mean you've been hiding that this whole time? Who would be upset about this? I get two for one!"

Taberi nearly sobbed with relief as Vin leaned down to kiss him, slipping his tongue in his mouth, and thoroughly tasting him. Vin then knelt down and used both of his hands to stroke Taberi's dual length. When Taberi arched off the ground, Vin leaned down and kissed him right below his sternum. Leaning his head back, Taberi shook as his release slammed into him. He could feel his colors shifting out of control as Vin stroked him until he jolted from overstimulation.

Taberi lay on the ground breathless as Vin sat next to him and stroked a finger down his side.

Having a tough time holding back his emotions as his thoughts came rushing back, Taberi struggled to calm his breath. Vin could sense his uncertainty and pulled him into his lap, continuing to rub his hands over Taberi's skin. Vin held him there for some time before Taberi turned to him uncertain, "What about you?"

Vin grinned back at him, "Today is about you, not me. You're not quite ready for my tastes yet." Taberi wasn't sure what that meant, but he hoped to find out.

After Vin washed himself, they redressed and filled the water jugs, then made their way back from the stream. They arrived to find the guards had killed two deer, and all the other Respers had already eaten. Nera passed Vin some blood to drink and when she did, she sniffed the air and smirked at him. He noticed and jabbed her in the ribs with his elbow.

FORTY-EIGHT

ALISOT – UTC BASE DISCOVERY MISSION

It took a few days, but they made it down the mountain and camp had been set for the night. Cinis and Nera had already curled up on their mat as Vin and Taberi sat close together next to the fire. Tressa stood behind Lock as she applied ointment to the top edge of his wings. "Thank the gods, we made it over those mountains. I've never prayed so much before."

Lock hissed as she touched a tender place, "Your gods didn't answer your prayers. You and your blood did."

Frozen behind him, she tried to decide if it was worth an argument, but after the days of hiking they just did, she was on edge and her temper maximized. She *knew* the gods had heard her. She could feel her skin burning. "How could you say that? I know Jupiter was there to help us. He is the God of weather and nature."

After thousands of years of atheism on Alisot, he couldn't take any more of the god talk. He regretted asking her to pray when they were flying. Lock shifted to face her. "Your God's don't exist."

Tressa dropped the ointment on the ground and stormed off into the woods. Frustration and fury tore through her as she boiled over. Lock let her go and planned on allowing her to cool off before he went looking for her. Tressa stomped through the trees and tears streamed down her face as she whispered, "He didn't mean that. The gods are real. They have to be." The gods had to be real! There was no other explanation for why the universe had been blasted into existence. It had been Jupiter who lifted the winds under Lock's wings. It had to have been. The god's had been the only ones who had kept her from losing hope back on Emendo. They had nothing else to believe in there except their gods.

Tressa was still too upset to return as she checked behind her and could no longer see the campsite. With a snarl, she turned back toward the open woods and kept walking. She walked for an hour before she finally collapsed on the ground with a sob. She reached down and grabbed a handful of small twigs and began breaking them, one by one. By the time she reached the last one, she heard a crunch behind her, and she dropped it.

Terror filled her, she had not been paying attention, and she was in the middle of the woods. Night had fallen, and she was alone.

"What's a pretty human like you doing on this planet?" A masculine voice she didn't recognize came from the darkness. She moved to leap forward, but she wasn't fast enough as a hand wrapped around her neck, and she was lifted off the ground.

A second man came out of the darkness. "Did you catch us something fun?"

The one who had ahold of her replied, "I believe I did. Who is going to go first?"

The man in front of her, easily Lock's size, reached up and grabbed her face, "I want this one first. You got to have that winged one first. This one is mine."

Tressa tried to grab a knife from her side, but the man in front of her grabbed her hand.

"Not happening." He pulled her knives out and tossed them into the woods.

She reared back and tried to kick the man behind her, and he hissed, "Fuck you bitch!" He brought his fist to the side of her head and struck her hard enough she had stars shoot across her vision. Memories of the last time she had been beaten flashed through her mind when she had been left bleeding and shoeless on the side of the road.

"Meck, she's all yours." The man shoved her to the ground on her back and pulled her arms up and held them.

Tressa shrieked, "No!"

Meck leaned down and began unbuckling her pants, and she kicked her legs, as a scream released from her throat.

Just as she leaned her head back to shriek again, Meck shoved a cloth in her mouth and struck her once more in the face. This time she was too dizzy to tell up from down as she felt as her pants being ripped down. Tears sprouted in her eyes, and she cried into the cloth as Meck climbed over her.

She desperately screamed through the cloth as she felt him take her leg and forced it up. Tressa fiercely kicked at him with everything she had in her, landing one kick against his chest.

A rush of cool air blew over her exposed flesh, and she brought her head up to find Meck gone.

The man holding her arms down disappeared in a flurry. What was happening?

A sickly wet sound was followed by a blood curdling scream. Tressa pulled the cloth from her mouth and flipped around to see Meck stuck to a tree with a knife through his shoulder. She slowly turned and found Lock holding the other human man up by his neck. He pulled a long knife out and held the man against the bark as he slammed the knife through the top of his chest, pinning him to the tree. The man growled and tried to grab at the knife as Lock rushed to Tressa.

She had pulled her leather pants back on, but she had fallen back on the ground, trying to regain her balance.

Lock fell to his knees before her and took her face into his hands, "Are you alright? Did they strike you? Did they penetrate you? I need you to answer me clearly."

Tressa nodded, "They hit me, but you arrived here in time." She trailed off as tears poured from her eyes.

Lock leaned down and kissed her forehead and whispered, "I'm going to play with my dinner tonight. Do you want me to call Nera to take you back to camp first?"

Tressa knew precisely what he meant, and she looked at him through the tears filling her eyes as she boldly answered, "I want to stay." Something inside of her spun out of control. She needed to see these two men bleed. Her inherent fear of Lock's violence changed in the matter of seconds. What was once terror and disgust, was now a thrill at what Lock would do, at the pain he would inflict. This wasn't the first time she had been physically assaulted. It commonly happened on the streets of Emendo. Retribution had never been served before, and she couldn't wait to see the blood smeared on Lock's face.

She felt euphoric over the idea of her all-consuming protector devouring her enemies.

Lock wiped her tears away and kissed each of her eyelids, "I was hoping you would say that."

Lock stood and casually stretched his arms over his head before approaching Meck who was hopelessly clawing at the knife in his shoulder.

Meck whispered, "Jupiter save me."

Standing before Meck, Lock licked his lips before purring, "The only god here tonight is *me*." Lock pulled a long knife from his side and lifted Meck as he screamed, stabbing it through his other shoulder and pinning him back against the tree.

Meck cried out in agony as Lock reached down and yanked at his pants. Once Lock had them down, he pulled a small knife from his belt and began slowly sawing off Meck's penis as he released unending, gurgling screams. After Lock cut off his penis, he lifted it to show him before shoving it into Meck's mouth. Lock wrapped a gag around Meck's face as his screams became piteous sobs.

Lock tipped his head to the side and tapped a knife against his chest, "Now what should I eat first?"

Lock knelt down by the man's thigh and stuck his knife under his skin and sliced a long layer of skin away as Meck screamed and fought against the tree.

He could hear the other man begin to sob; Lock made sure they were close enough they could see one another.

Lock peered up at Meck, "Don't die too fast. We are just getting started."

He took his knife and began cutting away the thigh muscle on Meck's leg as he gurgled and cried. When he had removed a large slab of muscle, Lock stood up and bit into it. He tore at the meat and swallowed it down. Meck shook violently before his eyes slowly closed as his heart stopped.

"I told you not to die too fast." Lock tossed away the chunk of the man's leg muscle as he turned to the other man.

The man whimpered and sobbed as Lock faced him, "It wasn't my idea! It was Meck!"

Lock tilted his head to the side and asked, "What is your name?"

"It's Perte. I swear to you it was Meck. He made me do it!" Perte's heart rate was soaring.

Closing in on the trembling man Lock asked Tressa, "Tressa, is Perte a liar?"

Tressa was standing and watching, "Not only is he lying to you, he and Meck admitted they raped and murdered a Resper."

Lock sniffed the air and could identify not one, but traces of two female Resper scents on Perte. Unable to hold back his rage, Lock sliced deep into Perte's abdomen and disemboweled him. His intestines spilled out onto the ground as Perte trembled against the tree. Lock reached inside of him and ripped out his heart, holding it up to his face before leaning back and pouring the blood from the still beating heart into his gaping mouth.

Perte's eyes froze open in horror as Lock ripped into the human's heart with his teeth.

When Lock finished eating the man's dripping heart, he turned to Tressa. He wasn't sure what he was expecting to find, but it certainly wasn't her standing calmly next to him paying witness to every single thing he had done. He studied how she was standing, her heart rate, and the way she was nearly panting. With blood dripping from his face,

Lock sniffed the air and tilted his head to the side in disbelief.

Tressa's body was radiating heat, and the scent of her sweat brimmed with excitement, not a hint of fear. She had enjoyed watching them suffer.

He reached out with his blood covered hands expecting her to flinch, but she fell into them. The blood around Lock's mouth dripped onto Tressa's hair as she pressed her face into his soaked leather jacket. In the midst of the carnage, Lock dropped to the ground and pulled Tressa into his lap. She curled into him, and he held her there, stroking her back.

"I'll never stop you from praying to your gods," he whispered over her, guilt filling him.

She shook her head, whispering, "The gods didn't answer my prayers tonight. You did. You were there before I ever prayed."

Lock angled her face up so he could form the image in his mind. Tressa's face was already swelling, and his heart broke.

Tressa could see his concern, "Please don't look at me like that."

Lock furrowed his brow, "Shhh, I do not pity you. I am assessing your injuries, and I can't help it if I care."

Tressa closed her eyes, "How did you know?"

Lock brushed her hair away from the blood dripping down her face, "I heard you and followed your scent. You're not leaving my side again. Not ever."

FORTY-NINE

ALISOT – UTC BASE
DISCOVERY MISSION

The flitting birds chirping in the woods proved too cheery for the camp as they continued on their journey. A thick fog had just lifted and most of the Resper were struggling to move through the dense woods.

Up front Nera stopped and turned to the group, "Bensley, I need you up front."

Beside Nera, Cinis whispered, "I can lead. I can see pretty well."

Nera answered, "Bensley can see light and shadows better than the rest of the Resper in our group, plus he has a particularly keen sense of smell. I want you staying with me as we pass through the woods. Remember how I said protos like to ram?"

Cinis relented, rubbing their still unsettled stomach, "Point taken. I'll stay in the middle."

Behind them, a bruised Tressa and a particularly tense Lock had been silent after what had transpired the night before. Every Resper in the camp knew something sinister happened when Lock returned covered in the scent of human blood, human blood which clearly was not Tressa's.

Thunder cracked overhead, and Tressa jumped. Lock threw his arm around her and tugged her into him. "Do we need to take a rest?"

Tressa shook her head, "No, I'm alright, just startled. Lock didn't buy it for a moment. "I promise. I am alright. Back home I had been assaulted on the street more than a few times," Tressa admitted, trying to make him feel better but quickly realizing it was not the right thing to say.

Now boiling, Lock pressed his lips against her ear, whispering, "We will just have to find a way to Emendo so I can eat them, too." The old Tressa would have paled at his words, but instead, a thrill snaked down her spine. Something had changed, in her, and between them. She couldn't control herself as images of him covered in blood and avenging her sprouted in her mind. Sensing her change in disposition, Lock pulled her close to him and gently kissed her temple.

From the back, Vin asked, "Nera isn't there a road somewhere ahead?"

Nera answered, "Yes, if I had to guess, we have a half mile until we will reach it."

Taberi asked, "How do you gauge distance with no eyesight?"

It dawned on Vin Taberi likely never attended school, so to explain, Vin tapped below his ear. "We have combined precision and long-distance echolocation. When I send out a hypersonic sound, the time it takes for the sound to return is how I determine distance. Just like your eyes, my ears and brain work together to interpret the sound as imagery. The closer I am to an object, the better I can see it in my head."

"I guess it's not the same as me just closing my eyes. Now that I've said that out loud, I realize how silly it is," Taberi said, his mind blown.

Speaking of his sight, it struck Taberi that he wouldn't have to hide from Vin all his differences. He had been ridiculed by the other lab children who seemed fully human, then by anyone who noticed in his adult life. He seemed human which meant when humans came close to him, they would mock him, once they saw his tail or how his eyes were a smooth sphere and could move independently of one another. Vin, however, something about that made him feel at ease. Vin wouldn't put him down. Vin likely wouldn't ever notice, just like he also wouldn't notice his skin changing color. Something told him Vin would like those things about him, and his heart swelled.

When they reached the road, Nera retook the lead and turned left to head south just as a soft rain began. After a few miles, Trajen lifted his face to the sky and sniffed the air. "Nera, I smell a structure head of us, off to the left of the road. It's abandoned."

Inhaling deeply, Nera agreed, "Some rotting wooden boards, a fireplace, and a berry that grows up north. Good catch."

They turned down a side road within a few minutes and followed it for a while, before they passed through a gate with a guard station and just around a few trees was a large, traditional Resper homie. As they approached the front door, Nera pointed to the insignia of a tree above the door. "This is the former residence of the house of Ferosi. If I had to guess, this home is over six hundred years old. They abandoned it and moved south along with the rest of the west coast about twenty years ago." She tried the door, and it was locked, so she turned to Trajen, "Can you fly around to their wing gym and see if you can break in?"

He did as she instructed and within a few minutes, he unlocked the massive wooden front doors. The home opened to a formal seating area before leading to a lush garden in the center. The glass that had been the ceiling at one time, now lay shattered all over the tile floor in the center of the home. Scratches from protos' claws ran down the walls of the courtyard, and Lock pointed them out. "We should take care not to attract any attention. If they've been here before, they could return at any time."

Everyone silently agreed as they all headed up a wide set of stairs to the right of the front door and dispersed to find rooms to sleep in. Heading to the rooms facing the front of the house, Lock and Tressa took the first room as Vin and Taberi went in the second. The guards each selected a room facing the center of the home's courtyard. Nera and Cinis made their way to the main room of the home on the back, outer corner. The room had sparse decor, like much of it had been taken when the family left. It was dusty but otherwise clean. Cinis opened the closet and found clean blankets as Nera lay her bags next to the couch.

Like many Resper homes, this one had no beds. There would likely be fold out cots somewhere in a storage room, since most of the blood Resper sleep upside down and had no need for a bed. This room had been shared by a couple; the sleeping bar was long enough for two. Cinis spread out their bedroll under the bar and added the blankets they found in the closet on the floor.

After briefly running a faucet in the bathroom, Nera came up from behind them with some towels she found. "I'll see if someone can find the water furnace. This home doesn't have gas lines, but it does have running water. I bet we can have hot water in less than thirty minutes."

Recalling the water tower outside, Cinis nearly danced over the idea of a bath. "I would probably do some highly questionable things to have a bath right now."

Parting her lips and using her hypersonic range, Nera called out for Halso. He popped his head in her door moments later.

"Can you find the water furnace and get it running?" Nera asked as she sat on the couch and began digging in her bag. As Halso nodded and shut the door, Nera tossed Cinis a bag of dried fruit, and they greedily devoured it. Nera guzzled down a thermos of blood before storing it back in her bag.

Cinis began undressing, and Nera stopped and listened to every second of it, meticulously building the image of them in her mind. They unbuckled their jacket and slid it off, revealing the thin cropped t-shirt underneath. Pulling off their leather pants, they blew the dust off a small table before laying their pants over it. Nera couldn't tear her attention from Cinis's round behind, and she was filled with the desire to sink her teeth into it.

Cocking her head to the side, Nera demanded, "Come to me."

Cinis carefully approached Nera and stood in front of her.

Nera reached up and slid her hands around Cinis's waist, pulling them closer. She ran her tongue up Cinis's side, causing them to gasp and tense. Nera gently took Cinis's hands and held them behind their back with one hand while she reached up their shirt to gently stroke her thumb over their nipple. She leaned forward and whispered against their skin, "I am lost. My heart begs for you to stay, but my mind demands for you to be sent off, to be rescued from here."

Cinis moved to straddle her, "Please, Nera. I'll do anything to stay with you."

Nera held them at arm's length for a moment then lifted Cinis shirt off and used it to tie their hands behind their back. She guided Cinis to sit down on her legs. "Don't move." Nera knew exactly where Cinis loved to be touched, whether they admitted it or not. She rubbed her hands gently up Cinis's sides, and they gasped as she brought up them up to their needy peaks. Cinis head leaned back as Nera circled their nipples with the tip of her finger.

Nera leaned in and kissed Cinis's chest, "The hot water is working."

She scooped Cinis up and padded into the grand bathroom, setting them down on the edge of a bathtub. She didn't turn on the bath, but instead turned on a stone tiled shower similar to one they had back at her home. The water fell from the wide spout like a heavy rain shower. In moments steam billowed from the open shower as Nera stripped off her leathers. She hooked a finger for Cinis to come to her, and they complied. As they neared Nera, she untied their hands and pointed to the floor, "Lie down with your head here."

Cinis did as instructed, and Nera leaned over them, re-tying their hands with their shirt. She pulled their hands above their head and slipped the shirt over a small hook meant to anchor a curtain. Cinis's heart raced wild with need as heat formed low in their belly and they resisted the urge to rub their thighs together. Positioned under the falling water with their eyes closed, sensations were intensified. Something cold squirted onto their chest and stomach, causing their breath to catch.

Cinis shivered as Nera spread the floral scented soap over their body. She took her time, rubbing the soap gently over Cinis's stretched body. Nera savored feeling Cinis's fit, athletic body tremble under her hands. She ran her fingers over Cinis's nipples, causing them to arch off the floor. Nera moved down their body and thoroughly washed them between their legs. When her finger grazed Cinis bud, they tensed and released a breathy whimper. Nera couldn't resist teasing and toying with Cinis's body. She loved to drive Cinis mad. It was her favorite thing to do. "Are you ready, my little human?" Nera asked as she ran her fingers delicately down Cinis's sides.

Cinis leaned their head back, and all but cried out, "Yes, please, Nera, I'm begging you."

Nera grinned as she leaned over and took one of Cinis nipples into her mouth, and they shook with anticipation. Unable to help it, Cinis's thighs rocked, and Nera pressed her hand down on their leg. Cinis pulled at the shirt holding their arms as their body squirmed under Nera. Knowing she couldn't keep edging Cinis forever, she finally moved down their body and ran a finger down the center of their heat.

Nera licked the water from the valley of their hip before sliding her tongue between Cinis's thighs, eliciting a sweet whimper. She wanted to hear that sound a thousand more times. No, she needed to hear it forever, however long that may be.

Grabbing their hips, Nera ran her long tongue through Cinis heat again, this time circling their most sensitive place. Nera devoured Cinis, drawing their Little bundle of nerves into her mouth and mercilessly flicking it with her tongue. Cinis didn't just shatter. They imploded with a silent cry.

Their body quivered uncontrollably as Nera continued, taking them toward a second round of pleasure. This time taking longer to reach their climax, Nera held the rhythm and didn't allow Cinis to move their hips under her iron grip. She lifted them up high enough so only their shoulders still touched the floor. They squeezed their legs around Nera's head and arched their body up as the second wave slammed into them like an earthquake. Their mind scrambled as their body could only comprehend pleasure. Cinis leaned their head back and cried out unintelligible nonsense trying to speak as Nera licked them through a blissfully intense orgasm. When she finally pulled away, they collapsed, panting on the shower floor.

Cinis heard Nera walk into the bedroom and wondered what else she could possibly have planned for their spent body. Quickly returning after rifling around in her bag, Cinis felt Nera hover over them.

She kissed Cinis in the center of their chest as they felt her hand feel for their entrance. They felt Nera line up with them, was she going to? Cinis didn't get to finish that thought as Nera slowly entered their heat.

The toy Nera was using was the perfect size and shape for Cinis and their breath caught as she hit the sensitive place inside just right. Thrusting her hips, Nera once again brought Cinis to the edge of a precipice of pleasure. She leaned forward and rocked into them, Cinis leaned their face to the side as they curled their body, fighting their tied wrists above their head.

Cinis fell over the edge a third time, their body hardly able to take the pleasure. They released a breathy moan, giving Nera the sound she was craving.

Nera tossed away the toy and reached up to free Cinis hands. They lowered their hands to wipe the water from their eyes. Cinis moved toward Nera and slid onto her lap, leaning their head against her shoulder. Nera rubbed her thumb against Cinis jaw, "I don't think I can live without you, my little human."

Hearing her words, Cinis wrapped their arms around Nera.

She kissed Cinis on the forehead, "When Respers mate, it's for life."

Cinis's eyes flew open, and they sat up. "Are you saying what I think you're saying?"

The corners of Nera's lips tipped up, "My love, I want you to be my mate."

Overjoyed, Cinis leaned forward to kiss Nera and whispered against her lips, "I need to touch you."

Nera closed her eyes and leaned back in the water as Cinis straddled her. They cupped Nera's full breasts, gently rubbing her taut nipples. Cinis caressed down her luscious body and found Nera slick and ready. They twirled their finger around her bud, sending a tingling fire burning through her body with the pleasure of Cinis's touch.

Nera didn't need much more than a few strokes before she was shattering and a shiver of pleasure slithered up her spine.

FIFTY

ALISOT – UTC BASE
DISCOVERY MISSION

As they neared the area around the coast, the weather began to shift, and the air became sticky and warm. The group stored away their jackets in their bags, and they all wore thin, sleeveless t-shirts.

Abandoned stores, apartment buildings, and homes became more frequent along the side of the road. Other wide roads branched off leading to more homes and businesses. They traveled through the sprawling suburban area until late in the day when Nera found an old market.

The market was set up for individual vendors, so it was fairly bare inside. The space large enough for everyone and metal bars suspended over the vendor tables. The bars once held up items such as slabs of meat or bags of fruit and vegetables but would provide the Resper a place to sleep. The guards moved the tables back while Tressa, Cinis, and Taberi made up their pallets under the bars and pulled out their dwindling bags of dried food. Even with the roasted meats they've been eating, the humans supplies were dwindling since Taberi joined the group.

Lock knelt on the bedroll next to Tressa and pulled out one of his last thermoses of blood. They would need to go foraging and hunting before the end of the next day if they wanted to keep everyone fed.

Bensley sniffed the air and made his way off down a dark hallway in the back of the market space. When he reemerged, he held a wooden box and brought it over the group. He sat it down and opened the box lid, "A vendor must have left it behind in the storage room. It's packaged cured and dried meats with jars of cucumber pickles." Tressa all but flew from her spot by Lock and dove into the box. She grabbed two jars of pickles and two packs of dried meat before returning to her spot on her bedroll.

Lock adjusted his wings so he could sit on the ground next to Tressa. She handed him the jars to open as she tore open one of the packages of meat. Tressa reached into the bag and took out a piece of meat and brought it to her open mouth. Lock snatched it out of her hand, "You do not want to eat that."

Horrified, Tressa shoved the bag away from herself and gulped, "That's human meat isn't it." On the bedroll next to hers, Taberi gagged and slapped his hands over his mouth as Lock also took the bag from him. Smiling Lock tossed the dried meat in his mouth and licked his lips before taking another piece from the bag.

Tressa repeatedly blinked at him trying to find her words, "Thank you for not letting me eat that." Lock laughed to himself as he popped another chunk of human meat into his mouth.

Shocked they hadn't heard a word from Cinis about it, Tressa leaned forward to see why. Cinis and Nera were entangled with one another so intensely they had both drowned out the rest of the world. Since the group left the

Resper mansion that they stopped at a few days prior, they had been entranced by one another.

Lock pulled Tressa back and placed his lips to her ear whispering, "I think Nera asked Cinis to be her mate back at the Ferosi house."

Nera answered Lock without taking her attention from Cinis, "I did. Mind your own business, droopy wing."

Lock leaned his head back and replied, "Speak for yourself spewing spangler."

Vin braced himself as he laughed, "I forgot all about the tiara she had on!"

"Both of you can drink bowel blood," Nera retorted.

Vin and Lock laughed as Tressa sat confused. Cinis grimaced, remembering the story Nera had shared with them. Tressa noticed their knowing expression, and now too curious to stand it, Tressa asked, "Where did those nicknames come from? I can't be the only one who doesn't know."

Lock sighed, "Mine was from when I was a kid. I had a bad habit of dragging my right wing. Nera's is much worse. We all drank too much liquor one night, if I remember correctly, and we had given Nera a little coronation ceremony with a tiara after she ranted about her linage being the old royal line. We had a meeting with the head of a great house the next day, so when we woke up hungover and deep in the woods, we had to fly back home. As we passed over the house, aiming for the wing gym around the back, Nera threw up on our special guest as he walked inside. She had the tiara on the entire time and had forgotten all about it." Tressa, Cinis, and Vin all laughed with Lock as Nera groaned.

Without a warning, Trajen leaped off the table he was

sitting on and pulled his knives from his belt as he gave a hypersonic alert to the group that they had company.

The Resper leapt to their feet with their wings snapped tightly behind them. They each drew their weapons and formed a protection circle around the now standing humans. The guards moved into position in front of Nera, Lock, and Vin as seven massive protos charged at them from the hallway.

The Resper were outnumbered, and Tressa pulled one of the long knives from Cinis's belt. Lock spun and seethed, "Don't you fucking dare, Tressa!" Before he turned back to block the incoming assault. Ignoring him, Tressa held her knife up and crouched in front of a terrified Cinis and Taberi. Steadying her breath, she swallowed down her terror and gripped her knife with all her strength.

When the first proto-bat rammed into Trajen and Halso, the chaos began. Trajen hit the ground as the snarling bat reached down and ripped out his throat. Blood gushed from the wound and Trajen shook as he gargled and choked to death on his own blood. Beside him Halso sliced at the proto pinning him just as another slammed into Bensley. Halso stabbed the bat in the side as it clawed at his chest. The massive bat tore open his flesh as Halso screamed and stabbed it again, this time higher in its rib cage.

As the three Domitia's prepared to engage the next line of protos leaping over the downed guards, Tressa squared off with a blood dripping proto-bat behind them that had slipped through the others. She raised her knife as it charged for her and she planted her boots firm on the ground, leaning forward. Tressa remembered what Lock had mentioned, *I don't weigh nearly what I seem.* It echoed in her mind as she dropped down low and angled her knife upward. She heard both Lock and Nera cry out in pain as the proto rushed for her.

Clenching her jaw, Tressa shifted her weight forward as she crouched down low and thrust her knife up into the gut of the proto. The creature reached down as it slammed into her, slicing up her left bicep as she plunged the knife into its abdomen. Tressa ripped the knife down through the gut of the beast as it fell over her.

The force of its body crashing into her sent them both into Cinis and Taberi huddled behind her. Cinis was ready and slid their knife across the throat of the beast as it frantically clawed at them. Blood poured from the bat's mouth and neck as it slumped over. Taberi yelped at the blood and entrails spilling over all of them. Tressa rolled out from under the bats legs and checked to be sure Cinis and Taberi were uninjured before grabbing her bleeding arm and hissing at the pain. Wiping away the proto blood dripping in her eyes, she scanned the room and found Lock standing with a ripped open thigh. He leaned over a dying proto to plunge a knife in its throat, making the final kill.

Vin and Nera began assessing one another's wounds while Bensley and Halso crouched over Trajen's lifeless body. A long gash ran down Halso's calf, dripping on the floor. Bensley had some minor scratches, but was otherwise alright. Kicking away what looked like a kidney, Cinis turned around and helped Taberi, who was still in shock and unable to speak.

Tressa wiped her bloody face on her shirt as she met Lock halfway. He slid his thumb along her jaw, seeming to study her. Lock shook his head as he licked his bloody lips. "Your kill was impressive. I have to admit, I think I'm prouder than I am pissed off this time." Tressa grinned with blood smeared on her teeth and Lock pulled her in for a kiss before raising her arm. He licked the oozing wound, and it began tingling.

Tressa couldn't help but ask, "How does that work?"

"Enzymes and hormones." he answered as he continued to run his tongue along her wound. His leg was dripping onto the floor when he finally acknowledged it, "Nera, I need help with my leg." She came over and licked along the rip as he hissed, "I have a leather repair kit in my pack. Take off your damaged clothes and set them by Tressa's bed."

Behind them, Vin found a distraught Taberi. Taberi's eyes spun in shock. He held his tail with a white knuckled grip and his grayed body shook. Vin helped Taberi find a place to sit and wrapped him in a blanket. He then called over Cinis to sit with Taberi while he and Nera began cleaning up the intestines and kidney that had fallen out of the proto Tressa killed. Once the guts were back inside the beast, Vin dragged it away.

After a long, grotesque clean up, the two remaining guards reinforced the back of the building as the rest of the group tried to regain a sense of calm. Taberi's bedrolls had been saturated with blood, so he was curled up in Vin's lap, who had reclined up against a wall. Vin's wrapped around them both sheltering the still shocked Taberi. Tressa thought Vin looked worn out, but he seemed content.

When the guards had discovered the protos entry point, they returned with news. Halso approached Nera with a grim expression. "There are hundreds of them flying over, but we have the building secured now. Bensley will watch the back, and I'm going to find a position up front."

Nera nodded as she tugged Cinis into her. They were still shaking with fear, but as the adrenaline faded, the exhaustion hit. Within a few moments, they faded off to sleep, and Nera lay them down on their bedroll before perching above them.

Lock curled up with Tressa, who wiggled into his warmth behind her, before wrapping his wing over her. "I feel so bad for Bensley and Halso, they seemed close to Trajen." Tressa whispered.

Lock inhaled roughly, "The three have been inseparable since childhood. They will mourn him as a brother."

Tressa couldn't hold back as tears sprouted in her eyes and silently wept until she, too, slept.

FIFTY-ONE

ALISOT – UTC BASE
DISCOVERY MISSION –
YONIC CITY

Bensley and Halso towered over the freshly piled mound of dirt as the rest of the group stood back. They had just finished burying Trajen, and the two heartbroken guards sniffled as they quietly spoke their goodbyes over their lost friend.

Matching their moods, the sky was overcast, but balmy, as they solemnly walked down the desolate streets. After a brief warm rain, the sky cleared, and a sticky humidity set in.

"I can't tell where we need to head with all these buildings around. I need to fly around so I can plot our course." Nera announced as she stepped away from the group and flew into the sky. After circling above, Nera landed by the group, "The main city buildings are this way." She headed to the southwest, and the group followed behind her.

After a few miles Vin offered, "Lock, aren't your wings healed up? Why don't we just fly there?"

Nera stopped and turned to Lock, who shrugged, "Why not? It will save us half of a day of travel time."

Taberi was the only one who didn't seem on board as his skin changed color, wildly rotating from light cream to dark brown with green splotches and back to cream.

While Vin couldn't see Taberi's outward reaction, he could detect his increased heart rate. Vin pulled Taberi into him and assured him, "It's alright. Just shut your eyes, and we will be there in no time." Taberi reluctantly crawled up Vin's body and clung to him as the rest of the group swapped gear around and prepared to launch into the sky. Once they were ready, Nera took a running start and took off gently with Cinis wrapped around her body. Vin and Lock followed Nera's lead as the guards shot into the sky, finding their positions above the rest of the group.

An uneventful short flight ended with Nera angling down to a sprawling building with columns lining the front entryway. She landed by the stairs leading to the great building and set Cinis down. Lock's boots hit the pavement behind Nera and asked, "Is this what I think it is?"

Nera nodded as she answered, "Yes. It's the Alitos Galactic Library that the First Humans built when they were trying to sway us into trusting them."

When everyone was on the ground, and they were sure they had not been spotted and followed, the group climbed the stairs that wrapped around the building. One of the main doors of the library hung to one side from a broken hinge. Halso moved it out of the way to allow everyone to file in before he wedged it in the door frame from inside. He blocked it with a heavy table before jogging to catch up. They entered the main library, an oval shaped room. Along the walls were recessed bookcases and a mezzanine balcony spiraled up seven levels to a glass dome ceiling.

The library was breathtaking, and Tressa couldn't help it as she ran her hands over the intricately carved balustrade. It struck her how smooth the woods finish texture was. How could any of the Respers see how incredible this building was if every surface is smooth? She could feel Lock behind her, so she asked, "I think this library may not be as beautiful to you as it is to me."

With his curiosity spiked, Lock asked, "Why do you say that?"

Tressa leaned into his warmth, "Every surface in the Domitia and Ferosi homes had a unique texture. The surfaces here are all smooth and polished."

Lock reached out and ran his fingers over the carved wood. "You're right. I can't see a lot of detail in my mind. It's not clear." Intrigued, Lock approached the intricately carved edge of the bookshelves and angled his head as he felt along the wood. He turned back to Tressa with his hand still resting on the edge of the bookshelf. "It's almost as if the First Humans who funded the build for this library, made it this way for a reason. This was a primarily fruit bat city before Alisot fell."

Hearing their conversation Nera butted in, "We should stop speculating. We know they built it this way as part of their ploy to make the fruit Respers develop a greater desire for sight. If we stayed in here long enough, I'm sure we could find evidence of the humans implying the sight of eyes is standard or superior."

Tressa agreed, "This smells just like the First Humans." Raising her eyes to the ceiling, she noticed something written on a plaque on the fourth floor. It appeared to be *flat*. Tressa took Lock's hand as Nera headed off to find the map room and led him up the angled balcony until they reached the giant plaque.

"Lock, can you read what is written on this plaque," Tressa asked.

He scowled, "I can't find any words. It's too smooth."

Tressa bit her lip before she read it off, "Alitos Galactic Library Number sixty-seven, funded by the First Humans. This library was built to show the Resper that humanity is grand, and we bring prosperity to their world. The First Humans seek out a long-lasting alliance with the Resper for the benefit of the Galactic Center and humankind everywhere."

Lock repeated the last part, "For the benefit of the Galactic Center and humankind everywhere. Not for the benefit of the Resper. They spelled out what they thought of us on a plaque inside the very peace offering they built."

Disgust filled Tressa, and she acknowledged, "I understand why you hate humans so much. We, as a people, are cruel and exploitive. We destroyed your beautiful world."

Lock wrapped his arms around her as he purred, "It sounds like we're perfect for each other."

Scoffing, Tressa replied, "I'm starting to think out of Resper and humans, humans are the real monsters."

Lock paused and angled his head, listening, "Let's go. Nera found the map room."

Heading down, passing by thousands of books, Tressa vowed to herself she would work on her reading and writing again with Cinis. They were always offering to teach her, but Tressa didn't care before. She believed she already knew enough. Now, passing thousands of books is dawned on her what she was missing out on. Even if it meant forcing Cinis to author short stories so she could read, she was going to make it happen.

Following Lock, they passed by the front door again and made their way down a darkened hallway. Natural light came from around a door at the end of the hall, and Lock reached for the handle to open it.

Nera, Cinis, Vin, and Taberi were all searching through stacks and piles of thick relief maps. Nera didn't look up as she spoke, "We are searching for map, six ninety-four."

Tressa went to work reading labels on the sides of the three feet by three feet maps. The labels were in Latin and duplicated in the raised Resper symbols. A few hours passed by, and they hadn't had any luck in finding the map, but there were three more relief map storage rooms to search through. Each of the maps represented a portion of the Alisot planet. They just needed the one for where they were. Nera knew it was somewhere inside the city. She just didn't know where exactly and hoped there would be some kind of clue on the map.

Halso appeared with a basket filled with fruit. "There is an overgrown orchard in the city gardens next door. Bensley has two more baskets, and he's heading to a store across from the library to see if they have any gas. He's going to bake some of the fruit to dry it."

Nera nodded, "Thank you. I know you haven't slept, so when Bensley returns, Vin and I will take early watch." Halso seemed relieved as he set the basket of stone fruit down and went to join Bensley. Starving, Tressa was already half through a peach slurping up the juice running down her arm before the door shut behind Bensley. Lock reached around her and bit into a plum just to pucker his lips.

Lock chewed a few times before asking, "You really like this? It's just sugar?" Tressa stared at him like he was stupid and licked up another trickle of juice sliding down her forearm.

Cinis came up and grabbed two apricots before biting

into one and groaning with pleasure at the flavor. Nera was behind them and snatched one of the apricots from them, taking a bite. She grimaced and had to make herself swallow. "No, thank you," Nera handed Cinis back the rest of the apricot. Taberi reached in and took a handful of cherries and a plum before sitting down in a chair and meticulously eating each cherry in tiny bites to avoid chomping on the pit. By the time they finished their meal, Tressa could hardly inhale a full breath.

Taberi rubbed his stomach as he admitted, "I have never been this full before."

Next to him, Vin asked, "Are Bensley and Halso going to hunt tonight?"

Nera peered up at Vin and shook her head. "They need to rest. You and I have first watch tonight." Vin's mouth dropped open. He was starving and out of blood. That meant he would have to feed from Taberi. This was *not* good. Lock patted Vin on the head as he and Tressa headed to the door following Cinis and Nera. They would all need some privacy as they fed on their partners, it was almost a guarantee a feeding also meant sex.

That was the only respite Vin had as he turned to an already wildly nervous Taberi. He already knew something was wrong as Vin noticed his tail curled up tightly. When the door shut, the words all but raced out of Taberi's mouth, "What are you not telling me? What is about to happen?" There was a bench at the end of the room by a wall of windows looking out onto a lush, overgrown garden outside. Vin took Taberi's hand and led him to the bench. Vin slid his hand on Taberi's thigh, "I'm sorry. I wish I had more time to make you feel comfortable about this. I am starving right now and because Trajen died, Halso and Bensley aren't hunting tonight."

Taberi knew Vin couldn't see it, but his skin was rotating color so rapidly his skin color was blinking, "Are you saying you're going to make me give you, my blood?"

Vin eased a panicking Taberi into his chest, "I won't force you. I would rather go hungry."

Taberi's heart broke, "Vin I want to help you, but I'm just so fucking scared. I hate being half Vultus. They're such *cowards*."

Vin kissed Taberi's head, whispering, "What if I told you I could make it feel incredible and every Resper's wet dream is to feed and fuck at the same time. If we do this, it will be all about you."

Taberi reared back with his wide eyes pivoting wildly. "That sounds equally fantastic and terrifying."

Vin took his hand gently and asked, "Do you trust me?" Taberi thought long and hard before he gave Vin a slight nod. Vin smirked as he breathed, "I need you to say it."

Taberi was shaking as he finally said the words, "I trust you."

Vin lifted his hand and kissed Taberi's palm before turning his face gently toward his and kissing his lips.

They continued to kiss only stopping when Vin removed his t-shirt.

Standing, lifting Taberi with him, Vin returned to Taberi's lips while carefully unbuckling Taberi's pants, and tugging them down. Taberi's length sprang free as he shimmied out of them. Vin's mouth watered when he found Taberi already hard and ready.

Scooping him up, he carried Taberi to the padded bench. Vin arched his leg over the bench to hover over Taberi. Their hands greedily roamed one another, and Vin could hardly contain himself when he felt Taberi's hands slide up his abs to his chest. Vin twirled his tongue over Taberi's nipple, and he arched up from the bench with a gasp. Sliding his hand under Taberi's back, he held his body up as Vin peppered kisses along his collar bone. Vin gently grasped Taberi's length with both hands as he whispered, "Try not to move your neck, alright, baby?"

Taberi's mind spun when Vin called him *baby*, "I'll be good. I promise."

Vin licked up the side of his neck and again at the place where Taberi's neck met his shoulder. Stroking him a few times, Vin gently pressed his fangs into Taberi's neck and made sure to dose him with his saliva. Vin knew the moment his dose hit when Taberi's hands began roaming Vin's muscled chest. The blood flowing from Taberi was as delightful as Vin knew it would be. Something was deliciously different about it, and he was in heaven.

Taberi rubbed little circles around Vin's nipples causing him to gasp as he lapped up the blood. When Taberi began rubbing his thumbs over Vin's nipples, he rocked his hips forward. His length was so hard it was painful, pressing against his leather pants. Vin continue to stroke Taberi as he licked up the last of the blood and kissed him on his neck, right below his ear. Vin could hear the end of Taberi's tail slapping the pad on the bench and his heart leaped.

Taberi begged, "I want to touch you," as he ran his hands down Vin's cut abs to cup the bulge in his pants.

Vin obliged as he kissed down the center of Taberi's neck, "You don't need permission to touch me. I belong to you."

His heart pounded in his chest. Vin was a gentle giant, and Taberi made quick work of his buckle. When Vin's length was finally released, he tensed in anticipation as Taberi reached down and stroked him for the first time. He was hard and thick. Taberi felt a thrill burst through him at the thought of more with this man. Vin made him want *everything*. Sliding his hand down and back up, thumbing the tip before gliding back and pressing down. Above him, Vin closed his eyes and gasped before his hips angled forward.

It didn't take long, and Vin came with a groan, spilling his hot cum all over Taberi's stomach. A moment later Taberi followed and released a breathy moan as he erupted too. The pleasure he experienced with Vin was more than he ever dreamed possible.

Taberi peered up at Vin as he tried to catch his breath and admitted, "You were right, that was fun."

Vin threw his head back and roared with laughter.

From the back of the second relief map room, Nera jumped to her feet and bolted out of the door. Confused, Cinis stretched their arms over their head, as they followed her. The hard floor in the library had been uncomfortable to sleep on even with their bed rolls. They missed their bed. Rubbing their neck where Nera had bitten them the night before, Cinis tried to catch up with Nera, who was nearly running.

Nera went straight to the front of the building and stood still in the entry way. She pointed to a glass case with various ancient vases and sculptures behind it and asked Cinis, "Is this clear glass?"

Understanding fell over Cinis, "Of course you can't see on the other side. It's just old pottery that came from the K'hornibus home world."

"Are there any other glass displays?" Nera asked.

Cinis spotted one across the room. "Yes, follow me." Sure enough, when Cinis approached, they found the relief map they needed under the glass.

"It's in there isn't it." Nera tapped her foot standing behind Cinis.

"Yeah, it's in there. It even has a miniature library building. It has all the major buildings in the city. How the hell did you know?"

Nera smirked as she pulled out her knife, "Humans are predictable. They love miniatures, displays, and collections behind glass."

Feeling rather called out, Cinis bit their lips together. They had a quite extensive tiny rock collection when they lived on Portum. Who were they kidding? They already had over ten little, smooth rocks lining the sink counter in their room back at the Domitia house.

Nera felt around the display edges before taking her knife and wedging it under the glass. After she had it pried loose, she set it aside. Finally able to form an image of the miniature city, Nera smiled. She found it. "What's that right there?" Nera pointed to a place that seemed as if it had been redone or fixed.

Cinis reached down and picked at the teeny faux bushes, revealing a grey rectangle underneath. It still had lines of glue on the inside edge from where it once had a building. "It looks like they removed a little building and put bushes on top." Cinis explained.

Nera tapped on the spot, "That's where we're going to start." She turned around to call the rest of the group and they all arrived shortly after. "Cinis and I found the suspected location of the base. When the fruit Resper began planning to turn on us, they must have buried the existence of the base and erased any knowledge of it. Just like they wanted, over time it became a blood Resper legend. Pack up. We head out now," Nera commanded.

Within a few minutes, they were gathered by the front

door of the library with their gear. Bensley had an extra bag filled with the fruit he had dried at the restaurant across the street. He handed Cinis, Taberi, and Tressa each a bag before he stowed away the rest into the packs on his thighs.

After moving the tables blocking the door and replacing it, the group made their way around the building and began heading north. It just took a few minutes, and they headed up a hill toward the location Nera suspected.

As they neared the top of the hill, it seemed as if nothing had ever been there. Tressa searched the area, "Are we positive it's here?"

Nera pointed to an area with some bushes. "Right there. We need to pull up the shrubs."

Bensley and Halso began rocking a bush back and forth to pull it up. After some effort, the roots below the surface began breaking and they were able to pull up the plant along with its bundle of roots. Vin and Lock repeated the process, and all the plants were in a pile within a few minutes.

Nera knelt down in the dirty mess and began pulling up roots, "Found it!" She knocked on the metal and everyone dug in, pulling roots away. With their hands, they cleared off the soil revealing a metal door with a round lock on it.

Cinis recognized the signature teal tarnish on the surface. "The metal they used is copper. We should have no problem using the electronics below if we can make the backup hydrogen generator spark up."

Bensley pulled a hatchet from his pack and started hacking away at the base of the lock. It didn't take long before the round lock flew, and Bensley pried up the door.

It creaked as it opened, and light streamed down into a

small entry room with a reception table on one side and two lifts on the other.

Nera, Cinis, and Lock dropped down into the room first. Cinis studied the processor, and just as their hand reached the power switch, they stopped, "Oh fuck. We can't turn this on or it will get zapped. How are we getting into the base?"

Nera knocked on the lift. "We climb down." Flashes of their time at the UTC base on Portum flooded their mind. They began sweating and plopped down in the seat at the desk, tossing a cloud of dust in the air. Nera was with Cinis before they could take a full breath. Kneeling at their feet, Nera asked, "What's wrong?"

She slid her hands over Cinis's arms and legs searching for an injury. Nera took their hands.

Cinis's voice shook, "The last time I was in a UTC base, it was overrun with Iungo that had lost their mind from a fungal infection. They killed a lot of people. We had to barricade the door. They slammed against it, trying to get in. I didn't think we were going to survive."

Nera rubbed her thumbs over the back of Cinis's hands, "Are you going to be able to join us in the base?"

Cinis nodded and furrowed their brow. "I'm not going to be the reason for a delay."

Know damn well Cinis was lying Nera whispered, "Do you want me to dose you?" Taking a relieved breath, Cinis nodded avidly as Nera squeezed their hands. They wanted a version of her saliva as an anxiety medicine, anything to make this tolerable.

As everyone except for Bensley and Halso dropped down into the room, Nera leaned over Cinis and planted a kiss on their neck before sinking her teeth into them. The small amount of the substance shot through their veins, quickly making Cinis relaxed and ready to climb down the lift.

After Vin pried the doors open, he tried to shake the maintenance ladder. It didn't budge, so he climbed down first, Taberi followed close behind. Lock went next and Tressa reluctantly reached for the ladder and did her best not to look down. When it was Nera's turn, she waited for Cinis and helped them onto the ladder. Remaining close, Nera guided Cinis down.

It took several minutes of climbing before Vin asked, "How far down should we go?"

Cinis knew that answer, "If it's like any other human design, the main computer is at the bottom level."

They all heard a harrumph from Vin as he resumed climbing down. It took several more minutes of climbing before Vin reached the top of the lift.

Halso stuck his head into the lift shaft and called down, "Bensley killed a deer. He's draining it now. I'll send down some thermoses when they're filled up."

Nera answered, "After you send down dinner, can you replace the door over the entry room? We don't want to flip on the electricity just to have it all fried in minutes."

He nodded as Nera and Cinis were finally reaching the bottom. Lock opened the hatch above the lift, and Vin dropped down the hole. Lock guided Tressa down the hole into Vin's arms. Taberi and Cinis went next. Once Vin had the maintenance door pried open and the lift wasn't so crowded, Lock and Nera dropped through the hole and joined the group.

They entered on the second to last level, and it was too dark for the humans to see.

Nera took Cinis's hand, "Where do you suggest we find the backup power?"

Cinis replied, "If it's like the standard bases, there should be metal doors somewhere leading to the emergency staircase. From there we just need to head downstairs."

Nera led the group to a set of double metal doors and passed through them, finding a staircase. At the bottom, Nera opened the doors to find a guard station, stacks of boxes, a particle replication machine, and what must be the main computer in the center.

Nera asked, "Do you want to start at the main computer?"

Cinis replied, "Yes, I just hope it doesn't send us into a lockdown when I boot it up on battery reserve. Hell, I hope the battery reserve hasn't corroded."

"What happens if it is?" Tressa asked from somewhere off in the dark.

Cinis sighed, "I'll have to build a generator which will take time." Running their hands over the main computer console, Cinis found the switch they were searching for and flipped it. The computer burst to life, and they could have kissed it they were so relieved.

Now able to see, Cinis rounded the console and read the options. Start up main power, base intruder lockdown, mainframe diagnostic, and engage backup hydrogen generator. Cinis selected engage backup hydrogen generator and the screen changed. *Please enter a valid security clearance.*

They huffed, "Fuck me sideways, I need a security clearance." Shifting their gaze to the guard station, they bet they would find it written down somewhere. They peered around the desk and sure enough, there was a strip of paper attached to the bottom edge of a dusty screen. They pried it off and brought it over to the screen to read the code. It was a UTC security access code. They typed the numerals and letters carefully and held their breath as they hit enter.

A message flashed on the screen. *Engaging back up hydrogen generator. Stand by while the system warms up. Time remaining, twenty minutes.*

Cinis was ecstatic. "Now we just wait. Power should be on in a bit."

Vin heard the thermoses of blood clink on the top of the lift as one of the guards lowered them down and went to retrieve them. They all heard the thick copper door of the base slam shut as the guards above sealed them in.

Returning with three thermoses of blood, Vin handed one each to Nera and Lock as he asked, "What's through the doors across from here?" Cinis was confused. There usually wasn't doors to the left in any UTC base unless this base contained an underground ship's bay.

Nera sensed Cinis's heart rate spiking and gently wrapped her hand around their arm, "What is it?"

"There might be a ship through those doors," Cinis admitted.

Vin leapt up, ran across the room, and headed for the doors.

When Vin opened the doors and walked in, he whistled as the rest of the group followed. Nera and Lock each gasped. Cinis already knew what was there before the lights flickered on. Before them stood an imperial command ship, appearing to be in perfect condition. Above the ship was a rolling bay door. The room was a sealed, underground launch bay. Nera was too stunned to speak as Cinis slipped their hand into hers. Cinis squeezed Nera's hand, "It looks like we might have a way off this planet after all. I'll get to work on it as soon as I can."

Behind them Lock asked, "What level is the medical lab?"

Cinis replied without taking their eyes from the ship. "It's up at the top level of the base. The UTC usually has it on the ground level, but here it should be on level ten. The bedrooms and mess hall will be on level eight and nine directly under the lab. Levels two through seven will be holding cells."

Approaching the ship, Cinis climbed the stairs to open the airlock. They needed to access the bridge to run a diagnostic. Nera followed Cinis while the rest of the group left to find the rooms and lab. The airlock whooshed as it opened and Cinis stepped inside, heading straight down the center walkway to the bridge ahead.

They took a seat in the captain's chair and began scrolling through the ship's readings. "It's space-worthy with some minor routine maintenance. It's fully stocked with magnetic charges, an old fashion wormhole engine, and a full tank of radioactive fuel for the thrusters. We just need a command code to access navigation controls."

"What the fuck happened to those people?" Lock breathed as he opened the door to the lab.

In the center of the room stood six shattered glass paned holding cells with black Iungo bones littered inside of each of them. Each of the skulls had wilted grey mushrooms protruding from their head.

Behind him Tressa gasped, "I think those are Iungo skeletons. Cinis told me all about the fungal infection the UTC tried to weaponize." Tressa followed Lock to a counter in the back of the lab with the lab's main computer and a large screen.

Patting the counter next to the keyboard, Lock asked, "Would you mind being my eyes?" Tressa approached the keypad. She wasn't all that great at reading and writing but she would do her best. "We need to start by locating the chemical formula for the gas we used before to eliminate the overpopulated protos. It's a compound of arsenic and fluorine," Lock explained.

Tressa typed in the words he said, unsure of how to spell them. Nothing came up the first time, so she tried again. The third time the computer gave her a list of options. Tressa scrolled through the database results and tried to sound out the first one, "Arsenic penaflour triple right-bonded enchanter."

"Arsenic pentafluoride triple right-bonded enantiomer, got it. We will set the replicator to form molecules designed to disintegrate and go inert like the gas we used before. We don't want to destroy our environment trying to save the world. Cinis said the computer would have a formula synthesis program and the canisters should be somewhere in the lab's lower cabinets. We will need to bring the canisters down to the bottom level and attach them to the particle replicator. Cinis warned it may take a few hours for us to have the formula entered correctly in the replicator."

Using the base intercom, Tressa went over to the wall and reported down to Cinis who was working on the mainframe computer. "We already found the formula for the gas we need to produce. I'll be down with some canisters in a few minutes, do you need anything from up here?"

Cinis, staring at a blinking entry field on the screen replied, "No. I'm in the middle of trying to find a way around this command code request so I can search for a way to turn off the satellites around the planet. Well, maybe a snack would help."

Tressa went back to the computer screen and asked, "So, how do I copy this from the screen?"

"Tressa, you're going to have to copy it down on some paper."

Tressa snarled, "Great." She opened the drawers

around the computer and found a stack of paper and a few pens. Taking one sheet and a pen, she began writing out the formula. It took her over thirty minutes to transcribe it all, but once she was finished, she was damn proud of herself. It looked identical to the screen, or so she hoped.

Tressa took a deep breath and turned to Lock, "I think I have it copied correctly."

Raising his eyebrows, he replied, "I sure hope so, if you don't, we might blow ourselves up." Tressa's mouth dropped open. Lock laughed, "I'm sure the replicator would have a safeguard if you missed something."

Narrowing her eyes at him, Tressa snapped, "You're an ass."

He took her hand to help her from the chair. They made their way to the kitchen on level eight to collect some food for Cinis before heading down to the bottom level.

Lock and Tressa found Cinis rubbing their forehead and hunched over the mainframe computer screen. Cinis startled when Lock tossed a bag of dried fruit on the counter next to them. They turned and huffed, "I think I'm going to have to pry off the back of this damn thing and re-route a few pathways. Every time I think I've found a way around the command code request pops up."

Patting them on the back, Tressa reassured, "You're going to figure it out. You always do." Cinis knew what she meant. They had always taken care of Tressa and Nan. They always found a way, no matter what they had to do.

Lock and Tressa moved to face the particle replicator, and she began entering the formula. It took her a full twenty minutes and when she finished, the screen threw up an error message with a warning tone. "I'm guessing that means the replicator said no?" Lock asked as he leaned against the wall behind her.

Tressa scowled, "I'll try again a few more times before we go back up to the lab." Behind her Lock remained quiet and patient. He knew this was going to take some time due to Tressa's lack of formal education. This was all just going to take a little while, and he had no reason to rush anything.

The intercom above crackled, and Vin could he heard clearing his throat, "Hello? Oh, it's on. Is there anything I need to do before we go to our room for the night?"

Nera answered from the launch bay comms, "We're wrapping up for today. You can head to your room."

Vin held the door open to their room for Taberi. Vin went straight over to his bag and dug inside for his thermos. Taberi crashed down on the bed and asked, "Does it hurt your wings to lie down on them?"

Vin finished guzzling the rest of his thermos of blood and replied, "No, but sometimes they have that crawling feeling, like when you sit on a limb for too long."

Taberi cringed, "I slept on my tail wrong once and that happened. It drove me so mad I had to slap my tail until it stopped." Still kneeling by his bag, Vin became quiet after he wiped the blood off his face. "Is everything alright?" Taberi sat up and curled his tail behind him.

Vin moved to sit on the bed by Taberi's feet, he flared his wings out in the gap behind the bed as he lay back against the cement wall. He didn't speak right away. A few moments passed before he answered Taberi. "I want to know more about you, but I feel like every time I ask, I say the wrong thing."

Taberi lay his hand on Vin's forearm and replied, "It's not that you have asked the wrong questions, it's just my life before was hard and lonely."

Vin took Taberi's hand, "You had to have found joy somewhere?"

Taberi smiled, but as he did, a lump formed in his throat. Vin noticed his shift and became visibly discouraged. Taberi sighed, "I had a best friend. He helped the Iungo gain their freedom by hacking into the UTC broadcast system. He sent out a message with the truth about their species, and Tressa recorded it for him. I miss him a lot, but we never really talked. We just played games or listened to other hacker broadcasts. Sometimes he would invite me over when he was working a big job and let me watch. I never even knew his real name, but none of the hackers ever reveal their names."

Vin pulled Taberi over to him, "We will have to make new happy memories to take up for what you didn't have before."

Taberi's heart wanted to leap out of his chest. "That has to be the nicest thing anyone has ever said to me."

He leaned his head on Vin's shoulder as Taberi whispered, "I feel like I've found my home with you. I've never felt like my home was anywhere before."

Vin kissed Taberi on the forehead. "There's only one more thing I need to talk to you about."

Taberi looked up at Vin, "Anything."

"I naturally have an insatiable appetite for blood and sex, but I've only had one of them consistently."

Vin's words sunk in and Taberi understood, "I'm nervous, but I want more."

Biting his lip thinking about Taberi's dual length, Vin offered, "I like to be dominant, but I don't mind changing it up. What if I let you be in control?"

Taberi's voice shook, "How do I ever repay you for being so gentle with me?"

"You repay me by fucking me tonight." Vin pulled Taberi over his lap to straddle him.

Taberi's breath caught in his throat, did Vin say he wanted Taberi to fuck him? Not waiting for an answer, Vin guided Taberi to sit down on the rock-hard bulge in his pants. He grabbed his hips and ground Taberi down on his length as he implored, "Don't make me beg."

Taberi's breath was quick as he answered, "Yes. I'll have sex with you if you're sure that's what you want."

Vin laughed as he pulled Taberi's shirt off, "I want anything and everything you're willing to give me."

Vin leaned in and met Taberi's lips with his. He ran his hands up to Taberi's chest and rubbed along his collar bone with his thumbs as he deepened his kiss. Vin could feel Taberi's length press on his lower belly, and he reached down to free it. Taberi gasped as Vin unbuckled his pants and pulled him up so he could slip them off. Vin tossed his shirt away and pulled his pants off so quickly they turned inside out. He kicked the inverted ends of his pants off his feet as Taberi moved to climb onto the bed. Vin lay flat and Taberi crawled between his legs before he leaned down to continue their kiss. Pulling his legs up, Vin stopped their kiss, "I almost forgot something important."

Vin leaned over the side of the bed and grabbed his bag, opening the left side. He dug deep in the bag and produced a little bottle.

Showing Taberi the bottle he shrugged, "I almost forgot the lube."

Taberi laughed as he took the little bottle, "I was wondering how that was going to work."

Vin ran his hands up Taberi's body and pulled him in to continue their kiss. He couldn't keep his lips away from this man. Vin heard the bottle open, and he angled his hips up as Taberi guided his length to Vin's back entrance. Taberi slowly pushed himself inside, and Vin's whiskey eyes fluttered with anticipation.

Vin leaned his head back and shifted his hips as Taberi hit just the right spot, "Damn, baby, you feel so good."

Taberi released his held breath and gently thrust into Vin. The look of delight on Vin's face gave Taberi all the confidence he needed to loosen up and allow his natural instinct to guide him. Moving inside of Vin, Taberi felt the desperate urge for his length to split in two. The inner flesh was beyond sensitive, and he readied himself for the onslaught of stimulation. As his length parted, Taberi curled and whispered, "Oh gods!"

Vin's eyes widened and he let out a breathy moan as he felt Taberi separate inside of him. The rolling of the two parts had Vin's hips shaking uncontrollably, it was better than he could have ever imagined. Vin released a loud high-pitched sound as Taberi's length rotated over his most sensitive place. Vin felt like he was blasting into outer space as Taberi pressed in and ground against him.

Feeling the pressure build, Vin felt his explosive end nearing and wrapped a cloth over the end of his length. His head popped up before he slammed it back against the pillow. He grabbed his knees in a bruising hold, and he unabashedly moaned as he tipped over. The first sign of cum spilled into the cloth just as Taberi began to tip over with a gasp. With one last thrust, Vin's orgasm detonated, and he nearly bounced them both off the bed. As Vin curled up his body with mind altering pleasure, Taberi spilled inside of him with a soft groan.

Grasping for air, Vin raised his head up and absently

rambled, "Your cock deserves a standing ovation and a metal for just existing. That was the best sex I've ever had."

After Lock and Tressa successfully replicated the poisonous gas, they spent hours of digging in the lab computer, and the search results produced an immune suppressing medication for Tressa's disease. Lock planted his hands firmly against the counter next to the computer, "You cannot tell me there is nothing but a drug that kills your white blood cells. The UTC labs have had genetic base sequence editing for thousands of years."

Tressa sighed, "Everything is owned by the wealthy. They hoard all the medical and technological advances. I had a feeling we wouldn't be able to find anything. I'm sure some rich asshole on Melior owns the formula."

"We are not giving up. I can sense your internal temperature runs warm and you sweat at night. You're getting worse. I know the side effects of immune suppressants, and they're only marginally better than the symptoms you have now. I can't accept this. I won't" Able to build only flat surfaces in his mind from the computer screen in front of him, Lock grumbled, "If this equipment wasn't vision normative, I could use the damn computer myself and develop my own treatment."

Guilt consumed Tressa. This base and the library the UTC and FH built, only had humans in mind. First Humans had always disregarded disability at best and at their worst practiced eugenics against those they found lacking or even different. They failed to understand the beauty of life as it occurs naturally she decided.

Tressa did her best to explain her feelings, "Our deficits and differences according to the masses don't define us, but they do give us depth in heart and perspective in mind. They enrich this experience we call life by helping us grow in understanding. We may not have chosen these differences, but we can choose what we make of them. My own narrow perspective was destroyed and rebuilt when I discovered you could see with sound and not your eyes. I am inherently a changed person because of it. My perspective of thinking vision as central or normative was altered permanently. As for me and my pain? It's a reminder I'm alive. If we never find a treatment for this awful disease, I will persevere through life as all people do. I will find peace in acceptance, and I will give myself grace. I am not a diagnosis. I am a person."

Lock paused before he breathed, "I don't know if I deserve you."

Confusion fell over Tressa. "What do you mean?"

"I am a lot of things, but worthy of you is not one of them."

"You mean your brutality?" Tressa clarified. Lock was silent. Tressa continued, "Your actions are a direct result of your environment. You evolved from blood drinking bats. Similar, but much smaller, bats naturally occur on several worlds besides yours. Not one of those species is aggressive in any way. They are sneaky but never harsh. I read about it in a book once, my only book actually. I think you crave the taste of fear because of conditioning. I'm sorry for ever making you out to be a monster. I'll never complain about your eating habits again, even when human is on the menu. The real monsters are the First Humans. I'm halfway convinced they're genetically engineering them to have no feelings."

Struck by her words, Lock didn't know how to respond. It was as if she had peeled away his layers and revealed parts of him he kept hidden away from the light. He and all the other blood Resper had a deep-seated desire to return to the way it had been before their world fell. Sure, before the fall the fruit, Resper had long separated themselves as the elite of the Resper people, but the blood Resper had always been free and could travel within the galactic center.

Lock exhaled roughly, "After years of the fruit Resper demonization of the blood drinking Resper, the UTC voted Alisot to be banned from all galactic travel. No one on or off planet, and any blood drinking Resper caught off world would be sent back. When the blood Resper responded with force, the UTC unanimously voted to transform the planet into their long-needed prison world. Their prison space stations were overflowing, and the UTC took the opportunity when it was presented. Within a month of the EM pulse satellites being deployed, our once highly civilized and educated society crumbled into chaos. The UTC sent droves of drop ships with criminals from Emendo. It was a gory massacre every time a pod landed. The only reason I know any of this is because Nera's ancestors took meticulous records."

"What happened to your people was wrong. I wish

there was something we could do. If we just talked to the right people?" Tressa shook her head.

Lock gave Tressa a devastated smile. "I don't know how that could ever happen, Tres. How do you undo a thousand years of conditioning on both sides?"

Tressa squeezed her eyes together; she couldn't accept this. She could accept many things, but she just wasn't going to fold this time. "I will always reserve hope you and your people will one day rejoin the galactic community. I don't think anything could take away that desire."

Lock slid his hand over Tressa's shoulder. "Let's go check on Cinis. We haven't heard a report all day."

Knowing damn well Lock was changing the subject to avoid further discussion, Tressa relented. "Right, no news is bad news. We should go check on them. Cinis is only happy when projects go their way. One of my earliest memories is Cinis ripping up a drawing they couldn't sketch right."

"Well, we better go down there for Nera's sake then." Laughing Tressa rose up from the chair and they headed to the lift.

They could hear a clanking sound as they rounded the corner from the stairwell and found Cinis tapping a screwdriver against the side of the computer. Nera was a few feet away standing with her hands over her ears and her eyes closed. She seemed to be counting.

Lock bit his lip as he approached Cinis, "So, how are things going?"

"How do you think it's going?!" Cinis' eyes radiated anger as she stared him down.

Tressa knelt down to Cinis, "Please don't give up and burn it down."

Cinis laughed, "Shut up Tressa. That doesn't help anything."

Taberi and Vin came around the corner with their hands full of food and thermoses of blood. Vin handed a thermos to Lock. "Halso and Bensley found a drop pod with a malfunction. The human was stuck inside. They freed him, and he tried to attack them."

With his eyebrows raised, Lock acknowledged the situation by raising the thermos, and Vin continued, "They sent down his leg if you want it. I put it in the kitchen freezer, but it's still warm if you want it now."

Tressa patted Lock on the shoulder. "Go on and eat your leg. Come back when you're finished." The pep in Lock's step as he took off for the stairs made Tressa giggle under her breath.

Taberi grimaced and searched for something else to think about. His eyes fell on the circuit boards Cinis had unscrewed and was attempting to reroute. Bending down, he reached in and moved a few wires around. Taberi just solved the problem of the last three hours and Cinis watched in disbelief. "Why have you not been helping with this?"

Taberi shrugged. "I guess I didn't think about it. I worked in data entry, but I was always working on the consoles."

Narrowing their eyes at him, Cinis held back their frustration. "Well, you're on my team now. I need to bypass the security protocols, so we don't need to enter command codes. We have to disable the EM pulses, or we are stuck and can't access any off-world information."

Taberi understood. "Got it. Plug this wire here into this slot and reinstall this circuit board under it but use the second port. You'll need to connect the board to the power source through this wire, and the other circuit board goes here so we can connect them. This chip on top is the security firewall. Look how the pathways run on the board. We are going to need a soldering tool. Can the particle replicator make one?"

Cinis reached behind the console and handed Taberi the soldering tool they already made. Taberi made quick work of the plan and within an hour they were closing up the back of the console.

Standing in front of the machine, Cinis flipped on the power and the command access screen was the first one to pop up.

Cinis looked at Taberi' and he joined them at the keyboard.

He typed in the word 'Taberithebest' in the blinking space on the screen before confirming it and grinned.

The computer booted up and all the command control bans had been lifted. Cinis twirled around and yelled, "You did it!"

Taberi laughed, "Now what?"

The group crowded around as Cinis explained, "We just need to find the program that controls the satellites around the planet. It's somewhere in here. I just couldn't access the file."

Taberi considered for a moment, "The EM pulse only activates when it's detected a signal right?"

Cinis nodded and Taberi explained, "The program will be in a subspace communication file if they left a way to control it in this base." Cinis moved over and let Taberi work, and he began clicking away at the keyboard, searching through file after file.

FIFTY-FIVE

ALISOT – YONIC CITY – UTC BASE

Cinis pushed away from the console and threw their arms in the air cheering, "I'm in! The EM pulse is off!"

Taberi, who had dozed off on the floor, startled and staggered to his feet, "What?! I didn't do it! It wasn't me!" Behind him, Vin twitched and snorted before resuming his light snore, Taberi slowly twisted to look down at Vin as his mind cleared.

Cinis stared at him. "Are you alright?"

Taberi gulped and stared back, "Getting there."

"I broke into the UTC intranet. Why don't you and Vin go upstairs and go to bed. We've been working on this for two days. I slept last night, but you haven't really since yesterday."

Vin didn't seem uncomfortable face down on the floor, but Taberi thought it probably was best to go to bed. He leaned down and rubbed Vin's arm. Within seconds Vin stumbled up and began absently mumbling, "What are we doing? What's happening?"

Taberi answered, "We're going to bed." Vin blinked several times before his feet had enough coordination to make their way to the stairs with Taberi leading the way.

Lock had instructed Cinis privately to run a search for a medication he could replicate for Tressa, but he warned Cinis not to say anything to her in case it gave her false hope. Cinis hated keeping things from Tressa, but they knew this time there was a good reason.

They worked for a few more hours before heading off to bed, just to wake up a few hours later and head back down to the computer. Nera was irritated with them over their lack of sleep, but she would deal with it. This was important, and they couldn't keep it out of their mind. Lock had said there had to be something they could find for her, and they were both willing to do anything for her. Cinis knew if they found a safe treatment for her, they would also release the formula to the public.

Invigorated with the idea of doing something profound, something just and good, energized them, and they could feel themselves becoming enthralled. They helped save a world once, and the high from that experience was something they had never dreamed of. It was joy, but on a scale they didn't know how to express. Cinis would find that formula, even if they had to break some rules. *I hate breaking rules.* They were already trapped on a prison planet; how much worse could it get?

They typed away, planning to search every inch of the data base, when Nera appeared around the corner and wrapped her arms around Cinis. Nera leaned over them and asked, "What are you working on?"

"Lock asked me to find a treatment option for Tressa. I think if we find it, and we can obtain it, we should make it available to the public. I bet if we contact Rungi, she would want to help. She has been behind several medication formula releases now available for next to nothing. One is a medication for a deadly muscle wasting disease which used to be common in people with First Human ancestry."

Nera kissed Cinis temple. "Tressa means the world to the people I love. I think we should do what we can for her."

Leaning into Nera, Cinis replied, "I'll be back up in a little while."

"Liar." Nera kissed Cinis forehead and headed upstairs for some sleep. She was probably right. Cinis had just begun searching through various information files for a way to contact Rungi as well as looking for who owned the formulas to what medical treatments. The way it was organized, Cinis had to find the person's file and scroll through it to find the information they needed. For Rungi it was easy, but to find who had the T-cell gene therapy formula, meant Cinis would be there for a while.

A few hours went by, and Nera was again slipping her arms around them, pulling Cinis toward her. "I knew you weren't going to come back to bed.

"I found how to contact Rungi, and I've sent her a message. I had to break into a lab computer on Melior to access the broader galactic center internet. Once I broke through, I've been able to make a list of people who own medical formulas. I'm narrowing down who has the formula Tressa needs now. Lock said it would be a T-cell gene modification for inflammation."

Still scrolling through the information while they talked, Cinis found the name and couldn't believe their eyes.

"It's fucking Baiselle! You have to be joking. That's the damn map collector Jael smooth talked for the map to

Janus! That's how they proved the First Humans committed theriocide against over a hundred worlds. Baiselle probably hates us more than anything. She is the mother of one of the now disgraced commanders."

"We need to find a way to steal the formula. If you can't find a way to do it, we will just have to fly there and take it," Nera declared.

Cinis slowly turned to face Nera, "Are you suggesting what I think you are?"

Lock and Tressa appeared in the doorway behind her, and Lock answered, "Yes, Cinis, she's suggesting we plan a heist. I think I agree."

Beside him Tressa's mouth dropped open, "You cannot be serious."

Lock smirked at her, "Chaos is part of the package deal, Tres. You know that." Lock was fucking serious, and she knew he had no idea what it would involve.

"No. We cannot commit a heist on Melior against one of the great houses. Thura Baiselle will have us put to death if we are caught! Nera, you can't possibly be alright with this can you?"

Nera and Cinis turned to face Tressa, and Nera replied, "You are adored by people I care for more than I can put into words. If we can find a treatment like you have asked, and release the formula to the public, it could help millions of humans with your condition who are seeking treatment. It may even sway the opinion of blood Resper in the galactic center."

This was much bigger than Tressa; nonetheless, she hated putting her friends in danger.

Cinis added, "I've already sent Rungi a message. I should hear back within a few hours. It's early morning on Emendo right now. She will be all in for this plan. What do we have to lose anyway? We're all trapped on a prison planet, and we've made it this far. If we're going to be arrested and sent right back anyway, we might as well benefit. I mean what did we really think was going to happen if we left the planet? Eventually the UTC is going to notice the satellite EM pulses are turned off, and what then? I don't know what changed with me, but I'm itching to fight back somehow."

Tressa blinked slowly as she found her words, "You mean to tell me even the ultimate rule follower wants to go along with this? You have never once played a whole card game with me because you just *know* I will cheat, and you don't want an argument."

Cinis snapped back, "Tressa, you fucking said you just pulled one card, but I know you pulled two! You *had* to have cheated; I even counted the cards!"

Tressa's heart rate sped up as she clearly remembered grabbing two cards. Lock slowly raised his eyebrows and peered over at Tressa expectantly. Tressa's cheeks heated and elbowed Lock in the ribs, "Oh, you shut up!"

Cinis blue eyes went wide, and they hopped as they pointed and yelled, "YOU DID CHEAT! You fucker! You've been lying about that for years!"

Nera burst into laughter, "Lock, is this what we look like when we fight?"

Still hot from Tressa, Cinis twirled around to Nera, "Yes, it is!"

Nera giggled as she wiped her eyes, "How are we going to pull off this plan?"

Tressa harrumphed and crossed her arms as Cinis answered, "Rungi always has a list of heist ideas." A beep sounded behind Cinis, and they turned to look, reading a returned message from Rungi. They opened the file, and it was a link to call her. "This is it. Rungi has sent us a link to discuss a plan. She says the Iungo have reported us missing." Cinis explained as they clicked the link, and the video screen opened to Rungi's face.

Noticing Nera so close to Cinis, Rungi flared her eyes at Nera before meeting Cinis's gaze. "I've relayed a message to the Iungo world that I've found you two, but you tell me that's not all you need?"

Cinis replied, "My sister is not well. We need to break into Baiselles lab and steal the formula for a treatment she's refusing to make accessible."

Cinis calling Rungi with Nera by their side seemed to tell her everything she needed to know about how to negotiate with Cinis this time. Certain favors were no longer on the table. Considering her words, Rungi made an offer, "If you steal another of Baiselle's formulas, one to shrink an inoperable childhood brain cancer, I'll give you all the maintenance access codes I've collected for her labs. I just so happen to have a niece who was recently diagnosed, and I was actively searching for a team to perform the extraction. Labs on Melior are low security since the planet is limited to only the rich, so it will be an easy job. I'll tell the Iungo to keep quiet about your location until after the job is done."

Cinis looked back to Nera who nodded. "Let's do it." Planning began immediately as Cinis, Rungi, and Nera discussed options and strategies.

Tressa quietly headed back upstairs. She knew Lock heard her walk away. He would be following behind her soon. She just needed a few minutes after listening to the plan form.

She lay down on the bed and stared at the cement wall, wondering how they had possibly arrived at this point.

Why couldn't they just kill the proto-bat overpopulations and go home, back to the Domitia house? That wasn't all she wanted though. Did she really want to live out the rest of her short human life in peace with Lock, but with this disease constantly attacking her? No, they had to do something.

She felt Lock lie down behind her and his arms wrapped around her middle.

Tressa whispered, "Part of me just wants to kill the bats and go home. So much could go wrong."

Lock brushed her hair to the side and kissed the back of her neck. "That's not happening Tress, Cinis is going to start working on the ship in the morning. If this wasn't what you wanted, I wouldn't push it. I know it is though."

Sliding his hands up Tressa shirt, he purred against her ear, "I'm hungry."

Complying, she raised her arms, and he lifted her shirt to toss it away. He reached down and grabbed a leather strap off out of his bag and tied her hands to the top of the bed. She scowled at him. "What are you doing? I thought you said you were hungry?"

He hovered over her breasts, his hot breath warming her skin, "I am. I'm hungry for all of you." Lock descended on her breast and licked around her nipple before he closed his mouth over it. She knew what he was doing. He was distracting her, and it was working. Heat built in her lower belly as he moved from one nipple to the other. He never rushed and always made sure she was desperate for more when he finally moved on.

He started on her pants and pulled them down her body before crawling over her and lifting her legs. Furious with the metal bar keeping Lock from properly lying on the bed to lick her, he broke it off at the end of the bed.

When he did, he noticed Tressa's legs were clamped back together. He didn't like that at all. Taking two more straps from his bag, he tied her ankles to either end of the bar, and spread her out wide for him. "That's better,"

She peered up at him like an innocent, doe eyed fawn tied and unaware they're being prepared for slaughter. He couldn't wait to devour her, but first he wanted to play.

He lifted the bar up, and her body lifted up with it. He rested it on his broad shoulders and carefully wedged the bar between his back and his wings. He took his finger and ran it down the length of her spine before twirling his finger at her back entrance.

Tressa sucked in a sharp breath, "Lock?"

In answer, Lock grasped her hips and twirled his tongue around her back entrance before flitting his tongue over it. Tressa fought like hell while Lock licked her *everywhere*. She was half shrieking/half moaning as he ran a finger up and down her spine, just gently enough to make her groan with frustration as the twirls over her back entrance continued.

Tressa whimpered, "Lock, what..."

He peppered the inside of her leg with kisses before moving up to her entrance, finding her dripping. He growled as he licked up her center, collecting every bit of pleasure spilling from her. He planted both hands under her hips, lifting her completely off the bed. Her head was hanging and only her hair touched the bed. Lock slid his tongue up her center and found her swollen bud, desperate for contact. He closed his mouth over her and wedged her tender bundle of nerves between his front teeth before he began flicking his tongue. What started as Tressa shaking, progressed to her hips fighting his hands to no avail. He brought her to the edge, and just as she began to tip over, Lock pulled away.

Tressa tried to kick her legs to get away, "Uh! What the fuck!"

Lock ran his fangs over the place directly above her most sensitive place and sunk his teeth in. He had waited until she was about to cum to *start* feeding.

When she felt him close his mouth on her and suck, she bucked against his hands and her binds. The pleasure was all consuming. He lapped up her blood by running his tongue over her bud, over and over. Her breath caught in her throat, and she was frozen in place, trapped in a state of mind-bending ecstasy. Just when she thought she couldn't handle any more, he continued and she cried out with breathy moans as she felt something else building. Just when she didn't think it was possible to experience anything more, Lock began humming. Tressa *screamed.*

A second orgasm slammed into her so hard her vision blanked in and out, and languidly he licked her through it before pulling the bar up and over his head. He held it up, with her body still dangling and lined her up with his length. He lifted his other arm to hold the bar her ankles were attached to and slowly slid her onto him. Tressa's eyes rolled back as Lock began swinging the bar, slamming her against his length. Every swing was met with a thrust, and Tressa was sure she would crack in half. How could her body accept anymore? When Lock heard her mouth part in a silent scream, he exploded into her. He ground against her heat as he spilled over.

By the time Lock finished freeing Tressa, she was in a satiated sleep. He carefully washed her body before climbing in behind her. It was still early in the day, and he planned to keep her busy and spent when she awoke again.

He knew this mission to Melior could mean he might return to Alisot without her, or not at all and end up dead. Lock, Vin, and Nera all knew the truth. They couldn't just exist on this planet. They had to do something. The call inside to act was too great.

Their command code override didn't work, and Cinis had the floor pried up and on the circuits underneath as Taberi relayed instructions from the main computer.

"Pathway 879, re-route to connection 64," Taberi yelled.

Cinis grumbled, "879 to 64. What's next?"

Taberi answered, "That should be the last one."

Cinis looked up to find Taberi standing next to them, "How did you make it up here so fast?"

"I had some energy to burn, so I ran."

Understanding, Cinis asked, "So, do we need a password?"

"No. We just need to set you as the captain," Taberi explained.

"I don't think so. If anyone is flying, it's Nera."

Cinis eyebrows shot up with realization. "Oh. Oh fuck. This is a human ship. All the controls are flat and for people with vision. I'm going to have to learn how to fly, aren't I?"

Nera appeared behind Taberi, "Yes, you are, Captain."

Cinis knew this should be a compliment, but all they could think about was how they were going to learn how to fly a whole ship. This was the smallest of the old imperial command vessels and only needed a captain to run it. It was perfect to mask as a maintenance ship since many of the older command ships were repurposed after the UTC updated the fleet every few hundred years. They had to admit this plan was coming together well, and they just needed a captain.

Cinis nodded in uneasy acceptance, "Taberi, can you pull up the file location of the flight manual at the main computer so I'm not digging through ship files for an hour?"

"Sure, I'll be right back," Taberi replied as he took off down the ship's walkway.

Nera leaned against the bridge wall. "I'm going to the surface with Lock to hunt with Bensley and Halso one last time before we leave."

Cinis approached her for a kiss before giving Nera a sarcastic reply, "Have fun." Nera scoffed and softly flicked Cinis nipple through their under shirt before spinning on her heels and heading to the surface. Cinis rubbed their chest as Taberi came back with the manual instructions.

"If we get caught, what if all of us are sent back here, but you and Tressa are sent home?" Taberi asked.

Cinis popped their head up from the controls. "I hadn't thought of that. I guess just a heist wouldn't send Tressa and I back here, would it? We would probably be sent to a prison ship for a few years."

"So, we just can't be caught, right?" Taberi said.

Cinis nodded, "Right, we just can't caught. I trust Rungi. I think we'll be able to pull it off and escape without anyone noticing. We can just come back here and hide the ship afterward. If the UTC hasn't noticed the EM pulse grid is down, we might be able to turn it back on, giving us the option to leave again if we needed to."

"That makes sense. We could just go to wherever they all live."

"You haven't been there. I hadn't thought about that," Cinis admitted. Noticing Taberi's silence, Cinis continued, "It is a lot like the Feroci house, but the courtyard glass is intact, and it's much larger. It's beautiful, and I don't know if any description I can give you will do it justice. I can't wait to return."

Cinis did their best to refocus as they located the file they needed. They opened the flight manual and prepared to memorize a substantial amount of information.

Taberi saw Cinis fluster and sensed they were overwhelmed, so he offered, "Why don't we do it together so two of us are learning it. What if you need backup?"

Relief washed over Cinis. "That's genius, and I feel a hundred times better. Thank you."

Taberi sat at their feet as Cinis angled the captain's controls so he could see them. The two worked for a few hours and had already mastered the basic controls when Tressa came in with roasted meat from the fresh kill on the surface.

Bringing the warm bite to his mouth, Taberi paused in horror, "Is this?"

Tressa nearly spit her bite out, "Fuck no! It's pig! Ick, now I'm grossed out. I hadn't even thought of that."

Cinis kept eating and simply announced, "I'm just going to keep pretending the consuming of humans here doesn't exist."

Tressa shook her head at Cinis, remembering when

they sat at the dining table as she watched Lock, Nera, and Vin eat two criminals Nera had locked away in her room somewhere. "I'm glad that works for you." Tressa slowly raised another bite to her mouth.

Vin's large form darkened the walkway. "Pig tastes *just* like human, I honestly don't think any of you would notice a difference. Your senses of smell and taste aren't developed enough." Tressa, Cinis, and Taberi all stared at Vin before Taberi reached in his mouth and removed the bite he had been chewing. He sat it down on his plate and bit his lips together.

Vin's eyes went wide when he realized he may have said the wrong thing, "You know what? I'm just going to go back and join Nera and Lock in the kitchen upstairs, but I promise, that's pig!"

They all set their still full plates down, and Tressa collected them before heading upstairs.

Cinis called out as she was descending the ship's stairs, "Can you bring us some dried fruit or anything else?"

Tressa yelled back, "What do you think I'm doing?" Cinis rolled their eyes.

Hours later, Taberi and Cinis had mastered the thrusters and how to run the wormhole engine. It worked by creating a tiny singularity and detecting its frequency. Once the frequency matched, the ship would shoot a concentrated beam of the same frequency radiation into the singularity. It blew a hole in space-time, then created a destination location by the intensity and direction of the radiation burst. Cinis hadn't known how it worked before and thought it fascinating.

They worked for hours, went to bed, and spent another entire day on the ships systems. Cinis and Taberi went through each system multiple times before deciding they were ready.

At the particle replication machine, Taberi made them each current UTC maintenance crew attire, thin, sleeveless tunics loose pants in white. They found dust collectors, particle mops, and various other cleaning supplies in the base to take with them to extend their disguise. Rungi had sent them the floorplans of the lab with the formula storage location, access code, and maintenance codes. Taberi entered these into the ship's system, and with their weeks work, they were ready.

Cinis entered the command to open the bay doors, and moments later they heard rumbles from above. Darkness enveloped the ship as the door receded away. Night had just fallen over Alisot, which meant millions of the protos were rallying in the sky, fighting one another, and over hunting the ever-thinning wildlife. If something wasn't done to stop them, this planet would be completely unin-habitable soon.

Taberi had installed enough seats for everyone, and they each found a seat and buckled themselves in. Nera fluttered her wings over the seat, "These damn chairs are awful." After several attempts to find a tolerable position, she had enough and hooked her feet around the column holding up the seat and slammed her body backward. The metal creaked as Nera bent the seat back, "There."

Cinis stared at her, in disbelief but also quite impressed. They shook their head as they engaged thrusters and gently raised them from the launch bay. Bensley, who was remaining behind, shut the bay door from inside the base as they traveled into the sky.

When Cinis located the first concentration of proto-bats and the ship was in the best position, they released a canister of gas. The highly concentrated compound sifted onto the swarm of protos below them. Cinis reported, "The first drop is finished. Just six more to go."

Taberi kept a lock on the life signs of the bats. "It looks like the gas is working. The first group is falling dead out of the sky."

After all the canisters deployed, Taberi reported, "There is almost no more proto activity on this side of Alisot. I think it's safe to say our first mission has been accomplished."

Cinis replied, "Alright. I'm heading into the upper atmosphere. Taberi, begin the wormhole protocol."

Taberi clicked away at his controls as Cinis brought them into position. Taberi finished entering the coordinates, and the ship countdown began. A ball of carbon expelled out the front of the ship and within moments, the wormhole opened up. Cinis guided them inside and took them through the wormhole. Everything around them blurred and no stars could be seen, but it wasn't total darkness. The destination appeared in moments, and Cinis pulled them out of the wormhole.

When they emerged, they were directly above Melior. The ship's command controls lit up with the request for authorization codes, and Cinis sent them over. They responded within seconds, sending the ship the coordinates for their parking location on the ground.

"They accepted the codes. I'm taking the ship down," Cinis reported as they plugged in the landing coordinates. Within minutes they were lowering the landing gear and setting the ship down. They had done it! Cinis had just flown a spaceship. Never in their wildest dreams did they believe they would ever pilot a space craft. They rose from their seat, beaming with anticipation about the heist. If it was going this well, the rest of it would be likely be just as easy, or that's what they kept telling themselves. Rungi had seemed a little odd, but they were glad they could count on her as a friend after what they had together at one time.

Cinis lowered the ship's stairs, and they each filed down the steps with their cleaning gear. Recalling the map Rungi sent, Cinis guided the group to the back door of the medical research facility. Beautiful shrubbery, manicured lawns, and lush gardens surrounded the building. Every inch of Melior was picture perfect.

They entered the authorization codes into the door, and the seal popped, opening the door a crack. Cinis opened it up to a stark white hallway.

Entering the building, Lock shook his wings, "Something about this place is uncomfortable."

Tressa rolled her eyes at him. "Uncomfortable? What about our little dinner with the hunters?"

Lock smirked, "No, that was nice."

Ignoring his answer, Tressa and the rest of the team followed Cinis down one hallway and the next, around a corner, and through a door. It was the database for the lab, and one wall was lined with servers. Cinis approached a console with a copy drive and plugged it in. A code request popped up, and Cinis entered what Rungi had shared.

The copy drive opened on the screen, and Cinis searched for the formula for Tressa first. They copied it to the drive and moved on to the formula for Rungi. As it downloaded to the drive, the rest of the team pretended to clean the room in case anyone wondered in.

Cinis finished up saving the files and removed the drive, slipping it in their pocket, "Time to go."

The group headed out of the room and made their way to the back door. Cinis began feeling uneasy as they approached the door and paused a moment with their hand on the authorization keypad. Brushing it off, they entered the code, and the door seal popped open. They opened the door, and the group headed back toward the ship.

Nera, at the front of the group, stopped abruptly, "Oh fuck," as a spotlight hit their group and a team of UTC guards ran toward them with rail guns drawn, demanding they surrender. Nera was the first to fall to her knees with her hands up, and one by one, each of them followed. None of them could take a full breath or think as one of the UTC guards approached the group.

"We found them just where that arms dealer said we would. Let the station general know the two missing humans are in the group," The squad leader reported to one of the soldiers.

Cinis held back a sob as she watched Nera's head sink. They had trusted Rungi, and she betrayed them. They should have known by the way Rungi had flitted her eyes at Nera. Cinis should have known better. Their heart broke as Nera, Lock, Vin, and Taberi all had their hands bound and were being lined up to wait for a prisoner transport.

Cinis and Tressa were pulled to the side as the soldier asked, "Where is it?"

When Cinis didn't reply, he patted them down, reached into their pocket, and took the drive.

Cinis and Tressa stood with guards surrounding them, unable to take their eyes away from the people they loved. Cinis rubbed their shoulder against Tressa's, and she let out a quiet sob. When she did, they could see Lock's wings tighten behind him.

It occurred to each of them the Resper could hear them. Both began whispering *goodbyes* and *I'm sorry's*. Cinis swore to Nera they would find her one day. Tressa begged Lock to behave and that she loved him.

Nera and Lock leaned against one another as they listened to Cinis and Tressa. Vin and Taberi were doing the same, making their last moments together count as much as possible in case they were separated.

Cinis and Tressa couldn't hold back their sobs as the prison transport arrived, and Nera, Lock, Vin, and Taberi were forced inside. They didn't understand why Taberi was going with them, but he was, and there was nothing they could do.

In the transport soldiers shoved them into seats not meant for anyone with a tail or wings. A moment later, harnesses swung over the seats securing them in place before the soldiers found their own seats and buckled themselves in.

Vin was behind Taberi and whispered to him, "No matter what happens, don't tell them anything."

Taberi heard him and he nodded his head. Vin's heart

broke. He wished he had insisted that Taberi stay with Bensley and Halso.

The prison transport ship lifted into the air and headed straight for a prison station circling Emendo. When they arrived, soldiers and commanding officers poured into the ship and dragged Nera, Lock, and Vin into an interrogation room. They took Taberi into an adjacent room with mirrored glass. He was able to see into the interrogation room that held Nera, Lock and Vin.

When Taberi was sat down in front of the window, he knew what was going to happen. Nausea filled his gut as he watched the three Resper stripped nude before being strapped down to chairs with their wings smashed under them. The three Resper remained silent as sensors were placed all over their bodies.

A man in an unmarked black command uniform came in and directed a lab tech to stand at a control panel. He kept his hands clasped behind his back as he introduced himself, "I am the prison interrogations specialist, Kulat Moins. You may call me Sir. UTC command has requested that I ask you some questions." Kulat gave a signal to the lab tech and three Resper arched their bodies from a painful burning electric current pumped through them. They shook violently as their teeth clenched and the places where the sensors were began to smoke.

With another signal of Kulat's hand, the current was shut off, and they slumped with relief. Kulat spoke as if he was speaking to a class of children, "That was just a taste of what's to come. Is anyone feeling talkative yet?" They all remained silent, so Kulat continued, "Did you notice how incredible the pain was? My new interrogations device sends a specific current through your nerves, one specifically chosen because it makes your body feel like you're being burned alive. It's quite exhilarating to watch!"

Kulat signaled, and Nera arched off the chair as her body fought the horrific fire running through her. She couldn't scream or cry as the pain engulfed her. It went on and on, each moment she internally pleaded for death. When it finally stopped, her skin was steaming and Kulat smiled at her, "Are you ready to explain how you escaped the UTC prison planet? Where did you find the old command ship?"

None of them answered so Kulat whispered to Nera, "If that's how it's going to be, just know I am thoroughly enjoying this." Kulat signaled to the lab tech, and this time Lock was electrocuted. Blood trickled from his lips as he felt fire blast through his nerves. His mind thrashed against his skull as he begged for the pain to stop. He was sure his psyche would break if this torture continued much longer. Panting, Lock fell back into the chair as the current receded. His breath steamed as it left his throat, and he licked his own blood from his lips as he met Kulat's gaze with a scowl.

"Oh scary, scary! I'm so frightened of your mad little eyes," Kulat taunted. Lock smiled at him, his teeth covered in his own blood, and Kulat cleared his throat before throwing up another hand signal.

This time it was Vin. When the current entered his body, the chair Vin was strapped to groaned as his body clenched every muscle. His eyes fluttered as he believed he could hear himself screaming. The metal chair continued to creek as Vin viciously fought his binds. When it ended, the cries he could hear were devastating and tears slid from the corners of Vin's whiskey eyes. He couldn't tell if those cries of desperation were in his mind? Or were they real?

Frantic pounding sounded to the left of him, and a flat surface on the wall shook in the center like something was crashing against it. Vin was so confused.

Kulat clapped, "Oh what a joyous occasion! A couple!"

Taberi was drug into the room and when Vin realized what was happening, he thought he might die of a broken heart. With Taberi shoved in front of Vin, Kulat grabbed his shoulders and peered around him, "So you and the lab rat? What a cute couple."

As he raised his hand to signal, Kulat winked at Vin. The current slashed through Vin's body and he thrashed against the chair. Taberi's blood chilling scream filled the small room as Vin was electrocuted. When it was stopped, Vin slumped breathless, blood trickling from his eyes and ears.

Taberi's stood paralyzed with terror. Vin wasn't breathing. *Vin was dead.*

In a fit of blinding rage, Taberi fought Kulat's hold just as the current started up again, and Vin shot up in the chair with his eyes wide. Vin struggled to suck in a deep breath of air. He slammed back against the chair as he gasped for another breath.

Taberi couldn't hold back as he released a sorrowful cry and fell to his knees, "Please stop, I can't do it. I'll tell you whatever you want. Please, stop hurting him!"

Silent, bloody tears streamed down Vin's face as he was forced to watch Taberi sob at his feet. Vin knew what was coming next for he, Nera, and Lock, but he didn't have the heart to be angry with Taberi. Even in this moment of despair, Vin's heart swelled with love. No matter what happened next, Vin knew he had been loved, truly, deeply, authentically loved.

For the first time in his life, Vin felt truly complete. He couldn't help giving Taberi a weak but genuine grin as they pulled Taberi from the floor and drug him away.

Three more soldiers entered the room, and the three Resper were taken from the chairs and forced down to the end of the hallway toward a docking bay. They didn't have to see to know there was no ship on the other side. Only distant stars shone behind the glass doors.

Vin roughly exhaled as he turned to Nera and Lock, each of them well aware of what was about to occur. They were being thrown out of the airlock. Their secrets had been revealed and it was time for their execution. The soldiers lined them up, Nera first, Lock, and then Vin. The door of the airlock slid open, and all three were shoved inside. The door sealed and they heard the countdown from twenty begin.

Nera's thoughts turned to Cinis, and she did her best not to weep, but to only recall the brief, beautiful time they shared. Nera had to say something to her loyal friends. "Vin, our time was glorious, and Lock, your daughter will make a fine head of the Domitia house."

Lock tried to smile. "She will lead just like you have. You would have been so proud of her. She is almost as tall as my shoulder now." Lock hadn't told Tressa he loved her. He couldn't help but regret it after he heard her whispers. He would give anything to be able to go back and tell her.

Vin remained quiet, his mind engulfed with Taberi.

The countdown reached five, and Nera leaned against Lock's shoulder. Vin did the same from the other side. The three had spent their lives together, and not one of them was honestly surprised they were meeting their end together as well.

The countdown reached four, three… They each closed their eyes and prepared to be blown out into space.

FIFTY-EIGHT

MELIOR - UTC TRANSPORT

Tressa and Cinis were forced down the stairs of the ship, and outside. Shortly they were jerked to a halt and the wrist bands were released. When they lifted their eyes, they were surprised it wasn't a prison. It was a towering glass building, a Melior mansion. They looked at one another, bewildered, as they were marched inside the front courtyard. Through the garden courtyard, they found two Iungo as guards, holding open the doors to the massive Melior home. Tressa reached over and squeezed Cinis's hand as if to ask, *What the fuck is going on?* They were guided to a giant room with a long meeting table and made to sit at on a couch by a fireplace.

One of the Iungo guards behind them announced, "Empress Claudius of the United Trusts and Colonies and King of Aduro."

A regal, tall woman with brown skin and a shining head glided around the corner with two Iungo guards in tow. She wore a dark grey UTC military dress uniform with her house of Claudius insignia, on her shoulder. Her mechanical blue eyes glowed as she sat across from Cinis and Tressa. "You two can call me Livia. Cinis, I hear you helped my friends."

Cinis nodded profusely, "Yes, that was me and Tressa."

Livia could tell Cinis was desperate to explain, "Cinis, if you can explain yourself, I may be able to help."

Overwhelmed, Cinis did their best not to ramble. "It's such a long story, Tressa and I were picked up by a First Human commander, and he sent us down to the prison planet. We were saved by some genuinely nice Resper. Three of them, and we are very concerned about them. They were taken away in a prison ship. Oh, and Taberi too! He was the hacker's friend!"

Livia nodded, pretending to understand, "But how did you get off the prison planet?"

Cinis didn't hold back as they explained, "We hacked an old UTC base. Please, Livia, we will do anything. We need to know the Resper we were with won't be harmed. Please!"

Livia scowled and nodded before she hooked a finger at her guard to hand her a communication tablet. She tapped the screen a few times before bringing her eyes back up to Cinis. "I have informed the team holding the Resper and the half-human Vultus I want them for questioning. That's all I can offer you right now with what I know. I need much more information from you and your friends. You broke a list of laws, and I cannot just snap my fingers, especially with just some ramblings from one of you. What does house Baiselle's medical research lab have to do with this?"

Understanding fell over Cinis, and something told them to trust Livia as they apologized, "I'm sorry. I am nervous. Tressa is not well, and we had to leave Alisot to steal the treatment for her. We planned to release it to the public."

Pausing a moment, Cinis wasn't sure they could bring up Rungi without anger, but they continued, "We were betrayed by Rungi. She asked us to steal a formula for her, and in exchange, she would give us maintenance authorization codes. I think it's my fault she turned us in. One of the Resper, I, I care about her. Rungi and I used to be intimate, but that's been over for a long time. I think she became jealous."

Livia narrowed her eyes at Cinis, and confusion was written over her face as she spoke to one of her guards, "Please fetch our guest in the back."

Moments later, Rungi appeared around the corner. Cinis brimmed with rage and did everything they could to remain calm. Tressa reached over and took Cinis's hand, the action not going unnoticed by Livia.

Livia sharply pointed to a chair, and Rungi sat down. "Rungi, I've heard something interesting just now. I was just told you were formerly involved with Cinis here. That doesn't match with what you presented to me. I was told Cinis and Tressa were being held captive and being used by the blood Resper. You told me a half truth."

Rungi paled. "Blood Resper have a compound in their saliva to drug humans to be compliant and malleable. These two humans are under the influence of the drug and any relationships they claim are nothing but a fabrication of their own minds. The blood Resper are manipulative and void of empathy. There is a reason why they have remained trapped on their home world. If you will just hand over the Powe siblings to me, I can ensure to have them detoxed and back home in a few weeks."

All Cinis could see was red and an Iungo guard

stepped in front of them before they could charge Rungi. They wanted her blood. Fire burning inside, Cinis leapt up and thrashed against the guard's hold as Livia blankly peered at them. She observed Rungi feigned shock, like she hadn't anticipated this level of reaction, but a reaction had been expected.

Livia smelled a rat. Turning to her guards, Livia commanded, "Remove Rungi and send her home."

Rungi sucked in a sharp breath and protested, "You can't see Cinis is under the influence? Look at how enraged they are! They have never acted this way before. Cinis has always been gentle and mild tempered."

Having been manipulated for most of her life, Livia wasn't buying it. Cinis clearly wanted to rip Rungi's throat out after simply being nervous for her friends moments before.

When Livia ignored her and Rungi was being pushed out of the front door, Rungi cried out, "I won't forget this, Cinis!"

Cinis seethed, "I won't forget this either, not for as long as I live!"

Once Rungi was forced away, Livia stood and put her hands on her hips, "Let's go find something to eat, shall we?" Livia eyed her guards, "I'm safe with these two. Your team can move to position six."

They scattered and Cinis sighed with relief, "I would love some water."

Livia smiled at them, "Right this way."

Livia guided them through the house to the kitchen where they found a table covered with hundreds of different foods. A few off-duty Iungo guards filled their plates and shuffled off as Livia came in with the siblings following behind.

Cinis took a plate and couldn't help but ask, "They're alive right? I mean our friends. The Resper and the half-human Vultus?"

Livia tipped her head to the side before she approached a communications panel. She input a number, and when someone answered, she pressed an option to shield the sound from projecting through the room. Cinis and Tressa couldn't hear a thing as Livia spoke to someone at the prison. She nodded a few times and ended the call.

Livia turned around and replied, "I should hear back soon. I've sent my private royal guard to collect them."

Setting their plate down on the food bar, Cinis began to fade and asked, "Do you think I could sit down?"

Livia rushed to Cinis as they faltered and Tressa didn't look much better, "What have you two been through?"

Tressa finally spoke, and when she did, her voice cracked, "We love them. The Resper, they were good to us. Rungi is a gods damned liar. We just need to know if they're alive. Please."

As the hours passed, Cinis and Tressa began to lose hope. They hardly touched the food they selected from the spread. Livia hadn't asked them any more questions and sat quietly with them at her ornate kitchen table. A four-foot-tall flower arrangement stood in the center, filled with delicate fragrant flowers they had not ever seen before. Cinis was focused on the intricate petal when they spotted a familiar face hobbling through the back door of the kitchen.

Leaping to their feet, Cinis knocked the chair over backward as they bolted for Nera. Tressa let out a sob as Lock limped in behind her, and they slowly made their way to one another. Vin and Taberi came in last, arms wrapped around one another.

Livia watched the touching scene unfold as Cinis embraced Nera and Tressa frantically assessed Lock for injuries. Taberi and Vin both held their eyes shut as they quietly embraced, Taberi's tail curled tightly around Vin's leg. All Livia could see was genuine care from these supposed monstrous Resper. The fruit Resper had made such a compelling case long ago the UTC blindly went along with it. Livia decided a deeper look into these Resper must be made. After what had transpired with the Iungo and her own planet, Livia would no longer follow old assumptions and judgements.

After allowing the couples a few discrete moments, Livia approached and requested, "Cinis, please introduce me to our guests."

Stunned, Cinis stuttered, "O-o-oh, um. Empress Claudius, this is Nera, Lock, and Vin Domitia."

Livia grinned at Nera, who dropped her arms to her side and seemed as though she couldn't take a breath. In almost imperceptible volume, Nera asked, "Did you just say Empress Claudius?"

Livia corrected, "I am United Trusts and Colonies Empress Livia Claudius, and King of Aduro. If I am not mistaken, Domitia is the house of the former Kings of Alisot."

Pressed against Nera, Cinis could feel her wings tremble, not with fear or anxiety, but of delight, unhinged, chaotic delight. Nera softly answered, "You are correct, my ancestors once ruled Alisot. I am the head of house. Lock is my brother, and Vin is our cousin."

Livia politely bowed her head, "It is a pleasure to meet you, Nera Domitia. May I show you to your rooms?

Cinis was overwhelmed and their voice squeaked, "Rooms?"

Livia gave them a gracious smile, "Yes, you and your friends are my guests until I determine precisely what it is happening. I will decide what to do after I have heard the entire story, and I suspect we have a lot to discuss. I have informed my staff to prepare dinner for us. I am aware of blood Resper's food requirements and accommodations have been made for all menus. You will find clean attire in your rooms. Dinner is in two hours."

As they followed her down the hallway, a large, crimson Iungo man barreled down the hallway with a forest green Iungo boy chasing behind him. Both carried wooden swords and yelled gleefully at one another as they passed by.

Livia shook her head and ignored them. They continued down the long hallway until Livia stopped and gestured to the three open doors. "All three rooms have full baths. Please make yourself comfortable. Your door comm system will chime when dinner is being served." Livia casually strolled away, and Nera was left speechless as they all stood in the hallway.

Nera turned to Cinis for an explanation. "How do *you* know the Empress?"

Cinis nervously laughed, "I told you we helped the Iungo win their freedom. Tressa and I both helped their president. Livia must know them."

"Did you just call her by her first name?!" Nera's black eyes nearly bulged out of her head.

Cinis quietly responded, "Um, she said we could call her Livia."

Nera turned to Lock, "Do you understand what this could mean?"

Realization dawning, Lock nodded, "We need to clean up for dinner."

Nera and Lock all but drug Cinis and Tressa behind them as they went in their separate rooms, eager to bathe and spend a few moments alone with their loves.

Vin caught on moments later, and he nearly shook Taberi, "Oh! We are going to make a plea to the Empress!"

Taberi's mouth dropped open, and it was as if they all had fires burning under them as they took off for a bath.

Their excitement faded fast, and it took over an hour and a half before they finished with how slowly everyone moved due to their injuries. Lock knocked on Nera's door, she opened it and held it open for him and Tressa. Vin and Taberi already sat on the made bed by the wall and Cinis stood by the fireplace. When Lock and Tressa came in, Nera shut the door and leaned against it.

"I think we should come right out with it and tell the Empress we believe the fruit Resper made a deal with the First Humans for sight. We should invite Livia and diplomats of the UTC to Alisot so they can see firsthand. Once we have her ear, we can discuss the proto-bats," Nera proposed. Lock and Vin nodded in agreement as the dinner chime sounded over the room comms.

When they arrived at the dinner table, Livia had place settings for them all at one end of the long table. They found their seats, and Livia came from the back of the kitchen and sat across the rest of them, again with no guards. Nera deeply appreciated the gesture of trust.

Servers came out with trays of food and placed them on the table.

Once the staff finished, Livia stood up and invited, "Please help yourselves. We can eat, and afterward, we will have our discussion."

Lock stood first and reached for a bowl, but when he lifted it, he winced. Livia noticed, just like she noticed everything, and asked, "Lock, are you alright?" He slowly sat back down, and the table grew quiet.

Lock hesitated as he answered, "I will be."

Boiling in her seat, Livia did not accept that answer,

"Did your injuries happen during your incarceration? Please elaborate."

Lock froze, but Taberi had no problem telling Livia what happened. He blurted, "They were tortured. Some officer named Kulat interrogated them. He strapped them to chairs and electrocuted them over and over. It was the worst thing I've ever seen. They killed Vin and brought him back. I folded, and Vin won't admit it, but I know they were going to toss them out of an airlock. I wasn't supposed to know, but I saw where they were when the call came in to bring us here. They were led out of the airlock when I was taken out of the room by one of your Iungo guards." Tears streamed down Taberi's face as Vin pulled him close. Tressa and Cinis couldn't do anything but stare at Lock and Nera in disbelief. Lock and Nera said nothing.

Livia seemed unsurprised, but the clinch of her jaw indicated her fury. "If you will excuse me, I need to make a call to the prison." Livia made her way to her comm system in the kitchen, but this time she didn't shield the call. "Connect me immediately with Commander Tinslip." There was a brief pause and then she continued, "Tinslip, strip Kulat Moins of his rank and charge him with the assault and attempted murder of royal diplomats," Livia commanded.

The call ended abruptly, and the Livia found her seat across from her table of stunned guests. Noticing their shock, she explained herself, "I fell in love with an Iungo mine worker, one of my father's many slaves. The crimson Iungo man running the halls with the child we passed is my consort. He helped me overthrow my father and take Aduro. I plan to continue similar progressive work within my newly elected roll as Empress. The First Humans have done immeasurable damage to the Galactic Center, and I am facing much opposition. I feel this is an opportunity to move forward with the work I have challenged myself with."

Understanding fell over the group and each one of them slowly eased back in their chairs. Livia smiled, "Eat. Then we can discuss how we are going to fix this."

She hadn't even heard their words, and already they felt the swell of hope blossoming inside. Lock, Vin, and Nera drank fresh deer blood from wine glasses as Taberi, Cinis, and Tressa devoured plate after plate of fruits, roasted vegetables, and various meats. No one touched the pork, except for Livia.

Once they had eaten their fill, Nera sat up and readied herself to make her case. She did her best to steady her voice, "We believe we were betrayed by our species counterparts, the fruit Resper. We have reason to think the fruit Resper traded the blood Resper, and our mutual home world, in exchange for their people to be given eyesight."

Livia licked her lips after she sipped her liquor. "The blood Resper use echolocation?"

Nera confirmed, "Some of us have limited vision. Most of us use echolocation exclusively."

"You seem to see with your ears well enough that I had no idea, and I am trained to detect such things. If what you say is true of the fruit Resper, and their leaders once traded your freedom for their eyesight, we may have a case to present to the UTC which could result in a vote to send diplomats to your world. This could also help with a case I am building for a bill to outlaw gene editing without medical necessity. I am putting a team together to investigate as well as hire a third party. I will contact Portum to assist on behalf of Cinis and Tressa. There is one question though. We have been dropping humans on your world for a thousand years thinking your savage species were enacting the UTC's harshest form of death penalty. Please explain what *exactly* has been happening."

Nera began, but Tressa interrupted, "First the human is interrogated, and if the human is found to be a true criminal, they're eaten, sometimes brutally. The Resper are a product of their environment, and they were twisted to be this way when their planet fell. Besides that, they're kind people. If they had wanted to kill my sibling and I, they had many opportunities. Instead, we grew close, and they showed us who they really are. If we had any wish and we could go anywhere with anyone, Nera, Cinis, Vin, Taberi, Lock, and I would all go home to the Domitia house. Even if that means we're trapped on the planet, and we have no chance for a life outside of Alisot, it is still all I could ever want."

Tapping her finger on her glass, Livia tipped her head to the side in deliberation, "Give me some time, and I will test and validate your claims. You're quite the opposite disposition of your reputation, and I trust you will treat my home with respect. Having said that, the comms in your room are linked with a palace map. Please explore the entire grounds at your leisure, Anything off limits will be locked and inaccessible, so you won't end up in the wrong place. You may be here for a few weeks. You are honored royal *guests*, and my staff is at your service."

SIXTY

MELIOR – UTC EMPRESS PALACE

Everyone except for Taberi and Cinis sat on exam beds waiting to see the royal doctor. Nera, Lock, and Vin were sore and burnt. They were treated with burn ointment and encouraged to rest. Not wanting to leave her side, Lock stood next to the exam bed as the physician moved on to Tressa.

He drew a blood sample and peered at her over his glasses. "Livia said you have an immune system problem."

She looked up at Lock who answered, "I think it's an inflammatory joint disease. Her white blood counts are higher than they should be."

The doctor blinked at Lock, "What are you some kind of healer? I thought you were a blood Resper."

Lock replied, "I'm a butcher."

The doctor raised his brow in confusion and concern.

Tressa's eyes went wide, "Oh gods, the translators! He means he is a surgeon. It doesn't translate well from the Resper language."

The doctor's face softened with understanding as he

nodded and offered, "Well, you can help me then. I need to isolate her abnormal genes. Humans tend to have fragile genes that cause a multitude of diseases. You know, we aren't naturally occurring? Many humans deny that new revelation, but it is true. We have a gene editing lab here at the palace."

Tressa's heart raged in her chest, "How much is this going to cost?!"

The doctor scoffed, "Livia said nothing about payment. You'll be treated and sent on your way. Lock, follow me."

Lock limped slightly as he followed the doctor into the lab. The doctor turned to him, "Nera said you see with sound. Can you see our physical holograms?" The doctor turned on his holo-screen, and Lock sucked in a sharp breath as he bent down and studied the double helix rotating in front of him. "You *can* see it."

Reaching his hand out to touch it and finding nothing, Lock turned to him, "How does this work?"

"This type of holo-screen uses physical magnetic particles, magnets, and beams of light for the color. I had a feeling you would be able to visualize the view screen with this sort of design. I'll talk to Livia and see if we can't pass on the technology," the doctor replied as he inserted Tressa's blood sample in into the console.

Tressa's genes appeared on the screen and Lock leaned in closely, using his echolocation to build the image in his mind.

The doctor tapped his foot as the genes populated on the holo-screen, "Oh, let me make this black and white so the abnormal genes stick out and don't just blink a different color." He typed on the keyboard and the image changed, revealing the genes the computer identified as altered or damaged.

She had six genes that popped out, and the doctor pointed to them. "These five are faulty immune genes, and this one here is to make her live as long as you if she wants."

Lock hadn't considered the possibility. "You mean you can make humans live as long as the rest of the galactic center species average?"

The doctor looked over at him as he pulled his glasses down, "One hundred and fifty? Yes, I can do the same for the other two humans as well. I'm not supposed to tell anyone, so you didn't hear this from me. Livia plans on outlawing made to order babies, and beginning a free healthcare program similar to the Sarter Kingdom. Billions of humans in the Center will be able to receive this same medical care, including the species average life length option."

Lock just assumed he would have to live alone for many years at the end of his life. Naturally born humans usually didn't live long, so he was speechless. He wondered if that would be something Tressa would want. He hoped so.

"Blood Resper are not what I expected. I thought Livia had lost it sending you down here with no guards. I can see now why she trusts you," the doctor admitted.

Lock smirked, "That charming, eh?"

The doctor laughed as the computer chimed. "Young man, you certainly have the wit of a doctor. It's ready." He pulled a small cylinder from next to the console, and Lock followed him into the next room. Young man? Lock was forty! How young did the doctor think he was?

They approached Tressa and the doctor showed her the cylinder, "This has the ability to repair your genes and eliminate your disease. We can give you assistive devices and medication patches to help with the pain from your immune system damage. I also included a treatment in this serum for the broken gene which causes humans to die in their seventies, so you will be able to live as long as Lock here. The ancient creatures who made us didn't exactly do the best job on every gene code. I can do the same for Cinis. I just need a blood sample."

Tressa's gasped. She had heard of the gene edit to extend a human's life but never dreamed it would be offered to her. It was a luxury only the rich could afford.

She quietly nodded. "Thank you."

Once they finished in the royal clinic, they decided to heed the doctor's instructions to relax, and they headed out to tour the palace gardens. As they slowly strolled through the lush foliage, Tressa gasped, "There is a pool Cinis!"

Cinis moved to see what she was talking about. "So, we don't even know how to swim."

Tressa scowled, "So? I'm getting in."

She spotted a cabana and one of the staff was inside. "Hello, we are staying here. Is there any way we could have swimsuits and towels?"

The human woman smiled and gestured, "Just through this door, we have particle replicators you can use."

They passed through the double doors and found four machines. After plugging away at them for a few moments, swimsuits and towels were replicated. They noticed the large food and drink selection and ordered snacks to be delivered from the kitchen. Once they came out of the dressing rooms across from the particle replicators, the kitchen was already delivering their food and drinks.

Lock rubbed his hands together when he saw the raw slab of meat he ordered, "I'm starving."

Nera twirled around to Lock, "Please, use utensils."

Tressa beside him laughed as he scowled, "I know how to use a knife and fork."

Vin raised his eyebrows, "Since when?"

Shaking his head, Lock sat down by the tray with his food and resisted the urge to tear into it like an animal. He ate his raw deer steak and drank down two large glasses of blood as Tressa ate a salad with a white meat. Nera and Vin drank blood while Cinis and Taberi shared a flatbread covered in vegetables and cheese. The others chose a different heated pool, so Tressa went to the deeper one. Tressa jumped in the deep end so she could figure out how to swim, thinking it would all make sense once she was in the water. She was wrong. She kicked and kicked, but couldn't figure out how to stay above the water.

Lock dove in and pulled her to the side. "Do you want me to teach you?"

"Are you telling me you can swim with those big wings?" Just as Tressa spoke the words, she noticed his wings were tucked so tightly they weren't much more than two spikes over his shoulders.

He smiled at her as he kicked away from the wall and effortlessly tread water.

Tressa scowled, "Are you just going to show off or are you going to tell me what to do?"

Lock laughed and swam toward her, "I'm going to grab your legs under water and show you how to move them."

He dipped under the water, and she felt his hands grasp her legs. He moved one in a circular motion and then the other before coming back up. Lock brushed his wet hair off his forehead before grabbing the side of the pool, "Now I'm going to help you balance on the surface, and you try that motion away from the wall."

She kicked away from the wall with her hand in his and made the same motion he had guided her legs to do.

"Now faster," Lock explained.

She did as he instructed and he added, "Good. Now hold your fingers together, hold your arms out, and grab a handful of water with one cupped hand and then the other."

Tressa did as he instructed, and she could feel herself stay up. Lock's hand slowly let go of her stomach as she slowly made her way to the wall, on her own. He gave Tressa a dazzling smile, and she beamed with pride.

Lifting out of the pool, Tressa ran to tell Cinis, and Lock followed behind much slower. Tressa leaped in the shallow, heated pool, and splashed everyone before surfacing next to Cinis.

"I did it. I can swim now," Tressa boasted.

Lock smirked at her, "You mean you can tread water and not die? We have a lot more to go over if you want to learn to really swim."

Tressa laughed, "I've wanted to learn since I was a child. I've never even been in a pool before today."

Lock climbed in after her wrapped his arms around her, and they both relaxed in the warm bubbling pool. After a bit, Lock whispered in her ear, "Let's go back to our room."

Tressa agreed, telling Cinis, "We're going to go back to our room. Are you staying?"

Cinis nodded. They were leaned back next to Nera and both looked like they were having a desperately needed moment of relaxation. Vin and Taberi were enthralled in one another's gaze and hadn't even heard her.

Tressa followed Lock, and they grabbed their towels and clothes before heading back to their room. Lock grabbed the half glass of blood Vin didn't drink from the table and downed it with a shrug before they walked away.

Once they arrived at their room, Lock made his way to the bathroom and started the shower. Tressa followed him in and stripped her suit off as he did the same. Lock seemed nervous and Tressa studied him while she washed her hair. What was he thinking about that had him looking so uneasy?

Thoughts about what could be wrong flew through her mind as they finished showering and preparing for bed. Tressa brushed her wet hair out and when she sat the brush down, Lock was standing behind her. He was grasping his own hands, and Tressa had to ask, "Are you alright?"

"No. Yes. Um, I mean. I have something I need to talk to you about." Lock admitted nervously.

Tressa awkwardly smiled, trying to mentally prepare herself for the worst. "Sure. Anything."

He took her hand and offered, "Let's sit by the fire."

Tressa hoped it wasn't as bad as she feared. He guided her to the fireplace where they sat on pillows on the floor.

Lock took her hands, and she could already see emotion welling in his eyes as he started, "When we were lined up waiting for the prison ship, and you and Cinis were whispering your goodbyes? When you said you loved me, I realized I had made a mistake. I hadn't told you how I felt, and at the time, I believed I would never have the chance. I knew we were going to die, and we almost did. All I could think about was my daughter and you. I was filled with regret I didn't tell you I love you.

That whatever amount of time your human life had to offer, I wanted you to spend it with me. In that airlock I lived a lifetime with you in a flash. I saw you grow old, and I adored you through every moment. Having to lose you and live another seventy years alone afterward? If this was the price of loving, you? I had accepted it."

Tressa squeezed his hands, "I knew you loved me. I just didn't know how much. Now, I'm probably going to live as long as you, and we can be old together."

Lock gently took her face in his hands and kissed her, "When we go home, I am announcing you as my mate. You will be a Domitia, and my daughter will become your daughter. My family will become yours."

Tressa asked, "Is this like a marriage?"

Lock shook his head. "No, this is declaring you my life mate. This is above a loving union. For Resper we don't share last names, fortune, or family with our partners, even if we have children. A mate means I am giving you my life. You own me. What is mine is now yours. We are one. I share my family, my title, my fortune, and my life. Declaring a mate is the same as if I were a king, I would be making you my equal, the crowned queen, instead of a queen consort. So, as Nera's mate, Cinis would gain the title of Monarch."

Tressa drew in a sharp breath, "Aren't the Domitia's Alisot royalty?"

"Yes. If the line was still recognized, Nera would be a queen, and I would be a prince. Vin would have a title as well."

Tressa couldn't help but bubble with laughter, "Does Cinis know how any of this works? If not. Please tell me I can watch when Nera tells them? Please! It will be priceless."

SIXTY-ONE

MELIOR – UTC EMPRESS PALACE

Livia called everyone to the conference room, and they were patiently waiting for her to arrive. She was a few minutes late, and when she finally opened the door, she started in right away. "We found the evidence we need to file a grievance with a special council. I sent the files directly to my representatives, and they are filing the grievance as we speak. The council will review within the hour, and it will be sent out for a vote. I suspect the UTC will be sending diplomats within the week, and I plan to file a request to personally accompany them. We requested DNA samples from multiple fruit Resper on Emendo. They all showed a curious, inheritable color vision gene, and my personal royal lab proved it was not naturally occurring. With our proof, we were able to pull from the DNA database on Emendo and every fruit Resper born on the planet has the same altered gene. We moved from there and pulled records from when the vote went across to withhold the blood Resper from galactic travel. With those records, we put together the suspected media used to sway the vote and found it to be clips taken from footage of starved blood Resper who were used in the arena games. We ran everything through data signature software and discovered heavy First Human involvement. With the recent fall of the FH faction, I have full confidence in a resolution by this evening."

With Livia's announcement, they all seemed to release the very weight of Alisot which had been resting heavily on their shoulders. Each one leaned back in their chairs as the news sank in as Nera thanked her.

However, Lock knew they had one more important topic to discuss with Livia. "We have something else we need assistance with. There is a bat we share a common ancestor with. We call them proto-bats. They began taking over our planet and before the heist, we were able to eliminate much of the overpopulation with a toxic gas in the atmosphere. We need help finding out why they're over-populating, and how we can regain a balance before they devastate the planet."

Livia thought a moment then offered, "I'll send my research team, and I will have a report to you as soon as they discover something or find a solution."

Livia's tablet chimed and she read the message with a pleased smile, "The council has unanimously approved the filed grievance. It is now being processed for a vote. I will let you know the results when they are announced in chamber."

With that, Livia bowed her head and disappeared through the door.

They all remained seated, unable to fully process it all. It was too much to believe. Years – generations of manipulation and destruction could be over. They could reclaim and save their planet for their people, their future.

Nera finally spoke, "It's hard to believe this is real."

Lock agreed, "What are we going to do for the next few hours while we think ourselves to death?"

Nera laughed, "Do you know what we need?"

Vin leaped to his feet, "Leaf!"

Within minutes, they were all huddled around the particle replicator trying to find the options for it. One of the staff members passed through and Nera asked, "Do you serve leaf?"

The Rubus man answered with his bushy tail flitting back-and-forth behind his head, "Absolutely, what form would you like? We have a basket option with several smoking options, a variety of flavors with different effects, and it comes with the palace's favorite entrees all in single bite form."

Nera considered the options and requested, "The basket, and can you bring some blood for us, and snacks for everyone as well?"

Without hesitation, the Rubus man agreed, "There are accommodations for the basket through this door and down the path." They filed out of the pool house and made their way down the path, finding several comfortable couches arranged around a low table. They each found a seat and within a few moments the 'basket' was wheeled out. It was a three-level cart, leaf at the top, drinks and liquors in the center, and bite sized food at the bottom.

Once it was laid out for them the ladies took on the role as hostess. Nera lit a rolled cigar with a calming effect before passing around the glasses of blood. Tressa made herself, Cinis, and Taberi mixed drinks and passed around the trays of food.

After several leaf cigars and a few drinks, they were all quite contemplative. None of them could find words to fill this tenuous time of waiting. No amount of leaf or alcohol could take their minds off the reality that the future of their planet was now in the hands of a council who once voted to condemn them all. Each passing hour sent them all further into their thoughts. Gentle music from the palace played, and it was the only reprieve to their racing thoughts.

Melior's day was ending, shadows crept over the gardens, and the warm day cooled. The daylight star was setting when Livia approached. When she arrived at the table and assessed the state of her guests, she didn't seem surprised in the slightest. "I can't say I wouldn't be finding a way to eliminate some time if I were waiting on word about my own planet." Livia acknowledged as she looked at each one of them, all slumped in odd ways. They slowly sat up as Livia pulled her tablet out and began reading, "The United Trusts and Colonies has voted to move forward with the evidence presented. The council accepts the grievance and had the majority vote in favor of the house of Domitia. Diplomats are to be sent to Alisot to begin negotiations for a peace treaty and allocation of adequate funds are to be provided for planet wide reformation efforts." When Livia was finished reading, she looked up to find everyone standing before her, speechless.

Livia bowed her head to Nera, "I'll arrange one of my personal transports to take you home when you're ready. Consider the transport a gift to begin our negotiations."

When Livia was out of sight, Nera finally spoke and her voice cracked in relief, "We did it." She turned to Lock, "We have our planet back." Lock grinned and hugged Tressa tightly.

With Taberi in his arms, Vin was unable to hold back as

he sobbed, "We were just trying to help Tressa and now we have our world back!"

Cinis held up the drive with the formulas on it. "Livia slipped this to me before she walked away."

"And I know just the place on the galactic web to upload it," Taberi added.

The next morning, they prepared for the flight home and boarded the transport. Livia had already set the autopilot programed with the ship's course. Cinis sat in the captain's chair, and when autopilot pulled up the map of their journey, Nera and Vin stared at the hologram. They could visualize it and were every bit as mesmerized as Lock had been. Nera quietly asked, "How?"

Lock explained, "They have holo-tech that works with projection, magnets, and magnetic particles. It looks like they implemented the tech on this ship for us."

Cinis read the ship's log, "They uploaded the holo-tech development files, and there are three industrial sized particle replicators in the storage bay."

Nera was overcome with emotion as she commanded, "Cinis, take us home."

Cinis engaged the autopilot, and the ship lifted off the ground, heading toward the blue sky above them. They reached orbit over Melior and blinked out of existence.

Within seconds, they appeared over Alisot and found UTC collector bots already catching and loading the EM Pulse satellites into recycler ships. "What mode of travel did we just use?" Nera was stunned.

"I think we were given a ship with the Iungo jump drive. Electromagnetic waves are blasted at an enclosed space and with enough concentrated radiation, the result is a full particle jump. I heard about it from the Iungo president Oz when I was there." Cinis explained. Where are we going first, Nera?"

Nera approached the captain's chair, "May I?"

Cinis was delighted to watch as Nera found the location and entered the coordinates with the option of a slow decent with thrusters. The ship passed through the atmosphere and carefully descended onto a large slab of concrete. They landed in the center of a bustling city built by the edge of an ocean. Resper were in a large circle surrounding the ship, likely wondering why a spaceship just landed in their square.

Nera emerged first, and Cinis could hear whispers of 'Domitia' roll through the crowd. When all six of them stood in front of the ship, Nera stepped forward. She raised a hand to quiet the crowd and the hush rippled across those gathered. "I am Nera Domitia. We have been at the UTC imperial palace on Melior, and we have pled our case to the Empress. Our pleas were heard, and the UTC has voted to open negotiations. We will be accepting diplomats, and the Empress herself will accompany them. I ask that you pass on this message to all the heads of the great houses. As the highest-ranking house, I formally request the presence of every house tonight at the Domitia residence. This is a time to celebrate. We have officially regained our world's autonomy!" Cheers erupted as Resper bolted into the sky, and in moments, cries of joy could be heard as the message was shared through the streets. Before long the cramped, bustling city echoed with celebration.

Nera guided everyone back onto the ship and entered the coordinates to the gardens of the Domitia sea-side home.

When they landed, and Cinis looked up at the palace sized home, they asked, "Nera why is this house so much bigger than your home up north?"

She took Cinis's hand as they headed down a path in toward a door, "Remember, I told you the house up north was originally the guest house. Our former home was the Alisot Royal palace. I'll have to take you to the ruins some time. It was twice the size of this Domitia home." They passed through a few hallways before they emerged in a large open space where several Resper gathered around table with a freshly slaughtered pig. They all stopped and turned as the rest of Nera's group filed in.

Nera spoke over the group, "We just returned from Melior; Alisot is ours once again. The great houses are meeting here this evening, so we need to prepare. Send a member of the guard to familiarize themselves with the ship and have them retrieve Bensley and Halso from the old UTC base. I left the coordinates in the computer."

Speechless, they scattered to begin preparing for guests and to notify the guards. Staff emerged to clear the table as Nera turned to Lock, "It sounds like the people we need to make an announcement to are waiting for us on the balcony."

Lock grinned, "After you."

Nera took Cinis by the hand, and they all followed as she took them through a few more hallways leading to a large balcony which looked out over the ocean. Several regally dressed Resper, were enjoying the view. Tressa's attention was drawn to one adult Resper woman incredibly beautiful, and a young Resper girl who lounged in the bright starlight. Tressa knew exactly who the girl was, Pyra.

Lock put his arm around Tressa as Nera and Cinis stood next to them hand in hand. Vin and Taberi remained to the side and sat quietly in the back.

Nera couldn't hide her wide grin, "Family, Lock and I have some introductions and announcements. This is Cinis. I have chosen them to be my mate."

A beautiful brown-haired woman leaning against the railing glared at Tressa as Lock spoke next, "I have chosen a mate as well. This is Tressa." Some were smiling, but others seemed indifferent. The stunning woman pushed past them and went inside as the rest of the elder family seemed at a loss for words.

Tressa then realized this must be Pyra's mother. Tressa could see Pyra was concerned about her mother, so Tressa bit her lip and snarled, making a silly face. Pyra noticed and laughed, before approaching Lock.

Pyra timidly peered up at Lock, "Father, will you stay this time?"

Tressa's heart broke as he nodded, "Yes. You and your mother will be going back to our home up north with me soon."

Behind them Nera suggested, "I think it's time to build a new northern Domitia house. What do you think Lock?"

Lock pulled Tressa to him as he agreed, "I think that's for the best."

Nera walked about with Cinis, introducing them to each person before heading off to their room. Vin and Taberi had already slipped out in search of something to eat.

When the balcony was empty, save a few lingering elderly cousins, Lock asked, "Do you mind if I take you to our room then track down Pyra's mother? I think I need to clear a few things up."

Tressa more than understood after her reaction. "Do whatever you need to do."

Lock kissed her forehead and led her to their room.

Before Lock left, he pulled her close, kissed her on the forehead, and requested, "Wish me luck. This is not going to be a pleasant discussion."

Tressa laughed and patted him on the shoulder. "I think you can handle it big tough guy."

He rolled his eyes and kissed her again before closing the door behind him. It didn't take long to find Kellin walking along the beach. Lock called out as he spotted her down the beach.

She slowly turned and met him halfway. Kellin crossed her arms and approached him, anger radiating from her stunning face. "What do you want?"

"Do you have a problem with my mate?" Lock sighed.

"You mated with your dinner, what do you think? It is just as repulsive as fucking a slaughter pig," Kellin seethed.

Stunned, Lock spat back, "Tressa is the reason we won our freedom. You will respect her, or you will be removed as a guest of the house of Domitia. Nera has the scribe drafting the mating documents. They will be signed tonight."

Kellin's skin heated as she growled, "She can't give you an heir like I can!"

Lock paused as understanding fell over him, "I have never once considered you to be an option for a partner, mate, or a child of my own blood, so you can forget that fantasy. I already have an heir, and speaking of her, if you keep this up, I will be forced to have the scribes draft us a visitation agreement for Pyra. You will accept Tressa as my mate, and you will show her respect, or you will leave my sight. It's that simple."

Kellin finally began showing a hint of emotion. "I thought you were going to come back, and we would be a family, you, Pyra, and I. I don't ever want to see you again, Lock ever. We can swap Pyra every week."

"You're colder than a winter night, and we do not mesh well. You came back different, but you were never what I wanted. Why can you not see that? I think us drafting an agreement is for the best."

Emotion beginning to overflow, Kellin tore into the sky.

Lock had enough of Kellin and her always trying to force her wants on everyone around her. At one time, he had hoped she would grow up and mellow some, but he had seen she couldn't change. He wanted a healthy relationship with her as Pyra's mother, yet she didn't even want to do that. He wanted to build a strong relationship with Pyra and knew it would be easier if he and Kellin cooperated, but that didn't seem likely now.

He made his way through the hallways to his room eager to return to Tressa, but before he opened the door he stopped and listened.

He could hear Pyra giggling. Lock cracked opened the door, and Pyra sat on the floor with Tressa playing a game. They had cards out and Pyra was explaining how it worked, honestly. Pyra was known for her artistry in conning anyone to do anything she wanted. They were all lucky she had a good heart. He leaned against the door and watched as Tressa and Pyra eventually noticed him.

Pyra playfully asked, "Do you want to play too?"

SIXTY-THREE

ALISOT – VINTNER CITY

Whips of light clouds roll across the afternoon sky on Alisot as Vin and Taberi strolled through the tropical gardens. Taberi spotted a bench and pointed to it, "Can we sit for a few minutes?"

Vin guided them to the bench, and he put his arm around Taberi after they sat down. "Are you ready to talk about what happened?"

Taberi shook his head, "I'll never be ready, but I know it has to happen eventually. We might as well start now."

Vin paused before he pulled Taberi close as he spoke quietly, "When they brought me back to life, hearing your pleas? Watching you cry for me? I don't know how else to say this, but, if they would have blown me out of that airlock, I would have died happy and complete. My parents are mates, and I never dreamed I would meet someone I could one day consider a mate. I want to experience a normal life with you for a little while first, but I want to eventually introduce you to my parents as my mate."

Taberi was unprepared for Vin's heartfelt words. He sat quietly thinking, and then smiled up at Vin. "I love you. I'm not going anywhere. You can call me whatever you want. I just want to be with you." Vin kissed him, and Taberi melted.

When Vin held his hand out for them to return inside, Taberi admitted, "You could have told me you wanted me to be your pet on a leash, and I would have put the collar on myself."

Vin knew Taberi could not fathom the extent of his carnal appetite, and he laughed, "Careful, you haven't even scratched the surface of my sexual desires. You never know, you might look good in a collar." Taberi straightened in surprise, and Vin paused, "We can talk more about that later, but I can hear Nera speaking to Lock inside, the Empress' ship is in orbit. We need to get ready."

Vin and Taberi headed off to their room and prepared for the evening. Vin put on a black suit as one made for Taberi was delivered to their room. Taberi dressed quickly, and they headed down to dinner. When they entered the Domitia formal dining room, Nera and Cinis were already seated at the end of the table.

Nera shone in a sleeveless floor length, slim black shimmering dress with a plunging neckline. Cinis sat beside her in a black suit with a black shirt and they wore a tie which matched Nera's dress. Lock and Tressa came in next, Lock also wore a formal black suit, and Tressa was radiant in a sleeveless midnight blue gown with a slit running all the way up her leg.

Nera angled her head to listen, and shared. "The heads of the great houses are arriving now."

Moments later, Nera rose from her place at the head of the table and signaled for everyone to rise. Ten Resper dressed in ballroom attire filed in and selected places to sit directly across from Nera.

When every head of house stood before a chair, she motioned for everyone to sit. "I have gathered you here to discuss the rejoining of Alisot to the larger galactic center community. I will need a pledge from each of you that we will set aside our differences and unite under this common goal. It has long been our people's wish for such a reconnection. I am open to suggestions on establishing a government structure."

The head of the Antillosi house stood up. "We have already convened, and we unanimously agree we would like the former Alisot government to be recognized in its entirety."

Nera allowed his words to settle before she humbly accepted, "As you wish."

The head of Antillosi reached for a small case he had sat down next to him and from it he pulled a scroll of paper. Nera knew precisely what that paper was. They had already drawn up their pledge to the crown. She turned to Lock who seemed too bewildered to think, his face was a picture of disbelief. The roll was passed across the table to her, and she unrolled it. She found the ten great houses of Alisot had written and signed their official pledge of loyalty to the house of Domitia. Their blood seals stamped under each one.

Nera took a silver pen from the mantle behind her and signaled for Lock and Vin to join her at the head of the table. Lock stood to her right and Vin stood behind them. Taking a slow breath, Nera leaned down and signed the paper next to her new title, Queen. As the ink dried, it expanded and raised off the paper. Nera turned to Lock to hand him the pen and he signed by his new title, Prince. Vin signed as a witness on part of the Domitia's. When he finished signing, he rolled the scroll up and formally presented it to Nera. The queen took the roll as all the heads of the great houses stood along with Vin and all bowed to Nera and Lock. Tressa, Cinis, and Taberi watched in unison, somewhat confused at what was happening.

The head of Antillosi announced, "From this day forward, Queen Nera of the house of Domitia is our recognized sovereign by the ten great houses of Alisot."

The room grew quiet, as everyone waited for Nera's first formal statement. "My first order of business is a law prohibiting the consumption of live or deceased humans without consent. I need an assurance we can remain civil and enforce this law in order to regain trust with the humans. Our planet will no longer be a prisoner drop zone and we will treat all who come here with dignity and respect."

Nods all around told Nera, they had been yearning for change and would accept this compromise. She knew it was going to take years to change their people from seeing humans as food, but this was where it began.

Cinis reached over and grabbed Tressa's hand under the table. Tressa leaned over to Cinis, and they whispered, "What the fuck just happened?"

Nera leaned down between them. "You're being announced, stand up." They lost all color as Nera helped Cinis stand as she announced them, "Great houses, I must take this time to announce my mate, Cinis. They and their sister Tressa are the entire reason our world is once again ours." Nera watched as they each set aside any internal issue, and one by one, they respectfully bowed to Cinis.

Lock took Tressa's hand as he announced her, "This is Tressa. She is my chosen mate," and the great houses bowed to her as well.

Moments later, Empress Livia and her Iungo consort were ushered into the formal dining room. Everyone turned and bowed to the Empress and her consort before joining her in rapid fire discussion about reunification.

Cinis seemed ill, and Nera pulled them aside, "Are you alright?"

Their eyes nearly bulged from their sockets as Cinis replied, "Alright? Are you serious? You are the queen now?! Did you know this would happen?"

Nera shook her head, "I knew it was a possibility, but I'm just as surprised as you." She squeezed Cinis' round behind, then left them gaping as she turned back to the party.

Nera approached Livia and the heads of house, "We have food and drink out in the gardens. Please join me."

She linked her arm in Cinis's and Lock and Tressa followed them as they made their way out to the gardens. Vin and Taberi were enthralled in a conversation about Aduro with Livia's consort August and were the last to join the party. The garden was lit with twinkling light and the reflected in the crystal and silver of the table settings. Delicious arrangements of food and drink were offered to everyone.

Nera and Lock watched as diplomats of every shape, color and form arrived from all over the galactic center, beaming with hope for the future.

Behind them, Cinis and Tressa stood next to one another, holding flutes of a light bubbly wine.

The two toasted to their future and laughed as Cinis

leaned over and whispered, "I think this means we have golden pussies."

EPILOGUE ONE

ALISOT – DOMITIA PALACE

The bright system star warmed the air as Nera stood on the stone balcony of her rooms facing out to her family lands. The intricate maze of trees and grassy areas with winding pathways sprawled out before her. They had built a new Domitia family home many years prior. Built of a light grey stone with ornate décor and just like any Resper home, every surface was a unique texture.

Nera had hired an aspiring architect from Portum on Livia's recommendation. His design for an octagon shaped courtyard home, large enough that each balcony, inside and outside facing, capable of being used to land on was phenomenal. Even guards with the widest wings could fly inside of the Domitia palace. She peered around her lands from high enough people on the ground looked like ants. Her world had been rebuilt and thriving.

Cinis came up behind her, wrapping their arms around her and resting their head against her shoulder. Nera held Cinis' roaming hand. "We have Pyra's coronation as first heir tonight. We cannot be late."

Cinis slid their other hand under Nera's button up shirt, and cupping her breast. Nera leaned into Cinis, relaxing, and they slipped their other hand into Nera's loose gently caressed her lower belly, edging lower and lower until Cinis stroked her softly. They kissed down Nera's shoulder as she trembled before her release. Cinis rubbed her thumb over Nera's nipple, feeling the cold of the metal piercing there. Nera jaggedly exhaled as the orgasm gently rolled over her.

Removing their hand from Nera's pants, Cinis licked their fingers and Nera lost control. Nera grabbed Cinis and yanked their shirt off before pulling them onto the bed and shoving them on the bed. Cinis bit their lip as Nera pulled their pants down and flipped them over. Nera purred, "You've made us late and now you're going to pay."

She crawled up and sat on Cinis's legs before leaning forward and slapping their perfect, round ass with her strong hand. Cinis groaned and grabbed the covers above them to hang on as Nera landed another slap to their bare ass. After a thorough spanking, Nera lifted Cinis up and twirled her tongue through their ass crack before devouring their heat. Face down on the bed, Cinis writhed as Nera drew their bud into her mouth and slid her tongue back and forth over it. With another slap to their ass, they yelp into the blankets, and Cinis shattered into a whimpering mess as their pleasure burst.

Nera slapped their bare rear one last time, "Now, get dressed, I think we really are late."

EPILOGUE TWO
ALISOT – DOMITIA PALACE

Lock's bright green eyes gleamed as he watched Pyra receive her crown and title of Princess from Nera. Next to him Tressa beamed with pride. Tressa and Pyra had grown close, and Tressa loved her dearly.

With the formalities concluded Pyra walked about with Nera, greeting guests and meeting the many representatives present. Her new title meant she could one day need to negotiate with these guests or even lead them. She smiled graciously and sparkled in her shimmering black tea length gown. As the party ended, she finally had a chance to visit with Lock and Tressa, "I am going to visit my mother. I'll be gone for a few days, but I'll be sure to come back before it's time to start classes next week."

Lock reached out to hand her coronation papers to her and offered "Have Bensley take you in my ship."

He and Tressa each hugged Pyra before she called "Thank you!" over her shoulder as she ran off down the hallway.

Lock adjusted his regal suit with the Domitia insignia

of wings on the lapel, tightening his belt. He had a surprise for Tressa now the ceremony was over.

Tressa slipped her arm through Lock's, "We are alone without a thing planned for a few days."

Lock looked down at her with a wicked smile before swooping her off the floor. He carried her out to the balcony and leapt into the sky.

As he shot up, she grasped onto him and huffed, "Just don't rip my dress!" Lock snapped his teeth over her shoulder strap, severing it. Tressa's eyes went wide. "Do you have any idea how much this dress cost?!"

He didn't respond, but instead laughed and began hiking up her dress over her hips before he flipped her upside down. He set her thighs on his shoulders as Tressa shrieked, "What are you doing?!"

She could feel his wings brushing against her shins as they climbed higher into the sky. Tressa grabbed Lock's waist and wrapped her arms around him tightly as he tore her panties away with his teeth and began devouring her.

Tressa squeezed her eyes shut as she felt his tongue caress every inch of her before he sucked her center into his mouth. Lock held her most sensitive place between his teeth and began humming as he licked her slowly. He could hear Tressa suck in her breath. The humming sent her to a place of all consuming pleasure, and she panted as she felt the heat and tension building. It was overwhelming her senses, but all she wanted was more. She needed more. When her orgasm slammed into her, she groaned and squeezed her arms tighter around Lock. Her hips shook as he tasted her through every moment.

Her eyes flew open when he landed on their balcony and lay her down on her back over their long padded chair. She was upside down on the chair with her dress hiked to her hips and her feet on the headrest. Lock swung his leg over the chair as he unbuckled his pants, his length springing free. He slid into her, and she arched to him. Lock put his hand between her breasts and thrust into her, filling her again and again. He slid his hand around her neck and leaned in to sink his teeth into her flesh. He dosed her right before another orgasm crashed into her, causing her to writhe. Drinking her blood as he buried himself inside of her, he could already feel himself tipping over. When he spilled into her, he raised his face to the sky, blood dripping down his mouth and whispered, "Fuck Tressa, you make me cum too fast. You're going to pay for that."

Lock licked up the rest of the blood on his lips as Tressa's head flopped to the side. He peered over at her and found her fast asleep. He grinned as he slid out of her, "You want me to dose you before you cum and then your ass falls asleep." Lock carried her to their bed and cleaned her before removing her dress and tucking her in. He crouched down by the bed and listened to her soft breaths as she slept.

Lock had known she was perfect for him when her image formed in his head, and he had breathed in her scent for the first time.

A day had not passed when she didn't consume his thoughts. He only had one true regret. He should have buried himself in her the first night he awoke to find her under him, but he had told her to get out. What a mistake that had been.

Life was painfully short and terrifyingly delicate. Kissing Tressa's forehead, Lock swore he would make up for that single missed opportunity with all the remaining time they had.

EPILOGUE THREE
ALISOT – VINTNER CITY

Playing children could be heard hollering in the background as Halso spoke over them, "We've got this. They're in the wing gym, and I'm taking them back for a nap afterward. Just enjoy your vacation." A blood curdling scream erupted from behind Halso, and he continued, "Palic just pushed Venton. It's fine. They're over it already."

Taberi anxiously huffed, "Are you sure?"

Halso laughed, "Relax!"

Vin took the tablet from Taberi. "He's right. You've been stressing about the children all day. They're three-year-old boys. They are going to fight until they're seventy."

Taberi was lounging in a chair on the beach in front of the Vintner City Domitia house and Vin was kneeling next to him. Vin leaned the tablet over to show Halso sent a picture of their boys swinging from the tree branches in the wing gym and Taberi calmed.

"Now, can we please get back to our vacation? Pyra

will be here in a few hours to see her mother and we won't have five minutes alone again until after she goes back for school." Vin ran his hand down Taberi's bare chest.

"What did you have in mind?" Taberi asked with his eyes narrowed on his love.

Vin smiled, "You know exactly what I want."

Taberi paled as Vin lifted him from the chair and they bolted into the sky. Vin landed on the balcony of their room and carried Taberi inside to their bathroom. Vin flipped on the rain shower, and Taberi slipped his swim shorts off. Vin slid his shorts off too and tossed them away before turning Taberi around by his hips, "Put your hands on the wall,"

Taberi complied and put his hands up as he felt Vin reach for the lube on the shelf. Taberi felt Vin grab his tail and lube the tip after he had slathered his own length. Vin carefully slid inside of him and Taberi tilted his hips back to take him. Taberi slid the tip of his tail into Vin and pressed on his bundle of nerves. Taberi and Vin moved inside of each other and Taberi gasped as his length split into two. Vin reached down and wrapped his hands around either side, pumping Taberi's dual length as they thrust into one another. Taberi's tail curled inside of Vin, and he came with forceful thrusts and a deep groan.

Cum burst from Taberi as he whimpered and pressed his body against Vin.

When they had finished washing and emerged from the shower, there was a knock at the door. Vin opened it, and a staff member rolled in a cart with an array of fruit, liquor, and numerous ways to smoke leaf. In the center was a box with a bow around it.

Taberi beamed as Vin handed him the box. When he opened it, he slid his hand over his mouth. It was the ring he had wanted for years, a band made entirely of giant pearl, from clams only found on the Plana home world.

"Happy anniversary!" Vin wrapped his arm around Taberi as he slid the ring on.

Vin had asked Taberi to be his mate two months after Nera had been crowned Queen of Alisot. It had been ten years of joy, and Vin couldn't wait to see where else life would lead them.

ABOUT THE AUTHOR

Lauren Logan is a neurodivergent, disabled science fiction romance author from North Texas. After high school and junior college, she attended the University of North Texas and studied Psychology and History. She met her husband in 2008, married in 2010, and they now have two little boys. They all enjoy watching science programs about astronomy as well as staying caught up on the latest Star Trek episodes.

In 2015 Lauren developed a passion for hair and began a journey that would lead her to hair school in her thirties. She specialized in vivid color and within a year and a half she had been nominated as a top 100 pastel colorist in the

Behind The Chair global hair awards. Unfortunately, the ultimate hair honor had come too late. A few months before her nomination was announced, Lauren had been forced to quit her dream career as a vivid hair colorist. The loss was devastating and she fell into a dark place.

November of 2020, Lauren was formally diagnosed with an autoimmune disease, Rheumatoid Arthritis. The disease course is aggressive and effects nearly all of her major joints, as well as both hands and feet. She has developed deformities in her fingers, making any chance of regaining her former hair career impossible. On rainy days you can often see her walking with a cane because the changing weather can bring on a flare. Since her diagnosis, she spends much of her time unable to leave her bed due to the constant pain and fatigue. The medication she is prescribed leaves her immunocompromised as well as having many difficult side effects.

Refusing to let her disability steal her ambition and kill her determination, Lauren began writing at the beginning of April, 2022. Over the course of one year, she completed writing two full length Sci-fi novels. Since the completion of the Reticere Series, she is now working on several stand alone novels in the same universe. Writing gives her hope and being an author gives her a future. She pours everything she is into her stories and she hopes you love them as much as she does.

For more information visit:
www.AuthorLaurenLogan.com

facebook.com / authorlaurenlogan

instagram.com / laurenloganart

tiktok.com / @lauren.logan